WE FLY
BENEATH
THE STARS

BOOKS BY SUZANNE KELMAN

A View Across the Rooftops

When We Were Brave

Under a Sky on Fire

When the Nightingale Sings

Garden of Secrets

WE FLY BENEATH THE STARS

SUZANNE KELMAN

bookouture

Published by Bookouture in 2022

An imprint of Storyfire Ltd.
Carmelite House
50 Victoria Embankment
London EC4Y 0DZ

www.bookouture.com

ISBN: 978-1-80314-382-8
eBook ISBN: 978-1-80314-381-1

This book is a work of fiction. Whilst some characters and circumstances portrayed by the author are based on real people and historical fact, references to real people, events, establishments, organizations or locales are intended only to provide a sense of authenticity and are used fictitiously. All other characters and all incidents and dialogue are drawn from the author's imagination and are not to be construed as real.

In memory of Ian Stott, my very first boyfriend, thank you for opening up my heart to what was possible. You were funny, loving and kind and I will never forget you. There is a little of you in every love interest I write and you will always stay gold to me, eternally young in the midst of an endless eighties summer.

I look at the stars, at Orion, at Sirius and I dream of becoming an Astronomer... I know very well, the hour will come, I can die for the cause of my people... I will forget astronomy for a long time and I will become a fighter.

Zhenya Rudneva—shot down April 9, 1944, on the eve of her wedding (aged 22)

The war won't end soon
The thunder of anti-aircraft guns will not cease
    soon.
Silence over the crossing
And the sky is covered with clouds.
The engine is calling—fly faster
Hurry, crashing into the darkness of the night.

Natalya Meklin (aged 19 at the start of the war)—flew 980 night missions

PROLOGUE

Tasha looked over the side of the plane in awe as she watch.
the dance of the corn fields. As far as she could see, the.
shaggy heads were twisting and weaving in the wind like a vast
golden wave.

She had flown in many different planes since the war, and
she always felt the same, thankful for the beauty of the land
and grateful for this place of peace.

She remembered how proud she had felt in 1945 when
the USA had welcomed her in with open arms, grateful for her
service alongside her American and Allied brothers, rewarding
her for fighting against Hitler's evil regime. It felt so long
ago, now.

All at once, Nadia changed direction, flying the tiny plane
into the wind and wisps of her white hair snaked out from
under her leather cap and flicked at her eyes, already damp
from the wind and the emotion, causing them to brim with
fresh tears. She closed them to stop them from smarting and
tuned into the engine's hum, so familiar to her. But instead of
the feeling of joy she'd expected, the sound dragged her back,
pulled her back to the deadliest night of her life, back to a time

)erson that she used to be forty years before. Moztok,
a^nber 5, 1942 was a date and place branded into her
ry.

\s she drew in a short, sharp breath, she felt all the weight
er regret for that one action that had caused the most
ible chain of events, the worst mistake of her life, that had
ulted in the death of a person she'd loved with all her heart.
s her stomach twisted and her heart pounded, her mind
:ifted back...

———

...Gritting her teeth and setting her jaw, Tasha leaned heavily
on the throttle and lined up the plane for the most dangerous
part of its run. Gripping the shuddering joystick, she tried to
block out the deafening roar of the engine that screeched its
vehement displeasure at being thrust into such a deep dive.
Since Russia had joined the war against Hitler's evil army,
they'd been fighting every night, alongside the other Allies.

Breaking through the ragged gray clouds, the world below
exploded into view and she was momentarily blinded by the
expanse of white crystallization, brightened by a ripening
moon. Like frozen stalagmites, petrified trees were silhouetted
against the night sky, appearing to grow up from the snow that
was softened by a swirling, low-lying fog. The fairytale
mystique was instantly broken by the heavy artillery and
searchlights that roamed the skies. Tasha blinked to clear her
vision as she got her first look at tonight's target, a German
encampment, and aimed the nose towards it, her intense
concentration not wavering as over her shoulder, her sister
Nadia, now navigating for her, shouted their descent into the
communication tube: "Eight hundred feet, seven hundred feet,
six hundred feet."

Nadia flashed a signal to the two other planes and one of
the PO2s at their side roared forward as their comrade Irina

moved into position to draw fire away from Tasha's plane, heavy with its bombs. Drawing in the collar of her fur-lined jumpsuit and swiping at her frosted goggles, she fixated on the silhouette of Kira, Irina's navigator, as Tasha chewed nervously on her bottom lip, waiting for the sign to commence her bombing run. Even though she had done this hundreds of times, this was always the point her heart pounded and her stomach clenched as though it was caught in a vice, especially tonight where she rocked on the edge of her emotional cliff preparing to jump. She always fought with her common sense at this tipping point, as it screamed inside her that she still had a chance to turn and disengage. Swallowing down the dry, frigid air, sharp in her throat, she watched the plane ahead bob and weave in the billowing gusts. Teasing out a ragged breath, Tasha watched the navigator in the plane ahead of her, waiting for the signal. Kira slowly lifted her arm into the air, the wind frantically whipping the sleeve of her flying suit. In her hand, the barrel of the flare gun was solid and ominous against the night sky.

There was a muffled crack, and then the sky was ablaze with a blast of white light. It cascaded to the earth on its parachute, blinding them all for a second before illuminating their enemy and intended target. At this height, Tasha could now see ghostlike figures that swarmed around the snowy ground in their odd white camouflage as they hastily swiveled guns towards Irina and started firing.

As bullet trails lit up the sky around them, Tasha clenched and unclenched her fists to keep blood circulating in her hands as she shifted uncomfortably on top of the frying pan that attempted to protect her in their paper-thin biplane.

Tasha drew in a deep breath and slowed the engine to just above a stall, the most perilous part of their mission that had earned them the nickname *"Night Witches"* from their enemy. And like a whisper, they whooshed towards their target, making them virtually impossible to be heard or seen against the black expanse of sky. As she prepared to engage, all she could think about was staying alive as anti-aircraft fire continued to explode all around them.

"Steady on course and altitude!" Nadia shouted, and a band of perspiration gathered under her cap as Tasha stared at her altimeter, keeping the plane as straight as she could. Behind her she heard Nadia slam her hand down on the release button as the bombs began to rain down with a whistle. It only took a few seconds for them to hit the earth, exploding into a loud cavalcade of heat, light, and smoke.

Then, quickly accelerating the engine, she dragged the thrust back to her chest to climb the plane. As she leveled out, she drew in breath, knowing it was now or never. If she didn't take this opportunity, she may never have the chance again. Swallowing down her fear, she followed through with her plan, and instead of turning around as she was supposed to, she continued on across enemy lines.

"What are you doing?" Nadia yelled into their communication tube. "We should turn here!"

"I can't," Tasha screamed back, the tears burning her eyes. "I have to know for sure. That the Nazis have killed the man I love."

Nadia realized her sister's plan.

"Don't do it, Tash. Is he worth dying over?"

"I just have to see it with my own eyes."

The flak picked up around them as their position was now evident with the hum of the engine.

A string of bullets clipped their wings. "Oh my God! You're going to kill us!"

"It will only take a minute!" Tasha yelled back over her shoulder as she felt Nadia attempting to take control of the plane from behind her. "Just one minute, please, Nadia!" she begged.

Nadia released her grip and swore as Tasha headed towards the place she had memorized from the map. And there it was, like an ugly black insect marring the virgin snow. The burned-out wreckage of a Sturmovik fighter bomber, Luca's plane. Tasha let out a strangled gasp.

"Oh my God. Oh my God, Luca," she cried out as she dived lower to get a closer look. A wall of uncontrollable pain hit her all over again, rolling in icy waves throughout her body, seizing her chest and robbing her of breath.

Distracted by her grief, she lost all sense of altitude and didn't have time to react as a dense black mass suddenly appeared in front of her. They clipped the top of the tree; the branch snapped in two, spraying ice and snow into the cockpit as Nadia screamed behind her. The force of the collision knocked them off balance, and the whole plane lurched to the left. Trying to regain control, Tasha overcompensated, and it jerked them back far to the right, clipping another tree as her sister swore and they were sprayed with another shower of ice. Instinctively, Tasha pulled hard on the joystick with all of her strength as the muscles in her arms twitched and burned with the force, clenching her jaw she willed the plane to climb, feeling Nadia's strength also on the control.

"Come on!" she screamed at the plane through gritted teeth and jagged breath. In answer, it growled back at her before finally screeching into a steep climb. Alerted by the high-pitched whine of their engine, a German spotlight located them, blinding them as anti-aircraft trails lit up all around them and a rattle of bullets peppered the side of the plane. They both swore. All at once a deafening explosion ripped off part of their tail, forcing them both to duck below their cockpit as the heat roared forward, scorching the back of their necks. Without part of their tail, the plane began to plummet, and both pilots were instantly thrust forward, straining against their harnesses. Tasha fought to gain control but without a balanced tail it was impossible. As terror rose into her throat, she could hardly breathe with the chill of the frigid air and the speed that they plummeted towards the ground, the engine whining high-pitched in their ears.

"We're going to die," yelled Nadia in desperation.

In answer, Tasha could do nothing as the ground raced up to meet them. She could do nothing but brace herself and wait for the end to come.

1

AUGUST 1941

Tasha

"Have you any idea how much I love you?" Luca whispered into Tasha's ear, his heavy breath warming her face, as he seductively moved from kissing her lips to her throat and neck. His hands found her hips and he gently pressed her against the tree that they were sheltering under.

"Tell me again," she gasped in between kisses.

"Why don't I just show you, instead?"

Holding her tightly, he drew her even closer, his soft, warm lips finding hers again. Tasha slid her hands around his neck, tangling them into his thick, dark hair, crushing it through her fingers, losing herself in his passionate kiss. A full-body tingle worked its way down her spine as she felt the thrill of him so close to her. He deepened the kiss, pressing his firm chest against her own. In response she found a gap in his clothing, and she roamed his skin as goosebumps raised beneath her fingertips all across his broad back. Luca's breath became rapid, their desire intensifying.

Suddenly remembering, she opened her eyes and checked the time and, hitching her breath, pulled away.

"We can't, Luca," she whispered, breathlessly, her tone reflecting her frustration. "I have my lesson in five minutes."

"I can be finished in three," he rasped, his quickening breath warming her ear as he began kissing her again.

"And how much fun would that be for me?" she joked, pushing him off her with a curl of her lip.

"Can we meet later then?" he implored, closing in again and covering her face with tiny, gentle kisses.

"I can't. My sister is getting married, did you forget?"

He stopped, pulled away, and looked blankly at her.

She peered at him. "You have to be there," she demanded. "Otherwise I'll have to sit with one of my boring cousins at the wedding breakfast."

He stared down at her. "I can't believe your sister is marrying Ivan Kozlov. All he talks about is his work for the Party."

"I know, but it's what she wants."

All at once, a plane roared overhead, and they both stopped to watch.

"Yan is such a showoff," she commented, shielding her eyes from the sun as she began to readjusting in her clothes. "You're a much better flyer. I wouldn't want to be in the cockpit with him."

"I would rather be in a cockpit with you too," he said, returning to his position and nibbling her ear. "Who knows what we could get up to at five hundred feet."

She shook her head. "Do you only ever think of one thing?"

"I do when I'm with you," he mused, running his fingers through her long red hair. "And don't lie, you like it too."

She smirked her agreement as, slipping her hand into his, they walked hand in hand to the hangar.

"So, Nadia is getting married. She's such a skilled pilot, I always thought she would be an instructor or something."

Tasha swiveled on her heels and glared at him. "I don't think she's that great," she snarled.

"Well, not as good as you, of course," he backtracked, realizing his mistake, before grabbing her around the waist and nuzzling her neck, "but no one is. You are one of a kind."

"I always think her flying is a little too perfect," continued Tasha, laboring her point. "She leaves no room for adventure or risk. Where's the fun in that?"

"That's why I think she would be a good instructor. Whereas you should be flying for the circus."

She smiled at his comment as they arrived at the hangar and she brushed his cheek with another kiss.

But before she could walk away he pulled her back, his gaze searching her face. His voice became husky with the intensity. "Tasha, with your sister getting married, will you not reconsider marrying me? I know we have a good time together, but I want more, there is no one else in this world for me, it has always been you. I can't imagine a world where I am not your husband and you are not my wife. So why do we have to wait? Why can't we get married next week?" He looped a curl of hair behind her ear and drew her closer until the gentleness of his breath warmed her ear. "Yours is the last face I want to see as I go to sleep and the first face I want to wake up to. I want all of our children to look just like you and I want us to grow old together."

Tasha scanned his face as she considered his words, hearing the intensity in his tone.

"It's not you, Luca. You know I love you," she said adamantly. "It's marriage, I just can't see myself as a married woman. It's like I have this giant bird inside me trying to break free that wants to soar and see all life has to offer before I am tied down to taking care of children and a home. I want to experience something *more*. I know it doesn't make any sense. I am from a small village; where could I go, what could I do? But still that feeling is there, I can't help it. And until I figure out what that means, it would be wrong of me to marry anyone, especially you: the person I love more than life itself."

Luca looked crushed.

She grabbed his chin in her hands "I promise you, this is about me."

His piercing blue eyes met hers as he continued at a whisper. "I don't really understand, but I do love you and I guess that means that I have to wait. Because one day, I believe you will say yes."

She smiled reluctantly, and nodded her understanding before pulling away from him and, lightening her tone, she tapped his cheek.

"See you at the marriage office." Her lips brushed his as she squeezed his hand and walked past him.

His words had weighted the air between them as she moved past him into the hangar, feeling the conflict she always did whenever they had this conversation. Why couldn't she just say yes? She and Luca had been in love for years, she couldn't imagine spending one day without him either, but still she felt this tightening in her heart. After the death of her parents when she and Nadia were so young, she felt this huge obligation to do something or be someone, so that their sacrifices for her weren't in vain. And she felt it inside her, there was something she was meant to do, something bigger.

Arriving at the plane, she was shaken from her reverie by her instructor who was already marching up and down.

"Miss Petroffskaya, you are late."

"I am. My babka needed me to help her this afternoon as my sister is getting married. Please forgive me."

"Your grandmother was out there with you under that tree?" he snarled, calling her bluff.

She smiled. "Well, helping her made me late meeting a friend and I'm here now," she responded. Grabbing her flying jacket from the hook where she kept it and buttoning her leather cap and goggles, she tucked in as much of her hair as she could, as they walked towards the plane.

"You need to learn more discipline," he fired back as she reached the aircraft. "I want you to know that even though the man that runs this club has agreed to give you free lessons as payment for the work you do here cleaning, you should remember it is a privilege. And though they allow women here to fly"—he spat out this comment, with obvious distaste—"I do have some sway regarding students who are not up to par."

She turned and flashed her emerald green eyes at him and drew in a slow, tantalizing breath, her voice lowering to a sensual pitch. "I am so grateful for this privilege, Comrade Stein, and to also get to fly with such an experienced pilot as yourself. I do hope you won't say anything. I so enjoy our lessons together." She then brushed his cheek gently with her fingertips before climbing into the front seat, causing him to remain red-faced and flustered in his response. Letting out a frustrated expulsion of air, he climbed into the plane and took the seat behind her.

Hitting the contact switch, a member of the ground crew spun her propeller and removed her chocks. Giving him a thumbs-up, Tasha taxied the aircraft out of the hangar and waved to Luca, who was already on his bike, waiting to watch her take off. Pushing on the throttle, she sped off down the runway.

"Not quite so fast!" her instructor demanded from behind her.

"What?" screamed Tasha, the engine roaring so hard she pretended that it was impossible to hear anything as she pushed it to its full thrust and then gracefully lifted the plane into the sky.

Waving to Luca and thinking of the earlier comment about the circus, she tore into the air and yipped as she swung the plane into a steep climb and then a dive that made her stomach flip-flop. Even from this distance she could see Luca was laughing.

An angry, urgent voice came from behind her, and though she couldn't hear him against the roar of the engine she knew he was scolding her.

"Sorry," she screamed back towards her instructor. "My hand slipped."

She wasn't certain, but she was pretty sure he swore behind her as she aimed the nose of the plane into the clear blue sky. As she let out a long, comforting breath, she felt the usual thrill of excitement run through her body as she marveled at the freedom and exhilaration she felt flying through the air.

2

Tasha

Before Tasha could even open the front door, her sister, Nadia, pulled it open and scowled at her. "Where have you been?" she spat out. "You should have been here over an hour ago."

Tasha bit her lip and tried not to laugh at her sister's appearance. Half of her long, dark hair was out of rag rolls, the other was still pinned up on one side, and she looked a fright as she stomped back into the house.

Tasha followed meekly behind. "I told you I had a flying lesson today. You never listen to me." Tasha looked across at their grandmother, whom they lovingly called Babka.

She still stood in her place behind the chair in the bedroom, obviously in the midst of taking out the rags from the bride's hair. Babka lifted her eyes to the ceiling in a look of exasperation as Nadia sat down to retake her place.

"See, I told you she was coming," Babka cooed, stroking Nadia's cheek with her knobbly knuckles. "Now, you need to calm down. All that anger will rise up and show in your face. And a bride should be serene on her wedding day."

"What chance do I have with a sister like mine?" she sulked.

Tasha looked over her sister's shoulder and, fixing her in the mirror, spoke in a gentle tone. "I'm here now. What do you need me to do?"

Nadia paused, then said in a slightly exasperated tone, "I need help with my makeup."

"Okay, Babka will take out your rags and brush out your hair, and I will help you with your makeup."

Nadia's face softened. "I'm sorry, Tasha. I'm just so nervous. I want to look especially nice for Ivan; many of his friends from the Party will be there."

"Of course you do," said Tasha as she pulled out her sister's wash bag and, searching through it, found some rouge. "And you will be."

"Not too much, I get the impression that Ivan prefers women to look natural."

Babka and Tasha shared a taciturn look of their mutual dislike of having to please Ivan rather than Nadia, but Tasha dusted off some of the color from the rouge pad.

They continued to dote on their charge. Picking up an ancient wooden brush, Babka combed out Nadia's thick, dark hair, her eyes brimming as she mused, thoughtfully, "I wish your parents were here to see this. Your father would have been so proud and you have the same beautiful hair as your mother."

Both girls smiled at each other wistfully, acknowledging their own yearning for their parents. Cutting through the sadness that had suddenly descended on the room, Tasha stood up and squeezed her sister's shoulders.

"You should put on your dress," she whispered.

Removing it from where it was hanging, Babka and Tasha carefully pulled the wedding dress over Nadia's head and laced up the bodice. Then, as Tasha placed and tied the red-peaked *kokoshnik* on the bride's head, Babka carefully draped the long piece of antique lace that would act as a veil. In the bedroom, all stood to admire the beautiful wedding garments that had been their mother's in the mirror. An elegant red *sarafan*, the Russian traditional wedding attire, looked striking with Nadia's thick, black hair and on her tall, angular frame. As she turned back and forward to view herself from every angle, the white pearls in the heavily embroidered headdress shimmered in the candlelight. As Tasha watched her, she admired how the delicate fabric brushed Nadia's slender hips and hung from her tiny shoulders, noticing as she adjusted her headdress that her cream-colored skin, high cheekbones and brown eyes were gorgeous underneath the fringe of gold tassels. As she watched her turning in the mirror, Tasha noted once again the stark differences between her sister and her. The bride, at twenty-two years old, was only two years older than Tasha but at five foot seven was a full four inches taller. Tasha, with her flaming red hair, full breasts, and shapely hips, was a real contrast to Nadia's slender frame.

"And now for the flowers," said Babka as the bride tried out her new heels, following her into the kitchen, where her grandmother handed her the sweet-smelling bouquet she had just cut that morning. Tears brimmed in all their eyes as the bride's outfit was made complete.

"You look so gorgeous," Tasha whispered, the emotion obvious in her tone. "He is so lucky to get you."

"I feel lucky to have him," Nadia whispered, lifting and inhaling the fragrant roses. She smiled at her sister, and then a concerned look crossed her face. "You're going to get dressed, right? Tell me you're not going to wear that to my wedding?"

Tasha looked down at herself and laughed. She had completely forgotten she was still wearing her flying suit and boots.

"I'll be changed in a second," she assured her.

Rushing back into the bedroom, Tasha stripped off her clothes and grabbed the dress that Babka had already placed on her bed. As she tightened her own bodice and tucked most of her hair under the traditional red headscarf, she thought back over the words her grandmother had said. She wished her parents were here, too. They'd paid a high price in their family for the revolution. A terrible time of upheaval: Babka had barely survived, but the girls' parents hadn't fared so well. Making sure their girls got the lion's share of the food, they had died of influenza, weakened by the starvation prevalent in Russia during that time. Leaving behind their two young daughters to be raised by their grandmother.

It was strange how their personal tragedy had affected the sisters so differently, Tasha mused. Nadia was always so careful, counting every ruble, weighing every situation, always striving to be the best and the brightest at everything. It had the opposite effect on Tasha, who wanted to live her life fully in every way she could.

As she reapplied her lipstick, her lips still felt slightly swollen from kissing Luca, and she smiled as she thought of him.

She loved to fly with him and they had both been allowed to fly as part payment for helping out at the flying school, as had Nadia. But she had dreams of seeing the world from the sky. She wanted to see every bit of this world and not just stay in Russia.

As she came out of her room, the clock chimed the hour, and they all looked at one another. It was time. Walking to the wedding office, friends and neighbors waved and blew kisses as they made their way inside. Before the bride entered, Tasha slipped inside and took a seat. At the front she saw Luca. He had changed his shirt and combed his hair. She whispered to him as the accordion player began to play. "It seems you found time in your day to make it."

"I'm hoping that the experience might rub off on you," he joked back, as she shook her head and chuckled.

Nadia made her way down the room on the arm of a

cousin to meet her bridegroom, who stood stiff and upright in his red tunic, black trousers, sash, and boots. When she approached his side, she gave the tiniest of smiles as he just nodded his acknowledgment of her being there. Tasha wondered once again if this serious-minded, intense man was the best choice for her lively, beautiful sister.

They went through the ceremony. And afterward, they had the traditional wedding feast. Nadia's husband made an elegant, but not affectionate, speech and dutifully kissed her on the cheek as he smiled at his new bride. Luca whispered in her ear, "Do you think they will even consummate their marriage? They're both so clean and careful, I can't imagine it. You know, them being naked in bed together."

Tasha choked on her drink and clenched her jaw to stop from laughing out loud.

"Not like us," he continued. Then, sliding his hand down her thigh under the table, he added, "What are you doing after the service?"

She leaned across and kissed him then whispered in his ear, "Seeing you, of course. Usual place?"

He nodded, and she slipped her hand into his.

3

Nadia

On her wedding night, Nadia lay in bed watching the shadows from the candlelight dancing on the ceiling, as she reflected on the day and waited nervously for Ivan to join her.

Ivan had made it clear that he hadn't wanted to sleep with her before the marriage vows had been exchanged, and she had respected that kind of morality. But she had already been lying in bed for twenty minutes, and it sounded like he was still in his study.

Frustrated, she decided to go and check on her bridegroom. Pulling her dressing gown over her brand-new nightdress that she'd bought for the occasion, her feet were cold as she stepped onto the stone floor. Ivan disapproved of heating a house too warmly, so he ensured that the fires were out by 7 p.m.

Slipping out into the hallway, she made her way to his study and tapped on his door. He called out to her to come in. But his tone sounded absent, as though he was deep in thought.

She stood in the doorway and looked in. The room was

cramped and dark, the atmosphere chilly and formidable, even with shelves crammed with books. And even though it was small, it felt as if it was his empire. She hovered in the doorframe.

"Ivan?" she called out towards him.

He was writing at his desk, his head bowed over a pathetic nub of a candle as he frantically scribbled away. Finally, he looked up and went straight into an elaborate retelling of the letter he was writing. Communicating how angry he'd been that a man of influence, Comrade Abbots, was not being as loyal as he could be for his country. She listened, but preoccupied by her own desires she didn't really hear a lot of what he was saying. Finally, he swiveled around on his chair and slammed his hand down on the desk.

"Can you believe this, Nadia? We have the evil of Hitler at our heels; we need more than ever to be united."

Nadia looked at her strong, handsome husband, his dark hair tousled, his jacket now removed, which only emphasized his broad shoulders, with just his shirt—a thin piece of cotton—between her and his naked chest. Her eyes were instinctively drawn to his neck where he had removed his tie and unbuttoned his collar, revealing a triangle of soft, dark hair nestled there. As he continued ranting, oblivious to her growing desire for him, his eyes glistened with the passion he felt for his subject. It was why she had fallen in love with him: this radical passion. But in this instant, she wanted that passion for herself and tried not to show her disappointment.

She swallowed down her hurt as he turned back toward the desk and, moving behind him, she placed her arms around his neck, her body shivering with the closeness of his skin to her. He stiffened as she whispered in his ear, "This can wait till tomorrow, Ivan. Why don't you come to bed? It's late."

It was subtle, but she heard him suck in a breath. Was he afraid? Gently he unhooked her arms and distanced himself by getting to his feet and drawing away, picking up the letter and holding it up between them like a shield.

"I really need to get this finished, Nadia. I'll be with you soon." He nodded and squeezed her arm and without a second look sat down and pulled out another sheet of paper. "I must get this in the post first thing tomorrow. It cannot wait. I'm sorry. Was there anything else you needed?"

She swayed coyly from side to side. "I wondered if you liked my new nightdress."

Swiveling back around, he swallowed down hard and hurriedly ran his eyes up and down her body.

"Oh, yes, it is very..." He settled on the word: "lovely. It fits you very... very... well," he continued with an overcompensating smile.

She was a little disappointed at his reaction; Tasha had made her buy it, insisting she was ravishing in it. Nadia realized that maybe he was just nervous; this was new for him too and it was hard to move from the chaste way he had conducted their courtship to something more physical. So, she tried another tack; maybe it would go better if he felt more comfortable with her. "Would you like me to get you a drink?"

"No!" he snapped and then realizing his sharpness, softened his tone. "If I needed a drink, I would've got myself one," he said quietly. "I don't need to trouble you; you get yourself to bed. It has been a busy day."

Pausing for a moment, trying to find something to add to the conversation, she gave up and finally slipped out of his study, moving back toward the bedroom. As she walked, Nadia felt the pain of rejection in the pit of her stomach. And as she got beneath the covers, she wondered if she was being churlish about this. Indeed, there were many days for them to be a couple in a physical way. She just thought that maybe he would've put some of this work aside, just for tonight.

As she stared out at the moon through a gap in the curtains, she felt the sadness welling up in her and maybe a little doubt. She tried to push down her thoughts of concern. Ivan was a good man and she loved him.

She thought back to their very first meeting. He had arrived from another village to talk about the ideals of the Communist Party. Impeccably dressed, and handsome with his raven black hair and a small goatee that framed a strong chin, his warm brown eyes didn't miss the opportunity to linger and connect with each person as he towered over them, delivering his speech. She remembered how he spoke that night with such vigor and enthusiasm that the whole audience had been in awe of him.

It had been her first time hearing Ivan speak, and she had been invited by a friend. Nadia had some interest in the movement, but wasn't quite as enthused as many people around her seemed to be. She didn't remember much about the words but mostly remembered Ivan's hypnotic presence and that the town hall had been cold and drafty that night. Afterwards, Nadia and some of the other women had cooked a meal for them to eat.

Ivan had made his way around the room, talking to them all, and had finally found his way to Nadia after finishing her famous soup. His deep brown eyes met hers.

"You are the cook of this wonderful food, I hear," he praised her.

Nadia felt her cheeks flush. "Oh, it was nothing. Just something my grandmother taught me to cook."

"No, don't minimize the gift you gave us, it was delicious." Then bending slightly towards her he continued talking to her, his tone a little conspiratorial: "I'm glad you're part of our group, Comrade Nadia. You are good for our future. Good food with comradeship: this is the Communist way."

After he'd left that night, all the girls had buzzed around her as they'd cleaned up.

"He obviously likes you, Nadia."

"He's such a wonderful man. I wish he'd talked to me the way he'd talked to you."

"He barely noticed my chicken stew," said one of the other girls.

They talked about him as though he were a god. He was mesmerizing for sure, but Nadia was surprised. Wasn't it the Communist way that everybody was the same? No person better than the other?

The women around her continued to admire him, discussing all the elements of his speech, not to mention his charismatic presence and handsome looks, as she pondered these thoughts. When he returned the following week, he greeted Nadia first, and they struck up a lively conversation. She had a lot to ask on the subjects he had addressed the week before and many questions that he was more than happy to answer. Appearing to feel flattered that she had considered seriously several elements of his speech, he was pleased to elaborate.

As the meeting ended and they were leaving, he had approached her again.

"Comrade Nadia, I wonder if you would be open to continuing our lively debate over a meal one evening?"

She had felt her cheeks flush at his forthrightness and felt flattered that a man of Ivan's status would want to continue to answer her questions. She liked being able to discuss weighty issues. At home, Babka was more interested in the latest recipes she wanted to try and Tasha just rolled her eyes when Nadia had wanted to discuss the news of the day.

After that first meal together, he had asked her if she would step out with him. She remembered the glow she had felt around him. He was stable, calm, thoughtful about so many things, very intelligent, and could talk on a multitude of topics. They could talk for hours and she enjoyed the lively banter between them.

After years of taking care of Tasha, feeling like a surrogate mother and father to her sister, it was nice to have someone around her she could rely on, who made her feel safe. It had meant the world to her. They had continued meeting regularly, their debating continuing sometimes late into the night. He had a quick wit and sharp mind and Nadia loved being around him.

And when he had actually proposed to her, she had been so flattered that somebody like Ivan would want to marry her that she had quickly accepted. But had she been in love? At the time, she had thought so. But now, as she lay alone in her marital bed, she wondered, had she been too hasty? Something struck her as she lay there. During their courtship, there hadn't been a lot of physical affection between them. On the contrary, he had kissed her dutifully on parting and squeezed her arm more than once. The affection had always been implied, but never really acted upon. It was nothing like her sister's romance. All the things Tasha was getting up to with Luca made her blush, as her sister had enlightened her when they'd lain side by side whispering in their beds.

Ivan had been warm but distant, kind but conservative. At the time, it hadn't worried her. She knew that some men were that way. And after their wedding, they would allow their own desires to come forward.

But now, as she lay here alone on her wedding night, she wondered if it was more than just nerves. Would she ever know what Tasha had? Those heights of passion?

She blushed with the thought, but she also wanted it. She couldn't imagine what it was like to feel the way Tasha talked about feeling. Having somebody so in love with you that they wanted to be intimate all the time with you to make you happy.

Ivan finally came to bed hours later, and she'd already dozed off. Nadia woke up with a jolt as he sat on the edge of the bed. Turning to him, she saw his shadow in the flicker of candlelight he'd brought with him.

Slipping in beside her, he whispered to her, "I'm sorry, Nadia. Did I wake you? I tried to be as quiet as possible."

This annoyed her.

"No, it's okay. I can get back off to sleep," she said. Then, wearily, she turned her back to him.

He got in alongside her. "It has been a busy day," he commented with a deep sigh. "But I think now that's all behind us. We can start getting back to normal." Was this what he meant by "normal"? She turned to him and peered at him disapprovingly, studying his handsome features illuminated in the candlelight. "You look sad, Nadia. Are you upset? Is there something wrong?"

"Well, not really, but it is our wedding night."

He looked at her with confusion.

"You know I expected..." She nodded her head, as if trying to help him understand, and suddenly he realized.

"Oh." He seemed to shrink a little as he continued in a tightened tone. "I think there'll be plenty of time in our future for... having children if that's what you were thinking. Young comrades to continue our work." He smiled wistfully. "It has always been a great desire of mine to have children, Nadia. And you will be a wonderful mother. But tonight we should get our rest; we have had a hectic day. We will have plenty of time in the future." He settled down next to her. Then, as if it was an afterthought, turned and brushed her cheek with a dry kiss, smiled and squeezed her arm. Yes, he *was* nervous; as the candlelight swept across his face she could see it in his eyes. But what was making him so scared?

He turned over and was asleep within seconds. Nadia lay there feeling the heat of his body so close to her own, yet so far from her touch. As she listened to his breathing slowing to a regular rhythm, she was tormented by her own anguish and frustration.

4

Tasha

As soon as she opened the door to Luca a month later, Tasha knew something was wrong. His face was drawn and guilt-filled, his eyes cast down. Tonight, they were going out with their friends, meeting at the flying club's bar, and he would usually be upbeat and happy, but he looked grave.

"What is it?" she asked. "Something's wrong. I can see it on your face."

In response, he leaned forward and pulled her in and hugged her deeply, kissing her neck. She knew he was trying to avoid the question so she pulled away and, grabbing him by his shoulders, studied him.

"What is it? Tell me."

"It's nothing. There's nothing going on. I just had a hard day. Go and get ready. We'll be late."

He pulled away, but something in the pit of her stomach started to grind, balling itself into a knot.

She had known Luca all of her life. They had grown up together, and the only time she'd ever seen him like this before was when he'd been sent home from school for killing a bird with his catapult.

She changed her clothes, put on some makeup, and came back out to the kitchen. Luca was staring out the window. As she approached, he turned nervously and smiled too widely, apparently overcompensating for whatever he was thinking and feeling. She rolled back her shoulders and narrowed her eyes. She would get it out of him, but maybe she'd have to wait until he'd had a couple of drinks first.

They made their way across their little village, walking side by side, making pleasant small talk. She noticed he didn't take her hand or grab her at all. So un-Luca-like. Whatever it was, this was big.

Inside the bar, their own group of friends were already on their second drink, and they greeted them in a loud, jovial manner. "Here they are, the lovebirds. We've been waiting for you."

They both sat down and settled into conversation with those around them, much of it about the progression of the attack on Russia's borders by their enemy, Hitler and all the terrible things he was doing. As she talked, Tasha continued to glance across at Luca and could see his obvious preoccupation, though he was attempting to join in with the conversations around him.

From across the other side of the bar, Igor Tsyskowski approached the group. Another pilot, he was a large barrel of a man. His tunic was grubby and stretched tightly over his straining sash. On his head, a leather cap was set at a jaunty angle. Reaching the table, he slapped Luca and Mikhail, Luca's best friend, on their backs.

"Here you are, you rogues. Are you drinking your last before you leave?"

Tasha had been deep in conversation with her friend Olga, but she caught the comment and stopped what she was saying to listen. Go? Where were they going?

Luca looked sheepish and responded quickly by asking Igor if he wanted a drink.

"Don't pretend to be so humble," roared Igor, who was obviously quite drunk. "I think we need to have a toast." He held his glass in the air, and all the group looked around, bewildered. "To all the men that are going to the front to fight the Nazi evil, and to our newest recruits, Luca and Mikhail," he said, knocking back his vodka.

Luca's eyes flicked toward Tasha and he looked crestfallen.

This was what he had been hiding. He had signed up.

Jumping to her feet, Tasha screamed at him, "What?"

The rest of the group froze in the midst of their toast. Olga, who was also Mikhail's girlfriend, turned towards Tasha with concern. "You didn't know? He and Luca signed up yesterday. They're going to join the war against Hitler at the front."

Tasha turned to peer at her boyfriend. His face was cast down, looking at the floor.

"No, I didn't know," she said, "because Luca didn't tell me, did you, Luca?"

He looked sheepish as the whole group stared at him.

"You didn't discuss it with Tasha before you decided to sign up?" whispered Mikhail, looking shocked.

"Tasha and I think the same on everything," he said defensively, swirling the vodka in his glass. "I'm doing what's right for my country. She will understand. Right, Tasha?"

Tasha lifted up her own glass of vodka and threw it into his face. "This is what I understand, Luca. I understand you made a decision that would affect me without even considering me. You decided to go off to the war and fight, not even thinking how that would make me feel."

He jumped up too, wiping his hand down his face, which was red with the embarrassment. "It wasn't like that. They came here to the flying school. They were looking for recruits. They need people on the front that can fly. And why not? Here I'm just working at the mill day in, day out. This way, I'll get to go and do something worthwhile. I'll get to be in the air."

"Right up until you die!"

"I'm a good flyer. I won't die."

"Said every other young man that's been buried in a cemetery during every war," she responded.

Olga grabbed her arm. "He's doing a good thing, Tasha. You shouldn't be angry. He wants to do what's right for us. He's fighting against that animal Hitler for our safety."

Tasha pulled her arm away. "It's not that I don't believe that. I think that going to fight is a good thing. I just would rather have talked about it before he made such a huge decision without telling me." She glared at him. "It makes me wonder what I really mean to you if you can just do that without thinking." Pushing past the chair, she stomped away.

Out in the fresh air, she strode away, the shock of what she'd heard hitting her, and she felt tears stinging her eyes. Her stomach cramped and her chest tightened. Luca was going to the front. Her Luca, the man she loved with all of her heart. She couldn't even imagine being away from him for one day, never mind for the rest of the war. Then, predictably, she heard steps running behind her. He grabbed her by the shoulders, pulling her around to face him, his blue eyes filled with concern.

"Please, stop, Tasha, we've got to talk about this."

"What is there to talk about? You already signed the documents. You're already going."

He looked like a wounded animal. "I didn't do it to hurt you. I would never do that."

"Well, you hurt me anyway. Whether you intended to do it or not, I'm in pain. But you know what? Don't you worry. I'll find somebody else to take your place in five minutes," she lied, her anger and need to hurt him overtaking her as she strode away, although she could feel the anger turning to hurt and pain twisting within her stomach. She felt shocked and wrung-out at the same time.

He followed as she strode at a clip but kept at a distance, knowing she needed her space. Along the way, he called out to her; she could hear the fear in his tone. "You know how much I love you, Tasha. You know this is not about us."

"How could it not be about us?" she spat back. "You're leaving me, aren't you?"

"Then why won't you marry me before I leave? They are saying this war won't last much longer. Then we can have our whole lives together."

"No, thank you. I don't want to be your widow. I look terrible in black."

She glanced at him over her shoulder; he looked wretched. Racing to catch up to her, he grabbed hold of her arm and pushed her against a tree.

"Please stop. We've got to talk about this." He had tears in his eyes.

She fought him for a second then gave up, his strong arms keeping her in place.

"Why did you do it? Please, be honest with me," she said, finding it hard to keep the pain from her tone.

"Tasha, I would have been conscripted eventually anyway. That's what they're all saying. This way, I get to decide and I get to fly. You *know* how that feels." His voice cracked. "And I want you to be proud of me... Maybe you would want to marry me if I was something more than just a miller."

She sighed. "Oh Luca, I am already proud of you and I couldn't love you any more than I already do. Oh God, I can't believe you are leaving me! I'll miss you so much." She stifled a sob, her head dropping to his chest, tears now sliding freely down her cheeks.

He cradled her in his arms and smoothed her ruffled hair with his hand as he whispered into her ear, "And I'll miss you too,

Tasha. But I have not stopped thinking about the words you said ever since you told me about the reason you won't marry me. I have been thinking that maybe there was something missing between us and that this separation would be what we need to make our love stronger." The tips of his fingers gently swept away the tears running down her cheeks. "Remember when you said you wanted to live a bigger life?" She stared up at him, suddenly feeling guilty for sharing so candidly. Was she the reason for this decision; had her words driven him away? As if sensing her thoughts, he shook his head. "At first what you said hurt me. As if somehow a life with only me wasn't enough, that I wasn't enough. But then I started really thinking about it." He took her chin in his hand and gently looked directly into her eyes as he continued.

"And I realized something in that moment. I realized that I have always seen you, Tasha. Seen who you really are. Never a day goes by when I am not in awe that you chose me, you chose me out of everyone in this world to love. Because when I really think about it, I have always seen in you what you are talking about. And that desire I see inside you is everything I have always loved about you, and to try and cage that bird, that needs to break free and fly, would be wrong. It would crush you." His voice became hoarse with his emotion as he continued. "And I could never do that, because I love you too much to see you held back in any way. So, if I go away, it will be a good thing; maybe it will give you the time and space you need to experience whatever it is that is calling to you. And then maybe you will be ready, ready to trust me to love you for the rest of your life."

As he slowly pulled away, the moonlight streamed across his face and she could see the tears were now rolling down his cheeks, too. They looked deeply into each other's eyes and she understood. As though she was really seeing him for the first time too and just how much he really did love her. He loved her enough to let her go and be what she needed to be, and though she wished more than anything she could just be what he wanted, just settle down like Nadia, she also knew that she could never be happy when there was something else burning inside her, a destiny she had to fulfill. She hung her head in despair.

"Oh Luca, what if you get killed and it's all my fault for wanting more, making you feel as if you have to be more?"

He drew her chin upwards so she could see his expression clearly. The intensity in his eyes.

"Tasha, I promise you this. I promise you I won't die. I won't die because I believe with all my heart you and I have a destiny. I don't know how I know this; I just do with everything that is within me. Do you trust fate?"

"What?"

"Do you believe that we are supposed to be together?"

"Of course."

He gripped her shoulders and drew her closer. "Then we will take a chance. We will let fate decide. I love you enough that I can let you go, believing that there is nothing, not even a war that can stop us being together if that is what is meant to be."

She choked up again with his words. And, wiping the tears from her face with the heel of her hand, she rolled back her shoulders. "Oh Luca, I understand, and though I hate that this is where we are, you are right."

"I'm right?" His eyes shone, his tone playful. apparently enjoying her admitting that.

She responded with a half-hearted smile, her voice still tight with emotion: "Maybe just this once."

He chuckled, kissing the tip of her nose and pulling her close. She tried to rally. "You will be the best ever pilot we have; the Germans won't stand a chance with you at the throttle." Stroking his face, she went on, "You will defeat Hitler quickly and I will figure out what I need to do and I will be waiting here for when you come home a decorated war hero."

He kissed her long and lingering; his lips were warm and soft. Then, hand in hand, they walked back towards her home.

"When will you leave?"

"Next month," he said quietly.

"When were you going to tell me?"

"After I was gone," he joked, attempting to lighten the mood. She started to laugh and punched him on the arm. "Soon. I was going to tell you soon. I just wasn't sure how to put it into words."

"Do you know where you're going to be based?"

"First, I'm going to Moscow for basic training—I'll give you the address so you can send me wildly inappropriate love letters—then a flying training school in the south."

As they continued, they reached the place where they'd first made love, a small copse of trees not far from her home. She stopped and pulled him close.

"This is where it all started for me," she said wistfully.

He nodded, remembering.

She continued, "So it seems appropriate to do this now."

She turned to him and slid her hand inside his tunic, caressing him, feeling the downy hair of his chest as he shuddered in response.

Kissing him urgently, she removed his top and they slid to the ground below the covering of the bushes and began to make love, this time with all the fire of the knowledge of what was to come. This time with the realization that nothing could be counted on from now on.

5

OCTOBER 1941

Nadia

When she heard the latest news of Hitler's invasion, Nadia felt sick, rooted to her kitchen chair as Ivan read to her all the details of the latest developments from his newspaper.

"It appears that both Smolensk and Kiev have fallen, and Hitler is not going to stop and will now set his sights on taking Moscow itself. Also, it appears that the Germans have not penetrated further into Leningrad since they surrounded the city a month ago but apparently intend to hold the city under siege and starve the people out," he stated, rubbing his eyes with the fatigue.

As her husband continued, Nadia's mind wandered back to how it had all started a few months before when the whole of the Russian western front had been hit in one fell swoop in June. Up until then there had been nervousness throughout Russia for a while as the newspapers had been carrying the stories about the buildup of the German armies on their borders, but most people had hoped that Hitler's non-aggression pact would stand and he would be true to his word.

All their hopes of that had been diminished on Sunday, June 22, when Hitler had invaded.

"What does this mean for us now, Ivan?" Nadia asked her husband as he sat staring at the news in front of him. He hadn't even touched his cup of tea.

Finally, Ivan sat back in his seat and shook his head. "I'm not sure, but it's terrible. Look at the numbers. So many people have been killed in all the invasions already. Thousands of tanks, millions of German soldiers storming our borders, overrunning our cities. Our great leader has his hands full."

She tried to cover Ivan's hand with her own, but slowly he pulled it away, and she felt rejected again. Would he not even let her comfort him?

"We shall have to get a meeting together soon. I'll organize one here at the house. Will that be all right?"

Nadia nodded.

"We need to come up with a plan. We need to decide how to respond to this."

Three days later, the local members of the Communist Party arrived at Nadia's house. The look on their faces was bleak, their greetings to her subdued. It was a warm day, and the gathering in their front room was cramped, as so many of the members had decided to come. But they were afraid of being outside and being overheard and, when the soldiers arrived, being reported. There were many rumors about what would happen to fanatical Communists if they were found, and this group was so progressive.

As they sat to meet, one whispered to them all, "Did you hear Comrade Borovkov was killed?"

They nodded soberly.

Another added, "We're hearing such terrible rumors of what's going on. Comrade Devin and Dobrow were taken from Smolensk for being leading members of the Party. That is only two hundred and fifty miles from here and no one has seen them since. I thought that Hitler was angry just with the Jewish people. What does he want with Russian Communists?"

The whole room erupted into alarm and speculation as Ivan tried to calm their fears. "We're a long way from Smolensk, and we will do everything to find our brothers in arms, but we have to decide what we need to do. Hold on to our ideals; we must not let go of what we believe."

"Why is Comrade Stalin, our precious leader, not doing more?" said a short man at the back. His eyes were wild with fear. "Why has he not done anything to assure us?"

"He was taken by surprise," said another young man, rubbing his stubbly chin. "He thought that Hitler was Russia's friend."

"Which just proves you can't trust a fascist," said another one. "Hitler is only doing what he said he set out to do. I read *Mein Kampf*. I know what he wants to do, and having Russia as his play area, his garden for his Aryan race, was always part of his plan. No matter what he promised Stalin."

They all erupted into arguments again. Many of them voiced their concerns about Stalin. No one disparaged him outwardly; that would be too dangerous in a country where people sometimes disappeared for talking negatively about him. But they caged it in phrases such as, "Being our great leader, you would think he would do more to protect us."

Ivan turned to Nadia. "Can you get some food to calm them all down?"

Nadia had been cooking all morning to prepare and brought in food that they all stopped to enjoy. Though after they'd eaten, the argumentative discussion went on into the night, as everybody was so fearful and scared. Once they were gone, Nadia spoke to her husband.

"We need to know more; what can we do?"

Ivan shook his head. "I don't know. I have sent many

letters out to friends to see if they know what's going on, but Moscow is in terrible disarray, apparently. Of course, no one had any idea that this was going to happen, though, so it may be a while before we hear back."

As her husband continued to write letters and fret, Nadia hoped that maybe this would bring them closer together. She approached him once again in his study that night. Talking to him, she put her hands on his shoulders and started to loosen the knot that had formed there.

"Can I do anything for you, Ivan?"

He drew in his breath with her touch, and she gently tightened her grip.

"Like what? Are you planning to fight?" he joked.

She thought for a minute. "Maybe if that's what Stalin wants. Isn't it the Communist way that we are all the same, we are all one?"

He turned and looked at his wife with concern. "No, Nadia, you cannot fight. I don't want you in harm's way. I want you to be safe here in the home you love."

She felt a sting at his dismissal of her, not only from his reluctance to consider her contribution to this war but also at the way he now placed distance between them as he stood away from her at the other side of his desk.

As she watched him nervously moving papers around it, she pondered again what she was doing wrong. What had happened to him in his past that made him so afraid of intimacy?

They had finally consummated their marriage after they had talked in depth about their deep desire to have children, but it had not been any of the pleasures and delights that she'd heard of from Tasha. Nadia had practically had to throw herself at him. Because of his striking good looks and charismatic personality, she had assumed that there had been other women before her. But it had become painfully obvious by her need to guide him through their lovemaking that Nadia was his first lover. Instead of the passionately breathtaking embraces she had often caught Tasha and Luca in, Ivan had treated her more like a china doll. So much so she had to reassure him in the midst of it, "You cannot break me, Ivan. You can be more demonstrative if you wish." In response he had reddened and finally completed the act, but afterwards had apologized profusely for all of his inadequacies. Once he had finally fallen asleep, she had lain in bed bewildered, hoping this wasn't what she had to look forward to for the rest of her married life. Her husband loved her, she was sure of that, but there was something that he seemed so afraid of. She wished there was someone she could confide in, But, as an only child with both of his parents dead, there was no one she could seek out to see what in his past had created such a fear of intimacy for him.

Normally she would have talked to Tasha about any personal issues she was having. But she felt this would be a betrayal of her husband, especially since Tasha already felt Ivan wasn't the best choice for Nadia, as she struggled with Ivan's preoccupation with the Party. She did not want her sister to see her disappointment. Even so, Tasha was very conscious of her sister and often could tell what was happening, even if Nadia didn't say anything.

When Luca had announced he was joining up to fight their enemy, Ivan had commended him to her. When she told him over breakfast, he had said, "I am pleased to hear it. Luca will make a good soldier and an airman. We should have them over to celebrate his decision."

Luca and Tasha had come over to visit the next evening, and it had quickly become an excruciating experience as Ivan found out that Luca had very little care for the Communist Party and very little knowledge of the things that Ivan liked to talk about. Nadia could feel the frustration in her husband as he challenged Luca about his beliefs, to which Luca would just shrug or look at Tasha blankly.

"Whoever is in power, we have to respond. I have never thought it is right for one man to have so much power. If it is wielded in the wrong way it could be disastrous for us. I don't know much about Leninism or Stalinism. It's all the same to me. I look at the difficulty of my life and all the struggles we have been through as a country and I don't see our life as better for one or the other. I'm still at the mill working hard, and so is Tasha. So why is our life any better with one or the other?"

Ivan continued passionately, trying to make his point. "You don't understand our ideals. We're still becoming what we need to become. One day we will achieve this, and people who hold back, who do not embrace the Party, stop us from becoming a great nation."

It was then that Tasha had rolled her eyes at Nadia, before a long awkward silence caused Nadia to retreat quickly into the kitchen as soon as they had finished eating. Once they'd been in the kitchen alone together, Tasha hadn't wasted time asking her in hushed tones, "Are you happy with him, Nadia? He talks about nothing but the Communist Party."

Nadia hated the way Tasha always got straight to the point.

"He's a good man and a good husband," Nadia said defensively. "Just because he's not like Luca doesn't mean that he isn't a kind person."

"I don't expect him to be like Luca, but he barely acknowledged you as his wife throughout dinner. Where is his affection for you after just a few weeks of marriage?"

Nadia swallowed down her own frustration as she placed the plates down on the draining board. She jumped to defend her husband. "That is not what all of life is about, Tasha—affection. Other things are important. Stability, intellect, the building of the home."

"You sound like him. Is that where you got it from?" Tasha

smirked. "Look at you, Nadia," she hissed. "What is wrong with you? You need more than this."

"There is nothing wrong with us," Nadia spat back. "He is a good husband and I'm a good wife, and I hope one day to be a good mother."

"And I hope one day you will be too, but not like this," Tasha stated, starting to wash the dishes. "I would die of boredom. And so will you, unless he diverts some of that passion from his party to you."

"I'm not like you, I don't need a lot of affection to feel loved. We have amazing debates and he is so kind and considerate."

Tasha shook her head with deep knowing. "You're more like me than you admit to yourself. You have our mother's passion in your heart as well as our father's steadfastness. And one day that desire is going to roar up inside you like a lion."

Nadia turned her face away and busied herself with putting away the dishes, not wanting Tasha to see her flushed cheeks that she could feel burning. Nadia didn't want to argue with her sister because, deep down, she knew she was right. But she didn't want to admit the fact that she might have made a grave mistake in marrying Ivan.

6

Tasha

Before Luca left, Tasha tried to spend every single minute she could with him. His boss had been very accommodating at the mill, giving him some time off, knowing that he was just one of many who were leaving to fight the war. Each day of his last week, Tasha would call on him early in the morning and they would go out until late at night.

They went on picnics, they swam, she cooked him food, they flew together, and they made love. Often, urgently at first, their bodies quivering with desire and the desperation of their situation, their eyes always intently locked upon each other. Then, often they would make love a second time, this time long and lingering, watching one another shiver as they ran their fingertips over warm, soft flesh, their bodies moving in a slow, intense rhythm. After they were exhausted, they would lie panting and satisfied, drawn together in one another's arms, limbs intertwined, her head tucked under his chin. As Tasha caught her breath, she tried not to think about what the end of their week would bring.

"How will I know where you are?" she whispered sadly,

one afternoon, her head in his lap after they'd finished making love.

He cleared a few strands of flyaway hair as he studied her face and then ran his hand through the bulk of her messy red locks. His gentle touch sent a shudder right down to her stockingless toes, her summer dress creased from rolling in the long grass.

"I'll send you my address," he said, kissing the tip of her nose.

"Won't they move you, though? Won't you go to different places?"

"They'll always give me an address."

"It will feel strange to think I can't see you when I want to."

The back of his fingers brushed her cheek as he whispered, "We will make a place to see each other every day."

She looked at him quizzically.

"Do you remember the very first time we made love?"

She smiled. "Of course. Babka had sent me on that crazy errand before dawn."

"And I was on my way to work." He continued. "All I could think of was you and even though we were just friends, how desperately I wanted to kiss you."

She smiled at the memory as she remembered too. "That was the reason I was up so early; my stomach ached with my desire for you as well and I couldn't sleep. When Babka saw me so restless, wandering around the kitchen, she sent me out for mushrooms for breakfast to keep me busy."

"As I made my way to work, I was thinking about you and then when I turned that corner and saw you in the woods, it was like a dream come to life. You were searching in the forest with your basket, your hair glistening like copper with the rising sun at your back and I found I could not hold back my desire any longer. I didn't know at the time that you also felt the same way about me, but I knew if I didn't take this stolen moment between us and kiss you, I might lose my nerve forever."

She too remembered the preciousness of that morning meeting. "You were also all I could think about and then suddenly you were there in front of me; I remember how you made me jump and we both laughed. But before we could say anything you rushed towards me and kissed me. Your warm lips on mine with such passion. It was so quick I never had time to take in a breath and I thought I might pass out with the feelings racing through my body and the lack of oxygen."

Luca chuckled. "I was afraid I would never have the nerve again. It sounds so strange to say now, but I felt that if I hadn't tried to kiss you right at that moment, I would never know a way to put out the flames burning inside me."

She readjusted her position and sat between his legs, her back resting against his chest, and he wrapped his arms around her waist and gently rocked her as she continued. "Kissing you was so much more than I had expected; I couldn't believe that once your body was so close to mine, I wouldn't be able to feel satisfied until I had all of you. It was like a drug."

"For me too." He whispered as he kissed her cheek. "That moment in time lives inside me as the most perfect of my life so far. So, let's make that our address."

She studied his face to understand what he meant as he continued. "Every time I see the sunrise, wherever I am, I am going to replay that memory in my mind and send you all my love, and you do the same. Then we know at exactly the same time we are together, not physically but in our minds and hearts."

She stared up at the waning sun as the day was coming to a close, and smiled. It was a perfect way for them to connect and at least for a short time every day she could be with him, if not in her body, in her spirit. They sat like that for a while just replaying that beautiful memory until it became chilly and she stretched forward to retrieve her discarded clothes and to put on her stockings.

Luca stood up, brushed off the grass, and looked at his watch. Realizing the time, he started to bound through the high grass as he baited her over his shoulder, "Whoever gets to the aerodrome first gets to pilot the plane I have booked."

She squealed, still dressing, pulling up her stockings and snatching up her shoes to race after him.

They arrived at the flying club out of breath and laughing. Getting there first, he climbed up onto the wing and held up his arms in triumph. Not to be outdone, Tasha grabbed him around the shins and pulled him down onto the ground and then, climbing over him, clambered into the pilot seat and held up her own arms in victory.

"You little minx." He laughed, sitting up on the tarmac and rubbing his leg. "You could have broken my ankle."

"Would that have been such a terrible thing?" she sputtered back, swallowing down dry, burning hot air. "Then, instead of you going to war, I could have played nursemaid all day."

He flashed her a seductive smile, as though he liked that idea, before limping off to sign out the plane and file his flight plan.

While he was gone, Tasha fetched her goggles and flying cap and, fastening the strap, instantly tamed down her wild mass of hair. They buckled themselves in and he taxied the plane down the runway. She watched him seated in front of her and her stomach flip-flopped as it always did around him. His broad shoulders filled the seat, curls of his thick, black hair escaping from beneath his flying cap as he skillfully aimed the plane into the sky. She unbuckled her harness and, leaning forward, wrapped her arms around his neck, closing her eyes, enjoying the air rushing past her as wisps of his hair brushed her face.

"Hey, you crazy, wild woman, you had better sit back and

buckle in. I may be tempted to see what acrobatics I can perform before I leave."

She responded by drawing gentle circles with her fingers on his chest. "I love you, Luca," she whispered into his ear. "I love you so much it actually hurts."

He ran his hands down her arms and, lifting one of her hands, kissed the tips of her fingers. "And I love you, too, my wild woman. Want to give her a go?"

She kissed the back of his head in response. And leaning back into her seat, she affixed her harness and felt the power of the joystick under her grip. Looking over his shoulder, she turned the plane towards the sun, which was beginning its descent, and felt there was nothing more perfect than this moment in time.

———

The day he was to leave, she awoke early, tears already stinging her sore eyes. The fact she was saying goodbye seemed unreal to her somehow. She'd had a turbulent night's sleep, her dreams a jumble of images and intense feelings. Memories of them making love, his piercing blue eyes looking down at hers, his face watching her as she removed his tunic, the shiver of his body at her touch. She had also dreamed of playful moments, flying or reading together; once when she had cheated at cards and he had chased her down and pinned her to the ground, tickling her till she'd screamed in submission. So many moments of joy and connection.

When Tasha finally opened her eyes that morning, she remembered the pain of the day before. They'd spent quite a somber day together, unable to forget everything they were doing was for the last time. She'd even cooked him his favorite dinner, but they had barely touched it as they made small talk throughout. They had stayed up as long as they could, and that night on the doorstep, she had sobbed in his arms as he had held her so tightly it was as if he never wanted to let her go. It had been so hard, so much harder than she would have ever imagined.

Slowly dressing that morning, she put on her best dress and walked to his home, leaving without even eating breakfast. Inside the house, she could hear his mother already quietly sobbing in the kitchen, and his father looked soulful as he opened the door. Unable to speak, he just nodded to her to come in.

All at once her boyfriend appeared in the hall in his uniform, and she couldn't believe it was her Luca. Normally in a cream tunic and dark trousers, the boy she loved looked like a man. He looked so smart, smarter than she'd ever seen him. So incredibly handsome. She walked towards him, hardly wanting to touch him. Frightened she would crease him some-how, she ran her fingers down the fabric of the gray uniform.

"What do you think?" said Luca, quirking an eyebrow as he twirled. "Do you think they'll believe I'm a real pilot?"

She grappled with the emotion in her voice. "You look amazing, Luca. You'll be the best fighter pilot there is. But, please, will you stay alive?"

"I will, remember I have promised you." He took off his hat and kissed her on the lips. She could smell shampoo in his hair and the soap on his skin and her stomach cramped with desire.

After a tearful goodbye with his parents, when they affirmed how proud they were of him, she walked him all the way to the center of their village, where a bus would pick him up and take him to Moscow.

Arriving, she turned and looked into his eyes, and the tears started to stream down her face.

"Don't do it, Tasha," he said, his voice hoarse from his own emotion. "I can't stand it to see you cry." His eyes that searched hers were heartfelt.

As the bus arrived and other members of the fighting forces started to slowly board, she pulled him close and held him tightly, wanting to squeeze every inch of him into her. She closed her eyes to intensify the feeling. Running her hands down his body in the unfamiliar fabric, she tried to remember how every part of him felt to her touch. As he gently stroked her back and held her close, feeling the outline of his shoulders, her fingers danced down his own strong back. Reaching his hips, she moved her fingers around to his waist, feeling his toned stomach tighten with her touch. As she gently stroked his skin Tasha pictured him naked, and the many times that she'd seen him that way, and she so desperately wanted to have his warm flesh next to her own right then.

Choked up with the intensity of her touch, he pulled away from her.

"I have to go, Tasha."

She nodded her head and kissed him on the lips so hard her own tingled when she pulled away.

"Write to me, Luca. Write to me every single day, or I swear, I will marry someone like Igor."

Picking up his kit bag, he laughed. Holding her hand one last time, he brought it to his lips and kissed it. "Please take care of yourself. Know that I'll miss you every single day."

She nodded, already aching with the absence of his body close to hers. As he boarded the bus, she stepped back farther to watch him. As she did so, Tasha panicked. Everyone looked the same, and momentarily she couldn't find him in the crowd of men pushing their way onto the bus. And then all at once, there he was, seated next to a window, his dark hair crushed beneath his cap, his piercing blue eyes intent on hers. As she caught his gaze, he nodded and mouthed the words, "*See you in the sunrise.*" The memory of that special time and place immediately brought tears to her eyes as she nodded her reply and swiped away endless tears that streamed slowly down her cheeks as she watched the bus leave with her heart on it until it was barely a speck in the distance.

7

Tasha

"I see you're still crying," Babka said, sighing as Tasha lay face down, sobbing into her pillow. Sitting next to her on the bed, she stroked her back and began twisting Tasha's hair into spirals around her fingers to soothe her. "If you keep going, you will run out of tears," she warned ominously.

Tasha turned her head and looked up at her grandmother. "My heart is broken," she said through mournful rasps. "I don't think I could ever feel whole again. It's a terribly empty feeling, Babka. I think I'm going to die."

"Shh," her babka cooed, clearing away a stray tear from her hot, damp cheek with her thick, square thumb. "It feels like that now, but you will feel better, trust me. I remember when your grandfather went away to Moscow to study. I felt like you did, that my heart would break without him in my life. Every minute felt like an hour, every hour felt like a day, but you get used to it. Time will pass."

Tasha turned over and thrust herself up onto her elbows. "But it was different for my grandfather. He went away to study. His life wasn't in danger every minute. Luca chose to go off to fight the war."

Folding her arms around herself, Babka closed her eyes and shook her head. "The young men are under so much pressure right now. There is a war out there that is raging, a war where they get to wear a uniform, fight against those evil Nazis, and for what they believe in. You can't see it as a rejection of you. On the contrary, it's a desire for an ideal they all want. Luca is swept up in all of that. His friends are going. Cousins are going. He doesn't want to be left behind."

"But he's happy to leave me behind! I thought I could do this, but I can't," Tasha wailed back.

"I'm guessing he didn't think much about that at the time." Babka chuckled, tapping her granddaughter's cheek.

"How can he not feel this pain? I feel like I'm being torn in two, as though my heart will literally break in my body without him every day."

Babka pulled Tasha into her arms and held her close, smoothing her wild hair into tame, silky strands. "Men are different. It doesn't mean he loves you any less. He's just not so controlled by his heart as you are. You're a very passionate person. So different to him and your sister." Babka rocked her granddaughter as she continued. "When her husband is called up, which he will be, I imagine Nadia will be very practical about it. Though she might feel the same pain as you, she will tuck it inside and dutifully kiss Ivan goodbye. Just because people don't show it in the same way doesn't mean they don't feel it. You feel everything and wear it all on your sleeve. You always did. You're sensitive that way."

"I hate it, though. I hate who I am. Why can't I be more like Nadia? I want to care less. It wouldn't hurt so much then."

"You can't change who you are, my little one. As much as you think you are all grown up, you are still young, with your mother's adventurous spirit and your father's kind heart battling inside you. One day your emotions will not control you as much as they do now. I promise you, one day you will find a way to balance it all, and then you will become a formidable force for good. I just know you will."

Babka wiped the tears from Tasha's face with a large cotton hanky she always kept tucked in the band of her apron.

"Come, let me make you your favorite soup," she encouraged, then, planting a feathery kiss on her granddaughter's forehead, struggled to her feet. "We will soothe your broken heart with food," she announced.

Tasha placated her grandmother with a half-hearted nod as Babka smiled her satisfaction and, leaving the bedroom, was soon humming Russian folksongs in front of her stove.

Tasha blew her nose and tried to sit up. She'd have to eat some soup for her grandmother, even though she wasn't a bit hungry. There would be no arguing about it. Babka believed she could heal every broken heart, every sadness, every scrape and cut with something from her stove. As Tasha swung her legs around and sat on the edge of the bed, she felt dizzy and so drained. Drained and angry. She would do something about this. She would find a way.

After she had managed about five spoonfuls of soup, enough to make Babka happy, Tasha cleared away the dishes. Her stomach was still aching with the pain of her loss when she had a thought. Why could only the men go? Why couldn't she go too? Surely there was something she could do for the war. Even if they wouldn't give her a gun and put her on the front line, there had to be something she was capable of doing to help, nursing or flying supplies. That way she might be able to see Luca. They could even get leave together. She suddenly had a glimmer of hope.

That evening, after Babka had gone to bed early, she paced the kitchen thinking it through.

As the night wore on, and the sounds of day creatures gave way to those of owls and wolves, she made her plan, packing everything she had into a small bag. She would find Luca and fight alongside him. It was the only way. She left as the dawn broke, leaving a note for Babka. As Tasha slipped out the front door, she took in a long slow breath of the cold air and closed her eyes as the rays of sun warmed her face. She took a moment to connect with Luca before saying out loud, "I'm coming to be with you, Luca."

She was feeling a buzz of excitement that she hadn't felt in days. She now had hope: hope of finding him and being with him, and also maybe along the way fulfilling her own destiny. Looking back over her shoulder at the humble, warm cottage that had been her home for her whole life, she felt a stab of apprehension, then, swallowing it down, she was gone, gone away to find out what life outside of this village had to offer, and to be with Luca.

8

Nadia

Nadia sat down at her kitchen table, feeling the pain of disappointment at not being pregnant again this month. She knew they hadn't been married long, but still she felt a little grief every time that she wasn't pregnant with the baby they both so desired.

All at once someone was hammering on her door. Who was calling so early with such urgency? She wiped at her eyes that were brimming with tears and looked around her neat kitchen to see if it was ready for visitors. It was. She had scrubbed it clean the day before, though in the bedroom was an unmade bed, but she guessed whoever it was would not be going in there. Tidying her hair quickly in the mirror, she made her way to the front door and opened it.

On the step was Babka, tears staining her grief-stricken face. Nadia's heart lurched up into her throat. Something was terribly wrong. Her babka had never called on her in this way with such distress before. Pulling her grandmother quickly inside, she closed the door and sat her down at the table as Babka gasped, trying to catch her breath.

"What is it, Babka? Whatever has happened?" she inquired. Nadia's tone was high-pitched, reflecting her concern.

In return, the older woman just closed her eyes and shook her head vehemently, sucking in great gasps of air as she did so. Finally, she held out a crumpled piece of paper toward her granddaughter. Taking it from Babka's shaking fingers, Nadia walked to the window to read the letter. It was in Tasha's hand.

Darling Babka,

I can bear it no longer. I have to go away for a while. Please try not to worry. I will be fine. But there is something I need to do. Give my love to Nadia.

Please take good care of yourself.

Much love T xxx

Nadia shook her head and teased out a deep, slow breath. Her sister would be the death of her. Now, what was this foolishness?

"She left in the middle of the night," came the spluttered words from the kitchen table, Babka finally finding her voice, which was thready with emotion. "What should we do, Nadia? She can be so headstrong and willful when she has an idea." The older woman began to wring her hands in her apron.

"Don't worry about this, Babka. You know how she is. She'll be back in one day when she's hungry."

"I'm not so sure. She was heartbroken when Luca left. I've never seen her so sad. She can be such a foolish child. And who knows what trouble she will get into. So, you have to go after her and find her."

"Go after her? But I'm a wife now, Babka. I have a home. I

have a life. I can't just go after her. I can't be rescuing her for the rest of her life. She needs to grow up and face her own consequences."

"But you're all she has. So if you don't go, who will?"

Nadia felt a familiar stab in her heart. Since losing her parents, she had always felt responsible for her sister. Along with Babka, Nadia had been the one to take care of her, the one to pick her up when she fell, to cover for her when she made mistakes, to get her out of every scrape.

"I'll talk to my husband about it tonight, and we'll decide what to do. One thing I know about Tasha is she always falls on her feet. And she will do the same now. So please try not to worry yourself. Let me make you some tea to calm you."

Nadia put on the kettle as her heart went out to her grandmother, who sat looking at her hands, bereft. Her desperate expression betrayed the fact she was obviously dissatisfied with Nadia's solution. She suddenly felt angry. She loved her sister dearly, but why was Tasha like this? Why was she always creating so much difficulty in their lives? And what would they have to do to make this right?

9

Tasha

Tasha stood sheltering from the rain in the doorway of the address she had scribbled down onto a piece of paper and felt wretched. Catching the first bus from her village in the morning, she'd been buoyant in the hope of seeing Luca again. But on arriving in Moscow, the strangeness of a big city that had excited her at first now felt unfriendly and overwhelming.

As soon as she'd arrived on the bus, she'd made her way across town to the address of the base that Luca was stationed at. But at the gate, the guards had not permitted her entry. No matter how many ways she tried to beg them, they had stood firm in their refusal. She couldn't believe she was so close to Luca and yet couldn't see him.

Now it was the afternoon, and after walking around for hours, she was waiting outside the building where her cousin lived. A few years before, Sonja had moved from their village to Moscow, as many people had, encouraged by Comrade Stalin's vision of making the capital a progressive, industrialized city. Sonja had a job teaching here. However, Tasha wasn't sure exactly where. She wished she'd listened more carefully to Babka when she'd read her excerpts from her cousin's letters, as she'd already been waiting for two hours and had no idea what time Sonja would be home.

When she finally arrived, Tasha was soaked to the skin and frozen to the bone. Seeing her standing in the doorway, her cousin ran to greet her.

"Tasha, what are you doing here? You look so cold. Let me get you inside."

Putting her arm around her, Sonja let her into the communal living building she lived in. As Tasha followed her cousin into her housing complex, she was amazed. She had heard about them and knew they were prevalent in Moscow, but had never seen one before. The shared use of space meant that many people could live together in one building, and each of them rented an apartment with other families. They all had their own bedrooms and sometimes sitting areas, but they would share bathrooms and kitchen facilities. This made the housing very affordable, especially for someone like Sonja, who didn't earn much as a teacher.

Putting her own coat around Tasha's shoulders, Sonja led her up to her apartment, and once they were inside, she ushered Tasha straight into her bedroom, where she found her some dry clothes to change into.

It was after she'd warmed up and had a hot drink that she was finally able to tell Sonja her story. Sonja nodded regretfully after her cousin explained the situation.

"So many of our men are going to the war. I'm so sorry Luca had to go. I know the two of you are very close. You have been friends since you were children."

After they finished their dinner, which Tasha insisted on preparing, Sonja looked despondently over at her as they sat together in her tiny bedroom.

"I wish I could spend more time with you tonight, but I have tickets to go out with a friend to a musical concert. And unfortunately, it's sold out. Otherwise, I would love to take you. I've been waiting to go for three months. Would you hate me terribly if I didn't stay home with you tonight?"

Tasha shook her head. "Of course not. It's good of you that you will even put me up."

Sonja placed a small bed next to her own on the floor for her cousin as they chatted. "It's not ideal," she sighed, "but this housing is good for me and close to my work."

"Of course, I'm so grateful."

"What will you do now?" Sonja asked.

"I'm not sure. Somehow, I can't bring myself to go home yet. Would it be okay with you if I stayed a couple of days?"

"Yes, I would love that," Sonja enthused, throwing her arms around her cousin. "I'm so glad to see you. Stay as long as you want."

That night after Sonja left and she had been given her own key, Tasha went for a walk. Now that she felt safe and warm, it was thrilling to be in a city, so many sights and sounds to see, so many people, but she wondered if she could survive here as well as Sonja had. It was a very different kind of environment. She could find some work here, maybe, but Luca would be gone soon so what would be the point? She hoped if she stayed a few days, perhaps she would find another way to get to see him at the camp, for them to be with one another, even for an hour.

She was making her way back out from her walk when she passed the town hall. Gathered around the steps were many women talking excitedly about the upcoming speaker. She studied the poster on the board outside, where it announced that Major Marina Raskova, a prominent member of the military, was coming to talk this evening on her desire to see women flying in the Russian Air Force. Naturally, it piqued Tasha's interest. She didn't even know that women were allowed to fly in the military. But then, she suddenly had a thought. What if she did that? She might be able to be close to Luca that way. Reading the details on the announcement, she noted that it was free to attend and she made her way into the large building.

Inside was packed with people to listen to the major. Many of them were women about Tasha's age. Making her way down a row, she sat and waited in the cold, large hall. The excitement around the room was palpable. Finally, after a grand introduction, the major made her way out onto the stage amid rousing encouragement and started her speech.

"We are at a challenging time amid historical transition. Right now, Mother Russia has the chance to change history for women. Comrade Stalin has tasked me with the job of finding our next fighting forces amongst the brave and capable women of Russia. Our assignment is to take back our borders that have been attacked by that despicable fascist, Hitler. And that is what we are going to do!"

As the whole auditorium erupted into raucous applause, Tasha marveled on how exciting it was to be part of such a large crowd, feeling the resounding patriotism that was palpable in the room. As Major Raskova stood waiting for the audience to retake their seats, Tasha looked closely at this brave woman standing in front of her, surrounded by photos of her impressive aviation achievements, and couldn't help but be totally in awe. She had expected someone older, not this beautiful woman who looked not much older than herself.

Raskova held up her hand to quieten the room. "As part of an ongoing recruitment program, I am traveling the country to find women who would be willing to serve alongside their comrades and attack these invading forces. I am hoping that in this room there are indeed women who will respond to the call and will help me defend Russia. Then, after we have taken back the borders of our precious motherland, this group of talented female flyers will help me take us into the next decade, a model for the entire world. If you feel that you can help, comrades, I ask you to see me at the end of this event, where I will outline what I am looking for in our female pilots.

Be assured, with a strong, vibrant female force to fight along-side our comrade brothers, we shall not allow anyone to threaten our homeland."

People all around the hall jumped to their feet and started clapping. Moved by her emotional plea and speech, Tasha stood alongside them. She suddenly felt great excitement. Why couldn't she do this? Why couldn't she fight for Russia? She already knew how to fly. If they had mixed squadrons, then maybe she and Luca could fly together as she'd always wanted to. This was so exciting. Women had never been able to do what they were doing now. She wasn't entirely sure about Stalin and all his policies, but he was evidently a progressive leader if he felt that women were capable of much more than they were being allowed to do.

"We will show them..." Raskova continued over the applause, "We will show them what the women of Russia are made of. I have a plan. And with your help, I will be able to make it happen."

At the end of the event, many women went forward, and Tasha did too, pushing her way to the front of the hall. She waited in line to meet this woman who had so inspired her. Her stomach clenched with the excitement and the thought of what this could mean. She didn't have anywhere to stay in Moscow for the long term, and she didn't have to go home. She could do this instead.

As soon as she reached the table, she blurted out, "I want to sign up. I want to go."

Raskova looked up at the young woman before her, a bemused look on her face. "Nice to meet you, comrade sister, and your name is...?"

"Natasha Petroffskaya. I go by the name Tasha. I've been flying for a number of years at the flying school in my village. Where do I sign up? I want to go. I want to fight."

Raskova started to chuckle. "I admire your enthusiasm, comrade, but first, there are a few things that we need to complete. First, you will have to have a physical, and you will be assessed on your abilities. We are doing trials in the next few days here in Moscow. Do you live here?"

"I'm staying with my cousin nearby, yes."

"You can be available for this?"

"Of course," responded Tasha. "Do you want me to sign now?"

"First we have to complete all the tests. We want the best of the best. Here are the details of what you will need to do." She handed Tasha a sheet of paper with all that was required. "Come to my office, tomorrow, and we can get started."

Tasha nodded, and started to move away.

"Miss Petroffskaya." Tasha turned. "I want to tell you, I have a good feeling about you. Your enthusiasm is well received, and I hope you make it, as I look forward to flying alongside you in our first female flying squadron."

Tasha beamed her response and tucked the paperwork into her bag. She was excited that now she had a plan, now she knew what she was going to do with her life, and it felt right.

10

Nadia

When Tasha hadn't returned after two days, Nadia began to feel real concern. As unpredictable as her sister could be, she would typically be more considerate. She at least expected her sister to write to them and let them know all was well. She had wanted to broach the subject with Ivan that first night, but he had returned from work in a terribly dark mood and went straight to his study. Which Nadia had come to recognize meant he wanted to be alone. She had begun to see that as well as his charismatic personality there was this darkness. A heavy oppressiveness that she couldn't seem to penetrate no matter how hard she tried. He seemed so conflicted about something and appeared afraid to talk to her about it.

When Ivan went to work the following day, barely brushing her cheek with a kiss, Nadia went straight over to Babka's house, as she had each day since her sister had gone missing. Her grandmother was still fretting and had not slept much since Tasha's departure, and there were dark circles under her eyes that were heavy with worry.

"Any word?" Nadia asked, entering the house and removing her headscarf.

Her grandmother shook her head as she automatically shuffled to her kettle to make tea. "This is not like her, Nadia. I know she can be a little impulsive. But it has been so long, there is so much danger out there, and she is so beautiful."

Nadia placed her arms around her grandmother and hugged her. She was pretty sure that Tasha could probably take care of herself, but she didn't like to see her grandmother worrying the way she was.

"I'll go and make inquiries with her friends today. Someone must know something."

Babka nodded her head absently and, drawing out a long, sad breath, put out the tea things.

Nadia spent the rest of the day visiting all the places she would expect to find her, calling on different friends, at different places she knew her sister frequented, but no one had seen her. Even her best friend, Olga, knew nothing of what was going on, and the group she and Luca were part of at the flying club were none the wiser.

"She said nothing to us," said Olga. "We expected to see her at the club last night."

After leaving Olga's, Nadia was at a loss at where else to look. The only other place she could think of was to Luca's house, and of course, Luca was gone off to fight the war. Then she had an awful feeling. Would her sister have tried to follow Luca? Maybe tried to find him? It was the sort of impulsive thing that she would do.

Paying a call on Luca's parents, she asked for the address they'd been given of their son's base for the next few weeks in Moscow. And, assuming that she just wanted to write to him, they were happy to oblige.

"We miss him terribly," his mother sighed, "and I bet Tasha is beside herself."

Nadia smiled in a noncommittal way, not wanting to make her sister look unfavorable in the eyes of Luca's parents.

Back at her grandmother's house, she sat down wearily at the kitchen table.

"There is news?" asked her grandmother desperately, taking Nadia's hand.

Nadia so wanted to give Babka some hope, but she also needed to be honest with her. She shook her head.

"No one has seen her and she said nothing to anyone about where she was going."

Tears pricked Babka's eyes.

Then Nadia broached the idea she had been considering, carefully. "If she is not anywhere here in the village and no one has seen her, it is possible that she has gone further afield."

Babka looked confused.

"I think that it's possible she may have tried to follow Luca to Moscow. His unit is staying there for a few weeks before they head down to the training center."

Her grandmother looked horror-struck.

So Nadia quickly continued. "If that's the case, I know she has very little money, so if she went as far as Moscow to track down Luca, I'm sure she'll be staying safely with Sonja."

Babka's expression brightened with the prospect of her granddaughter staying with her cousin. "I just find it strange she didn't even say anything to you. You have always been so close."

Nadia swallowed down her own guilt. She had hardly given Tasha a second thought over the last few weeks. She'd been so preoccupied with her own life, adjusting to her marriage, trying to make a new life with Ivan.

"So, you will go and get her back then?" Babka assumed.

"I'll try to make a trip to Moscow. I have to talk to Ivan first."

Spending hours reassuring her grandmother, Nadia lost track of the time and suddenly realized with a jolt that she would be very late in getting home to prepare her husband's dinner, and she knew he would not be happy.

She got home just minutes before his arrival from work. Ivan found her in the kitchen, flustered and chopping vegetables; he looked concerned with no meal to greet him.

She could see he was still battling the demons inside him and his melancholy tempered his interactions. Never seeing this side of him before they married, it concerned her that these black moods were becoming more and more frequent.

"Was there a problem today, Nadia?"

"No problem," she lied. "I just got caught up with Babka at her house."

Normally, he would have conversed more, inquired about her visit, but instead he shrugged despondently and went into the front room to read his newspaper. Should she say anything to Ivan? Maybe he could help her look into where Tasha might've gone, but she was afraid to burden him more. He already seemed so preoccupied. She did not want to have this discussion this evening, especially as Ivan was obviously struggling.

As she tried to gauge his mood and what she could do to make him happy, she swiped at her damp bangs, and her stomach knotted as she felt the pressure of her whole life squeezing her. She was caught between her need to comfort her grandmother, worry about the trouble her sister might be getting into, and the constant needs of her husband. That, out of all of it, felt like a ceaseless weight. When she'd met Ivan, she'd been struck by his determined conscientiousness, his thorough, upright character, his strength. All the things she desired in a husband. But now that she was with him day after day, she realized he was more complex than she had originally thought. As if the man she had met had been a sham, a facade of the man he wanted to be, and more than anything she hated the way he didn't let her in. Didn't let her help.

She served up his meal that evening, and their dinner

together was very quiet. Just the sound of utensils scraping on the edges of their dishes. Nadia couldn't think of one thing to say to him. But as she spooned in soup, Nadia decided she definitely would not say anything about Tasha. Instead, she would go herself tomorrow and see her sister if she was there, and if there was still a problem, maybe he could help her then.

The next day, she set out to Moscow. Up until she had got married, she had worked two different jobs, secretarial work at the flying club and also some housecleaning. She had saved some money and had hoped to surprise her husband with something special, after their marriage, but so far, she had not felt very motivated; it seemed the longer they were married the less she knew him. So instead she used some of that money to pay for her ticket to Moscow. It was a two-hour journey, so she went as soon as Ivan had left. Arriving in the bustling city, she went first to Sonja's communal housing building, but no one was home, so she caught a tram and went over to Luca's base, hoping to speak to him.

The guards on the gate eyed her warily.

"We don't take women here. What do you want?"

"Can I please speak to Luca Baranov?"

"This is a training base, not a tavern," one of them snapped at her. "We don't have time to fetch recruits for their lovelorn girlfriends."

Despondently, Nadia made her way back into the center of Moscow. She couldn't go until she had at least spoken to Sonja. But every minute she was here it would make it more difficult to get back to her husband in good time.

Upon visiting the house again, an older man who was a resident of the same apartment answered the door and she asked about her cousin. Tasha appeared over the small man's shoulder.

"Nadia!" she exclaimed. "I thought that was your voice."

Nadia felt her stomach unclench for the first time in days.

Tasha threw her arms around her sister and hugged her,

then, pulling her into the room, told her the whole story about not being able to see Luca and how she had decided to join the female pilots.

It was hard to dash Tasha's enthusiasm, but she was angry about all this. "Tasha, do you think about anyone but yourself? Babka is so worried. And I have had to take a day to come here to make sure you weren't dead."

Tasha looked at her sheepishly. "I suppose it was a little irresponsible. I just missed him so much and just wanted to see him one last time and now we may be able to fly together. I was writing a letter, to Babka, see." She pointed to a letter that was barely started and was dated two days before. "Please don't be angry with me, Nadia. I want you to be happy for me. This is what I was born to do."

Nadia tried to picture her sister as a fighter pilot and was surprised to see how easy that was to imagine. And there was something else, too. Was that envy she felt? When Tasha had told her, there had been a sinking feeling inside her. Nadia suddenly saw her days ahead mapped out: cleaning her house, cooking Ivan's dinner, and sleeping by his side as he snored the night away. In comparison, her sister would be flying and defending their country against Hitler, their enemy.

"I leave in the next week, but before I go, let's go and celebrate," Tasha said buoyantly.

"I need to get home and cook Ivan's dinner," Nadia responded drily, her words sounding a little colder than she had intended.

Tasha laughed and, hooking her arm into her sister's, said, "God, let the man cook his own dinner for a change. I want to celebrate with you, and I don't know when I will see you again!"

11

Nadia

When Nadia returned from Moscow that afternoon, her heart sank to see that her husband was already home. She had rushed all the way and was jubilant to make it back an hour before he was due to arrive back from work, but seeing smoke twisting from the chimney, and his work boots on the step, she knew he was home before her. Having prepared some food the night before, she had planned to have dinner ready this time. Nadia opened the front door; Ivan was standing by the kitchen window, holding a letter in his hand. He turned, and there was a look of great disappointment on his face.

"Where were you, Nadia?" he asked, unable to keep the hurt from his tone.

She felt flustered and burbled, "I had to be out. I was doing something."

He peered at her. "Don't lie to me. Is there someone else you would rather be with? Do you regret marrying me?"

"Of course not," she spat back. "Why would you say such a thing?"

The rejection was real in his eyes. "First, I come home and

you are behind with cooking dinner. Now you're not even here. What else am I to think?"

Her shoulders sank, and teasing out a long, ragged breath and without even removing her coat or headscarf, she slumped into a chair at the kitchen table. "You're going to find out anyway," she sighed. "Tasha went missing."

His eyebrows furrowed. "Missing? What do you mean missing?"

"She got on a bus to Moscow. She was trying to follow Luca."

Ivan shook his head incredulously. "And I suppose you have been spending your days trying to locate her?"

Nadia was too exhausted to defend her sister's actions.

He turned away then and continued reading. Usually, he would have debated the merits of her sister's actions longer, but Nadia could see he was preoccupied with the letter he was holding.

"Is everything all right?" she asked, desperately wanting to change the subject.

He shook his head and placed the letter in front of her on the table. Quickly she read through it, then read through it again. "What is this?"

"It's my papers to fight in the war."

"You've been called up?"

"Yes, Nadia. We will all be expected to fight against Germany."

She looked at the date on the letter. It was dated weeks before, and she felt a stab in her heart and a growing anger. So, her husband had held this secret from her when they had only just got married? Weren't they supposed to tell each other everything?

"When were you going to tell me?"

He seemed surprised by her need to know. "As soon as it was necessary."

She stood to her feet and paced the kitchen. "Why did you wait so long?"

"Because I didn't want to worry you. It is something I have to deal with."

She folded her arms defensively. "This will affect me too. We're a married couple now. We're supposed to talk about such things, aren't we?"

He looked at her warily. "I don't think we should talk about everything. There are things we need to keep to ourselves. Things that could worry or..." He paused, looking for the right words. "...cause distress for the other to hear. Each of us should be able to have our own private thoughts and experiences."

What was he trying to say? Nadia looked into the face of her husband and realized something she had been trying not to admit to herself. As much as he was a good, upstanding man, he knew nothing of a relationship and what it was meant to be, at least what she'd hoped it would be.

"When will you go?" she asked softly, trying to come to terms with his cool indifference.

"Next week," he responded, folding the letter back up into its envelope and putting it away. "I thought you should know so we have time to prepare."

He made it all sound so matter-of-fact, as though he was going on a short trip. Did she have time to prepare? Time to prepare her whole life and heart to be without her husband for months, maybe years? Time to prepare for the fact that he might not ever come back? Time to come to terms with the reality that her marriage was a sham? So far this had been nothing like what she had expected, and now there would be no time for them to work at it, to maybe get closer. She wiped the tears from her eyes, more with the frustration of that thought than sadness.

"Now, now," he said, as if appeasing a small child, "there's no need for tears."

Her voice cracked with the brimming emotion. "Ivan, I may never see you again."

He pulled her towards him, and even though their bodies were close as he dutifully patted her back, she felt distant from him. It felt so excruciating to be this close to the man she loved and felt overwhelmingly physically attracted to, but not be able to really get close to him. In that moment she desperately wanted to him to hold her in his arms and kiss her passionately. Even throw her on the kitchen table and make love to her there and then. Anything so she could feel any kind of intimacy between them. Through her tears, she looked into his handsome face. His strong features and warm brown eyes. This close she could smell his newly soap-washed skin. Something he always did when he arrived home from work. Nadia wondered if she should initiate a kiss between them. Surly if their kiss was passionate enough he would have to respond in kind. But as she caught his eye with her need and moved her head toward him with parted lips, he pulled away, looking terrified, and quickly released her from his arms. She felt so rejected. What had happened to him that made him so scared to kiss his own wife? Embarrassed by her forthrightness, she moved away from him, catching her breath, her heart beating so rapidly in her ears she could barely hear.

"I should make dinner;" she said, blowing her nose on her handkerchief as she pulled onions out of the cupboard and the potatoes she had already prepared for a goulash. He turned quickly and left the kitchen, apparently desperate to put some distance between them. He didn't seem to have a clue about what she was feeling. He just wasn't connected to her in any way.

———

A week later, she walked with him to the bus stop and stood alongside the many other women saying goodbye to their loved ones. Ivan kissed her dutifully on the cheek and without a backward glance stepped quickly towards the bus.

As she watched him go, looking so strange in his new uniform, Nadia's heart was breaking, but not in the way she'd expected. She felt robbed of the life she had desperately wanted. She had wanted to be a good wife, to be a mother and to create the perfect home.

Tears pricked her eyes, but she suddenly realized they were not tears of sorrow at him leaving but of deep disappointment. Sadness at what she had endured for the first months of her marriage. And though she hated to admit it even to herself, alongside those feelings there was also relief. She could stop trying now, stop pretending. Stop trying to be in love for both of them.

She watched him take his seat on the bus and wave to her briefly before he became deeply engrossed in a conversation with another member of his unit. It was at that moment that Nadia felt her heart turn to stone. It was never going to change. This was her life with Ivan. And now she had to be the dutiful wife waiting for her husband to return, otherwise she would look cold and heartless. How long would that be? Months, years? Her growing older and him away. She would have to go on living this lie, and all at once she felt utterly trapped and alone.

12

Tasha

After Tasha passed her interview and physical, she was given a date to be at the station in Moscow to travel on the troop train to the air force training facility.

She had already sent a letter to Babka and Nadia, updating them on her acceptance and with her new address. On the morning she was leaving, Tasha hugged her cousin goodbye and felt incredibly brave and excited to be starting a whole new life. The kind of life she could never have imagined for herself in the world she had come from.

On the way to the station, so many thoughts rushed through her mind. What would it be like to fly for Russia, up in a plane day after day, maybe even bombing their enemy? Also, what would the other women be like? Would they all be from Moscow and be sophisticated and worldly, and would she feel just like a country peasant? And lastly and most importantly, what would Luca think of her decision? She hoped he would be happy.

Even though it was autumn it was a chilly day, and when she arrived at the Moscow station, the wind whipped around her legs that were frozen in her skirt, and she shivered in just the thin coat she had rushed to bring with her from home. Taking a deep breath, she stepped onto the platform and was surprised to see, instead of a group of women as she had expected, that the station was packed full with servicemen. Refusing to be intimidated, she rolled back her shoulders and started to stride down the platform as a general hubbub of wolf whistles and catcalling followed her. One serviceman who was leaning against the wall smoking a cigarette raked back his gray cap and stepped in front of her.

"Hello, I'm Sergei. Where are you going, princess? You must be the entertainment our government has provided for our trip."

Tasha was just about to give him a piece of her mind when from the crowd someone reached out and grabbed her arm. Startled, she turned to see a young woman with long, dark, curly brown hair and soft, brown eyes smiling at her.

"We're in here," she said, pulling Tasha towards a small waiting room.

Inside, huddled around a tiny stove, sat a group of women.

"Well done, Eva," a tall, thin girl with long, straight, black hair encouraged. "You've rescued another one."

Eva squeezed Tasha's arm. "They're like a pack of wolves out there. We only know when another girl has arrived by that ridiculous display."

Tasha sighed, and her heart, which had started pounding, ready for a fight, started to calm.

"I'm Kira," said the girl with the long, straight hair. "And your rescuer is Eva."

The short, curly-haired woman smiled and patted her hand. "You feel so cold. You should get warm."

The girls automatically shuffled down the wooden bench they were sitting on to make sure Tasha was the closest to the fire. And she suddenly felt calmer. These women, though very different, were kind and friendly. Not snobbish as she had feared.

The girl who was sitting next to her had blonde, wavy hair and was wrapped in a warm woolen coat. She was busy knitting what looked like a scarf. "I'm Liliya," she said, pushing back the cuff of her coat, fixing Tasha with striking blue eyes and shaking her hand. "Are you from Moscow?"

Tasha shook her head and told her the village she was from.

"That's just down the road from where I grew up," said another girl enthusiastically. "I'm Katya. I moved here a few years ago, which is where I met Kira." The girl with the long, straight, dark hair bobbed her head in agreement as she continued. "Kira is a very active friend and talked me into learning to fly. Which is how I got here."

"Only because you wouldn't hike or go rock climbing with me," Kira added in obvious disgust.

"Do you all fly already?" Tasha asked.

Most nodded. A couple shook their heads.

"I'm hoping to learn, though," said a quietly spoken girl with mousy brown hair. "Really, I don't mind even if I'm ground crew or something. I just think this is such an amazing opportunity."

"That's Anastasia," Eva added, leaning in towards Tasha to be heard.

"I'm not sure I'll remember all your names," Tasha admitted.

"We'll soon get to know each other," said Liliya as she gave her a warm smile and hooked another stitch. "We're all going to be working closely together."

All at once, the men outside became rambunctious again, with a fair amount of calling out and wolf whistles.

"Eva!" Kira encouraged.

"I'm on it," said the small woman with the curly hair. But before Eva could even get to the door, a roar of laughter went up in the crowd, and as she opened it, an irate woman's voice could be heard in the midst of a rush of expletives.

All the women eyed one another with interest as they started to chuckle.

Soon Eva was back in the door with a red-faced woman with thick, dark hair and green eyes.

"This is Mila, and she punched him, that ringleader out there, Sergei!" Eva informed the group as she pulled the girl inside. They all cheered and clapped.

"Good for you," said Kira as the dazed young woman entered the room.

The first words out of her mouth were, "What the hell was that about?"

All the girls laughed and Kira responded, "They're your unwelcoming committee!"

When it arrived at nine o'clock, the male recruits crushed onto the train, and a woman in her green dress uniform greeted them and checked off their names. All the girls were ushered into a separate covered wooden carriage with benches inside.

"We'll have to huddle together and keep warm," said Eva as she made room for Tasha to sit next to her.

"I hope it's going to warm up," stated Mila as she paced the carriage, looking out the windows.

"How fast can you knit?" inquired Kira, looking over at Liliya, who chuckled.

"Not fast enough to knit a blanket," she responded with a smile.

"They told me we'll be traveling for a week," added Katya. "I hope I'm not going to regret you talking me into this, Kira."

Kira laughed. "I'm sure you will! But what an adventure it will be."

"This trip will toughen us up for the front," Mila added as she cleaned a circle on the cold windows.

Even though the carriage was basic, they had it to themselves, and with them all huddled together, it was also quite warm. They had been told by the woman who had greeted them that they would stop in about three hours and get something to eat.

As the heaving train slowly made its way from the station with a puff of gray, acrid smoke, the men in the other carriages started to cheer and then sing crude drinking songs that Mila knew all the words to. She entertained them with a lively rendition of each one. As she did so, Anastasia blushed and the other girls laughed.

Making their way from the city into the vast landscape that was Russia, Tasha suddenly felt in awe of her situation. Yes, she'd started this to find Luca, and finding herself joining this group had been serendipitous, but now she felt different. She felt a camaraderie with these women. There was a real reason for why they were doing this. Stalin had put a call out just a few weeks ago, asking all of Russia to fight back against Hitler, and doing this made her feel patriotic.

On the way, Liliya continued to knit. Eva, who was brilliant at sketching, showed them a picture she had drawn of all her family. And Kira and Katya talked about all of the crazy adventures they had been on together. Mila told them stories about being the only girl in a horde of brothers, and Anastasia listened and read her book. When Tasha told them of her dramatic dash from home and trying to get into the camp to see her boyfriend, the girls clapped and laughed.

"And he doesn't know you have signed up?" Kira affirmed.

Tasha shook her head, and all the girls seemed impressed with the amazing amount of bravery that had resulted in her being there. They all talked and joked, and the time went fast. After three hours, the train pulled to an abrupt stop, and hooking arms with each other, they sauntered into the tea room on the station platform.

There, food and drink had been provided for them. And it

was pretty evident from the beginning that they weren't going to starve.

"I'll get as fat as a pig," said Mila as she worked through the pile of food in front of her. "I thought there was a war on?"

"They obviously want to make sure that we are good and fighting fit," offered Kira.

"They'll have trouble getting my plane off the ground like this," Eva added, pushing half the plate of food away.

As they finished and Kira and Katya lit a cigarette, a group of the male recruits came past them and eyed them with distaste.

"I didn't realize that Russia was so desperate that now we are hiring little girls," said Sergei, the one that Mila had hit. He wasn't very tall, with a slender frame. One of his blue eyes was bloodshot, slightly swollen in his baby face. He had thin, blond hair and a wispy mustache, that betrayed the fact he was still young.

"Are you afraid we'll show you up?" sneered Mila, taking a bite out of an apple.

"I'm afraid *you* will show *us* up," he spat back. "It's embarrassing that our country would allow women to fight. We'll probably have to spend our time saving you. Though maybe as soon as you girls have a little bit of discipline, you'll all be crying and running home to Mama."

All the men jeered around him.

"Don't be so sure of that," responded Tasha, jumping to her feet and cutting across the hubbub. "You may just be surprised. Maybe we'll end up saving your lives!"

The cadet backed off, apparently afraid of Tasha blackening his other eye, and he strutted away to get his tea.

"Are you concerned at all about how people will think about us?" asked Liliya, who had started her knitting again.

"My mother was so angry," whispered Anastasia. "She couldn't believe that I'd want to fight like a man. She cried for three days when I told her I was coming. I tried to explain to her, Mama, our leader has asked us, he has asked us to all help, and I can do this. I have wanted to fly for as long as I can remember. I used to read about it in the books and always thought it would be amazing."

"I've never even been near a plane," Eva mused wistfully. "I just wanted to do something and they chose me because I'm good at navigation and willing."

"We'll all make Russia proud," stated Kira decisively. "You wait and see."

"What do you think they'll have us do?" asked Tasha.

"Major Raskova rumored that they will have some of us fly as our own unit." Kira nodded.

"An all-female unit?" Anastasia responded, looking up from her book, her eyes widening.

"Now that would be amazing," stated Katya.

"It'd be better than flying with the likes of them," Mila added, pointing towards the guys that were now looking over and sneering.

"Let's just make a pact," said Eva, placing her hand outstretched in the center of the table. "We will have our own set of commandments. The first one will be: we are proud to be women."

"Yes," they all echoed, placing their hands on top of Eva's.

"We are proud to be women, but we will fight like men," added Mila.

They laughed as they made their little pact. Then, finishing their meal, they made their way back to the train.

The girls continued to become close as they traveled. It took so long to get there that they had plenty of time to get to know each other. En route, Tasha looked around the group. They were all so different, yet they all had something in common. Eva was almost like the little mother of the group, always checking on them, making sure everyone was all right. She could also tell that she and Eva were going to be firm friends. Kira and Katya, already such good friends, weren't exclusive at all. They encouraged all of them into their warm bond of friendship as they shared all the fun they had experienced together. Liliya and Anastasia were the quieter members. Liliya was warm and kind and she never stopped knitting the whole trip. Anastasia was so quiet, she preferred to listen and read but was always engaged, taking everything in. And lastly Mila, the tomboy of the group. If she ever found herself down over enemy lines, Tasha hoped Mila would be with her. She had a natural survival instinct, and Tasha really liked her straightforward, no-nonsense way.

By the time they arrived, they knew everything about each other's families, their loves and their losses. Tasha just knew they were a strong team. When she looked back years later, she would remember the train trip as one of the highlights of her life. It had been a time of excitement, of promise and antici-pated experiences. She was glad that ignorance was bliss, because if she'd known where they all would be in a few years' time, she would not have been so enthusiastic to join the war.

13

Tasha

When they arrived at the Engels School of Aviation, near Saratov in the south, Major Raskova was there waiting for them.

There was a flush of excitement as the girls realized and filed in to stand in front of her.

"My dear comrade sisters, I wanted to be here to welcome you all even though I am still on a very busy tour of recruitment around our country. I just had to be here to see the faces of the women who will usher our motherland into this new age. I know that as women there will be many challenges ahead of you, with a war to fight and especially around your male counterparts. Believe me, I know something about that, having spent most of my career in a male-dominated world myself. But I want you to know that, whatever hardships you face, I am proud of every one of you and know you will not let me down. Strive to not only do your best, but to do it with dignity and enthusiasm. Eventually we will win over some of the prejudice we see in our male military units, but only if we execute our work to the highest of standards. I shall be watching from afar and in the meantime commend you into the very capable hands of your new leader, Commander Bershanskaya. She is well respected among our ranks, and it will be a great honor for you to serve with her. Do me proud and I hope fate will favor you as you all go forward to join our fighting forces to defeat our enemy."

She gave a slight bow of her head as she motioned to the commander standing by her side to come forward. All the women clapped enthusiastically, and Tasha felt such a sense of pride to be part of this exciting new opportunity.

Commander Bershanskaya described the procedure and began by telling them they would all be issued uniforms, but because there had never been women in the forces, she explained to them that they would be getting male uniforms.

"You should know that as our dear sister, Comrade Raskova, has already mentioned, there is some opposition to having women in the training school. So they refuse to offer any concessions for the fact you are women. But I hope, like me, you are stubborn. They may throw bulky male uniforms at us. They may force us to fly in the older planes. They may insist that we train in six months when the male cadets have much longer. Even so, I believe that one thing that women know how best to do is work against the odds. I know there isn't one of you who hasn't stretched two meals out of one potato."

There was a snigger around the room as many nodded their agreement.

"I want you to promise me this: that you will rise above all that we face and, as Major Raskova said, shine in spite of it all."

Once the speeches were over, they were taken to their barracks. They were very simple buildings with rows of wooden bunk beds. At least it was a little warmer in the south than it had been in Moscow, but still, when the wind blew it was drafty and cold. As soon as they settled in, they received their uniforms and then shrieked in surprise to also be handed large male boots.

"How am I supposed to wear these?" said Eva, holding them up. "These are way too big; my feet are small."

"We shall use this," said Mila, pulling out some of the stuffing in her pillow. "We will push it into the toes."

"But I'll have to get used to walking up and downstairs in these huge monstrosities," responded Eva, putting them on and looking down at her feet. "This is so ridiculous."

"Mine are a little smaller," said Kira, swapping hers with Eva. "My feet are bigger. You can have mine."

They all tried on their boots and guffawed at the way they looked.

Then they got into their large male uniforms and, in the mirror, Tasha didn't recognize herself. She looked just like a man. This was the last way she had wanted Luca to see her. She had always envied the fact he could wear trousers every day, but she didn't want to have the freedom of that experience in this way. Even tightening the belt and making a few extra holes still left a good three inches of excess material at her waistline. The only saving grace was that the officers had conceded to giving them skirts with their dress uniforms, which were green with red stripes.

All around her, the girls laughed at one another in their huge boots, baggy army trousers, and bulky tunics. Mila began parading up and down the barracks, her knees bent, her feet pointing sideways. "Look, I'm Charlie Chaplin!" she announced, pretending she was twirling a cane and twitching an invisible moustache. The girls guffawed at her antics and began pantomiming their own versions of male characters that were popular.

They were interrupted in their performance when Commander Bershanskaya came to find them.

"Ready to get your hair cut?" she asked in an upbeat manner.

Defensively, Tasha ran her hand through her long red curls. Luca loved her hair the way it was. "How short will it need to be cut?" she asked, unable to keep the panic from her tone.

"As short as mine," their commander informed her, turning her head to show the length of her hair, which didn't even reach to the collar of her uniform.

Tasha felt sick. She knew, on the one hand, it was ridiculous to be so vain, but she hadn't been prepared to let go of all her femininity at once when she joined up.

Sensing her unease, Bershanskaya continued, "I know it might feel harsh right now, but trust me, in a few weeks you will soon love how easy it is to take care of and you will wonder why you didn't do it a long time ago. There are many things you will find to worry about during your training, but hair won't be one of them."

Tasha nodded but couldn't help but feel sorry for herself as tears of regret pricked the corners of her eyes.

"Come," their commander continued. "The barber is waiting for you all."

"Barber?" Tasha mouthed to Eva.

"They even mean to cut our hair like men?" Eva whispered back, looking reluctant herself as she ran her fingers through her own curly dark hair.

Kira ran up behind them both and hooked her arms into theirs.

"It'll be fun. Don't worry, there will be no one here we want to impress and we'll all look the same."

Ten minutes later, they all stood nervously in line as, one after another, they had their hair sheared off. It felt criminal to watch the layers and layers of thick glossy curls dropping to the floor as the barber murmured complaints to himself, obviously not relishing having to take care of a group of women with so much hair. When Anastasia asked if it could at least be left to the base of her neck, he blew out his cheeks and informed her in a disgruntled monotone that he been given orders to cut everyone's two inches from their collar and that was what he was going to do.

"Well, that'll be easy to wash!" Kira laughed as she swished her head back and forward, running her fingers through the tiny brush of hair she had left.

When it was Tasha's turn, she couldn't stop the tears from flowing down her cheeks, even though she tried her best to be brave. The barber tutted at her. "God help Russia if you're this upset about a haircut. It just proves that women are not fit to fight." Tasha swallowed down her sadness and swiped at her eyes. She remembered her commander's words, to shine above it all, and told herself she could do this.

Once her hair was sheared, she looked down at the pile of her long red curls and just stopped herself from picking up a lock of it to keep.

As she turned her head back and forward, she couldn't believe how much lighter it felt, and Eva put her arms around her.

"I know this is the last thing you want to hear, but this haircut suits you." She turned her friend around to look in the mirror. "Look how beautiful your eyes look with your hair so short to frame them."

It was a shock to see herself without her hair, but her eyes did look bigger and even greener without all the hair that had hung like thick curtains to her shoulders.

All the girls linked arms around each other and made their way back to their barracks.

"You know what, Kira? From the back you would make a very handsome man," Mila joked. All the girls started to laugh.

"Well, at least I know I can attract women," she said with a joke. "That will be a relief from all those men trying to get one thing out of me!"

. . .

After they had eaten dinner in the dining hall, the group made their way back to their barracks, exhausted after a full day of orientation. In the days they had been together, Tasha had grown very fond of Eva, growing closer during their journey. She was always so kind and thoughtful, but also fun to be around. When they had arrived, they had decided to bunk together, and Tasha climbed up on top as Eva snuggled down below her. But as lights-out was called, Tasha started to feel uneasy. She had never really been this far from her family, and she missed Luca so much it hurt.

Eva must have sensed something because she heard her whispered voice through the darkness. "Tasha, are you all right? You were so quiet during dinner."

"I just feel strange, uneasy about all this. I'm wondering if I was too impulsive signing up as I did."

"I know what you mean, but I think you might just be homesick. I know I am."

"I miss my boyfriend so much," Tasha continued, "and it struck me tonight that even if we end up flying in the same unit, nothing is ever going to be the same. Our whole lives have changed."

"This war has changed all our lives," Eva responded wistfully. "Even if you had stayed at home, it would have been really different, I'm sure. We have been robbed of our innocence. And I fear that nothing will ever be the same again wherever we are until Hitler is dead and this is all over. But at least we have each other," she encouraged.

Tears welled in Tasha's eyes as she smiled at her new friend's reassurance, then joked, "You may live to regret befriending me."

She heard Eva chuckle. "I'm sure I will, but at least it's nice to have each other."

"For me too."

"Good night, Tasha."

"Good night, Eva."

And as Tasha turned over with a creak of the wooden bunk and settled down, she pushed past the strangeness of her short hair and sharing her space with a roomful of sleeping women. Because there was also a sense of excitement and fearful anticipation in equal levels. At least she was doing something from under the shadow of her sister, and away from her village. She knew it wasn't going to be easy, it was going to stretch her, and she welcomed that experience.

14

Nadia

After Ivan left, Nadia's days became long and lonely. Once they'd got married, Ivan had wanted her to give up her work at the flying club, so she had nothing to do with her time. She tried to stick to a routine. Waking early, she would drink her tea and read the paper to keep up with current events and would try to make the experience stretch out for a long time. Then she would clean and organize her house, cleaning her already-tidy kitchen, often washing linens and sheets that were already clean. Then in the afternoon she would write letters to Tasha and Ivan before making dinner and going to bed, early. As she busied herself, she tried not to think about the fact she was alone, though the hardest thing to come to terms with was the quiet. One morning, a dripping tap alerted her to its presence, and once she'd walked over and screwed it tightly, she was so startled by the sudden silence, she felt tears prick her eyes. Everything she did just seemed to reinforce her loneliness. She had no one to cook for, no one to care for. She still took food three times a week to share with Babka. And though her grandmother was always glad to see her, now that Tasha had gone, it was as though her babka had found a life of her own again, spending more time with her own friends and enjoying their company.

Ivan wrote her dutiful letters, talking in detail about his training and the other comrades he'd met; his life seemed so full and busy, filled with many stories of what he was doing. They were beautifully crafted letters—he was a gifted writer— but they still rang hollow when it came to affection or love for her. He never said he missed her or loved her. If he mentioned Nadia at all, it was in the context of housekeeping. "Ensure that the chimney is swept soon," or "Don't forget to check for mice in the grain store." In return, she found herself putting off writing to him for days, hoping that something would happen in her life to write to him about. Without a deep emotional connection between them, filling the letter with any affection towards him seemed redundant. Especially now, she seemed to be doubting her own feelings and their marriage. She felt so trapped between duty and staying in a marriage with no affection or husband at home, or moving on in some way. She just didn't know what to do.

She was shopping in the village one day when she met Olga.

"I haven't seen you for a while. How is Tasha? Is she doing well? I can't believe she joined up."

Nadia felt the usual pang. "She's doing well, I hear. But, unfortunately, she doesn't have much time to write. I think she's having a good time, though. The last letter I got told me she was going to a training site in the south, and I think she's hoping to see Luca there."

"What an amazing opportunity," Olga gushed. "I know no one wants to go to war, but I bet she loves it. I wouldn't have the courage to do something like that. I thought you might go, though, Nadia. I'm surprised you're still here."

Nadia felt something strike her. Why was she still here? There was nothing for her here any more, only Ivan's words about taking care of their home. And yet he was gone, enjoying time with his comrades. Tasha was gone. Babka was happy. There was no reason for her to walk around an empty house. She could do something herself, something for the war.

As she walked home, she considered it. What if she did something more meaningful with her time? She could make a difference. She would use the rest of her money and travel to Moscow the very next day. She would go and talk to the recruitment people there and see about doing something to help the war effort. Maybe she could train as a nurse or do some bookkeeping, as she used to at the flying club. There had to be something she could do.

As she put the kettle on, Nadia suddenly felt a new sense of excitement. It didn't just have to be Tasha who did something to help their country to fight against Hitler; she could help, too. That evening she visited Babka and told her the plan. Her grandmother was sad Nadia would also be gone, but she was also pleased. "I think it would be good for you, Nadia. You have not been happy since your sister and Ivan left. Don't stay around here. There is nothing for you. Go and have your own adventure."

Nadia went home that evening feeling excited for the first time in a long while. Finally, after months of feeling stagnant, she could feel some hope on the horizon. Her only nagging fear was how to tell Ivan. She knew he would not be happy with her decision and she wondered how long she could keep this secret from him.

15

Tasha

Waking up the next day, Tasha stared at the ceiling and tried to get her bearings. Where was she? Momentarily confused, she ran her fingers through her hair and realized with shock it was gone, and then it all came back to her. She had barely had time to come to terms with her new reality when lights were flicked on, and the commander shouted down the barracks, "Everybody up, get out of bed."

As she stumbled out of her bunk, tripping over Eva's bedclothes on the way down, Tasha moved groggily to the bathroom to get ready. The commander continued to bark instructions.

"Get washed, get your uniforms on, and let's see you on the parade ground. You've got five minutes."

Groaning, all the other girls joined her in the communal bathroom, still stiff and tired after many days on the train.

Still bleary-eyed, Tasha began to dress in her uniform. It was uncomfortable and the fabric stiff. She slipped her tiny feet into her huge boots, laced them up, and along with the other women, rushed outside as the commander shouted to them to all move faster. They raced through the barracks, their feet echoing loudly on the wooden floor as they all attempted to stay upright.

As soon as they were out on the parade ground, they were taught how to line up, stand to attention, and march, which was very difficult in their huge boots. Tasha kept kicking Mila in front of her, who got very cross. "I'm sorry," she hissed. "It's like my feet don't belong to me any more."

They were dismissed and sent for breakfast an hour later, all tired and hungry. Over the next week, they were trained hard in the military disciplines of being an air force cadet, and it was exhausting. At the end of the day they would all compare their blisters and practically fall asleep in their clothes.

"I think I've lost weight," commented Anastasia as she attempted to cinch her belt even tighter. "Just what I need in these trousers. I'm frightened that I will salute one day and they'll end up around my ankles."

All the girls laughed.

"I wish I had lost weight; instead I have gained muscles," moaned Eva. "Look at my arms. All that marching and rifle work. I look like one of my brothers."

As well as drill during the first week, they worked on other skills, too. How to take care of their planes, ballistics, and navigation.

They would sit for hours learning how to plot coordinates and use navigation tools, understand how bombs were dropped and how far before a target they had to aim for a successful strike, which was all incredibly boring to Tasha, who would almost fall asleep in her classes.

The first day they had arrived for a joint class, the male recruits had stared at them with curiosity, like they were strange animals at the zoo. Then came the snide remarks and jokes about their uniforms and boots. The girls, in turn, attempted to ignore them. When they all marched out onto the grounds to practice firing a machine gun, Sergei jeered at Tasha as she moved in front of him. "Look, here's a very beautiful girl with ugly hair," he scoffed.

She was about to give him a piece of her mind when Kira grabbed her arm and shook her head. "Ignore him. They will eventually get used to us."

They worked in teams of two to learn the anatomy of the machine gun and how to feed the bullet strips into it. Eva and Tasha paired up and Eva fired the first round, practicing hitting a moving target, which in this case was a small train car running on a rail. When it came to Tasha, she had trouble lining up her shot and started to get frustrated. Eva encouraged her, "Just pretend it's Sergei's head." And whether it was that or the fact she suddenly got the hang of it, she didn't know, but Tasha began to hit the target with ease as her friend laughed by her side.

The next day they were working on their armory skills. Because she was already a pilot, it was understood that she would probably be flying rather than working as ground crew, but all the girls had to learn these skills, which included placing a charge inside a bomb head.

As she was carefully hooking the charge into the bomb, Sergei came up behind her and shouted, "Boom," into her ear, making her jump. And even though she was working on a dummy bomb, it made her drop the charge into the mud, and she swore as she rooted around while he walked away laughing. She found she had never disliked anyone as much.

"I don't understand," she complained to Eva after the class. "Don't they want us to win this war? You think they would be encouraging us, not trying to make it harder."

"Oh, having us here threatens their fragile masculinity," her friend commented. "They like to think they are all the strong ones and we should just be pretty little wives at home." Eva batted her eyelashes.

"Phuf," responded Tasha, "I would never be like that. I'm

beginning to wonder if I will ever get married. I'm starting to go off men completely."

"What about your boyfriend?"

Tasha pursed her lips. "I'm scared, Eva; the longer I am away from him, the more I doubt our relationship. And honestly, he is not like Sergei, but what if his own masculinity is affected by me joining up? He may take one look at me in these ridiculous boots with my boy haircut and wonder what he saw in me."

Eva linked her arm and squeezed it. "He won't," she assured her. "If he really loves you, he will be so glad to see you, I'm sure."

Tasha responded with a reluctant smile but *she* wasn't sure. It had been such a long time since she had seen him, she wondered how it would be if they were ever to be together again.

Towards the end of the week, they were sent out on a navigation exercise to work with their maps and compasses. Again, the men were partnered with some of the women. Sergei was placed in Tasha's team along with Liliya, Eva, and Mila.

"I think I should show us the way," he said airily as they all studied the map, "since I am the man."

Mila balked. "And what makes you think that you're superior to us?"

"Men are more skilled in this area. And besides, I don't believe that you girls will be around very long. I think it has been very amusing having females... for a while." He mimed a plane crashing.

"You're more likely to get killed because your big mouth could be heard by the enemy from anywhere," stated Mila acidly. The three other girls agreed and laughed as they started to make their way.

For the exercise they had to use their maps and coordinates, using navigation points to guide them. They got about halfway when there was a dispute. Sergei thought they should go in one direction, and Eva thought they should go in another. Tasha studied the map. Navigation definitely wasn't her strength, but Eva was the best in the group.

"I think Eva's right," she said, looking down at the map.

"Well, you would say that," spat back Sergei as he thrust the map back at her. "But if I go this way and end up in the right place, you will look very, very foolish."

"And the same for you, if you end up in the wrong place," said Eva.

"We have to stay together," encouraged Liliya.

"Would you miss me, princess?" he said sarcastically as he flicked at her hair.

She slapped his hand away. "Don't touch me," she growled.

"We have to make a decision," said Mila. "Which way are we going to go? I think Eva is right too."

"You have to come with us, Sergei."

He sat down on a log and stretched back, placing his hands behind his head and closing his eyes. "I'll wait here while you go that way. And once you have gone around in a circle, you can come back and get me."

"We can't leave you," said Eva, "as much as I would like to."

They argued for a while but he wouldn't budge, just yawned and kept his eyes closed. They eventually had to leave and went off in the direction that they had decided on. They were frustrated when they got farther down the road and realized the markings weren't correct.

"I'm infuriated Sergei may have been right," said Eva as she studied the map from every angle.

"We can't go back," said Liliya. "It will be too humiliating."

"What else are we to do? If he was right and he knows he's right, we'll never hear the end of it."

"We'll never hear the end of it anyway," said Tasha. "We may as well go back and get him."

They started to double back on themselves and found him still sitting on the log, waiting; he mocked them as they arrived back. "I see you're back. Did you enjoy your trip into the forest?"

Tasha wanted to smack him. But instead, they started to make their way down the way that he had said. Nothing gave her greater pleasure when she realized he was also wrong. He would not be able to throw this in their faces.

After walking for twenty minutes, they also found that none of the landmarks they were looking for were there.

Eventually, they found the right way, as Mila stepped up and managed to navigate them in the right direction, but they were the last to arrive back at the camp. When they got back, there was a cheer in the group, and Kira came over to talk to them.

"Were you lost? What happened?"

"We had an idiot with us who didn't help because he confused us."

"Sergei?" suggested Kira with a curl of her lip.

"How did you know?"

At dinner, Sergei was back with the male recruits. But Tasha could hear him talking about them as she passed his table. He was implying it was their fault that he'd got lost and that if he had been given a proper team, he could have got back first.

She went up to him. "Are you such a small man that you cannot own up to your own mistakes? You had as much trouble as we did." The recruits around him stared at her as she continued to get angry. "We're going to be together fighting in this war, whether you like it or not. And your lack of support is not helping. You'd just better get used to us. You're a pathetic excuse for a cadet."

One of the guys started to chuckle next to him as Sergei's face flushed red. "You won't be in this war. I will put my odds on it. You and your little group of knitters will have to leave the winning of this war to the men."

"I'm glad they have taught me how to use a gun, because if ever I get a chance to kill you, don't worry, I'll take it," she snapped as him as Eva pulled her away, encouraging her to not upset herself.

"That might be possible if you ever learn to shoot straight," he shouted back after her.

Eva kept her moving so she didn't retaliate, but Tasha was fuming.

16

NOVEMBER 1941

Tasha

"There's a new troop train in," Eva said excitedly as the rest of the girls sat in their barracks, relaxing after a busy day. "I think I saw more girls coming to join the camp as well. That's what I hear. It will be exciting to have some new faces. And some of the men don't look so bad either." Eva smiled.

Tasha felt her heart quicken. Every time a troop train came in, she hoped that this would finally be the time that Luca would join the training school. He had been in Moscow for six weeks now doing his basic training. They hadn't even bothered with that for the girls, making them learn as they went along, sending them straight to the flying school, their training being shorter.

Jumping down from her bunk where she'd been lying, Tasha hurried out, hoping to catch a glimpse of some of the new recruits. Out on the parade ground was a swarm of gray uniforms. A billowing cloud of new recruits jumping down from military lorries, all chatting with one another, an excited hubbub of frantic activity. Tasha glanced quickly from face to face as then, with a sinking heart, she realized once again Luca wasn't there.

She was just moving away when something caught her eye. Just the way a cadet's body moved seemed familiar. Staring at where she had seen the movement, she scanned the crowd then, looking for that individual, and hitched her breath as she saw him, for the first time in weeks. He had been at the back of one of the trucks and had only just jumped down. Pulling off his cap, he wiped his forehead, and there was the dark, curly hair so familiar to her. She couldn't help but stop and stare at him in awe of how handsome he was. Butterflies fluttered in her stomach and she felt as if she were seeing him for the first time. It was definitely him, but he looked so different. He'd always been broad and handsome to her, but since he'd been in Moscow, he'd filled out, his body more muscular than she'd ever seen it. His jaw set as though the military had even changed the way he held his head. She daren't hope.

She saw him talking to a small group, and slowly she walked towards him.

"Luca," she called out.

He turned quickly and looked around, curiously. Then, seeing her, the shock on his face was unmistakable. She ran to him then and threw her arms around his neck, hugging him tightly, and it felt so good to finally be in his arms. The group of soldiers that had been standing talking to him stepped back in surprise and started jeering and calling out to him. Luca quickly pulled her arms from his neck and dragged her to one side.

"What are you doing here?" he hissed. "You can't come to a camp like this. You're crazy. If they find you, they'll arrest you, maybe even charge me too. Did you follow me all the way here? I wondered why I wasn't getting letters from you."

Pulling away, she felt rejected. "You're not happy to see me?" she asked, the disappointment obvious in her tone.

His shoulders dropped, and he sighed. "*Of course* I'm

happy to see you. But I don't want you to get into any trouble."
He looked her over and softened. "Oh my God, Tasha, I have
missed you," he said. And then, pulling her into his arms, he
hugged her deeply. "It's good to see you. But you have to go
now. You have to get out of here, before someone sees you."

"Get out of here? I can't get out of here. I live here now."

He looked at her, trying to understand what she was
saying. "You're helping out on the base?"

"Luca, I joined up."

The look on his face was unmistakable. He was so
shocked. He didn't speak for a minute. He just stared at her.
Was he not happy to be with her? Had he not realized that
she'd done this for him?

"What do you mean?" he finally whispered, incredulously.
"What do you mean, you joined up?"

"Like you, I joined up. I'm going to fly."

"But you're a woman. You can't fly."

"Says who? Major Raskova came to Moscow recruiting.
They're going to start an all-women's flying squadron, and I
joined up."

"Oh my God, Tasha. What is wrong with you? That's so
dangerous!"

"I thought you would be happy."

"Happy that you're going to be in a battle day after day,
you're going to fight in a war?"

"You didn't seem to have any problem with you doing
that."

"It's different for me."

"Why? Because you're a man?"

He blew out air. "It's not that, Tasha. I don't want to be
worried about you. I want you to be home and safe with your
grandmother."

"But our country is at war with Germany. I want to be
with you. I can't believe you're acting this way. I thought you
would be glad. We might even be able to fly together."

He looked crestfallen.

"Well, I'm sorry I bothered," she said. "I came all this way, through all this training. I let them cut my hair."

He looked at her, then.

"I know I look ugly," she continued.

"I wasn't thinking that." He smiled, looking at her wistfully. "I was thinking how you look so young. It reminds me of when you were a little girl. Remember when you cut your own hair?"

She laughed. "I do. Babka was so angry." She softened. "I did all this for us, Luca. I wanted us to be together."

He shook his head slowly, looking sad. "Of course you did, and I'm very flattered, and God, it's good to see you. But now I have more than just my life to worry about. And you shouldn't have done this, Tasha; you were too impulsive."

Suddenly, they were all called to attention, and he had to leave. He fell into line, and she walked away. "I wish I'd never bothered," she snapped at him, as she felt the raw sting of rejection.

17

Nadia

Nadia felt her stomach tighten as the train came to a stop. She had been traveling for days and was ready to get off but was also concerned about what she might find when she did. She was hopeful that Tasha would be glad to see her, but she also had a niggling suspicion that her sister might not be as excited about this development.

"Here we are," said Irina, grabbing her arm. "Time for us to start our new life." The girls she had traveled down on the troop train with had been really friendly, and they were all ready to serve their country, including Nadia.

When she'd gone into Moscow to see if she could do something for the war effort, they'd asked her about her skills. When she had told them about being a pilot, they had more than encouraged her to join the fighting forces on the front line with the new women's fighter squadrons that were being assembled. She had to admit the excitement in her had compelled her forward into taking the test, preparing to leave, but there had also been a great reluctance. The worst thing was that she hadn't yet told Ivan. She kept telling herself she would write him a letter and explain. She knew he would not be happy. He had made it very clear he did not want her in harm's way, but she couldn't stay at home. Not when everybody she knew and loved had already gone.

They had talked to her about nursing as well. But when she thought about rolling bandages or taking temperatures while her little sister was flying in the sky, it all seemed to pale in comparison. They bustled off the train and made their way to one of the many trucks that would take them to the flying school. She took a deep breath of the warmer southern air, ready to get started.

Of course her sister would be happy to see her, wouldn't she? So, they rattled along in the truck, chatting amongst themselves, and it wasn't long before they arrived and were introduced to their commanding officer. She looked up from her notes and glanced toward Nadia. "You are Natasha Petroffskaya's sister?" Nadia nodded. "Interesting. It will be good to have two sisters together. We already have such a strong bond here with each other, I think you will fit in well." As they were making their way across the parade ground, Nadia spotted Tasha with another girl just leaving the dining area. She hardly recognized her at first. Her hair was short, and in her new uniform, she looked so different and more formal than she usually dressed. As their eyes met, she gave her sister a halting smile. Tasha's eyes grew larger as she raced towards her.

"What are you doing here, Nadia? Is everything okay? Is it Babka? Why have you come?"

Her commanding officer turned to her. "Your sister has come to join our crew. She will be one of us."

Tasha's face went visibly from worry and concern to anger. Pulling her sister aside, she looked furious. "You have come to join? You have come here to be the same as me?"

"Surprise," her sister said, trying to lighten the moment.

"I can't believe you did this to me. I can't believe you

couldn't leave me alone to do something for myself for once," she spat out and, turning on her heel, was gone.

Commander Bershanskaya took the new recruits into the canteen where all the girls were eating. When she informed the cadets that their newest recruits had arrived, a cheer went up around the table where they had all just finished their dinner.

"Thank you, cadets, I know you will make them very welcome. Let me introduce you to them all. This is Irina Volkova. She has been a pilot before and is looking forward to joining our ranks."

A short woman with tight blonde curls blushed as she nodded her agreement.

"And this is Zora Belsky. She has been a navigator before but is fairly new to flying and I know you will all help her."

Zora was striking, with high cheekbones and a wide smile.

"This is Maria Popov. She has a lot of flying experience and will be a great asset to our ranks."

A woman with mousy brown hair and lively eyes nodded to them all.

"And lastly, this is Nadia Kozlov. She is a pilot too and also Natasha Petroffskaya's sister."

Everyone cheered and clapped and Nadia felt uncomfortable because of her sister's cold greeting.

"I'm sure you will want to be with your sister," continued the commander, "so why not take the same set of bunk beds. Eva, please move your things so the two of them can be together."

Eva nodded.

Acidic bile crept up into Nadia's throat. This would make Tasha feel manipulated, as though it was Nadia that had created the situation.

"There is no need for that..." she began to say.

"Nonsense." The commander beamed. "We know you will want to be together. All families do."

Nadia wasn't so sure.

Tasha found her half an hour later while she was having her hair cut. She strode towards her, her face still red with anger.

"Why are you here?" she spat out.

The man cutting Nadia's hair looked up in surprise but carried on doing his job quietly as Tasha paced in front of her sister's chair.

"You can't stand it, can you? You can't stand for me to have my own life. You can't stand to see me do well at something. And instead of you just saying, 'Wonderful. Well done, Tasha, I hope it goes well for you,' instead, you have to follow me here and make me look foolish."

"How does me joining the Russian Air Force make *you* look foolish?" Nadia protested. "I'm just doing my job, serving my country. I'm a pilot like you. So why shouldn't I be flying as well?"

Tasha continued pacing, her arms tightly folded. "Because I know it's not what you want, Nadia. You already chose the life you wanted," she continued sardonically, "your perfect little house with your wonderful husband. Everything so tidy and precious. Fighting for Russia is not what you wanted. And how does your husband feel about this?"

"Ivan has gone to the front," Nadia responded flatly.

Tasha stopped pacing for a moment, a look of surprise in her eyes. "He was called up?"

"Yes."

Tasha scoffed. "I'm surprised. I thought he would find some medical complaint to stop from having to go. He doesn't seem like the heroic type to me."

"That's because you've never bothered to get to know Ivan. He's a good man and wants to do the right thing for his country. As do I."

"That still doesn't answer the question of why you're here. And don't tell me again that it's to serve our country."

Nadia teased out a frustrated breath. "Babka wanted me to be close. She worries about you. You know how she is."

"So, you came to watch over me? You don't think I'm capable of taking care of myself?"

"I *know* you're not capable of taking care of yourself," snapped back Nadia as the man cutting her hair let out a low chuckle.

"I've been doing very well so far, I'll let you know. I've already flown and completed some training and I'm still alive. So, I don't need my big sister to hold my hand. And don't give me these lies. You came because you wanted to see if you could master something else and maybe to outshine me as well. Well, you won't, because I'll become a better pilot, and I'll outshine you for a change."

"This is not a competition, Tasha."

"It has always been a competition for *me* because I've always had to measure up to your amazing talents. 'Look how quiet Nadia's being.' 'Look how well she is playing.' 'She is coloring so nicely. Can you not color nicely just like Nadia?' That's all I've heard my whole life, and this was my chance to prove myself for who I was. And as soon as I try to branch out, and do something for myself, here you are. I will not forgive you for this, Nadia. And don't expect us to be friends while you're here. I'm furious and you should stay out of my way."

And with that, her sister strode off. Nadia watched her go, and her heart sank. There was some truth to what Tasha was saying. She'd seen right through her ruse. As much as Babka was concerned, Nadia had wanted to do this, prove something to herself, not to outshine her sister, but to be part of something exciting. What Tasha didn't realize was it wasn't easy being this way. Nadia had always felt the pressure as the oldest to set an example and in return she had set high standards for herself. Tasha had never understood that Nadia never felt as if she ever hit the mark, no matter how she was viewed by others. She wished she could be a little reckless now and again, throw caution to the wind in the way Tasha was so gifted at. But she always felt this need to be in control, to be doing the right thing, and that sometimes felt more like a curse than a blessing.

18

Tasha

Not long after Nadia arrived, they started bombing practice. Nadia was paired with Mila and they made a formidable team. Tasha tried desperately not to let it show just how disappointed she was that Nadia was here and had already performed so well. She didn't even have to try. It was who she was and it annoyed the hell out of her sister.

"It must be lovely having Luca and Nadia here," Eva commented one morning as they headed out to the field.

Swallowing down her frustration, Tasha turned to her navigator, who was tucking her hair into her leather flying cap as they walked. "Well, Luca still isn't speaking to me. He wants me to go home. And as far as Nadia goes, Eva, can I be honest with you?"

Eva stopped and furrowed her brow with curiosity. "Of course."

"I wish Nadia hadn't come. For my whole life I have been compared to her. And don't get me wrong, I love my sister with all my heart, but this was the first time I was doing something on my own, instead of in her shadow. And it felt good to make friends without someone saying, '*Ah, you're Nadia's sister; we love Nadia,*' then feeling their disappointment as they got to know me because I wasn't anything like her." The wind whipped up and blew Tasha's short bob of hair into her eyes. She pulled it free and started to tame it beneath her own flying cap, noting the kind concern in Eva's eyes as she continued. "She just excels without even trying, and it was nice to have a fresh start for once without that feeling of being something less."

Eva grabbed her arm and squeezed it. "I don't think of you as less. She is good, that is true, and if she carries on, she will probably be promoted. But you are so different, and not in a bad or lesser way. I think you too will have your own moments to shine."

Tasha put her arms around Eva and gave her a huge hug.

At that moment, Kira and Katya came up behind them. "Already saying your goodbyes before we've even handled the bombs?" Kira joked.

Tasha and Eva exchanged a conspiratorial glance between them, neither wanting to share what they had been talking about as they strode out with the other girls onto the field.

As they arrived at their planes, Commander Bershanskaya stepped forward to address them.

"I know there has been some resentment because the men will have better aircraft than we will. And it feels like we are being patronized, which, of course, we are."

There was a general snigger as the girls exchanged a look of agreement between themselves.

"It may seem unfair that our all-women flying unit has been allocated the training planes to fly during the raids. I know many of you were hoping for something better. And for the cadets who will fly in that unit, you will have to learn to be more tactical. But here is the good news. The German planes will not be able to catch you. This is because your planes travel at such a slow speed the enemy cannot stay behind you without stalling and falling out of the sky. So, they can't shoot us down in the air the same way they would with our male fighter squadrons. But we are still very vulnerable. You will have no radios and no guns. You will have no way to navigate apart from a compass, a pencil and a map."

All the girls looked horrified.

Bershanskaya nodded her understanding of what they felt before adding, "But we are going to show them that we don't need any of that."

Kira raised her hand. "May I ask a question, Commander?"

Bershanskaya nodded.

"How will we communicate at night with one another on a bombing run without radios?"

"I have given this much thought, cadet. And though it is rudimentary, I think I have a solution. For runs with the 588 Squadron, which many of you will be in, you will be bombing during the night and you will be able to use your flashlights. We will create our own code. Today while we are practicing I will have you use the hand signals you have been taught."

The group looked around at each other in amazement as their commander continued.

"We're going to show them that we can do just as well without all the equipment. That, of course, includes a parachute."

There was a general hubbub of disbelief throughout the ranks.

Bershanskaya held up her hand and continued. "Because of the weight in the plane, you won't be able to have one, but because of the height you will be flying at, there will not be enough time to deploy it fully anyway. This means you will have to fly more carefully. Today we will practice a bombing run in formations of three. We will also practice taking your engines down to a very low speed. This will make you tactically challenging to find in the sky."

Nadia looked over at Tasha. Tasha avoided her gaze.

"In the first run, I will have Nadia and Mila and Kira and Anastasia and Tasha and Eva work together." Bershanskaya allocated all the girls to teams, then continued, "I know you have all practiced what a run will feel like, but it can be different when you're working in formation and carrying ammunition. We have targets set up, but we are not too worried about you getting direct hits today. Just practice the process of working together in your teams and dropping your bombs."

They all fell out and strode towards their planes.

Tasha hoisted herself into the cockpit as Eva tapped her shoulder with encouragement. She took off first, and her plane led the way, the two other planes following. It was a beautiful day as they soared into the sky. The visibility was very good, which would be helpful for targeting the bombs.

Approaching the coordinates of the allocated target area, Nadia signaled and moved in front. The other two planes fell in behind.

As they approached the drop area, they could see that thick, red crosses were painted on the targets to help the girls with their aim. One target was a battered, old, burned-out car, the other a stack of flour sacks.

In front of them, Nadia dropped her speed in order to straighten up towards the targets. Tasha and Eva watched in anticipation as her sister came in as low as she could, descending toward the ground as she prepared to drop her bombs.

"She's released," Eva shouted as they both watched the first bomb plummet to the ground, landing very close to the car and bouncing away. Eva shook her head with admiration. "That was good for her first try."

Nadia and Mila came around again and bombed the second target, hitting that one head-on, and flour sprayed into the air, signifying a direct hit. Nadia was good at this, and

Tasha's stomach cramped with the realization she was never going to be able to beat her.

When Tasha circled back around to drop her own bombs, she was close to the targets but not as close as Nadia. At least she fared better than Kira, who had trouble timing her bombs to even drop in the right field.

After a successful afternoon of bombing runs, they finished for the day. It was obvious Nadia was exceptionally good at this.

After they landed, Eva went off to get something to eat, and with her stomach churning, Tasha walked back to her barracks wishing she could just go home. She got into bed early that night, still fuming, and though she wasn't asleep, ignored her sister when Nadia approached the bunk asking if she was still awake.

———

The next morning as she left her building, she heard someone call out to her. Turning, Tasha blew out a stream of frustrated air as Luca ran to catch up with her.

"I'm not in a good mood, Luca. If you have come here to argue with me again, don't bother."

Luca stopped her by taking her by the shoulders and turning her to face him.

"I've come to apologize," he said softly. "It was wrong of me to tell you what to do, and once I calmed down, I realized that it was actually very flattering. You came here to be with me."

She looked up at him, her frustration still etching lines across her forehead.

He pulled her out of sight behind one of the barracks.

"I love you, Tasha. It was a shock seeing you here. I thought you were safe at home with Babka. I should have known better than to think you would sit knitting with the old women for the war. But now that I've got used to it, I don't think the Germans stand a chance with you flying in our squadrons."

Tears pricked her eyes. "Honestly, Luca, I'm having some serious doubts. I think, as you said, I was too impulsive, *once again*. I just missed you so much, and that's all I could think about. But now I'm walking around in this horrible male uniform and these huge boots, my hair makes me look ugly, and we're both so busy we're exhausted and we hardly have time for each other, and Nadia is here and already outshining me."

Luca chuckled and pulled her close to his chest.

"Oh, Tasha, no one could outshine you. You are a one of a kind." He placed his lips to her forehead as he whispered his reassurance to her. "Yes, Nadia is good, we all know that, but you have some skills she will never have. If I had to fly into a dangerous battle, I would always pick you. You are brave and smart and one of the best pilots I know for maneuvering an airplane. And as for as the way you look, I would find you attractive in a flour sack. You have no idea how hard it is seeing you around the school and not being able to make love to you."

She pulled away and met his intense gaze. "I miss you in that way too. And sometimes I worry that we might never get to have what we had before. This is all so real and serious. Luca, do you think we're even going to survive? I'm hearing about so many deaths on the front and I'm not even sure we can make a difference."

"Of course we're going to survive. I promised you, remember? I promised you that I would not die; don't ever forget that. One day we can get married and have lots of great-grandbabies for Babka."

She started to laugh. "Who said anything about children?"

He raised his eyebrows humorously and smiled broadly. He had cheered her up just as he always did.

He turned and looked out across the flying field, toward the sun that was just beginning to rise in an amber glow.

"Look," he whispered to her, "it's our time of day."

Turning and drawing in her breath, Tasha closed her eyes, allowing the golden light to redden the inside of her eyelids, as she relived that magical morning so long ago.

Gently Luca slipped his arms around her waist, pulling her close till her back nestled against his firm chest. He leaned forward and she got a scent of his shaving soap as he whispered into her ear.

"I can still picture you there as though it was yesterday. God, Tasha, I can't believe how much I love you. I think my love has grown even more since we've been here." He leaned forward and kissed her neck, making her shiver with the warmth and gentleness of his lips, and everything inside of her relaxed. Everything always felt right when she was in his arms, as though nothing around them ever mattered.

Hearing someone approach, he quickly pulled away from her, squeezing her hand tightly as they parted and both started to walk towards the dining hall. A cadet walked around the corner and they all nodded to one another. "Comrade," Luca said respectfully as they passed one another, and then, giving her a sideways glance, they both shared a smile as she brushed his lips with a quick kiss and they made their way inside.

19

Nadia

To her frustration, Tasha continued to be cool with her as they progressed with their training. They learned many skills they would need in battle, especially how to drop their bombs. After they had perfected their bombing skills during the day, it was time to learn how to bomb at night. One evening, Nadia stepped out of her barracks and tightened the belt of her uniform. In her hand, she carried her navigation map, leather flying cap, and goggles. It was a cool, brisk evening as she strode to the briefing room, where the girls were already gathering. Inside, the girls sat huddled together on wooden benches. She moved towards them, and Anastasia shuffled over so she could sit down. She patted Nadia's leg with a smile as she joined the group.

Tasha was sat close to the front, and she barely glanced at Nadia as they all turned back around to face their commander.

Commander Bershanskaya started the briefing and explained what they would be doing that evening for training.

"Over the last weeks, we have been improving your bombing skills. Tonight will be your first night flight. You could find the darkness very disorienting, and in order to see your target, one of your team will set off a flare to illuminate the sight. Try the best you can. It would be good if you can hit at least one of the targets, but it can take a while to get used to lining up for a drop at night. After that, we will do two or three passes with each of you and see if we can improve your score. The ground crew is getting your airplanes ready. Good luck, girls."

The girls chattered excitedly with each other as they strode outside. Nadia tried to catch her sister's eye, but Tasha just looked down at the floor as she continued on her way. Nadia walked alongside Mila.

She felt the thrill she always felt when looking at an aircraft. She was always surprised at how basic it was. She knew the men were flying in something much grander than this, and it was unfair that the women had just been given these crop-dusters, but she wasn't complaining. It was this or stay at home staring at the walls.

As she pulled herself up into the cockpit, the ground crew gave her some last-minute instructions before she checked through her instrumentation. Once she'd finished her checks, she gave the thumbs-up for them to start the engine. Stepping back in front of the propeller, a girl gave it a yank to the left, and it began to spin furiously as the engine roared into life. Pulling on her leather flying cap, she tightened the strap underneath her chin and snapped it shut. Setting her goggles into place, she gave another thumbs-up.

Taxiing towards the runway, Mila's voice cracked through their talking tube. "We're going to fly northwest, so head off towards the trees over there." Mila pointed over to where there was no more than a mass of dark trees in front of them.

Nadia felt the exhilaration teasing its way through her body. She loved to fly, and this just felt so exciting. She knew her life would be in danger, but what an incredible experience. She eased forward on the throttle, feeling the balance in the plane's wings as she headed towards the runway. As they picked up speed, she pulled back gently on the control stick at the end of the runway and gracefully took off over the trees and soared high into the sky.

The cool briskness of the air instantly chilled her face, wherever it wasn't covered by the goggles. She couldn't help but shiver, with excitement as much as the cold. The moon peeped from behind ragged gray clouds as she flew towards the area that had been designated.

"We have to look out for a bridge," her navigator yelled to her.

They both started to look down below them.

"There to the right," Mila said, pointing over Nadia's shoulder.

Nadia looked down and began to veer towards the area.

"And then there is a lake further down, about half a mile away," Mila informed her as they found their way.

"We should be passing the target area soon," Mila continued.

"I'll do one pass over it first so we can get the lay of the land," added Nadia to her copilot, shouting to be heard over the roar of the engine. She dipped the plane slightly so they could get closer to the ground as they started to approach the area with the targets.

As they passed over the top, Mila released a flare, and the two of them looked out over the side of the plane to identify what needed to be hit. Then, as they pointed the targets out to one another, Nadia nodded.

"I'm going to hit the one on the left first." Nadia visualized the site judging the trajectory in her mind, calculating quickly when to release the first bomb. She'd always had a good head for this kind of calculation.

Circling the plane, she brought it back down lower over the trees as the navigator prepared to release the bomb. She lined up in front of the truck as its wreck came into view and the red cross became obvious. Easing back on her throttle a little, she shouted, "Release," and felt the slight jolt of the plane as the bomb sailed towards the target. They didn't have a chance to check if it hit the mark because the next target was so close. Banking slightly to the left, they released the second bomb. As she veered the plane back around, the girls both looked back and in the waning light of the flare could see a plume of flour coming up from both targets.

"Oh my God, Nadia, you hit both of them. I don't think anybody's done anything like this even in the daylight."

Nadia smiled with exhilaration. "You still have two to go," she said. She wheeled the plane around and lined up for her next run.

The engine's pitch lowered to a growl as she moved in a little slower to be able to hit the next target. "Release!" she shouted as they lined up again, and the plane rocked one more time. "Release!" Their third target was a little bit off. But the fourth one hit dead on.

Mila whooped behind her. "You are brilliant, Nadia," she screamed into the communication tube. "They can't complain about that."

They did two more passes, and Nadia did well again. She was pleased as they sailed for home.

When they arrived back on the ground, there was a great buzz of excitement from the girls as they all got down from their cockpits and gathered together for their results.

"I did better this time," said Kira as she pulled her leather cap from her head. "At least my bombs landed in the right field."

"How about you girls? Did you hit anything?

"Nadia hit all of them," stated Mila proudly. All the girls responded enthusiastically and Nadia turned just in time to see her sister was behind her. But Tasha just rolled her eyes and walked off in the opposite direction.

One hour later, they gathered together for their debriefing.

"You all did very well," the commander said. "But Tasha, you came in far too low for your last run, almost clipping the trees. I understand that you want to bomb your targets, but not at the cost of your crew or at the destruction of one of our planes. Please be more careful in the future. You are important to us. I don't want to lose you before you've even started."

Nadia glanced across at her sister, whose face was flushed bright red. She wasn't surprised at the comment. This was what she feared more than anything, that in order to outshine her, Tasha would take unnecessary risks. They were the kinds of risks she had always taken, but now they made the stakes so high they could cost Tasha her life—a thought that terrified her.

20

Tasha

One morning, they were all called onto the parade ground, both the male and the female cadets. Standing to receive them was one of their instructors, who the women knew did not look favorably on the women recruits.

Tasha marched into her line, trying to look for Luca out of the corner of her eye, but she couldn't see him anywhere.

As she waited at attention, the cold air whipped around her hair and she was glad to be warm in her flying suit.

The commander spoke to them all.

"Today, we will be testing your navigational skills in the air. You'll be under all sorts of duress when you're flying, so you need to get very astute at knowing where you are and where you need to be. You will be doing a navigation hop, which means you'll navigate to one point, then you'll navigate to another point, and then a third point before flying back. During that time, you won't be able to land. You should have enough fuel to get you around the whole course and a little extra in case you get lost. Watch your fuel gauge and make sure you land your plane in plenty of time. It is essential that you follow your maps and course correctly. I've assigned you in teams so you can all practice your skills."

He started to read out the list of the teams that would be going up together, and Tasha noticed he was putting all the women with the men, the women in the navigator seats. When he announced her partner, she groaned inwardly. Just to have to be around Sergei in the training center was bad enough, but to have to sit in a plane with him for an afternoon was going to be excruciating. It made it even worse that Nadia had been paired with Luca.

"Are there any questions?" the commander asked.

Tasha stepped forward and saluted.

"I have one, sir. I noticed that you put all of the female cadets in the navigation seat, when most of us are training as pilots. Would it not be wiser to have more of us get a chance to pilot the planes?" She knew this was pushing the boundaries of what was acceptable, but she really did not want to get in a plane with Sergei.

The commander's displeasure was obvious. "I am well aware of what I have done, cadet. You will step back into line and do as you're told. Even as a pilot, you will need to learn how to navigate well. At any point, your navigator could be injured, and you would have to be able to get yourself home through flak and even maybe from over enemy lines."

Tasha felt her heart sink as she glanced across at Sergei, who looked like he wasn't enamored with the prospect of being with her either. Leaving the parade ground, the girls went off to get ready.

"Bad luck for getting Sergei," said Eva sympathetically.

"At least Sergei can fly," muttered Kira as they walked back to their rooms. "I'm with Boris. I don't think he knows the back end of the plane from the front."

All the girls laughed with the truth of it. It had been rumored he was in the training center because his father was high up in the government.

"Maybe you can help our comrade by painting the front of the plane red to remind him the direction to fly in," Irina joked.

They all left for the field, and, putting on her goggles and fixing her leather cap, Tasha strode out to the plane. Sergei was already waiting in the cockpit. He watched her approach.

"Well, Miss Petroffskaya, we get to navigate together again. I'm hoping you can do a better job in the air than you did on the ground," he snarled as he continued. "And this time, I get to do what I'm good at, which is piloting, and you get the privilege of learning from me."

She wanted to slap him, but instead gave him a tight smile as she clenched and unclenched her fists before jumping up onto the wing and hoisting herself into her seat.

She looked down at the navigation map they'd all been working on an hour earlier, her finger tracing her penciled lines as she tried to focus on what she had to do.

Sergei took off with ease and the plane lifted into the sky. As he flew, he felt the need to commentate everything they were seeing. "We're passing over a small village, and there's a group of trees to the east and to the left and some bushes over here to the right."

"I'm quite aware of these things, Cadet Yezhova," she snapped. "I have eyes. That's my job."

"Just thought I'd better check. I know, as a pilot, you've probably become sloppy with your navigational skills."

She gritted her teeth, but controlled her temper. As they started to fly to their first navigation point, Tasha helped direct him, though this wasn't one of her strengths. She found herself distracted by the instrumentation, her mind drifting to piloting. As he flew, she kept checking his height and levels.

Something in the plane would distract her and she'd have to look down at her map again to scrutinize where they were. All at once, with much relief, she located their first point. She informed Sergei that the railway station was just below them.

"Amazing, I would give you a round of applause, but I'm busy using my hands in a much more important pursuit."

She ignored his rudeness and shouted, "We need to go due east for five miles now. I mean west," she corrected herself. He had her on edge.

"Well, is it east or west, comrade? Surely they taught even women to know the direction of the sunrise and sunset at schools in the country?"

"West," she responded forcefully, ignoring his comment. "Definitely west."

"Don't worry, Comrade Petroffskaya, maybe if you aren't good at this, they will give you a little job outside the plane. You could wash them for us when we get back from defending our country. That would seem to suit a country peasant like you better."

She could hold her tongue no longer. "You can be as disrespectful as you want. I know it's because you are afraid that I, a lowly woman from the country, will humiliate you by being a better flyer than you, which I would be, if I was given half the chance," shouted Tasha into her speaking tube.

He started to chuckle in a long, low rumble. "You're being very rude to me. I need to talk to your boyfriend when I get back. He needs to take you in hand. Luca seems like a nice comrade, but he obviously has no idea how to deal with his girlfriend."

"That's why he does *have* a girlfriend," barked back Tasha, "because he is nice. You are the exact opposite of my boyfriend, which is why you are still single!"

He turned and glared at her then, his face flushed red, and she could see his hands gripping the joystick harder.

He leveled his voice. "You're right, comrade. I don't have one girlfriend. I have many. And that's the way I like it. I don't plan to settle down ever. And you are lucky to be in my company. There are many women that wish they were up here with me."

"Ha!" she scoffed, though she couldn't believe his arrogance. "I would rather ride with a snake, but there were none available," she snapped back.

They continued to bait one another, and Tasha was so caught up in their argument that she missed several navigation points. Once she realized, she tried desperately to figure out where they were. On the map there should have been a river, but there was no river in sight. She looked nervously at her stopwatch. They should have approached it at least one or two minutes before. She swallowed down hard, not wanting to tell him that, or admit to him that she was struggling to figure out where they were.

He picked up on her silence.

"Ah, you are so quiet now. You have given up being rude to me, I see." Mistaking her quietness and concentration for a response, he continued, "Maybe one day instead of your peasant boy, you may be interested in seeing what it's like to be with a real man."

Tasha bristled at that, but had lost all the steam in her argument as she continued to look desperately at her map. Finally, she thought she had figured out where she was.

"I think we need to head east now," she said nervously.

"Are you sure?" he said. "With my recollection of the map before we took off, I believe we were west for another two miles."

"No, no. There's a river down here. We need to go east," she said.

"No. You're mistaken, cadet. I will continue on this route."

"I'm navigating. Aren't I supposed to be telling you what to do?"

"Just because you're sitting there with the map doesn't mean you have control. I have an excellent memory. I'm the pilot, and I get to decide."

He continued to go west.

"If you take us in the wrong direction, we may run out of fuel," she insisted.

"I know what I'm doing," he spat back.

With sheer frustration, she grabbed hold of her own joystick in front of her. She didn't know what possessed her; she was just so angry with him and started to move the plane back towards the direction she wanted him to go.

"Take your hands off the controls," he shouted at her. "How dare you do that? That was incredibly dangerous. I get to choose."

She knew it was wrong. She took her hand off the joystick straightaway, but now she was furious with herself for allowing her anger to get the better of her. So without comment, they continued on their course for another two miles, but as she looked down at the map, none of the landmarks were correct and she could see him squirming awkwardly in his seat in front of her. He'd obviously started to realize the same thing.

"What was the next landmark we were looking for?" he demanded.

"There's a railway station we're supposed to see down to the east of us. But I'm seeing nothing but these hills."

They argued back and forth for a little while longer till, eventually, he agreed to at least try the route that she had suggested. They soon found that she was indeed right. And once they got back on track, it had taken them half an hour to go the round trip from where they'd first gone off course.

She could feel his frustration and anguish in front. This would make them very light on fuel, she knew, as Tasha checked the gauge. There may be enough to get back, but they should finish the rest of the course and be back as soon as they could. They continued on to the third navigational point in virtual silence, and she found it with ease once he stopped baiting her, which meant she could just look at the map and concentrate. But as they started to head home, she looked at the fuel tank. They were really low.

"I think you should land early, Sergei. I don't think you'll make it to the school."

"Nonsense. It's fine," he shouted back at her. "I know what I'm doing."

Her stomach clenched as the tiny plane, buffeted by the wind, was reading empty, and they were a long way away from their training camp.

A mile from the base, the engine started to splutter.

"I told you, we need to land."

"I will make it," he snarled.

She could see his hands gripping the controls in front of her as he started to bring the plane down, ready for a landing. Two fields before they landed, the engine cut out completely. All that could be heard was the wind whistling past the plane as the propeller windmilled uselessly and the ground rapidly approached.

Tasha gripped the side of the aircraft and didn't speak. It would take all of his skill to land safely with the two of them. He started to coast towards the ground. The plane clipped the top of some trees and she sucked in a breath as he managed to hop over a hedge and bring them down on the runway without crashing the plane. But the wings had been damaged by the scrape.

He brought the plane to a stop and jumped out of the cockpit.

"You are an evil woman," he shouted back at her. "If you hadn't been arguing with me, we wouldn't have got off track. And if we hadn't got off track, we wouldn't have nearly been killed. You are dangerous. You should stay out of the sky." Then he strode off as she sat trying to pull herself together in the plane.

An hour later, they were both summoned to the commander's room. He paced back and forth in his office as they both saluted and stood to attention. "I see you finally made it back, but the plane is in a terrible state." He fixed his gaze on Sergei. "What happened? Why did you not land early?"

Tasha stared at him too, waiting for the commander to ask her opinion. But he was peering at Sergei.

"I felt I could land safely, and I wanted to bring it back all the way to the training center. We wouldn't have got off track if it wasn't for Cadet Petroffskaya and her terrible navigation. Also, she grabbed the controls at one point and tried to fly the plane."

The commander flashed an incredulous look towards her.

"This is highly, highly irresponsible," he said. "You never take over piloting unless the pilot is injured or he asked you to do that. What possessed you to do that, cadet?"

She saluted and spoke, her voice quivering with the altercation. "Sir, Cadet Yezhova was going in the wrong direction, and I knew he would not listen to me or take any kind of instruction. He is very rigid."

"Sometimes that is needed," responded the commander. "We make no concessions for a girl's temperament in the armed forces. You need to control your emotions." Striding to his desk, he turned again. "You will both be disciplined. Cadet Yezhova, for not landing the plane earlier, and Cadet Petroffskaya, for endangering the flight. You are both dismissed."

They each turned and exited the room, and scowled at one another as they headed off in different directions.

21

Tasha

As they came to the end of the first six weeks of their training, they had all become much more adept at the skills they needed, and it was time for all the cadets to undergo a series of tests to ensure they were ready, first to continue their training and, eventually, for what would be awaiting them at the front.

That evening after dinner, the girls sat huddled around a table as Eva read out the list of tests they would be doing.

"On Monday, they'll be testing us on how to arm the bombs, load the airplanes, and also on our landing skills."

All the girls at the table groaned. The bombs were heavy, and though their smaller, thinner fingers made it easier for them to arm the bombs, getting them to the planes took a lot of upper body strength.

"Do you think we'll be time-tested?" asked Kira.

"I don't know," sighed Eva. "It doesn't say anything, but we should be ready. Tuesday, they're testing us on navigation. Wednesday, our combat skills, then Thursday through the weekend, we're going on survival training in pairs."

"Well, that should be fun at this time of the year," said

Tasha, looking out at the freezing cold evening already icing up the windows.

"It's a good job I'm knitting you all thicker scarves then," said Liliya as she placed a half-finished project still on the needles around Tasha's shoulders to test it for the desired length.

"Yes," added Kira. "Wool, our own secret weapon."

Sipping their tea, the girls all laughed as they peered over at the table of male cadets. Sergei, the ringleader, caught them looking and muttered something quietly to the other cadets, probably off-color by the way the men leered over at them and started to laugh too. All except Luca, who looked across at Tasha and gave her a gentle smile.

Tasha's heart ached at the gesture. She didn't know what was worse, being away from Luca or being so close but never having the opportunity to really be together. They often had short, hurried hugs and quick conversations in passing, but were both so busy and exhausted it was hard to have time to be any closer.

After they had finished eating, Tasha slipped from her seat at the table and went to catch up with him, he was just finishing his meal.

"Hey, how are you?" she asked, sitting down next to him and surreptitiously squeezing his thigh under the table.

He smiled, placing his hand on top of hers and squeezing back. "Tired, and you?"

"Same."

"Any news yet on what squadron they'll send you to?"

Luca shook his head. "What about you?"

"I spoke to my commander and asked if I could be assigned to the mixed squadrons. But we won't know until closer to the end of our training."

He nodded, and she studied him as he finished his food. In the last few months he had changed so much. She wasn't sure if it was the severe haircut they had given him on arrival, the uniform, or the way his body had filled out with all the extra exercise, but it was as though he was a completely different person to the one she had grown up with. He was still loving towards her, but he seemed more serious, more thoughtful, and preoccupied all the time. She wondered if he viewed her in the same way.

He finished his drink. "I have to go; I have to study." His serious eyes met her gaze.

She nudged him. "Do you remember what that used to mean when we were at school?"

He started to chuckle, obviously recalling their romantic trysts when they had pretended to be doing just that. "I'm afraid that would be more challenging now," he said regretfully.

Before he stood up, Tasha crushed his fingers. "I miss you," she said with an intensity that she hoped communicated more than just her regret about not being in each other's company.

"I miss you too," he whispered, but was unable to say anything more as Sergei, who was leaving the dining room, caught sight of them and called out to Luca.

"Hey, Baranov! No fraternizing with the enemy; we have studying to do."

Luca nodded towards Sergei and, squeezing her hand one last time, got up and made his way to the door, turning for one last look towards her before he was gone and her heart ached with the distance between them.

22

Nadia

Nadia looked around the parade ground on the first afternoon of the tests. All the girls looked nervous, as Commander Bershanskaya took them through the procedure for the week.

"Each day, we'll be testing a skill that you will need on the front, skills such as landing your airplane under challenging circumstances or having to load your own bombs. First aid in survival, hand-to-hand combat, all the skills you've been training in since you arrived. For an added incentive we will we awarding you points on how you execute these skills."

Nadia couldn't resist a side glance at Tasha, who had always been very competitive, and noticed she was scowling at her, her desire to outdo her sister etched deeply into her expression. Nadia's stomach contracted. Why did Tasha have to be this way? Why couldn't she just be comfortable with her own abilities? Why did she feel she needed to outshine her sister?

The first test that would put them through their paces was how to do a controlled gliding landing. After they fell out, Nadia could hear her sister, who was very good at this type of landing, giving Eva tips and desperately wanted to join in and add her opinion. But she bit back her desire, knowing that she had to wait until her sister was ready to talk to her again. Anything else would be perceived as interference on her part. She hated when Tasha was angry at her and always wanted to put it right as quickly as possible, but she knew from past experience that it was better to wait until her sister was ready.

For this particular exercise, all the girls would be going up individually with flight instructors in the navigator seat. At any time, without warning, they were told the instructor would just cut the engine and they would have to execute the controlled gliding landing.

Out on the field, the girls lined up as they prepared to go up one at a time. Kira was up first, and as she walked past the line of girls, they each squeezed and tapped her arm to encourage her as she nodded her head, pulled down her leather flying cap, strapped it on, and placed on her goggles. Then, jumping into the cockpit, the instructor got in behind her with his clipboard. When she was ready, she gave a thumbs-up, and the ground crew started her propeller.

They watched Kira take off first and make the terrifying maneuver look easy, albeit with some wobbles on landing.

Nadia was up next and started out towards the plane. She turned to look over at her sister, hopeful for any sign of encouragement, but Tasha just looked away, which saddened her a little. She tried to put her thoughts of Tasha out of her mind, as she really wanted to do well at this assignment and wanted to prove herself. Nadia loved being a pilot, and knew she had a real knack for it; it was just something that came naturally to her. As she climbed into the cockpit, the instructor was calm and offered her direction in a monotone.

"You will fly as long as I ask you to, then you will turn back towards the field. As you approach the field, at some point, I will cut the engine. Please remember, cadet, that you will stall us out of the sky if you go below thirty miles an hour, so I will be watching for that. If at any point I think that you are incapable of bringing this plane in for a landing, I will take over. Do you understand?"

Nadia gave him a thumbs-up as the ground crew started the propeller. Her body vibrated slightly and her stomach lurched a little as with intense acceleration she climbed the small plane into the sky. They flew for about five minutes before the instructor told her to turn. As they approached the field, she wondered what he was doing, as they were getting closer and closer. Finally, they were midway across the field when he cut the engine. This would be very tricky for Nadia; this was a skill she was good at, but one that was hard even for the most competent pilot. She would have to overshoot the field and do a complete turn to bring the plane back around to glide it down. She could feel the sweat building up under her mask as she carefully watched her speed: thirty-four miles an hour. She had to keep it up so she didn't stall the plane and have it drop out of the sky.

Carefully, she brought the plane around, very gently dipping the nose. Not too far. She didn't want it to lose control. She eased it round slowly. It felt like she flew forever without an engine, and the quiet was disconcerting and hollow, the propeller twirling in the wind in front of her. She took in a deep breath and held it. She could do this. She looked towards the field. Nadia thought she might be a little high, so she dipped the plane again and the speed went up to thirty-six.

She heard the instructor rustle uncomfortably behind her, but she took her nose back up a little bit just to keep the speed down as she made her way towards the field. The ground came in hard and fast, even though she was going at such a slow speed. She swallowed down her fear as her stomach clenched and hoped they wouldn't have a hard landing. But as she righted the plane and lifted the nose the right amount of degrees, the wheels bumped down gently, and she let out the breath she'd been holding as the aircraft came to a full stop.

The instructor didn't say anything behind her. But she could see he was marking something on a scorecard. She was just relieved to have landed.

As she stepped out of the cockpit, she could hear the cadets clapping and cheering her and noted her legs were shaking. Wobbling across the field, she pulled off her leather cap and goggles, and she looked over once more at her sister, who had her arms folded, ignoring her and talking to Eva.

Tasha was up next and Nadia watched her sister stride out to the plane, thinking how grown-up she looked. Sometimes she forgot that her sister wasn't a little girl any more, but a young woman in her own right. However, she still couldn't shake off her desire to make sure she was safe. She just prayed that in her need to try and outdo Nadia that she didn't do anything dangerous.

Tasha took off and disappeared from view and, as she did, Eva sidled up beside Nadia.

"It must be very difficult to see your sister up there, and not feel some apprehension."

"It is," responded Nadia. "Especially when there is tension between us as there is now."

Eva squeezed her arm. "I'm an older sister too; it's hard not to always be looking out for them, making sure your siblings are safe. But she is a great pilot, don't worry; I love flying with her."

Nadia nodded, grateful for the reassurance but desperate to hear Tasha's plane return and see her safely on the ground.

The sound of an engine droned towards the landing field, and Nadia held her breath, waiting for the disconcerting cut of her sister's engine.

This time the instructor waited till she was well across the field before he cut the engine. This would also be precarious. Tasha would have to turn the plane and bring it back around full circle. They all watched as Tasha skillfully spiraled her aircraft into position and made it look easy to the rest of them.

She kept her plane at the correct speed and descended for an almost perfect landing, as though she wasn't gliding at all. The girls all clapped as their commander nodded and smiled, noting a score on her own score sheet.

Tasha marched back to the group. As Eva gave her a big hug, over Eva's shoulder she made eye contact with Nadia but instead of it being warm, her look was smug; she was pleased with herself. That look communicated her desire to win. Nadia had seen it before and it scared her a little. Her sister would do anything to win.

23

Tasha

The following day, their scores were posted on the message board. Both Tasha and Nadia had full marks and shared the first position, but Nadia's name was written before Tasha's, which made her burn with anger. Why was her sister's name always first? She knew that on one level her anger was ridiculous, but she had so wanted to do something alone, to be seen for the person she was without once again seeing Nadia's name ahead of hers.

She arrived with Eva at the gym where they would be assessed for their hand-to-hand combat skills. She was concerned about doing well at this test. It was not something she was naturally good at.

The girls lined up on one side and the men on the other, all wearing their exercise clothes. Tasha pushed away all thoughts of beating her sister when she noticed Luca was there, and her heart quickened. She missed him so much. As she watched him, waiting with the group, she ached with desire for him, imagined putting her arms around him, feeling his body close to hers. She remembered the last time they'd made love. It felt such a long time ago now. Did he feel or think about it too? He caught her looking over at him and he slowly smiled, that warm, loving smile that was only for her. The one that communicated everything she felt was reciprocated, that their bond was mutual, and unbreakable.

Their brief interaction was interrupted by the instructor.

"If ever any of your planes come down and you find yourself behind enemy lines, you all have to learn how to protect yourselves. You have learned many skills over the last few months about how to do that, and now you will have to be trained to protect your plane, your lives, and the lives of your squadron. We'll be tackling a number of scenarios that you need to respond to. I'll be your target."

The women looked from one to the other. They'd had some rudimentary training in this area but they hadn't actually practiced on a man before, only on each other.

He must have seen their expression because he added, "And for you female cadets in the field, it is highly unlikely that you'll be dealing with another woman in the German army. So, you have to learn to be clever, more skillful. Use a man's weight against him because I don't think they will be drawn in by your female wiles."

Tasha folded her arms. She didn't like how patronizing he was being. But he was tall, almost six feet with a stocky build. He would be hard to tip over, and she started to plot some ideas of how she would tackle him.

Finally, they all sat down on each side of the mat. Tasha smiled over at Luca again and he winked back. Her heart melted. She wished she was throwing him to the mat.

First up was one of the guys. He approached the mark from behind, putting both arms around him, attempting to disarm him of his gun and get him to the ground, but the trainer was too fast for him, and with a quick twist of his wrist, he had the cadet on the ground. As he cried out in pain, they all cringed. This wasn't going to be an easy exercise.

"You have to fight to the death, recruit, as though your life depends upon it. You come at a man like that, halfhearted, unprepared, and you'll end up with a bullet in your skull. Go back, and you can try again in a minute."

The trainer signaled to Liliya. She looked nervously at the other girls as she got up, and they encouraged her as she passed them. Liliya was graceful and gentle but she was tall, so she could use her height in her favor. She came up behind him fast, jerking him around, elbowing him in the face, and tipping him backwards over her. He almost went as well. But he found his footing and swung her around and grabbed her wrists. When all else failed, she kneed him between the legs. All the men grimaced, but the target hit the mat. He was, of course, wearing some padding, but he seemed pleased with her attempt.

"Well done, Liliya. You were thinking on your feet. You had to change tactics halfway through, and you did what you needed to do to get me down. The only thing that was missing is you should have removed my revolver because even from the floor, I can shoot you, remember."

Liliya nodded.

Tiny little Eva was up next. Tasha didn't rate her chances very well. She was the kindest of them all, an incredible navigator, a brilliant shot, but she didn't really like hurting people, so this would be a challenge for her. She, too, came up from behind and, adding a blow to the kidneys, twisted his head around before buckling his knees. Even though it was rudimentary, it had the desired effect, and the mark tumbled to the ground. She pulled his handgun from his holster and held it to his head. All the girls couldn't help but clap. Eva was brilliant. A smile broke out on the leader's face.

"Not bad, cadet. I was expecting to have you down on the mat very quickly. You did well. You used my weight against me, and you were cunning."

It was Luca's turn now. Tasha hoped he didn't get hurt.

She watched his easy stride as he moved to the mat, his well-toned physique and broad shoulders tight beneath his exercise outfit, his long, strong arms that she was so used to having around her body moving gracefully by his side. He had a look on his face she had seen so many times before, intense concentration. Getting into position, he actually tackled the mark from the side, full force, slamming him to the floor before the trainer could respond. Luca threw him onto his stomach, his arm pressed behind him. His wrist twisted up, Luca's other hand removed his gun from his holster, where he placed it on the back of the man's head.

"Not too bad," said the trainer, "though that would've made a lot of noise and could have brought other troops. It's better to do something quicker and cleaner, but it had the right effect. Well done."

Nadia was up next and as she moved toward the mat, Tasha couldn't help hoping that she would make a mistake, just a small one; she didn't want her sister to get hurt, but anything to help nudge Tasha in front. Anything that would put Nadia's name in the number two slot, below Tasha's.

Tasha watched her sister get into position. She approached from behind, and was like a gazelle the way she whipped her legs around him, tripping him, shoving the heel of her hand into his chin as he turned his head. At the same time, she grabbed his arm and then removed his pistol. She was so fast and so elegant. It was a blur of activity, and in two seconds, he was down on the floor with a gun pointed at his temple. She pinned him down and warned him not to move.

She was brilliant of course and all the girls clapped enthusiastically, and with a sinking feeling Tasha knew that performance would be hard to beat.

"The best yet," said the trainer, confirming Tasha's suspicions, as he jumped to his feet. "You were quick, you were quiet, and you did a good job. Well done, cadet."

Nadia smiled, handed back his revolver, and got back into the line.

Tasha was up next and now she was even more nervous of doing well. She wasn't very good at this. She didn't have the skills of her sister, but she had other things up her sleeve. She looked over at Luca, who nodded his encouragement as she got into position.

Approaching the mark from behind, Tasha grabbed him around the throat, her tiny hands digging into the soft flesh of his neck, but as quick as anything, he had hold of her hands and parted them. Before she had time to get a grip again, he turned both her wrists up, forcing her onto her knees, and pulled his revolver on her. She screamed out in agony and shouted, "I can't believe you did that." For a second, the guy looked surprised, bemused by what she was saying, and in that moment of weakness, Tasha pulled her arms down, releasing her wrists, jumped up and kicked the gun from his hand, grabbing it from the floor. She held it towards him.

"Not all our female wiles are powerless," she said with a smirk.

As he realized he'd let down his guard with her cry of pain, he started to chuckle. "Only as a last resort, cadet, but it was effective. Go and sit down."

All the girls were laughing as she sat back down, everyone except Nadia, who didn't seem to approve of her tactics.

Last, it was Sergei. She grimaced as she watched him. He swaggered up onto the mat, his wispy blond mustache twitching, his blue eyes catching hers with a defiant glare. She couldn't believe how much she detested him. He came up from behind and started out well. He managed to get the mark into a defensive position, and his weight was off balance. Instead of kicking at his legs or his knees to finish the job, Sergei paused and appeared unsure how to proceed. The mark took that moment to respond and get Sergei onto the mat, his arm behind his back, the pistol to his head.

"Never, ever hesitate, my friend. Even if it's the wrong move, you have to fight to the death. Do you understand?"

Sergei looked defeated, his face flushed red with anger and embarrassment. As he got up, Tasha couldn't help but smirk. He was so cocky.

All of the other girls took their turn, and they all did really well, using the man's weight against him. The men did okay, too, but Tasha could tell the instructor was impressed with how well the women had performed. She gave Luca one last smile as they filed out and made their way back to get some rest before they had to prepare for their night flight, when they would be searchlight hopping.

24

Tasha

As she had expected, Nadia had taken first place on the scoreboard and now Tasha shared third place with Kira.

"There are only three points in it," stated Eva, sensing her friend's concern as they both consulted the board as soon as the marks had been updated. "You could easily make it up tonight. You are really good at this."

Tasha *was* good at this. The following test would have them all flying at night, when they would gain points for maneuvering out of the searchlight and would be penalized for how long their plane stayed in the beam.

Maneuvering an aircraft was one of Tasha's best attributes as a pilot, while she knew Nadia was often over-cautious and not as quick as making the split-second decisions that were needed.

Eva and Tasha walked side by side into a freezing night. It had snowed that morning. There was a good couple of inches and the wind chill must have been minus ten. The planes were almost icy as the ground crew continued to warm them up with fires and ensure the engines didn't ice over. Then, finally, they stood out on the field, waiting for their names to be called. They noticed the male cadets were lined up to help with the spotlights and also to watch the girls at work.

The commander spoke to them all first.

"You'll fly into the sky away from the field. When we hear your plane approaching, we will flash on the searchlights. We have two set out here on the field. Whoever is manning the searchlight will listen for your engine and will try to find you. The minute you feel the light upon you, you have to move. Maneuver your plane in such a way that it will duck and dive out of it. Do whatever you need to do to get out of that beam. If both the lights lock on to you, you have much more chance of being shot out of the sky. Do you understand? You will do three passes across the field. We'll take away points for however long you're in that searchlight. Good luck, cadets."

Nadia and Mila were up first.

Tasha noticed that Luca was on the end of his line. She moved slowly over towards him. Seeing what she was doing, he edged tentatively towards her. It was hard to see what they were doing in the dark, as everyone's eyes were on the planes in front of them and the searchlights being set up on the field. While no one was looking, she slipped her hand into his, and he squeezed it. It was freezing.

"Oh my God, Tasha," he whispered into her ear. "I thought this would be better seeing you all the time, even though I didn't want you to come. But knowing that relationships are frowned upon here and seeing you and not being able to touch you is a nightmare."

She looked up at him through the darkness. His eyes were shining.

"Let's find some time to be alone. Tomorrow night?"

"Outside? It's freezing, Tasha."

"I can think of a way to keep you warm," she said, raising her eyebrows.

He gave her a half-smile as he shook his head. "I wish that

was possible. I can't tell you how much I have missed being close to you. Anyway, how do you feel about this test?"

"I'm not worried. I'm good at this. What about you?"

"I am not bad, but I'm up with Sergei."

Tasha rolled her eyes as Luca started to laugh. He pulled her hand to his lips and kissed it.

"Tomorrow night, after dinner, let's meet by the barracks for a short time."

She nodded and slipped back into her ranks.

They heard Nadia's plane start up, and though it was dark, they could just make out the outline of it on the field. She took off with ease, and they saw the dark silhouette of it against the night sky and could hear the engine moving away. Soon it was back approaching the field, and the searchlights were flicked on, bright beams reaching out into the sky as they roamed around, looking for the plane. Tasha held her breath; she didn't need her sister to do anything dangerous, just be her usual cautious self and stay a little longer in the spotlight than Tasha would.

One beam swept past one of her wings, and Nadia must have pulled the throttle quickly back. By the time they got back to the area, Nadia had moved. Tasha swallowed down her disappointment; she had hoped she would have been in the light just a few seconds longer to give Tasha a chance. It was only three points, Tasha reassured herself; she could make it up. The other searchlight followed the first. It swung around, caught Nadia's other wing, and traced it for a little while before Nadia managed to move out of it again and complete her pass over the field.

She had done well, even though she'd been in the light for a short time. On her second pass, she had more trouble and ended up being in the searchlight for a good ten seconds, where they saw both pilots illuminated in the dark. She finally swooped down out of the track of the lights, and Tasha felt her own tension ease. Her third pass was better, but still not perfect. She had done well, but Tasha knew she could do better.

As her sister landed, Tasha gave Luca a sideways smile and made her way out to the field and to her own plane.

Eva walked by her side, tapping her hands against her body. "It's so cold, Tasha," she said, quivering. "I'm frightened I won't be able to navigate. I don't think I can even hold the map or a compass."

"Don't worry, we're not going far," she responded.

They both got into the plane, taxied to the end of the field, and took off.

On the way back, Tasha plotted her course in her mind, knew exactly where she was going to go. As she approached the field, she swerved as far as she could to the left. Then, as the spotlights roved, having trouble locating her engine, she took it down to a dangerous pitch, slowing it almost to a stall. Her tactic paid off and she got all the way across the field without one searchlight finding her. She felt a sense of exhilaration. Surly that had to be worth an extra point or two.

"Oh my God," Eva said. "You scared me to death, but that was brilliant, Tasha! But you can't be that clever in your second pass. You have to do something else. They'll be onto you this time around."

Tasha turned her plane and dived so low, Eva started to panic. "You're going to crash us!"

"Trust me," said Tasha as she brought the plane in low.

Searchlights once again swiveled around and only caught the tail end of her as she left the field as Eva whooped.

"You're so good at this. Oh my God, they'll never find you, the Germans."

On her third pass, they got a small lock on her. And then she twirled out of the light, like a ballerina, climbing high into the sky and then diving down before swooping over the heads of everyone.

As she brought the plane in for a landing, she knew she'd

done well. She got out and started to walk across the field as all the girls were clapping and cheering her. She looked across at Luca, who was nodding his approval at her, even though the rest of the men didn't look very happy. As she walked towards him, she caught him mouthing the words, "All ready for the circus," which made her laugh.

Tasha was hands-down the best at this skill, and her commander seemed pleased with her efforts. All the girls congratulated her except one. As they made their way back to their barracks for the night, Nadia caught up with her sister and confronted her, grabbing her by the shoulder.

"What the hell were you doing up there? You didn't need to take that kind of risk just to win a stupid competition."

"Let go of me, Nadia," she spat back, jerking her shoulder out of her sister's grasp. "You are not in charge of me here and everyone else seemed to think it was all right. You just don't like the fact I did better out there than you did."

"At what cost!" Nadia responded, her eyes red with fury. "I know you are mad at me for being here, but you don't have to kill yourself to prove that point."

As their argument escalated, cadets peeled out of their barracks to see what was going on.

Nadia pulled her sister aside and lowered her voice. "Look, I'm sorry I came here without telling you first. I thought you would be happy. If I knew it would make you risk your life, then I never would have come."

"Then prove it," shouted back Tasha. "Leave! Go home to your perfect little life and take care of your house, and leave me alone to live my own life here."

Nadia released her grip on her sister's arm and looked heartbroken. "Is that what you really want? For me to go, for us not to be together?"

Tasha felt conflicted. She thought it was what she wanted but now she saw the hurt on her sister's face, she felt bad for suggesting she didn't want her in her life.

"Yes," she said without any of the fire of her conviction.

Nadia looked resolute and Tasha felt her anger flare up again.

"You can't, can you? You can't walk away from this because, once more, you want to be better than me!"

"It's not that. I'm signed up. I'm not allowed to just leave."

"You wouldn't anyway, even if there was a choice; I can see it in your face."

"I just can't go back to..." She hesitated, apparently trying to think of the right words.

"I prove my point," snapped Tasha.

"No," responded Nadia, "I just can't go back to that life."

Tasha saw it in her sister's eyes then: doubt, uncertainty, something she very rarely saw from Nadia. Still, she was too angry to ask her anything further just then. Leaving her sister looking exasperated, she stomped off to her barracks, fuming.

25

Nadia

They prepared for their next test. With Tasha's perfect score from the night before, Nadia was now only one point ahead of her sister in the evaluation, and she felt that pressure. She just had to get through this last test reasonably to stay on top and, as much as she hated to admit it, she wanted to win. Besides, Tasha had been nothing but hateful to her all week. But when she arrived at the parade ground, her heart sank when she realized Bershanskaya had partnered her and Tasha for today's task. With the growing tension between them so obvious to everyone this week, it looked as though their commander wanted to help them learn to work together.

In their next task, they would have to show they could arm their planes quickly. It was bitterly cold, and Nadia had been concerned about how that would affect her performance. To prepare ahead of time, Nadia and Mila, thinking they would be paired, had been secretly practicing lifting the bomb into place all week. Nadia hadn't factored in she would be working with her sister, who was always so unpredictable. As they headed towards the field, she shook out her hands, which were numb. It was still freezing cold and it had rained heavily the day before, and she knew the conditions would be really muddy.

When they got to the field set up for the test, she was surprised to see detonators on the table.

"We'll be arming the bombs as well?" asked one of the other girls.

"You will," affirmed their commander.

They had not done this before under any kind of time pressure, and Nadia was very nervous. She wasn't sure if these were live or dummy charges, and the commander wasn't saying.

Tasha looked at her sister, daring her to tell her to be careful. But with the mood Tasha was in, Nadia wasn't going to resume her big sister role right now.

A truck loaded with bombs pulled up as all the girls stood before their airplanes. "You have twenty minutes to unwrap your bombs, lock them into their position, and arm them," informed the commander. She consulted her stopwatch. "Starting from now."

All the girls ran straight out towards the vehicle. The mud was thick and they slipped, crashing into one another, and could hardly keep on their feet. This was going to make it really challenging. Nadia realized that they had been brought out to this particular field on purpose. It was supposed to be hard. She guessed Commander Bershanskaya felt that in the long run she was being kind because they could face situations like this. But Nadia was not enjoying it one bit as she watched Eva fall onto her back in the mud and Mila try and pull her to her feet. Two of the other girls also helped her, as they all slipped and slid towards the truck.

Arriving at the truck bed, sweating and breathing heavily, Tasha and Nadia unwrapped one of the bombs from its protective wired casing. They were about two feet long and solid. And even though these were probably dummy bombs, they were still incredibly heavy.

Tasha took hold of the bomb and attempted to pull it down on her own, but Nadia quickly grabbed hold of the other side of it, hissing to her over the top of it. "We are supposed to work together."

Anger flashed across Tasha's face. "I can manage; I don't need you to help me."

"I don't care if you need my help or not, we are still going to do this together."

"We would be faster taking a bomb each," insisted Tasha.

"No, Tasha, that is not what we are supposed to be doing."

"I don't care what you think we should be..."

Tasha never finished her sentence because as she fought, grappling to take the bomb from Nadia, it slipped out of her hand with the cold and crashed to the ground, missing Tasha's toes by inches.

Commander Bershanskaya eyed the two of them warily. "Please be careful; you must learn to work together as a team."

Nadia gave her sister one of those 'I told you so' expressions, which Tasha responded to by narrowing her eyes and clenching her teeth.

Allowing Nadia to take hold of half of the weight of the bomb, frozen breath chilled Nadia's cheeks as they struggled back towards the plane. It took a tremendous effort to haul it there with the sheer weight of the bomb and trying to stay on their feet. Arriving at the bomb cradle under the wing, Tasha hesitated, apparently trying to remember how to put the bomb in place.

"I know how to do this," said Nadia assertively. After a week of practicing with Mila, she could practically do this in her sleep.

"Of course you do," snapped back Tasha. "Just give me a minute..."

"We don't have a minute," Nadia shot back, her competitive side getting the better of her as she heaved the bomb into position alone.

"Now who's not working together?" snarled Tasha, as they headed back to the truck for the next bomb. Their commander shouted out the time they had left.

As Nadia swiped the sweat from her face, the sisters begrudgingly unwrapped the second bomb in silence, shooting daggers at one another as they worked. As they moved back and forward to the plane, it appeared all the girls were having trouble. They could've done it a lot faster if the conditions weren't so bad or if their hands weren't so cold.

As they finished hitching six bombs onto the plane, Nadia fought for her breath. Her arms were shaking with the exertion of carrying such a heavy weight, and her legs from trying to stay on her feet.

"We have to arm them," Tasha stated drily, also panting through a stream of frozen breath.

They slid towards the table and looked down at the fuses as Tasha picked the first one up, then moved towards the bomb.

"Be careful—they could be live," warned Nadia, before she could stop herself, which earned her another scowl from her sister.

Pulling off her gloves, Tasha eyed the charge warily, before tentatively picking it up and crossing to the first bomb. With sweat rolling down her face, she attempted to insert it into the nose of the bomb.

"You've got it upside down," hissed Nadia, stretching forward to take it from her. Tasha instinctively knocked her sister's hand away from her and in doing so dropped the charge in the mud.

"Look what you made me do!" she spat out as the two of them tried to find it but when Nadia finally succeeded, plucking it from the slimy ground, it wasn't useable and they had to go back and get a second charge. Tasha started the process again, before turning to her sister and saying, "Step back and stop breathing down my neck!"

"But you are doing it wrong," insisted Nadia as Tasha erupted.

"Of course I'm doing it wrong, I'm always 'doing it wrong' compared to you, aren't I, Nadia?"

All the girls stopped what they were doing and turned to see what was going on as Tasha continued to yell.

"So why don't you just do it on your own, Nadia; it's what you always prefer. I'm sorry you had me as a sister and that I'm always such a disappointment to you."

With that, Tasha turned and stormed off the field, leaving Nadia to finish the job on her own. Shaking her head with bewilderment, she couldn't believe that her sister had just abandoned the test.

When Nadia got back to the barracks, Tasha was nowhere to be found, and, changing out of her muddy clothes, she went for something to eat with the other cadets as they talked through their experience and how hard it had been. It was only after the test had been completed that the commander told them that nothing had been live, but without knowing for sure at the time, they had all found it frightening.

"My hand was shaking so hard, I could barely keep hold of the charge," Katya exclaimed. "Thank goodness Liliya was better."

"I closed my eyes and envisioned it as nothing more than a needle to thread. I wasn't going to be intimidated by a hunk of metal."

The girls around the table laughed as they drank their tea.

One of the commanders came by and whispered to the

girls that they had been faster than the male recruits, and they cheered. But Nadia's jubilation was tempered by the exchange with her sister.

26

Tasha

The next day, Tasha was summoned to Commander Bershanskaya's office. As she knocked at the door, she had a sinking feeling, knowing what this was about. Walking in, she saluted smartly. Commander Bershanskaya looked at her and nodded her head. "Cadet Petroffskaya."

She pursed her lips as she rose and strode in front of her desk to face Tasha, collecting her thoughts before she spoke.

Tasha felt nervous. Would they throw her out because of what had happened the day before? Had she pushed it too far?

As her commander met her gaze, the expression on her face wasn't one of anger, but more of calm professionalism; her tone was even as she spoke. "I'm sure you know why you are here."

"Yes, and I'm sorry about what happened yesterday. It's just that when I get with Nadia—"

The commander held her hand in the air to silence her, and Tasha, red-faced and flustered, waited in fearful anticipation. "This is the second time you have done something like this, cadet, the second time you have allowed your emotions to overtake you, and that is how people get killed. It is tiresome for me and challenging to continue to fight to keep you within this school." She paused, the sadness etched into her expression.

Oh, God, she was getting thrown out; Tasha was sure of it. The regret overwhelmed her, and the thought of going back to their village while Nadia and Luca were here flying was too much for her to bear.

The commander continued. "You have been warned before after the incident with Cadet Yezhova. Many male officers would like nothing better than to see you leave—all of you leave. Every time you do something like this, and it gets back to them, it fuels that fire, and we all suffer because of the consequences. Do you understand?"

Tasha nodded soberly, bracing herself for her banishment.

Bershanskaya's face softened as she spoke more intently from the heart. "I, too, am a younger sister. My sister was also brilliant, better at me in everything, and I always felt in her shadow. It is partly why I fight for you; it is why I connect with you and understand you. I see all of your brilliance, but I also see your immaturity. Even so, I know deep inside you that you have the ability to be an incredible pilot, even maybe lead a squadron one day. Your instincts are impeccable. Your skills in an aircraft are far above all the other cadets. But you take unnecessary risks to prove you are better than your sister. And every time you get in that plane, you not only put in danger your own life, but everybody else's too. You can't fly in combat with that chip on your shoulder because it is dangerous. I am fighting for you. I am on your side. But you've got to take what I am saying seriously. I'm afraid this is your last chance. I don't think I can fight for you a third time. So, I'm asking you to really think about the words I am saying. I implore you to put some of this competition you feel with your sister behind you and actually go up there and fight with, not against, the members of your squadron. Keep your mind on your work and do what you need to do. When you were up dodging the spot-light, you were brilliant, but you also took risks you shouldn't have taken. Now, I'm not saying there might not be a time and place for that. You have to be discerning. I want you to take all of that brilliance inside of you and channel it into your skills. And then, Cadet Petroffskaya, no one will come close to you, not even Nadia. But until you figure out how to overcome the burning desire inside of you to outsmart her, and while you are still flying in competition with her, you'll never be able to achieve all the greatness that I see in you."

Acidic fear burned in Tasha's throat as she attempted to clarify what her commander was saying.

"I can stay?"

"They wanted me to get rid of you. They feel that you are dangerous. I had to argue for a long time because I feel like sometimes we need a pilot with your skills. There is a time to be safe, and there is a time to take risks, and you are good at that and sometimes that is needed. But I had to compromise. I'm sorry to tell you that you will not join the main squadron with the men, which I know was your first choice. They feel you have trouble getting on with the male cadets. You'll become part of the 588 Squadron on the night bombing raids when you leave."

Tasha saluted her commander, the emotion tightening her chest. Her hope had been to fly alongside Luca, to be able to see him every day. Now there was no chance of that, and Tasha was devastated.

"If it wasn't for that, you would be out right now. It would be best if you learned to control your temper."

She nodded and saluted again. Tears of relief pricked the corners of her eyes. "Thank you, Commander; I will not let you down."

Her commander moved back behind her desk and nodded. "Now go and make it right with your sister. We are living in a perilous time; there may come a day when she is no longer there to buffet all of your frustrations, and I can tell you from my own experience that if that day comes, you will miss her more than you can ever know."

Nadia found Tasha sobbing on her bunk an hour later, and approached her tentatively.

Tasha looked up and, giving in to her feelings, pulled Nadia toward her as she sobbed.

Nadia gently stroked her hair, just as she'd done when they were children. She turned over and Nadia smiled as she pulled herself up onto the top bunk.

"Want to tell me about it?"

Tasha told her everything that had happened with their commander, and as her sister held her, she sobbed, "I'm sorry, Nadia, I've been so angry at you. I should have put this right before now."

Nadia nodded, brushing her hair away from her forehead. "No, it was wrong of me to come and not at least ask how you felt about it. I just thought you would be happy."

"I am, sort of. It was just nice reinventing myself, being somewhere with people who didn't know who I was. And when you arrived, it was as though I was just your younger sister again."

"No, it's not like that. You're good, Tasha. You were a good pilot when we flew at home, but since you have been here you have become so much better. You will help save the world from Hitler."

"We both will," insisted Tasha. "Let's hope there will be a world left to fight for by the time we get out there."

27

Tasha

For the last test of the week, they had to do their overnight survival training. Tasha was supposed to go with Eva, but Eva wasn't feeling well and had a temperature. As it was so cold outside, the commander didn't want to take the chance of Eva getting really sick. So, Nadia offered to go with her sister, as she'd completed her own survival training the night before. In the wagon that would take them out to the drop area, they huddled together in their flying suits, bumping along in the dark as blasts of frigid evening air lifted the canvas flaps at the back, chilling them to the very bone.

Nadia put her arm around her sister and whispered, "I have missed talking to you."

Tasha smiled. "I have missed talking to you too. It is right you are here, you're brilliant." Nadia shrugged and Tasha went on. "No, seriously, Nadia, you are three points above all of us; you will win the competition. I just hope I survive the night; that is all at this stage," Tasha said as her teeth chattered with the cold.

"We'll find a way," said Nadia optimistically. "I did it last night, and it was even colder."

"Does it ever get boring being so good at everything?" Tasha chuckled.

Nadia punched her sister playfully on the arm. "You'll be glad of how good I am if tomorrow we're both still alive," she joked.

The driver pulled to a stop and let them out. All they had on them was their guns, knives, their flint, a spade, navigation equipment, and some of the toffee they were given to survive on.

"No blankets, then, airman?" asked Tasha as the driver smirked back at her and made his way back to the truck.

"See you tomorrow, maybe," he shouted as he drove off into the night.

Nadia got out a compass to figure out where they were and studied the map. "We drove for about twenty minutes, so we have to be somewhere around here," she said, circling with a pencil the area she suspected they were.

Tasha nodded her head.

"The first thing we need to do is prepare for the night," Nadia informed her sister. "It's going to get even colder. So, we need to dig a snow cave like they taught us. It will be the only way to keep warm."

They trotted through the forest until they found an area that was quite shaded. Using her flint that was part of her emergency kit, Tasha started a small fire for light and heat. It was so cold, it didn't even really help warm them. Nadia began to meticulously build the cave as Tasha helped her.

"Can you believe we're doing this? Can you believe we're out surviving in the woods because we're going to be flyers and fight for our country?"

Nadia shook her head. "I never believed I would do anything like this. This is so beyond what I thought I was capable of."

"You never do really see your own value, do you? You're very skilled at what you do, Nadia."

Tasha saw a blush cross her sister's cheeks as she continued to press snow into a little wall she was building.

"I just do what I think's best, when it needs to be done," she said.

They finished their ice cave and sat looking up at the stars; the heavens were full of them with no light. They drew close to the little fire as they looked up.

"What do you think our parents would think of us if they saw us now?"

"I'd like to think they'd be proud," said Nadia. "I'd like to think that their sacrifices were not in vain and their daughters were fighting for the freedom of the country they loved."

Tasha shivered, and Nadia put her arm around her. "Are you all right?"

"To be honest with you, I don't like all the sounds I can hear in the woods at night."

"Remember when you were little and scared? I would make up stories for you," said Nadia.

"You were brilliant at it. You could have been a storyteller."

"Maybe in my next life. How are things between you and Luca?"

"I miss him," Tasha responded, barely above a whisper. "Even though I see him every day, it's not the same. Sometimes we get a few minutes together, but I miss the freedom of having real time together, just talking and loving and laughing."

Tasha felt her sister tense beside her. She looked up into her eyes that glistened gold in the firelight.

"What is it, Nadia? Is something wrong?"

"It's Ivan."

She heard the disappointment in her sister's tone.

"What about him?"

Nadia drew in a deep breath before she continued, teasing it out before she said, "Marriage was not what I expected, Tasha. When we were together, he was always so busy with the Party. It's as though I was invisible to him. From the minute he woke up until he went to bed, it was all he talked about. All he worked on."

"But I thought that's partly why you married him, because you wanted to be part of something that he was passionate about."

"I did. I thought I did. But I also want to be loved. Before he went to war, he hardly spent time with me, barely even kissed me." Tasha looked across at her sister with compassion. "I wonder if I'm just not attractive."

Tasha shook her head. "You're beautiful, and if he can't see it, that's his problem."

"But I want what you and Luca have. So why can't we have that and be passionate about what we do as well?"

"I'm not sure either of us can have exactly what we want. Isn't that the way life is? If I had what I wanted, I'd be living with Luca, my mother and father would still be alive, and we wouldn't be fighting this stupid war. What do you want, Nadia? What do you really want?"

Nadia looked out into the darkness, as though she was trying to collect her thoughts, as though she'd never even really thought about that before.

"I have felt compelled to make sure you felt loved, right from when we were children. As your older sister, I wanted you to grow up and feel safe. I saw the hurt in your eyes when you watched Mama die and then Papa. You were so heartbroken. I wanted to protect you, no matter what. I wanted to take that pain away. I know Babka was there for us, but each other is all we really have."

Tasha cuddled her. "And I did nothing but make your life a misery. For me, it was the opposite. Once our parents were dead, I didn't believe that life was fair. I saw it as something that was fleeting and could be gone so quickly, that I wanted to enjoy every single minute."

"Your character hasn't made it very easy for me." Nadia chuckled. "I feel like I'm always saving you from some calamity or other. But keeping you in line didn't mean I didn't love you, Tasha. I always wanted the best for you. I always wanted you to be safe and happy and loved."

Tasha hugged her. "You're my sister, my big sister. I know I don't say it enough, but the truth of the matter is, I don't know what I would do if you weren't there. I think part of the reason I'm able to push limits is that I know you're there to protect me. You'll always be there to catch me if I fall. I'm not saying it's right. I'm just saying it's how it is. So, I'm sorry I didn't want you to come."

"I understand," said Nadia. "I saw it on your face when I arrived and realized that maybe I'd gone too far in joining up. But honestly, I didn't just do it to check up on you. I wanted to do something for our country too. After the first few weeks of being married to Ivan, I was afraid I was going to die of boredom. I thought all I wanted to do was cook and clean for him, but it felt so empty. And then when I heard what you were doing, I wanted to be a part of it too. I didn't even tell him what I was doing, I know he wouldn't have approved and I thought we would enjoy being together. I didn't really think how it might affect you, how it might hurt you for me to be here."

"You found our mother's courage, I see. Though it still infuriates me that I can never get out from under your shadow and be taken seriously for who I am."

"You've done that here. You have a very good reputation as a pilot. All of the girls love you. I don't know one of them that doesn't wish they were in your navigator seat."

Tasha smiled. "Maybe we'll both find our feet here. But I am glad you're with me."

"And I'm glad I'm here too."

The girls finally fell asleep, tucked in each other's arms.

When Tasha woke in the morning, her whole body was frozen with the cold. The fire had gone out long before, and though the snow cave kept the chill from their bodies and stopped them from freezing to death, it was still bitterly cold. Nadia was already awake and moving about in the bushes, checking coordinates.

"Oh my God, I can't even feel my feet," complained Tasha as she tried to pull herself up and move around.

Nadia began building a fire, and Tasha moved to the side of it as her whole body felt rigid, a solid lump of ice.

"What do we have to do today?"

"Well, we have to start moving. But first, they'll give us more points if we can catch a rabbit."

"Catch a rabbit?" said Tasha incredulously as she saw that Nadia was setting a trap. "I think I'll just eat my toffee."

It took them a few hours, but eventually, they did manage to trap a rabbit. As Nadia screamed in excitement, Tasha looked uncomfortably at the sad creature she held up in her hand, and they decided to make their way back with their compass to the base. It was freezing as they clipped along, but it was also beautiful. The trees were full of ice and it felt magical. Nadia started singing a song they'd sung when they were children, and Tasha joined in. They stopped at lunchtime, but neither of them could face eating the rabbit, so they ate the rest of their toffee as they sat.

"Things may pick up with Ivan," Tasha said with further thoughts from their conversation from the night before. "Maybe he's just nervous. This war has got everybody on edge. Maybe after the war, he'll be a different person."

Nadia shook her head. "I'm not sure, Tasha. I'm not sure what I'm going to do."

"You don't have to stay married."

Nadia shook her head. "That's not an option for me. I

don't believe in divorce. So he will be my husband until one of us dies."

"Well, let's hope that's him soon," said Tasha drily.

"Don't wish that upon him. I still love him, even though it's awkward and strange. I just wish I knew what to do to get closer to him."

They carried on their walk and moved through the fields, arriving back just before dinnertime. They gained high marks for catching the rabbit and their ability to get back using their compass. But the girls were never so glad to see food and their warm beds.

"Oh my God," said Tasha as she put on every piece of her clothing and wrapped a scarf warmly around her ears. "Never again do I want to ever go out at night. Eva," she said to her navigator, who was tucked up in bed, still getting over her cold. "We're never going to crash-land, do you understand? If I ever go down, just shoot me in the head. I never want to go through a night like that again."

Eva blew her nose and laughed.

Tasha was glad for the time with Nadia. Even though they had been surviving, it had been precious, a moment in time for the two sisters to connect. However, she felt great concern for her sister's marriage too. She knew that she and Luca would not be like that. How could Nadia stand it? How would she be able to go on like that for the rest of her life?

She didn't know it then, but many things that neither of them had any control over were about to change their lives —forever.

28

Tasha

As the months wore on, the girls all continued to improve and get closer as a unit. After six long months they were exhausted, but jubilant. Towards the end of their training, they appeared on the parade ground in full military uniform. Since they had done so well, and impressed not only their own commander but the other instructors on the base, it had been conceded at last that they should have their own uniforms, properly made, that fitted them.

As Tasha had dressed in her uniform that morning, she'd looked across at Eva, who was in the bunk across from her now. She looked so smart. Nice they'd finally been given uniforms that fitted at last. And it was still hard to believe that they were all in the air force. They were women fighting for their country. After breakfast, they had marched out to the parade ground, and formed two lines, as they'd been instructed to do, and they stood to attention. Winter had set in and fingers of spiky weakened sunlight attempted to warm the icy morning, causing the parade ground to glisten with a thick coating of ice.

Their commander came out to greet them all. Her face was beaming. "Comrades," she said, her voice warm and husky with pride. "You have completed most of your training. And we want to commend you all. Even my superiors have been surprised at how well the female pilots have done. You know that it was hard for me to convince a totally male fighting force that women could do a good, if not better, job than their own recruits. But the loud voices of protest that I heard at the beginning of your training have become quieter as the weeks have gone by, and now they are nothing but a disgruntled whisper, as you proved over and over again that you can serve our country and win this war with your skills and deter-mination.

"You have completed the training, and you will now be assigned. Some of you will go on to work within the mixed squadron, fighting alongside your brothers in arms. I have been assigned to lead a unit and some of you will form a sisterhood with me in our 588 Squadron. There have been rumors that this is a lesser assignment, but I want you to know that every one of you is needed. None of you are lesser in any form. On the contrary, every single person that is fighting this war is vital against this evil; Hitler is butchering and enslaving our people as he moves through this country. You have surpassed every-thing we expected of you, learning all of your skills in six months when it takes the men longer. But, nevertheless, we will help them and be humble."

She smiled. And there was a ripple of laughter amongst the assembled cadets.

"Now, there is one last thing for me to do, which is to award you for your conduct during your training and read out your assignments. First, I have been commissioned to award one of the female cadets for outstanding achievement. And one has really stood out, a woman who is very studious, compe-tent, and a generous comrade, taking care of the other recruits as well as being an outstanding pilot. We would like to promote this person to squadron leader and award Nadia Kozlov for her incredible skill and abilities to be a leading example in our ranks. Please come forward, Cadet Kozlov, and accept your comendation."

Tasha looked down the line to her sister, who stood blushing at the end of it. She felt so proud of her, she deserved every bit of it, even if there was still a twist of jealousy in her stomach.

Nadia marched forward and stood before her commander as a medal was pinned to her chest.

They both saluted each other.

"Would you like to say a few words, Squadron Leader Kozlov?" her commander asked as Nadia nodded stiffly and turned to face the girls.

"I just want to say that I am so grateful for every one of you and to be able to serve our country, to defeat the evil Nazi forces. I feel privileged to be part of this group. You are all amazing cadets, and we are going to give the enemy a run for their money. I'll be glad to serve and be proud to be with any of you. Thank you all. And thank you to my commanding officers for this incredible honor."

Tasha could hear her sister's voice was starting to crack with emotion as she marched back into the line and all of the girls clapped for her.

"Now, I'll read out the assignments," said Commander Bershanskaya, and she started to make her way down the list. She read off the first two units that would be joining the men in the more powerful planes.

Tasha felt a sickening feeling, as she knew she would be in the 588 Squadron because of her conduct. She was so consumed with her thoughts that she didn't realize Nadia had not been called out.

"Now for the 588 Squadron," the commander said as

Tasha waited to hear her name. As she went down the list, she was relieved that many of her new friends would be with her. With great surprise, so was Nadia.

She looked down the row to her sister, who was just listening carefully. They were dismissed, and Tasha went straight over to her.

"Nadia, you're in the night squadron?"

Her sister gave her a knowing smile. "They asked me which one I wanted to serve on, and I wanted to serve alongside you, wherever you were."

"But you've done so well. You could have been on any of our squadrons."

She slipped her arm around her sister. "I wanted to be with you, Tasha. I don't care which squadron I fly for. It would be of no value to me to be in another area, serving Russia, knowing that you were somewhere else doing the same. I would much rather us be together, as Babka would want and our parents would've loved."

Tasha shook her head. "You're amazing. Sometimes I hate that I'm so different. I would've jumped at the chance of one of the other squadrons and not thought twice about you. No wonder they commend you and admonish me."

Nadia squeezed her sister's arm. "Don't say that. It takes incredible skill to do what you have achieved. Together, we will serve Russia and be proud to be a part of this work. Also, I have something for you."

Nadia reached into her pocket and pulled out a box. "I asked Sonja to get something for me in Moscow and send it. Here is a gift for you. Congratulations on completing your training."

Tasha looked down at the box with guilt. "I don't have anything for you."

"That's okay, I have plenty of metal I'm carrying around already," she joked about her new medal.

Tasha opened the box. Inside was a tiny good luck talisman in the shape of a bird in flight, on a necklace with her name on it.

"Oh, Nadia, this is beautiful. I'll never take it off."

29

Tasha

The first day that Nadia flew as their leader, they made their way out to the parade ground to get their daily instructions from their commander. Tasha stood to attention and looked out across the sky. It had already snowed a lot this winter, though it wasn't unusual to get that much snow in Russia, where it snowed seven months of the year. And today it definitely looked dark and ominous, as though more snow could be on the way. Her preoccupation with the weather was interrupted as Commander Bershanskaya spoke.

"Today, we have a special assignment for you," the commander informed them as Tasha shivered, a blast of the frigid air finding its way beneath her jumpsuit. "Today is the first day that Squadron Leader Kozlov will lead you. And for the first time, you'll be working together as a unit without supervision. We'll send you off in groups and we have an area set up half an hour's flight from here that you're all to navigate to. When you arrive there, the ground crew will meet you. They'll have food and refreshments and will refuel the planes. Then once you've had a break, you'll fly back. From the minute you leave here, Squadron Leader Kozlov will be in charge, and I know that you will fall into line to respect her new rank. I recognize that we have a very cold day with a chance of snow. Under normal circumstances, we wouldn't send you off with this kind of weather looming on this type of day, but you're training for war, and you will face many days with the threat of snow when you're at the front. So, it's good to learn to fly in all weather conditions. Good luck to you all, and we'll see you back here in a couple of hours."

As they made their way to the airfield, the temperature was bitter, icy cold. Tasha knew it would be even colder in the air. She put on her flying cap and goggles and tightened her jumpsuit, tucking the scarf that Liliya had knitted for her around her ears. Signaling to the ground crew, Tasha jumped into her plane. They started the propeller and pulled away her chocks. Tasha taxied off down the field and accelerated as her plane soared easily into the air. Eva reconfirmed coordinates as they went. Once they were in the air, they were joined by the rest of the first group, Nadia and Mila, Zora and Maria, Kira and Katya. Because of the biting cold, the length of the hop felt arduous. Tasha had to keep squeezing her hands to keep feeling in them and twirling her feet in her boots. Her goggles were already frosted up with the cold, and her ears were numb.

"You'd think within these bulky uniforms they'd at least have given us something woolen to wear," her navigator suggested, her teeth chattering as they both tried their best to brace themselves against the wind chill. It was a long, cold journey, and Tasha had never been more grateful to see the markings for their landing. All four planes landed safely.

"I've never been so ready for a warm drink," said Eva as they taxied to the base. "My body can hardly move, I'm so frozen."

Getting out of their cockpit, they made their way to the tent that had been set up by the ground crew ahead of time.

Inside, the girls huddled together, banging their feet and rubbing their hands to bring feeling back.

They hadn't been there very long when one of the ground crew came in to speak to Nadia. She saluted her, concern obvious on her face. "I thought I should let you know, Squadron Leader Kozlov, that there was some concern about the weather."

The girls hadn't even started eating yet, and all looked across at Nadia, who flushed, apparently realizing she would be expected to make her first command decision. Moving from the table, she walked to the tent flap and pulled it back. Outside, Tasha could see the sky was heavy with snow.

"I think we should start back earlier," said Nadia, with just a hint of a quiver in her voice at making the call.

"I'm starving, Nadia. Can we not at least wait until we've eaten something?" Tasha insisted.

"No." Nadia was firm. "It'll be dangerous if the snow comes in too fast. We need to get back to the base as soon as possible. You all fly out first. Then Mila and I will wait to bring up the rear."

The girls gulped down their drinks, and as soon as the planes were refueled, they raced back out. The air had turned bitterly cold, even colder than when they had set off. Tasha felt the sting of fear in the pit of her stomach as she rushed to her plane. She had never flown in snow. They usually grounded the planes when they had a snowstorm at the flying school.

"Be careful!" Nadia shouted to them all. "Don't take any chances, and if for any reason you're struggling, land. Don't stay in the air if you have any concerns."

Jumping into the cockpit, Tasha started her plane and, as on the outward journey, once the chocks were free, began to taxi down the airfield. She wasn't long into her flight when the snow started to coat her wings and blur her vision. If she'd thought it was cold on the way there, she'd had no idea how cold it could be with the wind chill and the wetness of icy cold snow burning her throat, chilling her face, and sliding down the back of her jumpsuit.

Eva gave her instructions from behind, and she could tell with the speed and her tightened tone that Eva was really nervous.

Before long, because of the blizzard, they lost sight of the other girls. They could hear the buzz of their engines behind them, but the visibility was so bad they could see nothing more than a few feet in front of them. Eva kept her head down, timing them, following the map with her compass and a stopwatch. She had to navigate blind, as everything below them was already covered by the snow.

Tasha had never been so scared. She was so grateful that Eva, though also afraid, was holding it together under pressure and navigating brilliantly. As well as the snow, freezing crosswinds would buffet them, attempting to knock their plane off course. And it was with great relief that Eva spotted a church she had been looking for, assuring them they were on the right course. All Tasha could think about was Nadia taking off last. She hoped she would be safe. The half-hour journey on the way there had turned into a one-hour trip on the way back.

Tasha did not want to fly too fast. Not wanting to miss any navigation points, she kept her speed down to be sure she got home safely with Eva. But as she started to lose sensation in her hands, she gripped the joystick with cold and fear, and she had never been so glad to see the flying school, gratefully bringing the plane in for a landing. Many of the cadets came rushing out to welcome them as she brought the aircraft to a stop.

"We didn't think you would make it back," said Liliya. "We thought that you must have landed somewhere else. They grounded all our planes not long after you left. They were very concerned. The snow was so thick. No one expected it to come down like this."

Placing blankets around their shoulders, they encouraged the girls inside.

But Tasha wouldn't move; she was too worried about Nadia. "I need to stay out here and wait," she said.

Eva understood. She grabbed Tasha's hand, her fingers frozen, even in her gloves. "I'll bring you a hot drink."

Tasha nodded as the girls left, and she stood waiting in the snow, her face icy and wet, her feet two blocks of ice. All around the field, instructors were there too, and she could see the worry on their faces.

All at once, Luca was there. News had quickly got around the flying school. Everyone was waiting to make sure all the female cadets returned.

He pulled her into his arms and held her tightly. "Thank God you're back. I was so worried."

Once she felt his body close, a sob escaped in her throat, and he knew without her having to explain.

"Don't worry," he whispered in her ear. "Nadia is a good pilot. Probably the best we have. She'll make it back."

Tasha nodded but didn't say anything in response. She was absolutely terrified.

All at once, they heard a noise from the sky, and she pulled away from his embrace. Then, through the blizzard, they saw it. A plane was being buffeted by the wind like a balloon, punched back and forward, bouncing around, and it was alone. As it drew closer, she knew it was Kira and Katya's. Tasha covered her mouth with her hand, willing Kira to land them safely as she lined up for the airfield.

As she watched the plane descend, something seemed to be wrong with it. It didn't sound right. She reached out and gripped Luca's arm.

"She can do it," Luca assured. "She's almost here."

Then, the plane suddenly spluttered and clipped the top of the trees as it came down faster than was safe. Kira touched down so quickly that the impact knocked the plane off balance. Instead of righting itself, it tipped onto its nose, flipped onto its back, stopping with its wheels in the air as they all gasped. Liliya crossed herself, and Tasha screamed and raced out with the recovery crew.

They all ran towards the plane, where the crew had already pulled the girls out. Kira looked so cold and still, and Katya had blood oozing from a wound in her head. Tasha looked down in shock at her comrades. They were alive but in a bad way and were transported quickly to the hospital.

With tears in her eyes, Tasha waited for Nadia. She kept praying that the wind would calm, that the snow would stop, anything. Then, all at once, with great relief, she heard a plane. It, too, was struggling. It seemed to be out of gas. Fighting the wind that had really picked up must have caused them to slow down a great deal. Eva had come back out to join her with a drink that Tasha didn't even touch. She gripped Eva's arm as Nadia slowly brought her plane in for a landing, righting herself as best she could as she was heavily buffeted by the wind.

"Come on, Nadia, you can do it," Tasha said through gritted teeth.

Slowly she descended, and even though the wind bounced her around, she was good at what she did and managed to right herself without overcompensating. Nadia finally landed, bouncing a couple of times, but kept the plane upright as Tasha rushed out to greet her.

"Oh my God, where have you been, Nadia?"

Nadia looked grief-stricken as she pulled herself out of the cockpit.

"We lost the other two cadets out there. We couldn't see each other with the visibility being so bad. We need to send somebody out as soon as the weather clears."

Her commander nodded.

It was several hours before the snow finally slowed enough so they could fly someone out to try and find the girls. In the meantime, they all sat numbly waiting for news in their barracks. Tasha tried her best to avert her gaze from Kira, Katya, Zora, and Maria's empty bunks. They finally got word from the hospital. Both Kira and Katya had sustained some injuries, but they would recover.

Time went slowly as they waited. None of them could say or do anything apart from hug one another or stare out the window. Finally, their commander appeared in the doorway. Tasha's heart pounded in her chest, she saw it in her eyes before she even spoke.

She looked around at all the expectant faces then slowly she shook her head. "I'm sorry to tell you that Zora and Maria didn't make it. Their plane was found about two miles from here. We think they got disoriented in the snow. They must have run out of fuel and couldn't bring the plane down safely. I'm so sorry. They were brave comrades and good pilots. I know that they will be greatly missed."

All the girls sat in shock for a minute, unable to take in the news. Then, finally, Nadia stood up from her bunk and pulled Tasha into her arms as, all around her, the cadets started to cry.

"Oh my God," Tasha said as she hugged her sister. "Thank God you got back alive."

"I feel responsible," stated Nadia somberly. "They were under my leadership. I tried to keep them with me but it was so hard." Nadia's voice cracked with the emotion.

Tasha hugged her sister tightly. "There's nothing else you could have done. Thank goodness you made us set off when you did, otherwise we may all have been lost. I'm sorry I haven't supported you as much as I should have. You will make a good leader, Nadia, and you can't blame yourself."

Nadia nodded, but a look passed between the sisters that reflected that this had changed everything, the seriousness of what lay ahead a silent understanding between them.

30

Tasha

After the snowstorm that claimed their comrades, the sadness of the accident hung heavy over the training school for the weeks before they prepared to leave for the front. They had a gathering to remember the lost pilots, and even Kira and Katya were well enough by then to attend. It took them all a while before they started to feel better, but also made them more serious about what they were doing still, as they prepared to face a war that badly needed their skills.

The cruelty of the Nazis was becoming known worldwide. Not only were they deporting Jewish people from their homelands to work in labor camps in Germany and Poland, but the ongoing siege of Leningrad, the stories of brutality and the starvation around that city were now widespread knowledge and further motivated the girls to fight to defend Mother Russia.

Even with the seriousness of what they faced, after they'd all passed out, there was great excitement about the upcoming assignments, but also some nervousness about traveling to the front to fight with their units. That evening the training facility held a party in their honor, and the cafeteria had been decorated with Russian flags and banners of all colors. There was even a small band playing patriotic numbers for them to dance to, and the men and the women mingled freely together as they all made their way into the hall.

Tasha couldn't wait to see Luca. Looking around the room, she found him and smiled. He was still in his uniform, his hair short, military length. He looked so handsome to her. Bounding across the room, she came up from behind him and kissed him on the cheek, almost making him spill the drink in his hand. He turned, his face blushing. "Tasha, we're still in uniform."

"I'm not," she said. "I've changed. I'm in my civilian clothes, so I can act like a civilian. You, however, must be more formal." She giggled at him. "I came to see if you wanted to dance."

He smiled at her. "I'm thinking about it. There are so many pretty girls over there for me to choose from." He signaled to the group of female cadets that had gathered at one of the tables.

She punched him on the arm as he put down his drink and turned to face her.

"Miss Tasha Petroffskaya, would you do me the pleasure of your company on the dance floor? Is that formal enough for you?"

She gave a comical curtsey with the words, "I'd be delighted, sir."

Then, taking her hand, he led her to the dance floor, and she drew his body close to hers. Whenever she was in his arms, she felt complete, as though their two bodies were part of one whole circle.

She slipped a hand around his waist, and he squeezed the other as they moved back and forth to the music. Placing her head on his shoulder, she breathed in his scent and closed her eyes so she could enjoy the experience of this man that she loved so deeply.

He kissed her hair and whispered into her ear, "Any change in your assignment?"

She looked up and sighed. "No, I'm still with the Night Squadron 588. We leave tomorrow. What about you?"

"832, we leave at the end of the week. But we're not that far from each other, just twenty miles. Maybe they'll even bring us closer at some point. It's not so terrible. We may still see each other."

Her eyes filled with tears. "But it won't be the same, will it? You'll be fighting with your unit in the day. I'll be fighting with mine at night. There'll be no time."

He pulled her chin up so he could see her face. "There's always time, Tasha. There's always time for what is right. Yes, we are fighting a war, and we have to do our duty, but we also need to be reminded of why we are doing that. So, I'll write to you every day, and we'll try and get some time off together if we can. Maybe they'll let us have leave together, who knows?"

She nodded, but Tasha didn't feel terribly optimistic. They read about how the war on their borders was in full throttle every day. The battles were savage and vicious, and Russia was doing all it could to keep the Nazis from advancing all the way into their country. After the scare of Hitler nearly getting to Moscow, many of them now knew the importance of what they were doing.

She looked up into his lovely blue eyes and smiled, and then not caring about who saw it or the fact he was in uniform, she pulled him in and kissed him deeply, placing her tiny hands on the side of his face so she could orchestrate the kiss. As his body moved hers closer to him, she closed her eyes and remembered the many times that she'd kissed him, the many times they'd been together. Their first kiss as awkward teenagers. The last time they'd been able to make love before they'd been here, so long ago now.

All at once, around them cadets began to whistle and she pulled back, laughing as she swept away a strand of his hair from his forehead that was glued down by a bead of sweat.

"That was intense," he said breathlessly as they started to dance again.

"I didn't want you to forget me. There will be other women from our units fighting over there with you. I wanted that kiss to last."

He started to chuckle. "You have no idea, Tasha, do you? You have no idea of how much I truly love you. All I want to do is be with you. Though some things have changed for me over the last few months."

He swung her around in front of the band and she stared up at him with concern as she waited for them to clear the loud music before he continued.

"Before, when we were at home, I loved you, but now it's different. Before I wanted to make love to you all the time, but now, as well as that, I want to be with you in any way I can. Talk to you, walk with you, just be by your side. I know it sounds corny, but this war has made it clearer for me. Sharpened my vision of what I truly want. Are you sure you won't marry me before we go to the front?"

She shook her head. "I told you, I will not be your widow."

"But I made you a promise that I was not going to die," he said earnestly. "Now, will you marry me?"

She chuckled. "Not like this, Luca. Let's wait. Let's wait until this is over. I want it to be special, with Babka, Nadia, and the whole of our village, not rushed in some government building in our uniforms. I can wait. I know you love me."

They enjoyed the rest of the evening together, and the following day she packed her bags, ready to go. She stood in the clean, tidy room, bunks all ready for new cadets, and lingered looking out across the parade ground through the window as she thought about her next step with fear and trepidation. There had been something extraordinary about being here, the camaraderie that she felt with all her sisters now, the incredible things they'd learned, and the things they'd done. The comrades she had met and the comrades she'd lost. Now that would all be over, and there'd be no time for them just to enjoy each other's company and the skills they were learning. Now they would be going to war. Every day would be vital and essential, and every day they could lose their lives. They would sleep in the day and bomb during the night. And as much as that made her stomach clench with fear, she also felt ready and equipped and excited to serve her country.

"Are you coming?" said Eva as she stood at the door, weighed down with her bags.

They strode outside and all the other girls were there, waiting to be taken to the train station. Nadia was already there and slid her arm around her sister and hugged her. At the train station, she saw Luca one final time as he blew her a kiss, and, making their way on board, she went with her unit to their new life, a life they couldn't even imagine, with no clue of what awaited them.

31

JUNE 1942

Nadia

Arriving at the front in May, they were finally thrown into action on June 12 when they were deployed to bomb river crossings on the Mius, Severny Donets and Don rivers, with the aim of pushing back the Nazi invaders. As they counted the cost of what they were doing, the weight of what lay ahead was etched into all of their faces when they arrived for their briefing. Things had intensified since the Russian army had managed to push Hitler's forces back following a severe winter, which had weakened his invasion, but seemed to have made him more determined. It made what they were doing seem so much more important. Between putting up their tents and making ready their airplanes, there was no time to relax before going on the attack. The German offensive was still very aggressive, and once they were unpacked, they were summoned to the briefing tent, where they were given their first campaign instructions.

In great fear and trepidation, Nadia prepared to lead her team in their first night-bombing raid. She could barely do the buttons up on her blue jumpsuit that evening, her fingers were trembling so much. She had been studying around the clock to prepare for the mission, and if she wasn't ready now, she never would be; but still, she was scared. It was one thing to make decisions in the air in training; it was another to make them under the heat of battle. She wasn't sure what it was going to feel like to move through the flak, avoid the Germans' retaliation, and guide her crew through the same.

After their briefing, they met in a circle that first night, just as the sun was starting to set. There was a nervous energy within the group as they waited to get last-minute instructions from their squadron leader.

Nadia spoke to her crew. "We have trained for this and you are all incredible pilots. Remember that I have your backs, and I will be supporting you all. Don't take unnecessary risks and make sure you look after your sisters."

They hugged one another and got into their planes. She double-checked all her instrumentation and went over the bombing route one more time with Mila. Because they would be navigating at night, there would be no chance to really follow the map, so she wanted to make sure she had it memorized. Also, because there were no radios, she would use the flashlights as they had been taught to communicate with her squadron, flashing the codes to them as they moved into position. Mila's job was to time their route so that they would hit the targets they'd been given.

As she bumped along the snowy strip, she felt the excitement of what she was doing. As much as she'd wanted to be a good wife and take care of her home, there was nothing as exhilarating as having a chance to be with these sisters in the sky, fighting their enemy.

She took off over the trees and headed in the direction of where she would drop her first bombs. The evening was chilly, her ears cold, and there was a clear sky, which gave her some concern. They would be easier to see against the night's gibbous moon.

They'd been practicing for weeks now to find a target in darkness, being careful not to be detected, as they had no guns they could fire. They would slow their engines right before the target, as they had been trained, making them much harder for the Germans to hear. This was a new idea, and no one knew if what they were doing would be successful or not. Nadia pushed away the fear that hovered on the edge of her thoughts.

Taking out her flashlight, she flashed her instructions, communicating with her team, who flashed their understanding back. As they neared the target bridge, her stomach began to contract with the fear. She could do this. She had been trained. Moving into an attack position, the planes fell in behind her as she got closer and closer to the enemy lines, the buzz of all their engines the only thing calming her as they flew.

"Twenty seconds from the target," shouted Mila into their communication tube.

Nadia nodded, gripping and ungripping the throttle with anxiety. As her navigator counted down, Nadia pulled the plane into position, slowed the engine, and started the quiet fall towards the enemy lines. The decoy plane flew out in front and the sound of whooshing air passed by Nadia's face in the cold as she dove down towards their target. The plane ahead of her set off a flare in a stream of white light, and she saw her enemy for the first time, groups of troops in white camouflage moving around in the snow as they swiveled their guns towards her. Her heart thudded in her ears and fingers trembled slightly on her joystick. It suddenly felt very real. Nothing could have prepared her in training for what she now experienced.

Mechanically she had moved her plane into a position, but her mind was exploding with the realization of the damage she was about to do. Nadia ran her tongue across her dry lips and forced air into her lungs, which hurt with the pressure of the fear. Trying desperately to push away the thought that she might be about to take someone's life, she concentrated on the target as she had been trained. All at once, flak exploded to the side of her, so much louder than she could have ever imagined. She suddenly felt so vulnerable in this tiny wooden plane, which she feared would go up like a tinderbox if anything struck it. Her heart jumped into her throat with the loudness of the explosions that continued all around her and she heard Mila swear behind her. But Nadia kept her eye on the bridge. There was more flak, but she could tell the Germans were struggling to find them, even though they could hear them. She sent a signal to her squadron, ordering them into position.

Her target was dead ahead, and lining the plane up, she willed herself not to lose her nerve as Mila pulled the release.

"Away," called out Mila. Nadia realized her whole body was shaking, her breath thready and stilted. Listening to the bombs whistling to the earth, she pulled the plane up. As she circled around, plumes of black smoke and fire erupted into the air all along the bridge as one after another the pilots released their bombs.

Below her, she saw their enemy forces aglow with the damage, and finally drew in a deep breath.

As they turned their planes back towards home to refuel and to reload their bombs, it felt surreal. She had done it. And from what she could see, none of their planes had been hit, so it'd been a successful sortie.

Tasha had gone up in the second group behind Nadia and had also completed her bombing run successfully. They would all be instructed to go back four or five times, as many as they could, until it became light. The idea was to exhaust the enemy so that the other Russian forces could attack during the day. Again and again she attacked, dropping her bombs, each time becoming a little more confident in what she was doing. At the end of her last run that night, a beautiful golden sunrise marked their route back to camp, and she felt a great sense of relief and accomplishment.

32

Nadia

They continued on their campaigns every night, but it didn't take long for Tasha's willfulness to appear. She was constantly overstepping the mark, pushing boundaries when Nadia asked her to do things. Finally, one perilous night, they were flying in the same team, against the wind, and Nadia quickly realized that they were only going to get one run with their bombs instead of the usual two before they would all be in danger of running out of fuel. As the crosswinds battered the plane, it took all of her strength to keep it on track. Her arms ached from the strain, and her stomach was sick from the lurching, but she kept her eyes on the task. She was also concerned about the navigation. Trying to keep the plane on the correct trajectory was challenging, and more than once, Mila was concerned they were heading in the wrong direction and had to readdress the course using her compass. They would both be glad when this night's campaign was over.

Nadia dropped her first set of bombs, then she sent a message down with a flashlight to all the other planes not to take the time for a second pass, saying that they needed to go back and refuel. They would only get the one run at a time tonight. All the girls acknowledged her instructions, apart from one, Tasha.

"I think I can do it," she flashed back. "I have enough fuel."

Nadia sighed, feeling her frustration, and flashed the same instruction again, telling her sister that she needed to return to base.

"I've got this," she flashed back as she zoomed towards the target.

Frustrated, Nadia circled the area, unwilling to leave Tasha alone as the other women headed back towards the camp to reload and to refuel. She swore under her breath as she fought to find Tasha. She waited as long as she could, and then she flew home, landing practically on vapor, to the relief of her navigator. Pulling the plane to a stop, she jumped out and looked up to the sky for her sister. But there was still no sign of her.

"Stubborn, reckless fool!" she shouted out into the air. Her stomach started to contract with fear. What if Tasha was down? Did she need to go back?

"Is Tasha not back with you?" inquired Alina, a member of the ground crew, as she came up to refuel the plane.

Nadia shook her head. She strode up and down, her arms folded as she looked into the skies, all the time hating the fact that that Tasha had done this.

Then, all of a sudden, she heard her.

Her engine was spitting with the lack of fuel, trying to make its way back to the airfield. She was swaying all over the place, being buffeted by the wind. At least she had a good tail-wind on the way back. But as she came in for a landing, she landed on just one wheel, barely managing to keep control of the aircraft before it came to a stop.

Striding out to her sister's plane, Nadia screamed up to her, "What were you *thinking*? I told you to turn around."

Tasha looked down at her defiantly. "I was bombing. That's what I'm here to do. I bombed the second target."

"But I told you not to. I told you to come back."

"You're always too safe, Nadia. There was plenty of time. Look, we made it back." She looked to her navigator, and Eva looked petrified.

"But look what you've done to Eva. You've scared her to death."

"We made it. You're making too much out of this."

The sisters continued to scream at one another until, eventually, somebody came and told them that they had both been summoned to the commander's tent. Striding into the command tent, they saluted their commander and waited.

"What happened, Squadron Leader?" she asked.

Nadia explained the situation.

"Cadet Petroffskaya, explain yourself."

"I felt we had enough fuel. I thought Nadia was too over-cautious. So, I continued to deploy the bombs on our enemy. And we had time. I made it back."

The commander sat down heavily at her desk and sighed. "Cadet Petroffskaya, when you are in the air, Nadia is your commanding officer. She tells you what to do. You do not defy her orders. On the ground, you can be her sister. You can do what you want when you're off-duty. But when you are up in the sky, you will always do as you're told. Do you understand?"

Tasha's face was bright red with anger. "But what if she's making the wrong call?"

"That is not your judgment," her commander said. "Your job is to do what you're told. Otherwise, I have to rethink whether I can have you in the air. We can't afford anyone to be too reckless out there. You endanger all of us when you're up in the sky, not just yourself. You have to think of the whole group. Nadia, how are you going to take control of Tasha?"

Nadia blew out air and shrugged her shoulders. "I've been trying to do that for years."

"Do you think she needs to be reprimanded?"

Tasha peered at her sister, her eyes boring into her.

Nadia let go of a sigh. "I think she may have learned her lesson, hopefully. I think it's hard for her because I'm her sister. But I think she knows what's right and wrong. Don't you, Tasha?"

Tasha didn't say anything. She just tightened her jaw.

"You girls are dismissed, but I don't ever want to hear of any of this again. Do you understand? Nadia, you need to get control. And Tasha, you need to do as you're told. Do you understand me?"

"Yes, Commander," was Tasha's stilted reply.

The girls saluted and walked out.

"Thanks very much, Tasha," said Nadia sarcastically as she strode away. "That was great. I really enjoyed that."

She could tell her sister was fuming but was also a little regretful. Now she was starting to become more confident in the air, this willful side of her sister's character was going to be more challenging than Nadia had bargained for. And up in the air where their life hung in the balance, she had some real concerns about how all this could end.

33

Tasha

Early one afternoon, Tasha was woken from a deep sleep by Alina.

"The commander wants to see you straightaway," Alina insisted. You have to come now."

Tasha forced her eyes open and tried to get her bearings. She had barely been asleep for three hours, and she screwed up her eyes with the insult of the morning sun that streamed in through the open tent flap. She would never get used to this weird schedule where she was awake all night and slept all day. It really upset her system, but to be woken like this caused her to have to take a moment to collect herself.

She tried to understand what she was saying as Tasha stared at Alina, who was looking intently at her.

"She needs you to come straightaway," Alina repeated, exaggerating her words so Tasha could understand.

Tasha nodded reluctantly, and slowly peeling back the covers, she heaved herself out of her bunk. Ten minutes later, she was dressed in her uniform and in front of the commander, worrying that she had done something wrong. The commander was marching up and down when she entered, and Tasha could see the concern etched on her face.

"Ah, good, Tasha, Alina found you. Forgive me for waking you in the middle of the day, but we have something very important that we need you to do. Tasha, we have a critical mission, and I feel that you're the right person to undertake it. But I'm not going to lie to you, it's very dangerous, and you will have to go alone, without even your navigator. But somebody must go. It would have been assigned to one of the men in one of the other units, but the area you will be flying into can only take a small aircraft that must be able to land without an airstrip at night. So that would be one of ours. They wanted to send one of the men in one of our planes, but I wouldn't have it, saying that we know the planes better, and we have girls as brave and as skilled as their crews. And I automatically thought of you."

Tasha felt bewildered and flattered as she tried to take in all that her commander was saying.

"Why me?" said Tasha. "Why not someone like Nadia or maybe Kira?"

"Nadia is well-equipped to lead our squadron, but we need someone who is, let's say, a little more of a daredevil, and I know you have those skills. If this is successful, I'll put you forward for a commendation, and I know that means a lot to you. Especially amongst your peers."

Tasha knew she was talking about her sister. Their rivalry was well-known throughout the unit.

"All right," she agreed. "What do you need?"

"You will go tonight, but you can tell no one what you are doing. Not even Nadia, do you hear me?"

"Yes."

"Go and get some sleep now, but report to me at seven p.m., and we'll go over the full plan."

Tasha saluted and left, wondering what she was undertaking. She tossed and turned in her bed for a long time, going over her commander's words before finally falling into a fitful sleep.

———

That evening, Tasha was getting ready to leave and she saw Nadia striding out towards the planes. She quickly rushed to catch up with her, noticing how smart and capable her sister looked in her jumpsuit, and her heart beamed with pride.

"Nadia," she called out.

Nadia turned around in surprise to see her. Tasha couldn't tell her what she was doing, but she also couldn't let her leave without her knowing that she loved her.

Nadia stopped and waited for her.

Reaching her side, breathlessly, Tasha tried to find the words without them sounding strange. "I wanted to wish you luck on your sorties this evening."

Nadia quirked an eyebrow, apparently not really believing in the sincerity of this sudden encouragement. "Thank you. You too."

Tasha smiled awkwardly, trying to find the right way to proceed.

Nadia looked amused. "Is that all?"

"No, not just that," she said as she started to pace. "I also wanted to say I'm sorry for everything I've ever done."

Nadia started to laugh. "Well, that was a pretty blanket apology. But all right. You're forgiven for everything you have ever done for your whole life. Apart from when you ruined my hair when you were testing out your homemade hair dye. I still plan on getting you back for that."

Tasha smiled briefly at the memory, remembering again how angry her sister had been when they had still been at school.

"Nadia, I know my shortcomings. I know who I am. But

you're my sister. I want you to know that I love you. I don't want you ever to forget that."

"Tasha, what's wrong? What have you done?"

"Nothing. Nothing is wrong."

"And you've never been able to lie to me. Now tell me, what is going on?"

"I can't tell you. I have been sworn to secrecy by our commander."

"All right, then." Nadia laughed. "But are you sure you're okay?"

Tasha sighed. "You're always so worried about me. I'm fine. I just didn't want us to part tonight without you knowing that I cared about you, even though I don't always show it. And even though I can be the worst sister in the world. And as much as I hate the fact that it's not me leading the squadron, I'm glad you are and that you're here. And I love you."

Nadia shook her head with bemusement and gave her a big hug. "And you know that I love you, too. So, you take good care of yourself, too, all right?"

Tasha nodded and, waving to her, watched her sister climb into her plane and hoped this wouldn't be the last time she would ever see her.

34

Tasha

Tasha arrived at the command tent at 7 p.m. as she'd been instructed. Commander Bershanskaya was waiting for her.

"Good, Cadet Petroffskaya. I'm glad you're here. I want to run over all your instructions for this evening. Have you told anybody?"

Tasha shook her head.

"It is imperative that nobody knows. As much as I'm sure that we can trust the girls here, information can get out, which is of the utmost secrecy. Do you understand?"

Tasha nodded.

The commander pulled out a map and, laying it on a desk, beckoned Tasha to her side. "We have a critical mission for you to fly. This morning, one of our military convoys were making their way from one secure location to another, with very highly sensitive documentation. And unfortunately, en route, they were ambushed, and many of the trucks were destroyed. We flew in another airman to retrieve the documents, but the airstrip was very difficult and he had a hard landing and was injured. Though he was able to radio us and he has the documents. The pilot is hiding in the woods there, waiting for nightfall, but it's only a matter of time before he is found.

"We realize now that the area you'll be flying into is way too small for one of our bigger aircraft. And to keep them away from this comrade, our forces have been keeping the Germans occupied all day. But we are concerned that once night falls, and they get some respite from the daytime onslaughts, they'll be more likely to find him. So, as the snow could be thick, we will put skis on your plane and have you land in a remote area and pick up the secret documentation and also the pilot, if possible.

"Now, this is highly dangerous, which is why we only want to send one girl in. But I want you to know that if you feel this is too much for you, I will understand, and we will send a male pilot. There'll be no humiliation and nothing on your file. But we need you to volunteer to do this and be prepared to go into a very dangerous situation."

Tasha hitched her breath, looking down at the map. It was about thirty minutes' flight from where they were, and would presumably be quite a large area of woodland.

"How will I know where to land?" she asked.

"He will light a path for you with some flares on the ground so you'll know where it's clear. But you won't have long. We're sending you in because you're used to traveling at night and can go in quietly, and you won't disturb the Germans who are all around the area. Do you understand?"

Tasha nodded.

"I'm not going to lie to you. There is a good chance that he may be dead already. And even if he's not, this extraction will put you in grave danger. Are you sure you can do this?"

Tasha nodded her head. "I can. I'll be in and out before you even realize it."

"I knew you'd be the right person." Her commander nodded, smiling. "Now, we don't have any time to lose. As soon as night falls is going to be the safest time to send someone in. We have rendezvoused with the pilot, and he knows to set the flares as soon as it's dark so you can find your way down."

Tasha nodded, and, saluting her commander, she moved towards the entrance of the tent.

"Cadet Petroffskaya," she called after her. Tasha pivoted around. "Good luck."

Tasha smiled and felt her stomach lurch as she made her way out. This was risky, she could tell. But she also felt a great sense of excitement. This was something she knew she could do.

A few minutes later, she was at her plane, which had already had its skis put onto it by Alina. She went over all her instrumentation and checked she had extra fuel. She wanted to make sure she got back. Alina was highly inquisitive, but Tasha explained to her she couldn't tell her anything. She headed out to the field, thinking of her comrade sisters already on their way for their first bombing campaign of the night.

Revving her engine, she slid along the snow, gliding up into the air and heading towards the place she was navigating to. It was a little more challenging navigating on her own using her map and a compass, a skill she still wasn't great at, but as she did, she looked down at familiar landmarks that she now was used to, marking her progress as she went. She was going right over German lines, which would make it perilous.

As she started to approach the target, she felt her stomach tightening. Her breath began to quicken as she looked around her. Though she couldn't see them, she knew that all below her were German forces. At the appropriate time, she slowed her engine, just the usual familiar whoosh, as she made her way towards the ground. Of course, they wouldn't be expecting an attack in this area, but still, she needed to be careful. As she approached, it was already quite dark but there were no flares, and she started to become concerned. So she circled around, kicking her engine back into life and searching the area—still, nothing.

She moved a little to the west to see if maybe she'd missed it. And then, as she approached from the north, she saw it—just a glimmer out of the corner of her eye, two small flares on the ground. Swallowing down her fear and tightening her grip on the throttle, she thrust forward gently towards the area. She had learned to land on skis many times, but she hadn't done it for a while. And she wasn't sure how thick the snow would be. Then, as she started to get close to the ground, she suddenly heard flak from behind her and then another gun.

Suddenly the air was alive with explosions that tore all around her, deafening her and heating up the cockpit. Wiping her goggles, she pressed forward. Lining up with the landing strip and pointing the plane towards it, she came down a little heavy on the skis and had to use her whole body weight to bring the plane to a stop on the very short landing strip.

As the Germans had detected her, she knew she wouldn't have long. They would know where she'd landed and it wouldn't take them long to get to the spot where she was. Jumping out of the aircraft, she looked around her, calling out. She didn't know the pilot's name, but surely he must be here.

Suddenly she heard a muffled cry from a clump of trees. Running over, she saw that the pilot had been injured and was nursing a wound that it looked like he'd had for a while. He'd used makeshift bandages to keep himself together. He was sweating profusely, and he was pale.

"I'm sorry it took me so long to light the flares. I'm in a lot of pain, as you can see."

As Tasha ducked her head to get close to his, she noticed there was something familiar about him. It was very dark, but she knew this person.

"Sergei?" she hissed.

His blue eyes flicked up to hers, and a knowing smile

curled his lips. "Of course they sent you. I should have known it."

She bent down to help him. "Where are you injured?"

"Go. I am fine. Get this important information where it needs to go."

"No! I can help get you ready to leave." She ignored his protests and started to check his wounds.

He shook his head. "They'll be here any minute. You need to leave."

"I have to do this," she said. "Stop arguing with me. Save your breath."

"Still as stubborn as a mule, I see," he croaked.

"And still as proud as a peacock," she shot back.

Sergei started to laugh, and then the pain took hold of him and he grimaced as she tightened his bandages.

"That should hold. Now we need to get you to the plane."

"Natasha, you need to leave me." He was serious for once. "I can't make it. I'm not well enough."

"Nonsense," she said, hoisting him up, "I can help."

He stifled a yell with the pain as she started to drag him towards the airplane.

"I always said that you would kill me one day. It looks like you want to do that with me being in agony."

"Shut up," she said, "and help me."

He tried his best to aid her as she dragged him towards the plane. A rattle of gunfire echoed through the trees, and behind them was the noise of the troops breaking through the woods.

"They've seen the flares," he panted. "You have to leave me."

"Oh no," she spluttered out, "and miss the expression on your face when you realize that I saved your life when you were sure that I would be the one that would kill you? That is too good a chance to miss."

He shook his head as she pulled him up onto the wing, and he cried out again with the pain as she helped him into his seat. They both ducked as the sound of gunfire exploded all around them again, and the sounds of German voices grew louder as the troops regrouped themselves to attack them.

"Quickly, Tasha," he said, "we need to go now."

She nodded. Starting the engine, she spun the propeller and jumped into her cockpit. She grabbed at the controls as two Germans approached the plane. One of them jumped onto the wing, a gun in his hand aimed at her, and tried to pull her out. Fighting them off, she elbowed him in the face and shoved him away from her. He rolled down the wing and off the side of her plane. She started to taxi forward as fast as she could as all around her explosions and the heat of gunfire stifled the air. She full-throttled towards the end of the field, kept her head down, and held her breath as the plane took off. All at once, a searchlight found her, and quickly she twisted out of its beam.

"You always were good at evasion," said Sergei's voice from behind her as he groaned. "But navigation, not so good."

"You're in the navigation seat," she shouted back. "You could navigate for me."

"Of course I can do that for you, in between bleeding to death," he mumbled with exasperation before he finally passed out.

She flew as hard and as fast as she could back to the camp. As she did, Tasha turned a couple of times to check on Sergei. He was so pale, he must have lost a lot of blood, and she wasn't sure if he would survive.

Her commander had alerted medical staff to be ready for them just in case. When they arrived at the field, they pulled Sergei out quickly and started to assess him.

Her commander met her in the field. "Quickly, Tasha, you must ready a hospital plane. We'll try and save this man's life."

Tasha nodded and rushed to the plane that was all set up to carry people in case of a medical emergency. It was fitted with a bed on the side that they could strap a patient into. As soon as they buckled Sergei in, Tasha started the engine. Looking over, she could see he had not regained consciousness.

A medical member of staff jumped into the navigator seat as she began to taxi again down the field. Taking off, she could see the medic working furiously with Sergei, and she willed him to stay alive. As much as this man had been an adversary for her, she also did not want him to die, not when she'd gone to so much trouble to save his life. And there was something satisfying in knowing that the man that had condemned her to the night flights would be saved because of one of them.

35

Tasha

A few days later she had got word that Sergei had pulled through, and she was dressing one evening, wondering how much she was going to enjoy throwing her heroic exploits into his face once he was well enough, when Eva came to find her.

"Did you hear Nadia is leaving?"

"What?" Tasha spat out incredulously.

"I just heard from one of the other girls that she's already packed her stuff and will be leaving today."

"That's impossible," Tasha responded, buttoning up her flying suit. "She has said nothing to me."

Pulling on her boots, she rushed out of the tent to find her sister.

And there she was. Nadia, dressed in her civilian clothes, coming out of the commander's tent, a suitcase by her side.

Tasha raced to her sister.

"Nadia, what are you doing? You're leaving us?"

Nadia's face was flushed, her eyes full of sadness.

"I have to go," she stammered.

"You don't have to leave if this is about me not doing what

I'm supposed to do," Tasha begged. "I promise that from now on, I'll do everything you say."

Nadia smiled and shook her head. "Well, as nice as that experience would be, this isn't about you, Tasha. It's Ivan, he didn't even realize I was at the front and now..." The words caught in her sister's throat, and the tears started to brim.

"What?"

She handed a letter to her sister. It was from Babka. She scanned it. Ivan had been injured, shrapnel in the leg, and had come home unhappy to find that his wife was not waiting there to help take care of him. Babka's letter said he was furious, and she encouraged Nadia to come home as soon as possible so she could sort this out.

"You're leaving because of him? Giving all this up because of your husband?"

"No, I've asked for extended compassionate leave. I've been given some time off to help nurse him, and while I'm with him, I'll talk to him about the importance of returning. Until then, Irina will lead the squadron. So make sure you take care of her and don't give her any trouble."

Tasha turned her sister to her. "Are you sure this is the only way? Why can't you write to him and tell him how important this is and how much we need you? How much I need you."

Nadia's expression softened. "I've written to him trying to explain, but he's written back insisting I return. He doesn't want me fighting. He says it's not right for a married woman. It's not what he wants his wife to be doing. With this injury, I have a chance to talk to him properly, make him see what I'm doing and how important it is. I promise I'll only stay as long as it takes to talk to him and get him on his road to healing. Then I'll come back."

Tasha took hold of her sister and hugged her so tightly she was frightened she might snap her. She didn't want her to go and hadn't realized how much she had got used to her being around. And though she would never admit it, she did like her sister being in charge. She knew that she was good at her job and was an incredible pilot.

"I'll miss you," she cried into her neck.

Nadia hugged her back tightly. "And I'll miss you too. Please take care of yourself. And be good to Irina."

Grabbing her suitcase, Tasha walked with her sister to the army truck waiting to take her to the train station.

As she loaded her suitcase into the truck, Nadia turned to Tasha. "Don't hang around here. You should get ready. You have tonight's campaign to fly."

A sob caught in Tasha's throat.

Nadia kissed her sister on the cheek and tapped her face. "Keep my plane seat warm for me. I'll be back soon."

Tasha nodded and waved to her sister as the truck drove off in a cloud of blue fumes, and all at once she felt a sinking loneliness. As much as there'd been tension between them during this time, they'd both grown so much together with this experience. They'd gone from being young girls to women, and to women fighting for freedom for the whole world. And she wasn't sure how she was going to cope without her sister there to help her stay the course.

36

Nadia

It took her days to travel home, but it wasn't until she was on the bus back to their village that Nadia felt a sinking feeling. She wasn't even sure how it would feel trying to fit back into her old life. She would have to get used to sleeping at night again with Ivan by her side. The whole experience seemed surreal compared with her ongoing life. So much had happened in such a short space of time since she'd joined the squadron. Could she just cook and bake now, keep the house clean? Her stomach knotted with fear and her reluctance. And she'd have to deal with Ivan. She knew he would not be happy with her choices.

When she arrived back at the house, Babka was there to greet her, caring for Ivan. She opened the door, and her grandmother pulled her into a flowery hug, kissing her warmly on both cheeks. "You look so well, Nadia," she said, standing back to admire her granddaughter. "There's so much red in your cheeks, and you look as though you've become stronger. Tell me everything, all about your adventures, and how is Tasha?"

"As willful as ever," stated Nadia evenly, placing down her bags.

Babka chuckled as she bustled to put water on the stove to heat.

"How is Ivan?" Nadia asked tentatively.

"As stubborn as ever!" Babka responded, her forehead creasing with concern, and her voice dropped to a whisper. "He's been like a bear with a sore head. Nothing is right for him. He was so upset about you not being here, I thought he was going to burst a blood vessel to go along with his broken leg."

Nadia sighed. "I'll go and see him."

"Here, take him some of my soup that I made, and maybe it'll soften him up," she said as she handed her a bowl.

Nadia made her way up the stairs and into their bedroom. She opened the door, and there was Ivan in bed. He looked like something from a newspaper advertisement. His pajamas were so starched and new. The bedclothes were not even creased as he sat up in bed, reading a newspaper.

When he saw her, he placed it down on the bed and stared at her. "The prodigal wife returns," he said sardonically.

"How are you, Ivan?" she asked as she came over and kissed him dutifully on the cheek and then seated herself on the side of his bed.

"As you can see, I'm a little worse for wear, though I have to tell you that the disappointment in my heart is much harder to bear than a broken leg. I couldn't believe it when I came home to find our house empty. And then to find out you trained and joined the war. Why, Nadia? Not just the fact that you went, but why did you go against my wishes when I was so clear about you not going to fight in this war?"

Why had Nadia disobeyed him? She didn't know. She just knew he wouldn't have let her go. He would have made her feel guilty for contemplating it.

"Would you have said yes if I'd asked if I could fly?"

"I never got the choice," he said defensively, but Nadia knew what he would've said. "I thought you liked being a wife and having your own home. When I didn't hear from you for a while, I just thought you were busy sewing or taking care of our house. I can't believe you're flying in the sky, with reckless abandon, putting your life at risk. I hate to think of the danger you are putting yourself in, day after day."

"Isn't risking your life what you've been doing?"

"I am a man, Nadia. I'm supposed to do this. You don't have to. Your job is to take care of our life, our home. I would hate anything to happen to you."

"Are you sure that is what you want or do you just want to control me, Ivan?"

Ivan was speechless.

Nadia folded her arms and began to stride up and down the room. "Okay, I admit, I should have told you, but I knew that you wouldn't want me to go, and I needed to do this for myself."

He looked hurt by her words, as if her being independent was somehow reflective on him. "I'll never understand, Nadia. I'll never understand why you did this." He sucked in a deep breath and then continued. "But at least you're home now and you've given it all up and we can start again."

She swallowed down the fact that wasn't the case. This wasn't the time to tell Ivan she had no intention of staying here full-time and that she was planning on going straight back out to fly with her squadron as soon as she could.

She handed him his food. "Babka made you her famous borscht. This should get your strength up."

"Your grandmother has been very good to me. I'm very grateful to her."

Nadia nodded.

"But now you are home, she will be able to leave and go back to her own life, as you are here to take care of me."

Something in his tone disturbed Nadia. His words were

cordial, but there was almost an underlying distaste she could hear, as if having Babka in the house was somehow beneath them.

Nadia sighed reluctantly and started to unpack her clothes.

That night, as she slipped into bed with him, she sensed him tense beside her. She had hoped their time apart had maybe increased his desire for her but he merely kissed her coolly on the lips and turned over. She, once again, wondered if she'd done the wrong thing in marrying Ivan as quickly as she had. He was a good man, but he was... what was it that Tasha had said? Caught up in himself, his passion reserved only for his party. Tasha had been right.

The next night, almost as if it was an act of desperation on his part to keep her by his side, he started to make love to her in his uniform way. It was orderly and precise, as though he was practicing a routine. But she sensed it in the rigidness of his body. He was holding back, and she didn't know why. When the candlelight flickered across his face, she was shocked to see that instead of looking at her, he had his eyes firmly closed as if he was really concentrating. During their lovemaking, in which he kept most of his clothes on, she couldn't help thinking of Tasha and Luca's passion, and she suddenly felt so resentful. Was this the life that she wanted? She couldn't even believe it now. Everything had changed for her. She was leading a squadron of women into battle each evening, respected by her commanders and peers. There was such a gulf between that life and this.

As Ivan left to use the bathroom, she turned over and tried not to cry. This felt like somebody else's life. Was she wrong to have other dreams or other things she wanted to do?

As if breaking through her thoughts, he spoke as he settled himself back into bed. "I do love you, Nadia, I want you to know that. And as your husband, I believe I know what is best for you."

Nadia turned over and looked out of the window at the moonlight streaming from below her curtains. They would be flying now, probably on their second run or third. Irina would be leading them, all of them engaged in the thrill of the hunt. It was a good, clear night with little wind. They would get at least four or five sorties in tonight, and there would be much celebrating tomorrow at the work they'd achieved.

All she had ahead of her was breakfast, lunch, and dinner and taking care of Ivan.

It was then she knew she had outgrown this tiny, boxed life. She could not stay within these four walls or she would go mad. But how would she tell her husband? How would she make him understand that she was more than this? She needed more than this. As she heard his breathing become even and steady in sleep, she allowed the tears to fall. She was trapped, and she couldn't see a way out of this without someone getting hurt.

37

Nadia

Nadia woke up again and felt strange. She hadn't slept at night for months. It felt disconcerting to be getting up in the early morning after continually being awake all night, participating in the bombing raids that had become a part of her life. Her home was so quiet and still: the light creeping under the curtains, Ivan sleeping silently by her side, a cockerel announcing the morning from a nearby farm. She slipped out of bed and found herself quickly returning to her former role as a wife as if it were a stiff uniform that she had just plucked off the back of the bedroom door. It felt restrictive and yet so familiar. The usual creak of the floorboards at the top of the landing and the smell of wax and lavender from her cleaning the day before. The chill of her feet on the stairs, the sound of the clock ticking on the kitchen wall. She started a fire to make Ivan's breakfast, moving through her cupboards in such a familiar way as she prepared what her husband expected. She looked out of the window and felt totally bereft.

She couldn't stand this; it was heart-wrenchingly laborious. As she prepared his breakfast, her mind wandered what felt like a thousand times to what she would be doing now with the squadron. If it was afternoon and they'd just woken up, they would be getting together to meet around the bonfire or do something together. Lately, they'd been putting on short musical performances, which were hysterical, she remembered with a smile. Most of the squadron wasn't talented at all. It was highly entertaining. She'd also started painting a mural on the side of her plane. Liliya had been teaching her. Here, she would not be able to do anything.

She watched a spider walk down the windowpane. Its slow advance felt like her life, nothing to do but amble through it, nowhere to be. She made Ivan's breakfast and took it up to him. He was already awake and sitting up in bed.

"Good morning, my dear," he said.

"I have your breakfast." Nadia slipped the tray onto his lap.

"Wonderful. Thank you."

"How long did the doctor say until you're up and about?"

"Why, are you ready to be rid of me already?" He smiled, taking up his cup of tea, his soft brown eyes teasing her.

"No, no, of course not," she lied. "I was just wondering if there was any kind of timetable for your healing."

"He said I should be walking fine again in about six weeks. Then, they'll probably just send me back to the front. So, we'll have plenty of time to be together. There are many people I have met, other comrades in the Party, who I want to tell you about. I have so missed our lively debates."

She felt her stomach cramp. Six weeks? How would she last like this for six weeks? She'd barely managed two days.

She tidied the bedroom nervously as he ate, even though there was nothing to really do. "I should think about some new curtains," she mused, brushing them off.

"New curtains? You only made those just before we got married."

"I know. But already I'm tired of the pattern."

"That's a waste of money," said Ivan. "You seem nervous, Nadia. Is everything all right?"

"Oh, yes," she said. "Just strange. You know? Coming back from what I've been doing."

He became serious. "We won't talk about that any more. I admire your patriotism, but there's no need for you to do that. You should be here with the other women of the village, spending time with them."

She felt a lurch in her stomach. Without Tasha around and many of their friends who had moved to Moscow in the last few years, there were no women she wanted to spend time with.

She spent the day cleaning their already-clean house and preparing lunch and dinner for her husband, wondering how long she could live this lie.

Finally, when Babka came by to check on her in the afternoon, she poured their tea, and her grandmother could instantly tell there was something wrong. "What is it, Nadia? You look so sad."

She sat down and shook her head. "I can't do this, Babka. I can't live this life any more."

Concern crossed Babka's face. "This life? Do you mean your life or your marriage?"

Nadia felt the heat color her cheeks. "He's such a difficult man to understand. He won't let me go back and fight. He says he wants me to be safe. But it also feels a little controlling. He appears to want me but..." She paused, too embarrassed to share with her grandmother their lack of physical connection. She settled on, "He seems to struggle showing his affection sometimes."

"Ivan is the same man you married," her grandmother said wisely, "but maybe you're not the same wife. There should always be room for movement in a marriage. It can take some time for you to get used to being together. I remember your grandfather was the opposite. He was very demonstrative and

I was so shy it took a while for me to feel comfortable with that. Ivan is a good man. You will find your way. But in the meantime, you need to make him understand that you can be a good wife and still fly, if that's what you want to do?"

"That's what I said. But he seems to be very resentful. He doesn't even want to talk about it."

"Then you need to make him see. Cook him some good food and put it plainly and simply. I can take care of Ivan until he is well if you want to go back. There's no need for you to stay."

Nadia didn't want to tell her about Ivan's feelings at not wanting Babka in the house, but she was right. There was nothing to keep her here.

After Babka left, she thought about her grandmother's words but hadn't the heart to say anything. Not for three days. By then, she was practically climbing the walls. It was after Ivan had managed to come down to eat a meal and they were sitting at the kitchen table. He had wanted to get out of bed and had got dressed and had shuffled down with a stick, as she'd made him his favorite meal. He was talking about something insignificant and out of the blue she stood up.

"I have to go back, Ivan. I have to go back and fly."

He looked at her curiously. He didn't seem to understand what she was saying. "Go back and fly where?"

"For the squadron. I want to go back to fight our enemy."

His face glowed red with frustration. "We've already had this conversation, Nadia. I want you to stay here and be safe."

"I can't. I can't stay. And if you really loved me, you would see that. Can you not see how unhappy I am?"

He looked devastated. "I thought that was because you were sad about me being ill. I didn't realize it was because you were sad to be here with me."

"It's not that, Ivan. I've enjoyed being with you," she said, though she knew she didn't sound very convincing. "But I belong there, and they need me. I lead the squadron."

"You're not going. This conversation is over."

"What do you mean it's over? I am going, and you can't stop me."

He looked at her then and tutted. "This is Natasha's influence on you. I was concerned about that with you being there, that crazy sister of yours."

"This has nothing to do with Tasha. This only has to do with me and what I want. If you really cared, you would let me go."

They continued to argue till late into the evening. And that night, when he went back to his bed, she didn't follow him. Instead, she curled up on the couch with a blanket and slept there. She felt so lonely. What had made her think that Ivan was the right man for her? When she woke up, she packed her things.

When he saw her bags, he looked bereft.

"I see now how you really feel, Nadia. I'm hurt to think there is so little love between us."

Nadia shook her head. "I think you and I have a very different idea of what that word means."

"What are you trying to say?"

"Love to me is intimacy and connection and being together, talking and sharing."

"Are you saying we don't talk? I've so enjoyed your fine mind. I chose you as my wife because of how clever and how insightful you are."

"I don't want to be insightful! I want to be desired, adored, loved."

"Romantic silliness," he spluttered. "We're not sixteen, Nadia, we're building a home together in the Communist way. You are my wife, not my..." He struggled for the word.

"Lover." She filled in the blank for him.

His face flushed as he turned towards the window.

She dropped her tone to a desperate whisper. "Do you not find me attractive, Ivan?" His face reddened even more.

"Answer me, Ivan, am I attractive to you?" She raised her voice. "*Answer me!*"

His eyes met hers and instantly she knew the truth and it shocked her. He didn't.

"I wanted to be." His voice was quiet and there was a slight quiver beneath his words. "I thought if I married you, the feelings would grow, but I have always struggled with a certain aspect of my..." He paused, as if deciding to finish the sentence or not, and then finally said quietly, "...identity on that level."

Finally, she understood. She had heard of men like Ivan, men who did not find women attractive. No wonder he so enjoyed the company of his male comrades.

She sat down heavily on a kitchen chair, the breath leaving her body with the shock. "Have you ever found me attractive?" she finally asked, desperately.

He looked towards her and for the first time she saw a genuine concern before he slowly shook his head. His voice was willowy, so unlike the man she knew. "Not in the way you would want me to. It is not you; it is any woman." He started to sob openly.

A thousand thoughts rushed through her head. Men that found other men attractive were taboo in Russia. She remembered a man in their village who had been uncovered as a "sodomite" and he had been jailed for five years with hard labor. It had broken him. And here she was with her own husband who was the same way and there was nothing she could do to fix this. She couldn't even share this burden with anyone, otherwise he too could suffer the same fate. No wonder he was so committed to his work. She suddenly felt such compassion for the man she had married. Also, a little relief. She hadn't realized it till now, but she had blamed his lack of desire on herself.

He was still looking out of the window as she moved to his side, the tears running freely down his cheeks. His handsome face was stricken with the pain he felt, as she finally understood, understood the physical distance between them, even though in so many other ways they had connected.

"Oh, Ivan," she said, and when she put her arms around him, he didn't pull away. He let her hold him tightly and it felt so good to her to finally hold her husband in her arms without him holding back his truth.

"I was so afraid, Nadia, that you would see it, that you would know. I know how beautiful you are, and every day I tried to will myself to find you attractive, to give you what you needed from me. I so longed to be the husband you wanted. I had no idea how hard it would be to be so close to another person in so many ways, except one. I pushed the thoughts from my mind of the perversion my body wanted and tried so hard to fix all that desire on you, but I have failed you, miserably. It preoccupied me day and night. Then when I went to the front and was with men in such close proximity I finally had to come to a realization that this desire was stronger than I could bear. I can't control it, Nadia, and I don't know what to do about it. I have been so unfair to you. You have no idea how much that troubles me every day." He paused then slowly continued, his voice barely above a whisper. "And there is another man, in my unit, like me. Nothing unholy has happened between us, I promise you, but we have talked candidly and he has helped me understand so much of what I am feeling."

They sat for a long time while she also cried and he told her of how hard his life had been, having these feelings and not being able to express them or even talk about them to anyone. As she listened, thoughts ran in a loop through her mind. She loved this man; could they overcome something of this magnitude?

Then he looked at her seriously. "I should never have done this to you, Nadia. It was wrong of me. But I so wanted to be different. I wanted to be a husband, and I still want to have children. And my work is so important, and if what I was became known, all the good work I am trying to do in the world would be lost."

She nodded. "I'm hurt and angry that you didn't share this with me earlier, Ivan. You married me without being honest. But you can't change who you are. Just like I can't change who I am. I want to fight, Ivan. I want to fly and I'm good at it."

He nodded his understanding and gently took her hand. "I now realize I was holding on to a picture in my mind of a perfect world I was desperately trying to create. A wife, a home, a family, in order to hide this side of my nature I am battling with. I was forcing that onto you without really taking into consideration your own needs and wants."

And ironically, as he told her they could never have the marriage she had always wanted, she felt that they really connected deeply for the first time. She tried desperately to swallow down all of her disappointment as she thought of what this would mean for her.

"What will you do, Nadia, with what I have told you?" He looked scared for a second.

"Your secret is safe with me," she assured him. "And right now, we have a war to fight that neither of us may make it through. When it's over, we can talk again. I'm not sure I can survive in a marriage without intimacy, Ivan, but this is not what we are dealing with today. Today I want to go back to my unit and I want your blessing to do so."

"If it is what you want. I am hardly in a position to complain."

She nodded and began to gather her things. "The bus goes in an hour. I'll get you a cup of tea and then Babka has offered to help."

He looked disapproving of the arrangement, but agreed all the same. As she moved to put on the kettle, he called out to her. "Nadia." She turned. "Thank you, thank you, for your understanding, and I'm so sorry."

She smiled back meekly and tried not to think about what

a marriage to a man like Ivan would be like. She thought of Tasha and Luca. And how she had once caught them in a passionate embrace. If she stayed in this marriage, she would never know that kind of love. But if she left it, would it leave him vulnerable to being exposed?

Later, she stood on her doorstep, her case in her hand, and he brushed her lips with a gentle kiss.

"Take care of yourself, Nadia."

She nodded. "And you too, Ivan. I'll write soon."

He nodded and she turned one last time at their garden gate to look back and wave. Her stomach churned as she battled with all her feelings of intense love for him, mingled with the crushing disappointment of his confession and wondered what all this would mean for them.

38

Nadia

In the first months of their campaigns, the girls were flying high. They had completed many sorties, often doing four to six a night. And the intelligence that had filtered through insinuated that there was a great deal of concern from the Germans about how successful their campaigns were. They had also found out with great hilarity that the Germans had caught wind of the all-female nature of their night squadron and nicknamed them "the Night Witches." Which they embraced with a great sense of pride. It was because of this euphoria that they started to forget the real danger of what they were doing. As if being witches also bestowed upon them their own secret powers.

One evening in the winter, it was a clear night, a perfect night for them to drop bombs. And they'd had a great afternoon together. But before they prepared for their night mission, Katya had a surprise for them all. For the past few weeks she had been instructing them in all the new dances. And they gathered around with excitement to watch her unwrap a parcel.

"My mother promised to send this from Moscow," she informed them with great excitement as they all watched. "A friend of hers was traveling to the south and brought it here for me."

Underneath the layers of paper, they all gathered around to look at the beautiful, polished mahogany box with an engraved silver needle. A gramophone!

"Well, that will be a step up from my fiddle playing." Irina, who had been the musical accompaniment so far, laughed.

Katya pulled one of the shiny records out of the cardboard sleeve, placed it carefully on the turntable, and gently cranked the handle. Instantly, music filled the camp with the delicate dance music that brought tears to all the girls' eyes. Nadia and Tasha had never been to a ballet or to see an orchestra play, and in the village, there was just the local musician who played an accordion for dances. They had never heard anything like the beauty of this music.

"When I was younger," Katya continued wistfully, "ballet was my life; this was one of my favorites to dance too."

"Play this one, Katya," Kira encouraged as the record finished. "Remember when we danced with those two airmen in Moscow before we left? It was to this tune. Katya knows it. She can teach us all the dance."

Katya began to show them the steps and they danced together, joking about how this was more fun than having men to dance with. Even in the midst of the darkness of war, this was a blissful moment of pure joy and Nadia knew she would always remember it.

"I like there are no men to step on your toes," Eva joked as she and Tasha partnered each other.

Once it was time to begin their campaign for the evening, they were in the mood for high jinks, all of them in good spirits as they flew towards their targets. There was a full moon, which was of some concern, though. They could be seen easier in the light, so they preferred it when it was cloudy or pitch-black. But as they'd already done this so many times before, they flew together, without much thought of what lay ahead.

As they moved into their bombing formation, Katya and Liliya took the lead to draw fire in response to Nadia signaling them into position. Nadia would drop her bombs first. Then Tasha and Eva would bring up the rear with their own deployment.

As they closed in on their target, as they had done a hundred times before, Nadia dropped her engine down to just above a stall for the approach. She smiled. Behind her she could hear Mila humming one of the songs they had been just dancing to.

Ahead of her, Liliya fired off the flare and Nadia lined up her plane, viewing her target with a little concern. It seemed as if there was more activity on the front line than usual, but nothing they couldn't handle. Nadia dropped her nose and moved gracefully through the night, swooping towards her target.

The flak picked up; above her, the loud hum of Katya and Liliya's plane drew the usual fire.

Mila called the bombs' release, and as bombs whistled through the air, she accelerated the engine and steeply climbed her plane, away from the lines. She was getting ready to turn for her second run when, all of a sudden, from behind her, there was an enormous explosion. As she'd only been supposed to be hitting an encampment, Nadia couldn't believe that her bombs had created such a huge impact. In the seat behind her, Mila screamed and swore. Nadia's heart started to pound; she maneuvered the plane around. Tasha had been right behind her, and she suddenly feared the worst. Had her sister's plane been hit?

Moving into view, she hitched her breath with shock. In the air was a fireball. One of their planes had exploded in midair, and she watched in disbelief as what seemed like a hundred burning pieces of it splintered and fell towards the earth.

At first, she couldn't believe what she was seeing. Frantically she looked around for the other plane. She saw it over to the left, just coming into view. It was Tasha and Eva.

Which meant that their dear friends Katya and Liliya had just been killed right in front of them all. It took a minute for her to register what this meant. They had been so confident, so cocky, thinking they couldn't die. After all, they were the Night Witches. But there it was, the evidence that they were human, the proof that they could all die. Her heart tightened with the pain and shock. The Germans must have got a direct hit and ruptured the fuel line, and Katya's plane had gone up like a firework.

Nadia didn't remember much about the flight back, just the sound of Mila, usually so stalwart, sobbing behind her, coupled with her own feelings of complete disbelief.

They all continued mechanically to finish their night sorties. But none of them had words. The shock throughout the camp was palpable.

As the sun rose, the girls all gathered that morning and huddled around the fire, trying to come to terms with their loss.

As the reality had now sunk in, many of them were weeping openly, their arms around each other. But it was Kira who suffered the most. She was distraught.

"It's my fault," she spat out through strangled sobs as Irina and Eva supported her. "I encouraged her to do this. She would still be dancing in Moscow if I hadn't talked her into all this."

"You can't blame yourself," Nadia responded sensibly. "She loved what she did and she loved your friendship. She wouldn't have been anywhere else."

They continued to tell stories about their friends as they commiserated with one another, each of them proudly wearing the scarves Liliya had knitted for all of them. They had all become so close, so much more than just friends, and Nadia realized, as much as she had known the danger, had been aware of it every night, she had believed deep down that nothing could happen to them. And the loss was acute to them all. It affected everything they did.

She found Tasha sobbing in her tent an hour later.

She put her arms around her sister. "Are you all right?"

"I just hate it," she spluttered. "All of it, this stupid war. Hitler. The fact Luca and I are apart. You and Ivan are apart. And now our friends are being killed. Nadia, I'm sorry I dragged you into this, too. You wouldn't have come if I wasn't here. We could be at home now, safe."

Nadia harrumphed. "Peeling potatoes and making soup with Babka. We didn't have a choice, Tasha. This is who we are. I didn't know that right away, but I know that now, we were always destined for this life. You can't focus on the death of our friends. You have to think about the hope of our future, the Russia that we are building for our children."

"If anything ever happened to Luca, I don't think I could live with another man and have any children."

"You don't know that," said Nadia.

"I do. I just can't even imagine that there would be anybody else out there for me. If he gets killed, I don't know what I will do. I think I will die."

Nadia held her sister until she calmed down.

That afternoon, before they flew, they had a service for their friends, bringing out a lovely picture Liliya had painted and playing music on Katya's gramophone.

Nadia huddled in her coat as Kira talked more about her dearest friend. "They say she could have been a great ballerina if it wasn't for this war. None of us will probably get to see our true potential because of it."

"But we get to be together and we get to do something for our country," stated Nadia, putting her arm around Kira. "And none of us will ever forget our fallen sisters. We will fly tonight for them and we will use our anger and pain to destroy our enemy."

The mechanics wrote *"For Liliya and Katya!"* on the side of all the bombs and the girls all agreed, and that night was one of their most successful campaigns. Every one of them hit their targets with great vengeance.

39

Tasha

In October they were deployed in the Battle of the Caucasus, defending the city of Vladikavkaz, and Tasha got word from one of the armorers who serviced all the camps that Luca's squadron was just a mile away. So, one night, just before the girls left for that night's bombing, she crept out at sunset, but not before her sister caught sight of her.

"Tasha, where are you going?" she asked sternly.

Tasha quickly pulled her sister aside where she could speak to her in a hushed tone. "Luca's camp is just down the road. I'm going to go and see him."

"Have you asked permission to leave?" Nadia asked, slipping easily into her older sister role.

Tasha knew she couldn't hide the truth from her. There was no point in lying. "I told the commander I wasn't feeling well and had stomach cramps. She told me to rest tonight."

Nadia shook her head. "As your squadron leader, I should report you."

Tasha looked up at her pleadingly.

Nadia sighed. "But as your sister, I understand. If you are

caught, you'll be reprimanded. We're working for the Russian Air Force now. You can't just take time off."

"Please, Nadia, you don't always have to do everything by the book. It's Luca, my Luca. I haven't seen him for months. I'll be gone for a couple of hours at the most. Can you not cover for me?"

Nadia rolled her eyes. "All right. I'll make this agreement with you: if no one says anything, I won't. But if they ask me a direct question, I will answer them truthfully. I have to be an example here, Tasha. I can't just allow this to happen because we are family."

Tasha hugged her quickly. "No one's going to ask anything. Thank you, and I can't wait to see him again," she squealed.

Nadia shook her head. "Get out of here, and don't be long."

Leaving her sister behind, Tasha moved quickly down the road to the area where the armorer had told her. It was pitch-black, but she dared not risk using light if the German forces were close by. She knew what she was doing was dangerous, and if they caught her, she would probably be killed, though she'd dressed in her civilian clothes, just in case, hoping she could fool them into believing she was just a Russian peasant.

Just when she was about to give up, she saw the camp, and she quickly found the entrance. Two guards stepped out from the darkness and pointed their rifles at her.

"Who are you? What do you want?" said a gruff-sounding man, heavyset and angry-looking, with a day's worth of beard.

Tasha placed her hands in the air. "I'm in the Women's Air Force, the 588 Squadron just down the road."

"Can you prove that?" said the other one.

"Of course, I have my paperwork," she said. "Will you let me put my hand in my pocket to show you?"

They glanced at one another and then nodded.

She pulled out her paperwork and held it towards them.

One read it in the beam of his torchlight.

"Natasha Petroffskaya?"

She nodded.

"I remember you from the flying school. You pulled that stunt with Sergei. He talks about it often. He never forgave you for that."

"I could say he pulled that stunt on me." She smiled, trying to be her most radiant self.

They chuckled.

"I suppose you've come for Luca. Weren't you two together?"

"Please let me see him for just a minute," she implored.

They exchanged a look, and the heavyset guy teased out a stream of frustrated air. "It's highly irregular to let anyone onto the camp, but I suppose I can at least let you speak to him. But you will have to come with me. We can't let you go on your own."

The heavyset man with a day's worth of beard waddled slowly ahead of her, acknowledging airmen as he went. They moved towards a large tent in the center of the camp. Even from a distance, she could hear their joviality. The men were in high spirits.

"They're finished for the day," he said, in the way of explaining what was going on as he opened up a tent flap, and they stepped inside.

The heat, the smell of sweat and tobacco smoke were what greeted her. Trying not to feel intimidated, she desperately searched the room for Luca. She saw a man with his colored hair and build. She put her hand on his shoulder, and the man turned around and looked at her. It wasn't him.

"What is this?" he said in surprise. "Are you here for me?"

"No, I'm looking for Luca Baranov. Do you know him?"

"Of course, but I'm just as good as Luca."

The group around him laughed.

Then, suddenly, she saw him over to the corner talking to

somebody. He stood to his feet as he caught sight of her and flushed red with embarrassment.

Rushing towards her, he took hold of her arm and pulled her to the edge of the room. "What are you doing here?" he hissed.

"That's a nice way to greet your girlfriend who you haven't seen for months."

"You could get us into trouble for being here. Both of us!"

"I wanted to see you," she implored. "Don't be angry. I've really missed you. Can you not get a few hours off?"

"I can't just take time off, Tasha."

"Please, just ask."

He blew out air. "Come on." They walked to the command tent and entered. Both saluted.

The commander looked up and cocked an eyebrow. "Who is this?"

"I'm Airwoman Natasha Petroffskaya, from the 588th Night Squadron, sir," she said, trying to sound confident.

"Petroffskaya," he said, narrowing his eyes. "I remember you from the training school. I'm amazed you're still alive."

She smiled meekly as Luca explained the situation.

"They let you leave your camp?"

"I spoke to my squadron leader. She knows about it," Tasha said, not wanting to elaborate that the squadron leader was her own sister.

"I suppose we can give you a few hours, Baranov. Don't go too far. There are Germans everywhere, but I know how hard it is, alone at the front, month after month. Be back before ten." Then he batted them away with his hand.

They strode out of the camp, and as soon as they were out of the eyes of the guards, he pulled her behind a tree and kissed her passionately on the lips. He'd taken her by surprise and she didn't have time to draw in breath. She had to pull away to breathe as they both laughed. He cupped her face in his hands.

"God, I've missed you."

"I missed you too," she stuttered back breathlessly. "I can't tell you how often I've dreamt of this." She looked at him, thoughtfully. "Is there anywhere we can go and be alone?"

He knew what she was insinuating, and his eyes shone with the prospect.

"Up here," he said, "there are abandoned farmhouses. Many of the local people fled when the Germans came this close, so they're unoccupied."

Taking her hand, he walked up the road until they came across a home in darkness. Stepping onto the land, they knocked on the door to ensure no one was there. Finally, after no answer, he led her around to the back of the house, where there was a barn.

"We should be safe up here."

Inside, the animals were gone, but it was clean and dry. He helped her upstairs into the hayloft, which was thick with fresh hay. Taking off his long coat, he laid it on the straw. They looked across at one another nervously, not sure where to begin. And then both laughed at the awkwardness they felt as he held out his hand and they sat down on his coat. He reached forward to kiss her again.

She noticed that his whole body was trembling. "Are you scared of me?" she asked with a smile.

"I'm nervous," he confessed. "It's been so long."

She laughed and pulled him closer. "I think I can remember what to do." Then, as she kissed him again, he drew his body close to hers and she slipped her arms around his neck and deepened the kiss.

"Oh my God, Tasha, I've missed you so much," he mumbled in between kisses.

"Me too," she responded breathlessly.

She noted the coolness of his cheek upon hers from the cold night, yet his lips were warm and sensual. Slowly his hands began to gently caress her in the way that she remembered. So artfully, he knew every curve and contour of her body, everything that made her happy and gave her pleasure. The whole experience was heightened by the length of time apart, and she could tell they were literally aching for one another.

Soon their clothes were off, and she shivered with the exhilaration of his body so close to hers. It didn't take long for their lovemaking to become heated as their need for one another intensified. She closed her eyes with the ecstasy of having Luca's naked body wrapped around hers, his lips kissing every part of her as they made love. Before long, they were lying panting in one another's arms. His chest pressing against hers, his hands tangled in her messy hair.

"Oh God, Tasha, that was intense," he spluttered, trying to catch his breath. Then, lifting himself up onto his arms, he looked down at her and laughed. "And unexpected," he continued. "One minute, I'm listening to a very boring conversation about the armory issues, and now look at me thirty minutes later, naked in your arms."

She laughed. "You should know me by now, Baranov. You should always expect the unexpected."

Still sweating and panting, he rolled over onto the straw next to her as beams of the moonlight streamed in and shone across their glowing flesh. She rolled over too and dotted his chest with gentle kisses.

"At least you remembered what to do."

He laughed. "It feels like a lifetime ago, doesn't it? Since we just did this every day and our life was so simple."

She placed her head on his shoulder and draped her arm across his chest. "It does," she whispered. "This feels so wonderful. I feel complete. Everything is right with the world and every minute I'm apart from you feels wrong."

"And we never get to forget this war."

She could hear the bitterness in his tone.

"I know," she said. "If I'm not thinking about fighting, I'm sleeping and dreaming about fighting. Every day feels harsh and unreal somehow."

Suddenly his face clouded with sadness.

"I don't feel human any more, Tasha."

She looked up at him with concern. "What is it, Luca?"

He closed his eyes, as if to push a hard thought away, and then she heard his breath quicken, as he must have decided to share what he was thinking.

"I had an experience last week," he whispered with great intensity. She waited as he paused to find the words that seemed to haunt him. "A battalion of German soldiers broke through the line to try and destroy the camp. It was a surprise attack, and no one had expected it. So, we literally had to fight hand to hand."

She looked up at his face, with shock. "You're all right? Were you injured?"

He shook his head. "They had probably been expecting support from the air, but it didn't arrive. Otherwise, I probably wouldn't be here now. During the attack, a German soldier came racing towards me from the woods with his gun drawn. I moved automatically into the training that we learned and, pulling out my pistol, fired quickly. Two bullets hit him right in the chest before he had a chance to pull his trigger on me. He didn't go down straightaway. He didn't move. His eyes just peered at me, and the shock of what I'd just done was desperate in that look. As he fell to the ground, his helmet rolled beside him and he no longer looked like a soldier, the enemy. He looked like one of us. He had brown hair and a youthful face, even a little acne across his cheeks. And I realized he was no older than me, early twenties at the most, and he looked just like Boris. Do you remember Boris? One of the guys we used to drink with at the flying club?"

She ran her fingers comfortingly through his hair as he continued.

"He looked just like him, not like some evil enemy, like a

person I could have a drink with. As I got close to him, I could hear he was still breathing, rasping his last breath, whispering something in German as he died. Something that sounded like, 'Oh God' and then the name of a woman. My heart tightened as I heard those words, and I thought about you. If I'd been slower, he would have been leaning over me and I would have been calling out your name.

"After he was completely still, I searched his pockets, as we were taught, looking for weapons. Instead of a gun or a knife, I found a photograph, a beautiful woman with dark hair and laughing eyes, with two boys in short pants and white shirts with the same eyes that he had. He had twin boys. His wife had one in each arm, the joy so obvious in her face.

"I couldn't stand it, Tasha. My stomach started wrenching and I was sick in the bushes. It all felt so wrong. Most of the time I don't think about it; I just fight. Stay focused, kill them before they kill me. But seeing his face and knowing something of his story changed me, Tasha. It haunted me and still does."

"You did what you had to do. He would've killed you."

"It's not that. I know that. But it's wrong, Tasha. What we're doing is wrong. Stalin and Hitler, with their ridiculous agendas, are like two gods over a board game moving us into position like chess pieces. They're not having to face those eyes, or kill people. It just makes me angry. So angry."

She put her arms around him and pulled him tightly to her. She kissed him gently across one side of his face and stroked the other cheek with her hand.

"I understand. It's okay, Luca. But you have to let it go. You can't hold on to the hate or the pain. You have to let it go."

He nodded, then all at once tears were streaming down his face. Pulling him towards her, she held him tightly as he sobbed in her arms. They walked back to the camp that night, and just before they got to the gate, he turned towards her.

"Tasha, as hard as all this is, I know that as long as I have you and the thoughts of us one day being together, I can go on."

She studied him for a second before she answered, her tone earnest. "Luca, I want you to promise me something. If anything happens to me, please don't live in regret or guilt. It's too painful. Please move on and find someone else, love someone else."

He balked. "I could never do that."

"You've got to promise me," she said. "Promise me now. You're too wonderful to not love and be loved."

"No! I won't," he said defiantly, "because we made a promise not to die, remember."

She beamed then. "That's right, we did, we are not going to die. I love you, Luca. I'll always love you."

"I love you too."

And as he gently moved in for a long, lingering kiss, she tried not to think about what lay ahead of both of them. She tried not to think about anything at all, apart from the joy of being in his arms.

40

NOVEMBER 1942

Nadia

The words on the telegram swam in front of her eyes. She had read them and re-read them, but it was still hard to believe that the end of her marriage was contained in one sentence.

Ivan was dead. He'd been killed at the front, just days after he had returned.

The sadness overwhelmed her. Was she heartbroken? She couldn't say that she was, but she was deeply sad. Since his personal confession before she had left home, he had opened up to her in his letters in a whole new way. As though her acceptance of him had softened him, made them allies, even moving towards friends. He was still Ivan, and his letters had been filled with his concerns about his beloved party, but there was also a tenderness to them, a kindness she had not seen for a long time. A genuine concern for her and what she was doing. Without the need of the pretense of physical attraction, he was free to pursue her in the way she had remembered when they had met. And even though she could never imagine a marriage without the intimacy she so craved, she'd wondered if there was some way they could have pieced together the

fragments of a relationship. Maybe even both turn a blind eye
to each other's lovers and still have the family they'd desired. It
seemed a little bohemian for what Nadia had planned for her
life, more like something Tasha would be comfortable doing.
But after facing life and death at the front each day, she found
that so many of her ideals were being challenged, and she
craved love in all its forms. Nadia knew that in his own way
Ivan had loved her, even if their physical lovemaking had been
so aloof. And now it was over.

She walked out of the tent to get some fresh air, and as she
strolled through the crisp, white snow, she protectively placed
her hand on her stomach, remembering the baby that was
growing there. She wondered if the letter she had sent to tell
Ivan about the good news had even reached him before his
death. She hadn't even told Tasha. She hadn't told anybody
here. She hadn't even believed it herself at first. They'd only
slept together that one time during her visit home. But when
she had noticed her breasts swelling and realized she had not
had her courses for four months, she knew it had to be true.
Though even now, with her slender build, there was still
hardly any change to her figure. Ivan had desperately wanted
children. Now with great sadness she acknowledged that this
baby would never have a father, and Ivan would never see the
child he had denied his true nature to have.

It seemed so unfair, and she would have to bring this child
up on her own. She wasn't afraid of that. Hadn't she been an
orphan herself with her grandmother taking care of her? But
still, she felt overwhelming sadness at her child's loss. She had
desperately wanted a stable home for her and her children.
Now all she had was this baby, and none of what she had
dreamed of seemed possible any more. She wondered if
anyone would want her, carrying another man's child. And
what would she do about the squadron? She decided she
would keep the baby a secret as long as she could. The last
thing she wanted to do was to have to go home and face an

empty house. This was where she belonged now. This was her family.

Tasha bounded up to her, the concern obvious in her eyes. "Somebody said you received a telegram. Was it... bad news?"

Nadia handed it to Tasha, who read it and shook her head with sadness.

"I'm so sorry, Nadia. I really am."

Nadia's eyes started to fill with tears, not with the pain of the loss, but with the fear of her predicament that she couldn't even share with her sister. Not yet.

Tasha reached out, thinking she was grieving Ivan's death. "I know your heart will hurt for a while, but I'm here if you need me. And people tell me the pain lessens over time. You should speak to the commander and ask her to give you some time off. I'm sure she'd agree."

Nadia shook her head. "No, I'll be all right. It's better for me to be up in the air with my mind on other things."

"He was a..." Tasha looked for the right words. "...nice man."

"Don't lie, Tasha," Nadia said. "I know you didn't even like him."

Tasha sighed, not even trying to defend that statement. "I know you loved him, though, so I am sad that you are in pain."

They walked to the bonfire that one of the ground crew lit every night, and as the flickers of golden firelight warmed them, they commiserated together.

Nadia remembered how excited she had been knowing she was to be a wife, how Ivan's eyes had shone as he had asked her for her hand in marriage. How at the time she had thought how restrained and respectful he had been towards her by only kissing her gently on the cheek when he proposed. As she looked back, she realized hints of Ivan's true sexuality had always been there. She had just been too blind with her own desires for a home and stability to see it.

She thought of those early days when she had been so

naive. Excited by a man who was so knowledgeable and passionate about his world. Their conversations had been dynamic, filled with his ideals, and that had excited her. They had shared books and ideas, but no affection. She would remember the good times, she decided. As she stared into the firelight, she decided when she looked back she would choose to remember those first days, those first days that had been so full of promise and the friendship they had shared.

Tasha wrapped her arms around her sister's waist and Nadia pulled her close, Tasha's head beneath Nadia's chin, and drawing in a deep breath, inhaled the scent of her sister's hair that was so familiar to her. It made her think of their childhood, and Nadia remembered all the times she had held her sister just like this through all of Tasha's heartaches. Because even though she and Luca had been together forever, as a passionate individual, Tasha had always seemed to be nursing some drama or other. Wiping away her tears of fear of the unknown that suddenly pricked her eyes, she gave her sister one last hug and got to her feet.

"We should go," she whispered. "We have work to do."

Tasha nodded, and with their arms around each other, they moved over to check their aircraft for the evening. That would keep her mind active, making sure that everything was working right for tonight's mission. News about the baby would wait. Wait until Nadia could figure out what she was going to do about it.

41

DECEMBER 1942

Nadia

Nadia had been getting ready to leave for her night mission a few days later when she heard the scream from outside. It came from a couple of tents down from her own. She knew who it was instantly. Rushing outside into the chilly evening air, she saw Tasha down on the ground, on her knees, her body hunched over. All the other girls were starting to peel out of their own tents and surround her as she wailed.

Slipping and sliding on the snow, Nadia rushed to her sister's side, calling towards her. "Tasha, what is it!? Are you in pain!? What's wrong!?" She knelt down in the snow beside her sister and, grabbing her shoulders, she turned her to face her.

As she looked up, Nadia saw it in her face. Her eyes were wild with the pain, the rest of her face screwed up into a ball with agony. Nadia grabbed her sister's chin, trying to steady her as the tears streaming down Tasha's cheeks rolled across Nadia's hands and pooled in her cuffs.

"What is it? What's wrong? You must tell me! Please tell me!" Nadia shouted, trying to get any kind of sense from her.

Tasha just shook her head and doubled over again in pain.

As Nadia tried over and over again to get through, Eva spoke to her in a whisper. "She got a letter from someone at home, and she ripped it open, and then she just screamed. I'm not sure who it was from."

"Is it Babka?" cried out Nadia, her stomach cramping with the fear for their dear, sweet grandmother. "Is she unwell?"

Tasha shook her head fervently.

Taking hold of her hand, Nadia unpeeled Tasha's fingers until she could remove the ball of paper that was screwed up in them. She straightened it out and didn't recognize the hand-writing on the letter, so she scanned it quickly. It was from Luca's father. Luca had gone down over enemy lines and was missing. The plane had been on fire at impact, which was never a good sign. And as they'd not heard from Luca, he was listed as missing, presumed dead.

Nadia's heart tightened with the news. Then, grabbing hold of her sister, she pulled her to her chest, held her tightly as the pain-wracked sobs continued to cause Tasha's body to contort violently.

Tasha finally screamed out words muffled by the tight grip against her sister's shoulder. "No. No. Not Luca."

As Nadia tried to calm her sister, her thoughts went to Luca, the boy she had known all her life too. She'd watched him and Tasha from when they had been small. First, the two of them, imps as children, finding frogs, digging holes, causing trouble. Then, as young adolescents, and firm friends, and finally lovers. He was like a brother to Nadia as well. And her stomach cramped with the pain of the loss. She couldn't imagine it could be true. She signaled to Eva to help her get Tasha back into her tent.

Tasha was almost impossible to move, a dead weight, unable to stand on her feet. They finally managed to get her onto her bed, and someone must have informed their comman-der, because she joined Nadia inside. "You will stay with her,

Nadia, this evening. Stay here tonight. Someone else will lead the squadron. She needs her sister right now."

Nadia looked across to Tasha, who had been thrashing about on the bed in pain and had now curled herself into a ball, her boots and flying suit still on. Nadia was grateful and nodded her agreement. It would have been difficult to lead the squadron with her sister back here in such a state. Her mind would not have been able to concentrate on their mission. She thanked her commander as she exited the tent to arrange cover for Nadia.

Sitting down on the edge of Tasha's bed, she started to peel off her sister's clothes gently. Tasha turned to her, the wildness still evident in her red, watery eyes.

"It's not true!" she screamed at Nadia. "I'll never believe it!"

"You need to calm down, Tasha," she said, cooing gently at her and stroking her hair. Then, pulling wet, matted strands from her warm cheeks, she continued, "You'll make yourself sick."

"I don't care," her sister cried. "My life is over. Do you understand me? My life is now over. He's the reason I'm here. The only reason. And now he's gone and I'll never ever see him again. I'll never be with him again. My body already aches with that thought."

"You can't be sure of that, Tash. He's only missing."

"There was fire! You know what that means."

Nadia did. It meant they had been in real trouble on the way down and probably hit the ground with severe impact.

She tried to calm her sister, dressing her in her night things, bringing her some water, but she couldn't seem to ease her pain or the violent sobs. Finally, after about an hour, Tasha fell into a fitful sleep, more out of exhaustion than ordinary tiredness. Nadia took a moment to stand outside the tent and look up into the sky. It was a good, clear night; the first raid would have already taken place, and the girls would be on their way back. She had chosen this life because of her sister, and her sister had chosen it because of Luca.

What would happen now? Would Tasha be honorably discharged because she couldn't continue her work? Nadia was committed to her unit and her squadron but also, if her sister needed her, what would she do? When she had left home, she had not realized how this new-found freedom and independence would feel and leaving her flying sisters felt like it would be a bigger wrench than leaving her village. She was also scared of what this would mean for Tasha. Her sister was unpredictable enough in good times. How would she be now? This would be a hard reality for her sister to cope with, and Nadia wasn't at all sure how she would get through.

42

Tasha

Tasha lay staring at the corner of her tent, listening to the clumps of snow as they slid down the sides of the roof and dropped to the ground with the heat of the weak winter sun. As she lay there, she tried to feel anything other than the pain that gripped her body like a vice and continued to tighten no matter what she did. Her mind was muddy, a muddle of thoughts through the lack of sleep. She had barely had more than two hours at a time since the news. When she did finally fall asleep with exhaustion, there were the constant nightmares, the many different visions of Luca dying over and over again and her unable to get to him no matter how much she tried. For the first time in her life, she understood how it was possible to die of a broken heart. She had thought when he had signed up she couldn't know a deeper pain but this was excruciating.

As she listened to the latest clump of snow sliding to the ground, the darkness of her thoughts grew in intensity, surrounding her and taunting her, threatening to consume her completely. She even had to will herself to breathe, as though her body had somehow forgotten how to do that naturally. As she rasped air in and out of her weighted lungs, she winced with the soreness of her raw throat, her dry eyes, red and gritty, and her stomach knotted into a solid ball of pain. All she could think about was the man she had lost.

As well as Nadia, Eva, who shared the tent with her, had been wonderful. She had been by her side all the time when she wasn't flying. Holding her hand whenever Tasha needed her. Even fetching a bowl and stroking her hair when she had thrown up after a particularly cruel round of wracking sobs that had overwhelmed her.

It was now the third day from when she had heard that Luca had gone missing, and Tasha knew she needed to get back in the sky. She needed to fly, but she couldn't imagine how she would be able to do that again. Although this was what she was good at, she had ultimately joined up to be with Luca, to be a part of what he was a part of. Now the endless emptiness that stretched before her, days of not having him be in her life, was unfathomable. She wasn't sure if she could fly, but she knew she could not go home. She did not want to face Babka or Luca's parents or be with their friends, certainly not anywhere that would remind her of him.

She felt trapped in her circumstances. The only way forward would be to get back in the air. But she felt so exhausted, so uncoordinated. How would she do it? There was also the feeling of disbelief that constantly consumed her. No matter how many times she reread the letter from Luca's parents or listened to her friends telling her he was only missing, she could not believe that Luca was gone, no longer with his unit, probably dead. It was surreal to her because she had not seen his body; she had not seen anything that would confirm this all to her. And that was very important to her for some reason.

She needed tangible evidence that her boyfriend was no longer around. That thought that consumed her plagued her for the whole three days that she'd been lying in this tent. And as she lay there, she started to develop a plan. Something that would help her, something that would hopefully help her move on from where she was. A way to come to terms with his death, if that's what she needed to do. So as the afternoon moved into the evening on the third day, she pulled herself out of her bed. Her body was still aching from crying. Her throat was still sore. Her eyes were still red. But still, she got into her flying suit. One thing was compelling her forward. One thing only. It was proving once and for all that Luca's plane had come down.

Eva eyed her nervously as she saw her approaching the tent flaps. "Are you sure you are up to this?" Reluctantly Tasha nodded and made her way outside to prepare for the evening.

43

Nadia

Three days after the news that Luca had gone missing, Nadia looked intently at her sister as she exited her tent wearing her flying suit. Tasha had taken a couple of days off to collect herself. But on the third night, she appeared ready to fly. Nadia approached her and asked if she was all right.

"I have to get back in the sky," she said, the seething anger spilling out from her heart. "What else am I to do? Just lie there in my tent every day? I've got to kill the people that killed him."

"Make sure you don't lose your focus, though, Tasha," Nadia cautioned, speaking not only as her sister but also as her squadron leader.

In reply, Tasha gave her a look that implied not to interfere. This was difficult for Nadia, finding the balance between being Tasha's sister and her leader.

They prepared for the next sortie. Nadia would be leading the mission again, flying with her navigator Mila. The other two planes coming with her were Tasha and Eva, and Irina and Katya.

During this run, it was Tasha's job to go in first, light up the sky with the flare, and then Nadia and Irina could get in with their bombs.

Moving across to their planes, Tasha seemed still subdued and incredibly sad, but Nadia hoped being in the air, which she knew her sister loved, and doing what she was so good at would help her restore her spirit again. They got into their cockpits and, taxiing down the field, took off one after another. It was a cold night and Nadia felt an eerie chill that didn't seem to have anything to do with the weather. As they flew towards their target, the collective hum of the engines that was usually calming for Nadia felt eerily like a prelude to a tragedy.

Nadia signaled when they were close to the target, and Tasha and Eva pulled forward to illuminate the run. Irina and Nadia fell in behind as they all moved into position to drop their bombs. Eva sent up the flare, and straightaway, Nadia knew that something was wrong with Tasha. She was usually quite an aggressive flyer, quick to draw fire but easily slipping out of the searchlights' glare. But something was dreadfully wrong with her tonight. It was like she wanted to get hit. She seemed lethargic, slow even. She wondered now if maybe she should have made her stay off another couple of days.

As the target lit up, Nadia throttled back, taking the plane to its low hum, ready to drop her bombs. With a whistle, they were away, and she climbed into the sky. But as she circled around, Tasha was still in the glare of the enemy's searchlights. She was usually fast at maneuvering her way out, ducking and diving with such skill the Germans couldn't keep up with her. But tonight it was as if her plane was on stage; the whole of the plane was lit up.

"Move out of the searchlights," Nadia begged through clenched teeth under her breath. "Come on, Tasha. You can do this."

Her sister banked in a halfhearted way, but it didn't even

free her of the lights. And then, all of a sudden, the sound of the ack-ack guns tore through the night as the Germans peppered the bottom of Tasha's plane. Nadia held her breath. It looked like it hadn't ruptured the fuel line, but something else was wrong. As she drew alongside her sister, she could see that Eva's head was bouncing around in the navigator seat, and she didn't look right. She signaled to Tasha, who told her that Eva had been hit.

"We need to get her back as soon as we can," Nadia signaled in reply.

When they arrived back on the ground, all the girls rushed to the plane and pulled Eva out as Tasha sobbed in front of her. Eva was breathing erratically. She had a wound in her shoulder that was bleeding profusely.

"Quickly, get her into the medical tent!" shouted Nadia.

They started to carefully take her out of the plane and over into the tent.

Tasha was hunched over in her cockpit, her face in her hands. "It's my fault," she said to Nadia. "I shouldn't have flown tonight. You were right."

"You know you will have to get back in the sky," Nadia encouraged.

"I may never be able to do it again. I can't do this, Nadia. I can't do this any more. I've lost my nerve."

As Nadia helped her sister over towards the bonfire to get her warm, as she was shivering, their commander approached to see how Tasha was doing.

Nadia explained the situation, and the commander spoke firmly. "You have to get straight back in the sky, Natasha. Or you'll never go up again. The medics are working on Eva now. She lost a lot of blood but they believe she will live. And if you stop flying now, the Nazis—the very people who may be responsible for Luca's death—will have won. You're one of our best flyers. So you have to find a way to get back in the sky."

"But who will fly with me? Look at them." They looked around the group that had gathered to see what was going on, and no one was coming forward. Everyone was nervous, Eva's blood still on their uniforms, and Tasha did not look as though she was capable of getting into a plane, never mind flying one.

"You have to get your confidence back," said Nadia, taking control. "You can do this."

"But no one will want to fly with me, Nadia."

Everyone looked uncomfortably towards Nadia.

"I'll fly with you," Nadia said without hesitation.

The commander, who had come to discuss this prospect, looked at her. "But we need you on another bombing run."

"I have to do this for Tasha. I'll navigate for her. I trust you," she whispered to her sister. "Do you hear me? I trust you."

The girls all looked at her with admiration, but she wasn't just doing this as their commander or as their squadron leader; she was doing this as Tasha's older sister.

Tasha nodded her head. "Are Eva's controls still working?"

"I think so," said the engineer who had been looking at the damage to the plane.

Before they climbed into the plane, the group discussed the next sortie. This time, just to be safe, Irina would lead with the flare and Nadia and Tasha would drop bombs. Tasha got into the cockpit, and she was shaking violently.

Nadia put a hand on her sister's arm. "You can do this, Tasha. I really do believe in you."

Tasha nodded and put her goggles and cap in place as they started to taxi down the field. She managed a smooth takeoff, and the three of them glided towards the next target.

Tasha was flying a little erratically, but nothing that Nadia much feared. She could hear her sister sobbing in the front seat as they got towards the target. Even though she had wanted to support her sister, she felt a great deal of apprehension. It wasn't just Tasha's heartbreak. There was something else her sister wasn't saying. Nadia had known her for long enough to know her thoughts were intense; she was plotting something and usually, that didn't mean anything good.

44

Nadia

The plane was out of control; Nadia knew it and there was nowhere to go for help. Tasha had taken them over enemy lines to find Luca's plane and now with their tail on fire the smoke caused her eyes to smart and choked the back of her throat. She could barely catch her breath as they barreled to earth. Even clenching the throttle and pulling up as hard as she could did nothing; Nadia could do absolutely nothing to help her sister control the plane—it was in a steep, unrecoverable dive. Seeing the earth coming up so fast to meet them, she sucked in breath and closed her eyes to prepare for the impact.

The first thing that Nadia felt was pain. The whole of her body hurt, and there was a searing ache across her upper arms and chest. Forcing her eyes open, she tried to get her bearings. Instinctively, she placed her hand on her stomach and hoped her baby was okay. Where was she? Something expansive and white was glinting far off in front of her eyes and a tree branch was right in front of her face. She obviously wasn't in her tent back at the base or home in her bed. It was also freezing.

Attempting to move her body gently, she tried to acclimatize herself to where she was. Her legs seemed to be working all right, but the pain in her arm and the pressure on her chest was intense. She realized she was in a plane and it was her harness that was pressing into her body. She would have unbuckled it, but she wasn't sure if she was hanging upside down, and she did not want to fall to the ground.

Slowly she got her bearings. The plane seemed to be wedged into a large tree. There was a nest of raw branches snapped all around her and it was a miracle the plane hadn't burst into flames.

Then it all started to come back to her. She and Tasha had been on a mission. Tasha had gone to find Luca's plane over enemy lines, and then their tail had been hit. They must have crash-landed, ending up in this tree. Realizing she was right side up, Nadia carefully unbuckled her harness, and taking a deep breath that hurt, she clawed her way forward and reached for her sister.

"Tasha," she called out. "Tasha!" Her voice was dry, her throat parched. There was the metallic taste of blood in her mouth. She looked down at her gloves. There was a gash on her hand, and the blood was seeping out up her cuff.

She took hold of her sister's shoulder and tried to shake her. "Tasha, are you all right?"

There was no response.

A horrific thought rushed through her mind, and she was just trying to come to terms with that prospect when she heard a moan from the cockpit.

"Thank God," she exclaimed out loud. "I thought you were dead."

She tore away at the branches surrounding her sister's head, noticing a large gash along Tasha's forehead where she must have hit the front of the airplane on impact.

"Tasha, can you hear me?" she yelled.

"Why," said her sister in a weary rasp, "are you shouting at me, when I'm right here?"

Nadia breathed out a sigh of relief. "We're in a tree, Tasha."

Her sister blinked open her eyes and appeared to try to focus on what was around her. Then, wiping her hand across her head, she noticed the blood and gasped.

"Tasha, are you okay?"

"I think so," Tasha croaked as she started to move her shoulders. "I can't breathe. This harness is gripping me so tightly."

She too released it and let out a sigh of relief. They both looked around the plane as the moon crept from behind a cloud and illuminated the area before them. The aircraft was tipped slightly on its side, sitting in a tree as if they had been placed there like a tree house. One of the wings had snapped off with the impact and was lying on the ground.

Nadia was just trying to figure out their next move when she heard voices. Tasha heard them too and their eyes met, the fear between them obvious. Nadia spoke some German and had always been gifted with languages. And she listened carefully. But with relief she heard her own language. They were talking about the plane's wing on the floor.

"Can you hear what they are saying?" Tasha hissed to her.

"They've seen the wing," she whispered back. "I'm not sure they've seen the plane yet."

Someone called up to them.

"Hello? Is there anybody up there?" said a female voice.

Nadia peered carefully over the side to make sure they weren't Germans trying to trick them and saw three women in their nightclothes, bundled into coats and boots, rows of curlers under headscarves.

"Are you injured?" shouted another voice. "We can help you."

Nadia shook her head at her sister, but Tasha's impulsiveness led the way.

"Can you get a ladder?"

The voices beneath them started talking amongst themselves.

"You are Russian?" asked one of the women.

Then, finally, Nadia shouted down. "We are female Russian pilots. We crashed in this tree. Can you help us?"

"You are the women that fly?" the same woman responded, sounding impressed.

"Yes, we are."

"We will help you down," said another woman in a deeper tone. She sounded older. "My grandson will get a ladder. None of our husbands are here. They're all fighting in the resistance, and so you're safe with us, don't worry. We'll get you down and take care of you."

Nadia and her sister both sighed with relief. Glad that even though they were over enemy lines, the first people to find them had been Russians.

It took about another thirty minutes, but a young lad in pajamas, coat, and boots scaled a rather large ladder then carefully helped them out of their cockpit. They both cried out in pain from their aching bodies and wounds, but slowly they made their way out of the aircraft. Fortunately, apart from a few gashes and the pain of the impact, neither of them seemed to be terribly injured. There were no broken bones.

By the time they reached the ground, slowly and haltingly, the first fingers of dawn were starting to rise above the horizon.

"When they find the plane, they will come and look for you," said one of the women as she placed a blanket around Nadia's shoulders. "We should hide you with us."

They shuffled towards the farm that the women had come from, and after they took them into the farmhouse kitchen and made them tea, Nadia told them their story of who they were. The women were full of admiration and clapped their hands. "I wish they would let all women fight," said one young woman. "War is so ridiculous. We've heard about you. They call you the Night Witches. Did you know that? My husband said all of the German armies are afraid of you. It's very embarrassing for them to be attacked night after night by a group of women."

"Thank you for being so kind to us," Nadia said, taking one of the women's hands.

The woman nodded. "We hate this war. It's ridiculous. I wish we could stop it. Hitler is a crazy man."

The women bandaged their cuts and treated their bruises and gave them some warm food.

"It would be better for you to stay. I'll send word to one of our groups. They can help get you back over the enemy lines. But in the meantime, we'll hide you in the barn. There's a secret room that nobody knows about."

The sisters were taken out there with a pile of blankets and pillows and it didn't take long for them to fall asleep quickly in the warm hay.

When Nadia woke up a few hours later, Tasha had managed to struggle to her feet and had limped to look out of the barn window. Nadia could hear her muffled cry.

"Tash, are you all right? Is something hurting?"

Her sister turned. Tears were streaming down her cheeks, and she shook her head.

"Luca," she mumbled back, a sob catching in her throat. "I can't imagine my life without him, Nadia. I can't believe he's dead."

Nadia got to her feet to go to her sister's side, putting her arm around her. "Nobody said he's dead. He's listed as missing. People come back."

"You saw the wreckage of Luca's plane, didn't you?" Tasha responded. "No one can come back from that kind of crash."

"We just did," Nadia said, trying to be optimistic.

"I'm scared. I can't *feel* him any more. I always used to be able to feel him, but now I can't feel anything."

"You've been through a shock. You have to fight these

negative feelings. It's possible Luca is alive, and if he is, we will find him."

"You don't feel pain about Ivan?"

Nadia swallowed down hard. "Of course I feel incredibly sad, but I just don't think about it. I put it to the back of my mind because there's nothing I can do about it. I just do whatever needs to be done right in the moment."

Tasha shook her head. "I'll never understand how you can always be so sensible." She slipped her arm around her sister's waist, Nadia having joined her at the barn window, and the two of them held each other, watching a group of geese honk their way across the frozen wasteland.

"Nadia?"

"Yes?"

"I'm sorry. I should have gone straight back to camp. You were right."

"Shh," Nadia responded. "It's too late for regrets. We're here now and we need to come up with a plan to get back into unoccupied territory."

45

Nadia

They stayed at the farmhouse for over a week, sleeping in the barn to gather their strength and let their wounds heal. Then, through contacts in the resistance, the grandson brought news that there had been some German troop movement and there were fewer soldiers active in this area now. They agreed to leave the next night, but realized they would miss their new friends. Each night, the older women had gathered around the farmhouse fire in the evenings, to sing songs, and tell stories, which had made Tasha and Nadia miss their grandmother so much it brought tears to their eyes.

The next day the women gave them some of their own clothes and a parcel of food.

"We will bury your uniforms in the garden so no one will find them. Then, one of the resistance groups will show you the way."

The sisters nodded their thanks and hugged the women as the following evening they began their journey.

At nightfall, a band of older men and some not old enough to fight called at the farmhouse. The only clothes the women had were about two sizes too big for the sisters, and the shoes already well-worn. They were getting used to wearing clothes too big for them. As they followed cautiously alongside the group, they hardly spoke, both preoccupied with their own thoughts. Nadia was thinking about the baby growing inside her, and her sister, she knew, was thinking about Luca. Every so often, a sob would escape her as tears ran freely down her cheeks. Nadia would squeeze her arm or hug her, and they would nod their understanding to one another as they continued their slow journey to a place that the resistance felt was secure.

The night was cold, and they felt great apprehension as they approached the lines where, ironically, they could hear the sounds of battle as their sister pilots dropped bombs on their enemy all along the line.

An older man with no front teeth and drooping eyes put his finger to his lips to signify they needed to be quiet. They all dropped to the ground. Not far from their position, two German soldiers had been spotted walking in the woods. With her heart beating like a drum in her ears, Nadia attempted to hold her breath, but Tasha shifted position, and a twig broke below her.

The Germans stopped talking and looked in their direction. Both sisters buried their heads into the undergrowth, hoping they couldn't be seen. Nadia listened to the Germans' conversation. One talked about rabbits and whether they could catch one, as they both were hungry. The other soldier did not seem enthusiastic, saying he didn't feel like setting a trap.

It was dark and cold. Nadia looked at the white of the men's eyes around her. The fear was palpable between them all as she thought about these men that were risking their lives for her. Then, finally, the soldiers started to move away, and they stayed in their position for what felt like forever, waiting for the resistance leader to tell them what to do.

Catlike, he got to his feet, nodded his head, and motioned

them all on. Slowly they started to creep through the grass, moving stealth-like towards the line. Then, all at once, a light flicked on and blinded Nadia. She turned to run. But before she could go any further, someone had taken hold of her roughly, and she heard her sister scream by her side.

Suddenly, there was a rattle of bullets in the darkness, and she turned quickly. Still blinded by the light, she couldn't see what was happening. *Oh God*, had her sister been shot? The two men holding her had her so tightly gripped that she could not see behind her, nor even perform any of the self-defense that she had learned.

A German officer approached her. "Who are you?" he asked roughly.

"We are just simple women," she said. "We are just looking for mushrooms. We are starving."

Suddenly she was aware that Tasha was being dragged to her side. Thank God she hadn't been struck by the bullets, but behind her, lying on the grass was the man that had led them, drooping eyes open and fixed, his gappy mouth hanging limp. Beside him the soldiers kicked at his body, to check that he was dead, confirming to their officer he was one of the resistance fighters they had been looking for.

"You are just women out looking for mushrooms, in the snow with Russian resistance fighters?" he said, an obvious irony in his tone.

Nadia's heart skipped a beat. As the guard held a rifle up towards them, grabbing hold of Tasha, the officer yanked off her headscarf and nodded his head.

"You are the women we're looking for. We found your plane. You're the Russian female pilots that came down. Aren't you?"

Nadia shook her head. "No, sir, we are German. I don't know what you're talking about. Pilots? We're just women that live here."

"So why do you look so well? Your hands show no signs of

hard work and you're out with our enemy. You're lying. I think my commander will be very pleased to see you," he said, gesturing with his pistol for them to move.

Two hours later, the sisters found themselves imprisoned in a makeshift jail in a German military camp. Being behind bars after having the freedom of the whole sky was suffocating. Tasha suddenly raced towards the door and battered it with her fists. Quickly Nadia pulled her away.

"Stop, Tasha, please. They will hurt you!"

She looked into her sister's eyes that were wild with her reaction to their situation and their incarceration.

"I can't breathe, Nadia; my chest is shutting down. I need to get outside so I can breathe!"

Nadia grabbed hold of her sister's face, staring intently into Tasha's eyes.

"You have got to calm down, Tasha," she snapped harshly, "or you will get their attention. Stop fighting and breathe; breathe slowly." Tasha's eyes were still wild, but she eased into her younger sister role, doing exactly what Nadia told her as she guided her through her panic, until she was breathing more easily.

They sat down on the bunk, as Nadia held her sister, whose face was ashen.

Her voice was childlike, scared. "I'm so sorry, Nadia. This is all my fault."

Nadia shook her head. "It was a long shot, anyway."

"What do you think they'll do with us?" asked Tasha.

"I don't know."

"I don't care any more," stated Tasha in her usual dramatic fashion.

Nadia placed her arm around her shoulders, aware of the pain her sister was in and the regret she felt. She considered telling Tasha about the baby, but didn't want to add any further to her guilt. "At least we're here together." She pulled her close as they sat huddled on their bunk that smelled of urine in their dark, dank cell, and Nadia thought about her baby and wished she was home.

———

Very early the following day, they were pulled roughly from their cell—two heavy German officers dragging them by the arms.

"Don't forget to let me talk," hissed Nadia.

Tasha nodded as she tried to blink her eyes awake with the stark morning light after being in such a dark cell all night. They were forced in front of another army commander writing at his desk, impeccably dressed and stolid. He wrote for a second before putting down his pen and looking up at the pair of them. His slowly studied them before he sat back in his chair and let out a deep sigh.

"So, you are the Russian pilots who have been terrorizing our troops, are you?"

Nadia spoke. "I don't know what you're talking about, sir. We're just simple women that live here and work every day."

"Is that so?" he said with a smirk. "Why are you wearing clothes that are too big for you?"

"My sister and I have had little food because of the war, and we've lost a great deal of weight. That's no crime, I take it. So why are we being held?"

"You're being held because you're lying to me," he spat out. "And why does she not speak?"

"She is very simple, sir. She doesn't know many words."

"She knows how to speak in Russian," he said in their native tongue.

Tasha flicked up her eyes at his words.

As the man stood to his feet and placed his hand behind his back, he started to pace up and down the room. "We have been waiting a long time to capture one of you. And now I have two. You've become very annoying to our troops. You must be punished. I have spoken to my high command, and we are in agreement. As much as I am supposed to shoot you..."

Nadia swallowed at the words.

"...you may be more use to us in one of our prisoner of war camps. In case we need to bargain you off one day. Meanwhile, your disappearance will hopefully send a clear message to the rest of the women in your unit who continue to bombard us."

Nadia tried again: "But we have families, sir. We live here. We have children. You cannot keep us here. I don't know anything about these Russian pilots you talk about. We are just simple women."

He turned and glared at her. "Don't lie to me and waste my time any more. You fit exactly the description of the women we are looking for. Your hair is short, which you have cut for your unit. You don't have the hands of working women. Your fingernails are too clean. And your faces aren't weathered enough."

"We have been sick, I told you. We cut our hair when it became too much to bear with our fevers."

"Take them away," he growled as the two guards came forward and again started to bustle them towards the cells. "You will go out on the next train."

"I'm begging of you," Nadia cried, "what about my family?"

"You should have thought of that before you chose to be a pilot and kill people. When you made yourself part of this war. You will surrender as a soldier would. We will find a good use for you."

46

Tasha

Tasha and Nadia were held, formally charged, and then told they were to be sent to a work camp in Germany. The next day they were taken by truck to a train station, then they were herded onto what was little more than a cattle train, with many other Russian prisoners.

"Where are we going?" demanded Tasha.

The soldier in charge responded by grabbing her arm and pushing her harder into the car. "You don't speak. You're a prisoner now. You just do as you are told," he spat as he shoved her toward her sister.

The Nazis continued to load the train until it was packed. The two were freezing in their thin, borrowed peasants' clothes. There was nowhere to sit, no chairs, and a row of open windows at the top of the wooden carriage, which gave a little ease of air, but also created a freezing draft. Tired-looking Russian soldiers, some wounded, were also stuffed into the car until it was so full they could barely move. Sliding down the wall and sitting on the floor, Tasha felt her heart sink. This was all her fault, and as usual, she'd pulled Nadia into it as well.

She thought about the resistance fighter, lying on the ground, his eyes glassed and fixed, and then of the man that Luca had told her he'd shot. The harshness of war, though it had been all around her, had never really been brought home to her like it was now. She'd watched it from above like an eagle or heard of it from others, but she hadn't been in combat face-to-face as many of the soldiers around her had. And it felt terrifying.

Nadia slid down and sat next to her sister, squeezing her hand. She placed her head on Nadia's shoulder, and Nadia put her arm around her.

"At least we're still together," Nadia said.

"I'm amazed you even want to talk to me. This is all my fault."

Nadia smiled. "Yes, it is. But you certainly know how to keep life interesting. If it weren't for you, I'd still be cleaning a house and wondering what to do with my life. At least this way, I get to see a little of the world. Even the difficult parts."

The train set off and rattled on. They looked out of the window together into the sky, and though Nadia didn't say it, Tasha knew she was thinking the same as she was. What were the girls doing today? Preparing for tonight? Meeting together around the fire? Did they wonder about where Nadia and Tasha were? Had they raised a glass of vodka to them as they had for Liliya and Katya? Who was flying the head of the formation? Where were they dropping bombs this evening?

The trip into the heart of German territory was not only uncomfortable, but very long, with little in the way of food or water. When food or water was thrown in, they would grab for it eagerly, fighting to get some of it from the dirty wooden pail. Nadia would also spoon some to the injured soldiers. One Russian soldier, called Anton, sat by their side and told them the story of his family, his beautiful wife, and his daughter.

"I hope one day she will grow up and be as brave as you and your sister are," he said to Nadia as she offered him water.

He was from a village not far from theirs, and Tasha thought she knew or had heard of one of his aunties. It seemed so strange to all be captured together like this.

The train rattled on for days, or that was how it felt. Night and then day and then night again. People even died in the carriage as they traveled. There was nowhere to sleep and definitely nowhere to bury their dead. Their own pain was minor in comparison to the stories of some of the soldiers. And some who had been thought strong enough to travel were practically dying from their wounds. They tried to help when they could, but a sense of fear and hopelessness permeated the whole carriage, as if they were all just lambs being led to the slaughter. Nobody knew where they were going to. They just knew that every mile took them farther away from what they'd known as home, into a country and to an army that was known to be savage and harsh in their treatment of Russian prisoners.

When they finally arrived, it was early evening and so much worse than they could ever have imagined. High barbed wire fences surrounded the camp, and the feeling of despair leaked out to greet them. Tasha could almost cut it with a knife. They were forced at gunpoint to the gate and thrust inside, the men separated off to one side and the women to the other.

They were paraded in front of the barracks, rows of dark-brown buildings that smelled of mold and mildew, and something worse: human sweat and suffering. They were assigned their hut and tentatively made their way into the darkened room, where they could make out clusters of rough wooden bunks, one on top of the other. Tasha grabbed her sister's hand, and the reality of where they were suffocated her.

"Nadia." Her voice was stringy and high-pitched, the distress palpable between them. Tears started to stream down Tasha's face. "I'm so sorry, Nadia. I'm so, so sorry."

From out of the darkness came a voice. For a moment, she thought it was in her head, but then Tasha heard it again.

"Save your tears. You will need them for the harder days you are to face. Now it is time to find your strength while you still have nutrition in your body and the memory of hope in your heart."

Tasha looked around the room to see where it was coming from. Now that her eyes were acclimating to the dark, she noted they were not alone. There were clusters of raggedly dressed bodies in the bunks, many fearful eyes looking out towards them. Then, out of the darkness, a woman approached them. She was of Slavic descent, but she looked nothing like them. Her hair was tied behind in a scarf, her eyes of the most piercing blue. When she stared at them, Tasha felt she was staring right into her very soul. Her clothes were odd and homemade, but like nothing that Tasha had ever seen before. She sidled toward them, eyeing them as a dog would eye a stray.

Are you friendly? she was asking. She looked them up and down, and then a smile moved across her lips. "I'm Gaia; I suppose I'm your welcoming committee," she said, moving towards them, holding out a weather-worn hand. She took Nadia's and Tasha's in her own. "If hell is a place on earth, then surely this is it. But hell is just a name, and it can only mean that to you if you allow it."

The sisters looked at her, bemused. What did she mean?

"You will learn many things while you are here, but more than anything, you will learn how to survive, and that is the most important." She ran her knobbly finger down Tasha's cheek. "Do not cry, little one."

"Where are we?" asked Nadia in a quivering voice.

"You are in Wiesenberg slave labor camp. They have brought us all here, those of us that are not Jewish. Trust me, from what I hear, this is luxury compared to what our Jewish brothers and sisters are dealing with."

"Why are you here?" asked Tasha.

The woman did not look like she was of fighting age. She was elderly.

"Why am I here? I'm here for you, my dear. That's what I choose to believe. I'm here to get you through. But how I got here is because, unfortunately, I was blessed with Romany blood. And just like you, we are not acceptable by Hitler. The rest of my family in the Romany camp died, so they put me in here.

"Come, I will show you where you can sleep. You'll soon get used to the hardness. The coldness, however, the fear, and the hopelessness, those are something completely different, things you will have to fight to overcome here every day. But you will survive because that is your only choice."

The girls followed her, and though they were afraid, they were also calmed by her words.

She showed them a bunk. "You are fortunate that Maria died yesterday, just in time to leave you somewhere to sleep. You will want to sleep together. It is warmer that way."

They nodded as they looked down at the hard, wooden bunk bed and gingerly moved onto it. They didn't even undress as they pulled the blanket over them and huddled close together, shivering, ready to spend their first night in the camp.

47

Nadia

The day after they arrived, the Germans put them to work in one of their own factories. They got up early for the roll call, where they stood in the freezing cold huddled together, answering to the call of their names. Then they were marched out the big metal gates into the town by guards. In one of the many factories that were there, Tasha and Nadia were commissioned to work on German winter uniforms.

The factory was also a mill, with the scent of clean cotton, linens, and sewing machine oil. The sound inside the factory was deafening, with row upon row of machinists tap-tap-tapping their way through uniform after uniform that they were making for their enemy. The building was enormous and was very cold and drafty. Nadia would try and wrap pieces of fabric around her hands to keep them from freezing as she worked on her machine.

They sat in long lines and had to work very long hours. But occasionally, when the German guards weren't walking up and down the line, they would stop and talk to one another for a short period of time. Nadia, Tasha, and Gaia were all close together. Gaia behind them, Tasha and Nadia side by side. One afternoon they sat back on their chairs as Nadia rubbed her thumb across her tender fingertips. She found this work challenging, the fabric coarse and unyielding, the work relentless.

"I'm so sick of looking at gray," Tasha said, days later. "How can there be this many people out there that we have to make these uniforms for? This is crazy. I'm so restless. I hate using my hands like this. I'm just not skilled in this kind of work. Why couldn't I work with their planes? I could have done that work. But, instead, this is tedious and monotonous."

"At least you are indoors," responded Gaia. "There are people out there digging ditches, or working in bomb factories where there is a constant danger. Here, at least, we are warm and dry."

"I only wish we had more food, though," said Nadia wistfully. "I had no idea how painful it could be being hungry day after day."

Gaia shrugged her shoulders. "We count our blessings when we can. Then we deal with what we have to."

Their conversation was interrupted by the sound of footsteps and they quickly bowed their heads over their machines again as one of the guards called their attention. Alongside him, their new foreman, Herr Müller, had come to introduce himself. He was a gently spoken German with cherub-like blond curls and blue eyes. He looked as if he would be more suited to being a poet or a history teacher than working in a factory, Nadia mused as she looked at him. He was pretty nervous as he spoke, explaining that he had been brought here from another factory to work with them all and, though they were all prisoners, that he would treat them with respect. The guard harrumphed at his comment as he even finished his little speech with a few words in halting Russian.

Then he smiled awkwardly and blushed a little before he left them.

Tasha beamed at the others. "He looks like he'll be easy to manipulate," she stated mischievously.

Nadia thought the same thing, but she wasn't about to trust any of them.

———

It was a week later that she got to find out for herself They had to eat in small groups and outside in the cold only, where the Germans gave them minuscule amounts of food. Tasha had gone with Gaia and two of the other women in the first group, and Nadia, wanting to finish something first before joining the second group, was alone at her sewing machine when a needle broke and the fabric got caught. She swore under her breath. Then the machine jammed completely. The new foreman heard the engine grinding and came over to investigate.

"It is Nadia, no?"

Nadia dropped her head and nodded, trying not to make eye contact as she had already seen what the wrong look could get from a guard in a bad mood hell-bent on punishing a woman.

"Let me look at that for you." He had delicate white fingers as he started to work the wheel back and forth, trying to free the material that had become caught, as Nadia looked for a needle to replace it.

"Such a pretty name you have. What does it mean?"

She looked up at him in surprise. "I'm not sure in German, but in Russian it means 'hopeful.'"

He smiled as he looked at her.

"It suits you. You have to remain hopeful. Mine is Hans. It means 'gift from God.' That's a lot to live up to." He chuckled, raising his eyebrows slightly.

Taken by his friendliness, she suddenly felt quite brazen.

"Why are you here?" she asked.

He blinked a couple of times at her and then looked away in the distance, as though he was thoughtful and afraid of saying anything that might get him into trouble. He appeared to choose his words carefully.

"Bad circumstances brought me here. They forced me to fight in the war. But war doesn't really suit my..." He looked for the right word, and she understood.

"Temperament?" she suggested.

He laughed. "Yes, that's right, temperament. Before the war, I worked creating beautiful soft furnishings for extravagant houses. It was a job that was very fulfilling to me. Then this war came along, and I was conscripted. Then, during an attack, my leg was injured, as you see with my limp, and so I've been put to work in our factories."

"You have no family?" asked Nadia.

He became quiet, his voice barely above a whisper. "My wife was killed two years ago with my young son in an air raid," he confided, swallowing down the pain that was still obvious on his face. "It has been a..." He looked for the right words again. "...lonely time. So many of us have lost loved ones." He nodded towards the white mark on her finger where the guards had taken her wedding ring when they stripped her of her possessions. "You are also married?"

"I was. My husband was killed a couple of months ago."

His face was crestfallen. "I'm so sorry to hear that." He covered her hand with his own. "It is a bitter pill that is hard to swallow."

She didn't like to tell him that Ivan's death hadn't been so hard for her, because she didn't want to admit what their marriage had been, but she felt stirred by this man's hand covering her own. Her enemy, a German. He must have realized straightaway that it was inappropriate because he pulled it away and apologized, his face blushing red as he continued to repair her machine.

He left her then, but she thought about him all day. How so many people, on both sides, were caught up in a war they didn't want to be a part of. But everyone was just a human being reaching out for connection, wanting to be loved and to love. It was easy when you were on the other side of a gun or above the sky in a plane filled with bombs to see the enemy as ruthless, harsh, something that needed to be dealt with, but looking into Hans's eyes, she'd seen his humanity, and it had really touched her.

The next day he arrived at her machine at the same time, and she felt a little awkward as he approached her. Looking around to make sure they were alone, he furtively handed her an apple.

"I noticed that you are having a baby, aren't you?"

She blushed with the confession. Tasha hadn't even noticed, she had kept it so well hidden. They were dealing with so much she couldn't bear her sister's sadness if she lost the baby, as she feared she might on their meager rations. She looked at him for an answer.

"My wife had the same look about her face when she was pregnant with my son, Jacob. I hope you don't mind, but you should eat more food than they are giving you here."

She nodded, grateful for anything.

After that, each day, he would secretly bring her food, a little cheese or bread, and slip it onto her machine when the others weren't at their stations. She was grateful for it and would've wanted to share it with Tasha, but then she'd have to explain where it had come from. She justified it by the fact that she was feeding her baby, and that was important.

A few weeks after their friendship began, she was inside sewing as usual during the first group of the girls' lunchtime, and just as he approached her, the air raid sirens went off. Before they had time to get to the shelter that was at the far end of the factory, bombs started to drop all around them, the whole building crashing and shuddering with the impact. The Allies were obviously dropping bombs right on their factory.

Quickly, he grabbed her arm and pulled her into a side room, which had stacks of bolts of fabric for the uniforms.

"You'll be safer in here," he shouted as he pulled her beneath a fabric shelf. It felt safe but barely had room for the two of them. Nadia could feel his breath on her cheek as they sat side by side and waited for the bombs to stop dropping. With one particularly loud bomb, she couldn't help but scream out, and he put his arm around her and pulled her close to him.

"Do not be afraid, Nadia. Continue to be hopeful. We will get through this."

She wanted to pull away—this wasn't right—but his arm was comforting around her, and she could hear the genuine care in his voice, smell the clean-scented soap on his cheek. The bombs continued to rain down until it became silent, and then they couldn't move until the all-clear. As they sat in the aftermath of the bombing, she didn't feel she could move, and she wasn't sure she wanted to.

As they sat there, he started to talk about his life and asked her about her own. He told her how he played the clarinet. And she spoke about how her father used to do the same. He spoke with fondness about his son and his wife. He also talked about his loneliness.

"It's hard to go home to an empty house every night. I miss my Greta so much. She was a quiet, happy soul, very simple in many ways, but she was the light of my life. The only mercy is that she and Jacob were taken together. He will have his mother in the afterlife, and she will have comfort, but it has left a hole in my heart that is hard to fill."

Nadia nodded and turned to look at him. He was so warm to be around, his eyes filled with genuine kindness. As she sat waiting, she started to feel something for him, even though she was fighting it, and she thought about what Tasha had told her, about being drawn to someone in an uncontrollable way.

It scared her and she needed to put some distance between them. "Do you think it's safe to leave yet?" she asked.

"We should wait for the all-clear," he said sensibly.

She shuddered.

"You are cold? I'll get a blanket for you."

She shook her head to protest, but he was having none of it as she continued shivering. It wasn't with the cold, though, just with the closeness of his body to hers and the feeling of acceptance and warmth after so much sadness and cruelty.

When the all-clear sounded, she hastily made her way back into the main factory building, wanting to check on Gaia and Tasha.

Inside the main room, the factory was in great disarray, and they were all ordered back to the camp while firefighters put out fires and dealt with the bomb damage.

As they lined up to leave, she looked surreptitiously across at Hans, who nodded and smiled gently to her. Then she felt something clench in her stomach, a connection. The same sort of connection that she had so desperately wanted with Ivan. But she felt instantly guilty. He was their enemy, and because of that, there was no chance of anything happening between them. But still, it felt good. It felt good to feel cared for, even in this small way.

As they marched to the camp, she thought all the way back of the words he'd said to her, the stories of his family, his life before the war, his love of music, and the way that he had talked to her, and she wondered what would come of it. Was it possible for love to bloom in such a strange circumstance during such a difficult time? She wasn't sure, but she had a feeling she was going to find out.

48

Nadia

As the days wore on, Nadia found herself being more and more attracted to Hans. The other guards were cruel and seemed to enjoy the brutality that they inflicted on the prisoners day after day. But Hans, not being a guard or even a Nazi but just someone also forced to do what was expected of him, seemed so different in comparison.

He would bring her something extra to eat every day, as the German guards and supervisors were given a little more food. Even though, on the whole, because of the war, food was becoming ever more strictly rationed, he still would halve anything he had with her. And as much as she wanted to reject his offer, she enjoyed their connection and reminded herself she had to feed her baby. They would always have just a few minutes between shifts. Tasha's group would move out to eat. And when Nadia's group was called, she would hang back just for a couple of minutes before the other team came back to start work for the afternoon.

It was amazing how much they packed into those few minutes. Sometimes they would simply gaze into one another's eyes, and he would hold her hand. The feeling of connection for Nadia was what she lived for every day in this dark and dreary world. With hard twelve-hour working days, lack of food, and uncomfortable beds, it was a moment of bliss she could count on every day. He often wrote her letters, which she would slip beneath her clothes to read later in bed when all the girls were asleep. In his letters, he told her more about his life, how he thought about her all the time, and how he too lived for the moments when they were together. She still hadn't told Tasha about her relationship with Hans, even though it was pretty innocent at this point. She wasn't sure how Tasha would feel. She had great animosity toward the Germans as a people, especially since Luca's plane had come down. She blamed all of them for his death.

But Nadia could see past that. Yes, Hans was living in the country where the Nazis were in power, and yes, he worked for them. But in his letters, he was also telling her of the terrible oppression that they all felt. The fear of speaking out against Hitler, and the fear about every neighbor or friend, and whether they would report you if any of your speech was not edifying to the Führer.

She was touched when he painted her a watercolor of a field of flowers in one of his letters. She hadn't realized how much she'd missed the beauty of life. It wasn't as though being in the camp with her squadron was full of art and poetry, but they'd had their times when they were together as a group. They had embroidered, painted or danced; they had written stories that they would share around the bonfire with the rest of the unit.

There was no time for that in this work camp. They got up so early and were marched out here for twelve-hour workdays, until their fingers sometimes bled, and were always just fed that same small bowl of soup with carrots or turnips in it, on which they were expected to survive.

Then, one day, when all the girls were leaving for their

lunch, he approached her and said gruffly within earshot of the guards, "Prisoner, I'm not happy about your work. You will stay and do your job correctly."

The guard nodded, smiling his approval as though he thought Hans was finally starting to learn how to treat the prisoners in the way that was expected.

Once they were gone, he really opened up to her. "Nadia, I need you to know, I've never felt feelings like this, not even for my wife. And she was the kindest and most wonderful of people. But the feelings I have inside for you are so strong. I think about you all day and imagine what we could do if we were alone together. I know it is wrong to have these thoughts. I know you are grieving your husband, and I am grieving my wife. But there is such small joy during this time. And honestly, I don't think Germany will win the war. Things are not going well for the Führer, and I don't know what that will mean for my country. I don't know what that would mean for us. You are Russian. I am German. Where would we even live if there was a future for us? I cannot think about these things because it is too hard. But I want you to know, I have these feelings for you."

She couldn't help herself. Lifting her fingers, she ran them down his cheek and cupped his chin. He leaned into her hand and sighed.

Reaching out slowly towards her, he brushed his hand down her arm and took her fingers gently in his own. Just that tiny act, with her body being so heightened in her attraction, caused her desperately to want more from him, the power of her feelings coursing through her body, and her heart was trying to beat out of her chest. Without a second thought, she leaned forward and kissed him on the lips. In response, he caught his breath. Then, enveloping her in his arms, he pulled her close, gently. She felt safe and secure. The feeling of being in his arms brought her such a moment of heightened bliss that she hadn't thought was possible. The whole of her body shook with the sheer joy and adrenalin that was running through it.

All at once, she heard a voice. Quickly pulling away from him, she knew who it was. "Get your hands off my sister!" screamed Tasha aggressively as she came towards him to attack him. "You Germans think you can do what you like with us. Well, you won't rape my sister. Not unless it's over my dead body."

Before Nadia had time to explain anything, Tasha had pushed Hans with such force he was thrown down to the floor, cracking his head on a machine on the way down. Nadia, without thinking, jumped down and kneeled beside him.

"Hans, are you all right? Hans, are you hurt?"

Tasha blew out air with shock and surprise. "Nadia, what are you doing? Take your hands off him. I won't let him touch you again."

Hans looked petrified and winded as Nadia cradled him and noticed there was a cut on the back of his head seeping through his blond hair, sticking his curls down to the back of his neck. "You're injured. You must have caught your head."

Tasha spoke again. "Nadia, what are you doing?"

Nadia looked up into her sister's eyes and saw the confusion and anger there, mingled with the adrenalin still running through her body.

Then Tasha realized. "You're with him?" she spat out with such vehement anger it chilled Nadia to the bone. "You're with a Nazi? You *wanted* him to kiss you?"

Nadia jumped up, as Tasha was getting louder. "Quiet, Tasha. Keep your voice down. Hans is not a Nazi. He's just like us. He's just a German. Many of the Germans have been forced to do this, just as we have been."

"He's our enemy, though," Tasha shot back.

"Just because he's German citizen doesn't make him our enemy."

"These are the people who killed your husband, who

killed Luca. And you have your hands on him and kissing him, so that's all fine, is it?"

"Hans didn't kill anybody." She got back down to the floor to attend to his wound, dabbing at it with a spare piece of cotton she pulled off from one of the sewing machines.

Tasha started to pace up and down. "Nadia, I can't believe you. I can't believe you would do this to the memory of your husband."

"Ivan is dead. Nothing that will happen from now on will bring him back."

"But this man is German!"

"But I really care for him," Nadia said, realizing it was the first time she'd confessed it, even to Hans. She looked down at him, gauging his expression, and saw joy cross his face as he spoke.

"And I really care for your sister. Please do not be angry with us." He slowly pulled himself to his feet and held out his hand to her. "I know how this must look for you, Tasha. But I love your sister. I've loved her for a long time. If I could, I would marry her tomorrow and be a father to her child."

Tasha stopped pacing and stared at her sister. "What?"

Nadia felt her stomach clench. This was not how she wanted to tell her sister she was pregnant.

"You're pregnant with this man's child?"

Nadia shook her head. "No, nothing has happened here. I'm pregnant with Ivan's child. I have been for five months. When I went back to take care of him. Do you remember?"

"And you never told me? We've been together all this time, and you never told me that you were pregnant?"

"I was afraid, Tasha, of you giving me your food, or..." She tried to find the words, but Tasha blurted it out.

"You were afraid that I would protect you and your baby at the cost of my own life."

Nadia didn't say anything, but her expression confirmed her sister's words.

Suddenly the room was starting to fill up with the other workers. They all looked in surprise from one sister to the other, and Hans, who was still holding the piece of cloth to his head where he was bleeding.

Nadia turned to him. "You should get that seen to."

A guard came in. "What is going on here? What has happened here?"

"I slipped and fell," said Hans. "Nadia and Tasha were helping me."

"Is that what happened?" said the guard, staring at Tasha.

She looked down at the floor and nodded. "My sister has some first-aid training. She was taking care of him."

"You should go to the infirmary and have that checked out," said the guard as he pointed a gun towards the two girls. "The rest of you settle down."

For the rest of the afternoon, Tasha did not speak to Nadia. All day, until they were alone in the hut. It was only later that she finally turned to her in the bed next to her.

"I just can't get over it, Nadia. How could you do this?"

Nadia turned over to face her. "How can you say that? Out of all people, I thought you would understand. The feelings I have for Hans are feelings I never had for Ivan. It's so strong it pulls me towards him whenever I see him, and I want to be in his arms all the time. And I know it's the wrong time and the wrong place, but—"

"There is no future for you, Nadia. How could this go on?"

"I don't know. But is it so wrong to want to be loved, particularly at this time? We will probably die in here of starvation or the diseases that keep coming to the camp. He brings me food and I have to protect my child."

Tasha pulled her sister close and put her arms around her. "I can't believe you're pregnant. Oh my God. You're having my little niece or nephew. Nadia, I so wish this had been under better circumstances." Tears started to roll down Tasha's cheeks. "I wanted this for you for so long. And I know it's what you wanted. But what hope have we in here?"

Nadia smiled. "We have to have hope, even with everything that's going on. Hans brightens my life every day. And now that you know about the baby, I can share the food with you."

Tasha shook her head. "No. You will keep the food for your baby, and we will do everything to protect you. Because if they find out, they will either make you get rid of it, or they will take it from you to one of those horrible orphanages they have here. We'll work together to protect you every day."

They were quiet for a moment. Then Tasha spoke again. "I still can't believe that you care for him."

"I just wanted... I wanted what you had, and now I have it, and it's amazing. I know it's not perfect, that it's not right. But it's amazing."

Tasha hugged her. "It is. And I can't be angry with you for that. I wish you love, Nadia. I always have. I know it'll be hard for me to come to terms with it, but if you need me, I'll be here for you as you always have been here for me."

49

Nadia

It was three days later that Hans approached her as they were all busy at their machines. "Prisoner Kozlov, I need to speak to you now," he snapped.

All around Nadia, machines stopped. Their foreman had never asked them for a moment of their time before. They were nothing but worker bees, invisible, anonymous, forced to sew from morning till dusk.

Nadia stopped sewing; her face flushed. She glanced at her sister, whose eyes had narrowed in that way that she did when she disapproved.

She cleared her throat. "Yes, certainly, Herr Müller. If I can be of any help."

His face reddened too. And, nodding, he bowed his head and walked towards his office at the back of the room.

Nadia did not look at her sister again. She didn't need to; she could feel her eyes boring into the back of her neck. She didn't care that she disapproved. She didn't care about anything any more.

When she reached the office, he closed the door behind

her, and she looked around. It was a depressing space—a large gray cement-brick room, with no natural light, except from a few tiny dirty windows at the top of one wall. Stacked high all around it were bolts and bolts of German army uniform fabric. One roll was laid out on his desk, still new in its brown wrapping.

She looked over at him, and when their eyes met, she heard him hitch his breath, and in response, her heart began thumping in her chest. Averting his gaze to break the spell, he moved towards the table.

"I feel that this fabric is not up to our usual quality, and I... I wanted your opinion."

She heard a slight tremor in his voice as he cleared his throat. She moved toward the table and stood next to him. Their shoulders brushed lightly, and as they did, she felt what was like electricity running through her whole body.

Reaching forward with a trembling hand, she picked up the fabric between her finger and thumb and started to rub it.

"It feels thin to me. What do you think?" he continued.

She had no idea what she thought. All she could think about was how everything inside her was alive and desperate to be closer to him. Finally, she forced down the emotion in her chest to clear her throat to speak. But when she did, her voice was willowy, just a thread of what it usually was.

"It feels fine to me, Herr Müller."

"Ah," he said, "maybe I was mistaken."

Their eyes met again, and gently he covered her hand with his, and she turned to face him fully.

"Nadia," he gasped, "Nadia, I'm so sorry about what happened. I don't know what came over me. It was wrong. You are a married woman. I am so, so sorry."

"But my husband is dead," she replied, unable to stand the look of guilt on his face any longer. Then unable to hold back her feelings any more, she pulled him towards her, her lips finding his in a passionate kiss.

If she thought the electricity was intense when his body was next to hers, or during their gentle kiss days before, she had not been prepared for how it would feel when she was kissing him this way. It was animalistic. Everything inside of her powerfully wanted him. She had never felt anything like it.

Responding to her kiss, he pulled her behind one of the shelves that hid them from the door. "Just in case," he panted.

She nodded and found herself doing things powered by the intense emotion.

Before she knew it, she had stripped off his brown foreman's coat and had started to unbutton his shirt, noticing as she did that it was buttoned incorrectly. It made her smile. This was the sort of thing she found adorable about him. Ivan would never have allowed anything like that to happen in his life.

Before she knew it, the buttons were undone, exposing his smooth, warm chest. Then, gasping with the exhilaration, he started to unbutton her blouse. "My marriage was never like this," he panted.

"Mine neither," said Nadia.

She covered his mouth again with desperate kisses. Then, as he started to kiss and caress her naked skin and she began to caress his, she suddenly stopped and pulled away. "We can't do this."

"You are right," he said, nodding his head. "It is inappropriate."

"No," she hissed, "I don't care about that. I am pregnant. I feel ugly."

He looked at her in disbelief. "What are you talking about?"

"My body is fat."

"Firstly, you could never be fat on what they feed you. And secondly, having a baby is not ugly." His hand drifted to her stomach and stroked her bump. "This is a miracle. This is the most beautiful thing in the world. This is new life. Your baby gives me hope that we will have better tomorrows. Never, ever hide that. Never be ashamed of it."

Tears filled Nadia's eyes. How did this gentle, wonderful man end up being her enemy?

They started to make love then pressed up against a bin of fabric rolls. Pulling clothes out of the way, half-naked as they allowed their desire to complete its course.

As he made love to her, Nadia could not believe how this felt: the desire, the exquisite pleasure of it. Everything felt so heightened and thrilling; the kissing, the touching, even the danger of being caught, excited her. She hungered to have him as close to her as she could.

It did not take them long to fulfil their desire. And as she lay panting on his shoulder, she started to laugh, gently. So, this was what Tasha was talking about. This was what she'd been missing in her marriage to Ivan. No wonder her sister had not been pleased with her choice.

Catching his breath, their bodies still half-naked and entwined, he gently started to stroke her hair, whispering into her ear. "Nadia, I know everything about this is wrong. We are enemies. If we are caught, we'll both probably be shot. But I can't seem to help myself. I wasn't looking for this. But I find I want you all the time. You are all I think about, every moment of every day. But we have to be careful. Do you understand?"

Nadia nodded. And, pulling back, looked at him; she caressed his cheek with her fingertips, getting lost in his gentle blue eyes, feathered with his white-blonde lashes.

"I think I love you, Hans," she whispered before she could stop herself.

He caught his breath with her confession. "I *know* I love you," he whispered back. "I daren't have hoped I could ever say those words again."

Just then, there was a noise outside on the factory floor, and it brought them back to their senses. Quickly, she started to dress. And he did too, buttoning up his shirt incorrectly again. Smiling, she undid it and re-buttoned it for him.

Smoothing out her skirt, she moved quickly out of the door. And he followed her, saying loudly so the girls could hear, "Thank you for your opinion, Mrs. Kozlov. I will speak to my superiors."

She walked quickly back to her machine. Her sister was sitting with her arms folded, watching her. "What did he need you for?" she snapped.

"Some of the fabric is inferior, and he wanted me to check it for him."

"And, how was it?"

"Fantastic," she said with a smile.

Tasha's mouth dropped open as she looked incredulously at her sister.

———

It was later when they were in bed that Tasha confronted her sister. "You made love to him, didn't you?"

Nadia giggled back her reply.

"Oh my God, Nadia, that is so dangerous; if the guards had caught you, they would have shot you both. This is so unlike you; you are usually so sensible."

"You're right, this is more like you," she gasped. "What does it feel like to be the sensible one for a change?"

Tasha rolled her eyes. "Do you have any idea what you are doing?"

"No," she sang back, "and it feels wonderful and wild and free and I am beyond happy." All at once she gasped and pulled Tasha's hand to her belly. A tiny foot pressed against their palms and both of them gasped again with delight.

"Oh my God, Nadia, I can't believe you are going to be a mother."

"I know none of this is how I would have planned it.

Having a baby in a work camp and being in love with a German. But what if this is fate? I can't feel upset because I have never been happier."

Tasha pulled her sister close. "Well, if you are happy, then that is all we are going to think about. I believe our own forces could free us any day, then you can give birth to this wonderful baby and live happily ever after with your good German. God, even saying any of that seems wrong." She balked. "I guess I'm just used to me being the one always in trouble."

Nadia agreed. "This, when I think about it, is actually a nice moment for me. Nadia is the reckless one and Tasha is the sensible one." Her sister punched her on the shoulder as they laughed quietly together.

"But seriously, Nadia, please, please be careful. If any of this gets out it could be so dangerous for you. And I can't lose you. You are all I have right now."

"You won't lose me; I will always be with you, even if I'm dead. You will know it is me by the sensible voice in your ear."

They snuggled together then, both of them feeling strangely happier than they had in a long time. Neither of them knowing the danger that was waiting for them just around the corner.

50

Nadia

As they continued their time at the labor camp, things did not get easier. The winter was long and cold, and as well as the grueling hours they kept at the factory and the lack of food, which they were all preoccupied with, there was always the fear of disease.

Both sisters had become bone thin. Nadia couldn't help but notice how her sister's cheekbones now pressed through her skin and her complexion was a sickly yellow color; Tasha constantly worried about Nadia's pregnancy and if they could keep it a secret. Because she too was so thin, she was barely showing, but still the women in the camp continued to find oversized clothes for her to wear to help hide the baby.

She and Hans would try and find time to be together whenever they could every day. Under the watchful eyes of the guards, they were unable to disappear off to his office together too frequently, but they found other ways to express their love. She found great pleasure in the brush of his hand across her shoulders as he inspected the lines, a flower on her sewing machine when she got back from lunch, and always his words of love that he would tuck in the pocket of her jacket for her to find later. In the evening, Nadia would read them and then tell her stories of love to her sister to give her hope as they would huddle together, freezing on their bunk, a thin sliver of a blanket to keep them warm. Nadia would also retell stories of their childhood until she heard her sister's breath slow and deepen to a calming rhythm.

The hopelessness they'd all felt was what she struggled with the most. Each night before she went to sleep, Tasha would make a mark on the bunk above her, marking the time that they'd been there. And soon she noticed that three months had passed.

"At least we are moving into the warmer months," she whispered into her sister's ear.

But as the winter became spring, a new concern arose in the camp: rats, which they all knew brought diseases with them.

One day, Hannah, one of the girls that shared their bunk house, came running into the hut before they'd barely got up. "Hut four!" she spat out, breathing fast. "Hut four! They have a disease there. One of the girls came out in a purple rash this morning. She has a high fever. They think it might be typhus."

Everyone stopped what they were doing and stared at her in disbelief. Life was so hard day after day, it was unfathomable that it could somehow become even worse. Nadia's stomach tied into a knot. Surely they would not make them work if there was typhus. But the roll call was called the same as ever. They moved out into the parade ground and stood to attention. Everyone looked fearful and thoughtful that morning as their names were called. Then, just before lunch, a young girl called Alice fell from her sewing machine to the floor. She sat only three seats behind Tasha.

Nadia could see from where she was that Alice was sweating profusely, and people went to attend to her. Hans, wearing a cloth around his mouth to protect himself, helped carry her out of the sewing room. The guards yelled at them to keep sewing, shoving two girls roughly in the process.

Alice was right in the next hut to them. Tasha looked across at Nadia, who shook her head. There was nothing they could do.

She looked at Gaia, who shrugged her shoulders, saying, "We are all in higher hands, and our fate is already written. There is no point worrying about it."

Nadia did not find this very encouraging. They continued to sew, the fear and trepidation like a weighty cloud between them.

At lunchtime, Tasha waited with Nadia to talk to Hans. "Why are they not going to segregate us off if people are sick?"

Hans looked as distraught as they were. "They don't care about you because you are Russian. They think of you as vermin of no importance."

Tasha paced up and down with frustration. "But it's so dangerous for us, especially with Nadia." She nodded towards her pregnant sister.

Hans nodded too, the concern obvious in his eyes. "Take this," he said. And he gave her his whole ration for the day, a small piece of cheese, bread, and an apple.

"I can't take all of your food," Nadia complained.

"Take it, Nadia," insisted Tasha. "You need it to keep your strength up. And it might help you fight the disease if it comes to our hut."

They were all very thoughtful on their march back in the dark, freezing cold, their fingers sore from sewing all day, their eyes blurring from the strain.

Arriving back, they stood in line for their evening roll call. Just as they were finishing, they were told that each hut would be visited and inspected to make sure they didn't have the disease.

The soldiers wore face coverings as they entered their bunk rooms. Inside they demanded that the women undo their blouses to see if there was any sign of a rash. It was humiliating and shameful.

Nadia held her breath and attempted to hold in her stomach, fearful that they would see her pregnancy bump. But as the soldier leered at her, taking more time than was needed, he didn't seem to get past her blossoming breasts.

Then, all of a sudden, from below the waist band of her skirt, she felt something drop, as the apple fell to the floor and rolled out into the middle of the room.

The soldier watched it roll to a stop. Then, picking it up, he held it up to her face.

"And where did you get this?" he spat out vehemently towards Nadia.

She didn't know what to say. If she said she stole it, she would surely be punished. But if she told the soldier about Hans, then he would surely get into trouble, maybe even lose his job.

Nadia just shook her head as he grabbed hold of her open blouse and pulled her towards him, until his face was an inch from hers, his breath stinking of garlic sausage. "Tell me where you got it!" he screamed. He began to shake Nadia violently and then backhanded her with a slap. "You stole it, didn't you, you little Russian rat? You stole this food from the kitchen! Well, we know how to treat people who are thieves here."

And as he picked up his rifle, Tasha jumped in front of him. "It was me! I stole it!"

He looked shocked and stepped back.

"No, Tasha, don't do this!" Nadia insisted.

But Tasha looked back at her with that willful expression that Nadia had seen her whole life. When her sister set her mind to something, there was nothing she could do to change it.

"Yes, bully me if you've got to bully somebody!" she spat at him.

All the women around the hut looked terrified.

He seemed to take pleasure in this as he pulled her towards him and punched her in the face, then as she bent double, he kicked her in the stomach. Nadia screamed, but two of the other women grabbed her and pulled her out of the way as the soldier continued to pummel Tasha.

Finally, he lifted his gun. At first, she thought he was going to shoot her. But then, with evil intent twisting in his eyes, he lifted it high and brought the butt down on the back of her head. Nadia screamed as Tasha fell to the floor and lay so still it was horrifying, thick blood starting to ooze from a wound staining her red hair. Before she could go to her, two other German soldiers whisked in and carried her out, and the commander locked the hut door behind them all. Nadia ran to the door, screaming, banging on it, calling over and over for her sister. The women, fearful of retaliation, pulled her away to comfort her. But Nadia was wracked with guilt. This was her punishment for loving Hans, she was sure of it, and she felt wretched.

51

Tasha

All at once becoming aware of her surroundings, the first thing to hit Tasha as she started to wake was the smell of sweat and blood and her heart sank. She had been having such a wonderful dream about Luca. They'd been flying together, the wind rushing through her hair. and the last thing she'd remembered was his wonderful, deep, barreling laugh. Now there was this stench of illness and death, and slowly through the murky depths of confusion she began to remember. She must be in the hospital, after the beating from the officer that she'd taken for Nadia. Though she didn't regret it for a minute, and was glad she hadn't been taken away and shot as so many were.

As she started to become more conscious, she could feel the pain wracking her body. Her stomach ached where she'd been kicked. Her jaw throbbed and felt as if it was out of alignment where he'd punched her. And then lastly, she'd been knocked to the ground by the barrel of his gun as it hit the base of her skull. The crunch of his weapon against the back of her head had been the last thing she'd heard as she'd blacked out. Drawing in a low, ragged breath, she forced open her eyes.

The room was dimly lit, and along with the smell of antiseptic, new smells reached her, sweat and rotting flesh.

She attempted to move her head, but the agony from her head injury was just too painful, so she slowly scanned the room with just her eyes. It was dark and dingy, and she was alone. In the corner there was just a small, dirty, barred window, and drawn by the light, she looked towards it. As she stared over at it, she realized she was still in a dream state, because looking in at the window was Luca. It made her happy and it also made her miss him terribly. She blinked her eyes and Luca's face disappeared. Her mind was playing tricks on her. Probably a result of the intense dream and the injury to her head.

Suddenly the door creaked open and the apparition was in the doorway. She peered at it, realizing it wasn't Luca at all. This spirit was far too thin. Closing the door, it moved swiftly towards her, and she became fearful. She'd expected her ghost to disappear.

She blinked to clear her vision again. But finally it reached her and she looked up into a gaunt face and serious blue eyes.

"Oh my God, Tasha, I couldn't believe it was you," he hissed. "I had to get closer to be sure. But, oh my darling, what happened to you?" He continued speaking in a hurried whisper as his concerned eyes searched her face and shone with tears.

Tasha's heart pounded in her chest, and she hitched her breath as she attempted to bury her head deep back into her pillow, unable to believe what was in front of her. It even sounded like Luca.

"Luca?" she rasped unsteadily, her voice gravelly from lack of water, her throat sore.

"Yes, my love." He smiled as he brushed a wisp of stray hair from her hot cheek.

Tasha's eyes filled with tears as her whole body shook with the realization that this might be real.

She began to sob loudly, overcome with all the emotions flowing through her body.

Quickly, he put his finger to her lips, signifying that she should be quiet.

She tried to make sense of it all, but her head hurt too much, her thoughts moving so slowly, as if they were underwater. He placed his fingers on her cheek, tracing her jawbone gently, where she could feel there were bruises, then running his fingers across her lips, he caressed her face as if he was trying to come to terms with the reality of her as well.

"You're dead," she said defiantly, realizing she needed to help this apparition on his way to the afterlife.

He chuckled and responded by leaning in and kissing her so deeply and tenderly that even in the midst of her pain she was aroused. Surely a ghost couldn't do that.

"My plane crashed," Luca started to explain gently as he pulled away. "The Germans found me. My leg was broken, and they brought me here. I've been here ever since." There was a noise in the hallway and he looked desperate. "I can't be here for long, or they'll see me and I'll be in trouble. I was just sent to move a body." He kissed her again, fresh tears brimming in his eyes. "I can't believe it, I just can't believe it's you."

Another voice echoed farther down the hallway.

"I have to go. When you're well, meet me over at the corner of the fence. There's a place where the male and female prisons intersect where we can pass messages. I have a way to slip out late at night after the camp is closed down for the evening. We won't have long, but at least I could see you."

She closed her eyes and hoped this was true and not a dream because suddenly she had a tremendous will to live, something she hadn't felt since she'd arrived here. Tears mingled with the feeling of joy at the miracle of the sight of the man she loved. Then, kissing both of her hands and brushing back her hair from her face, he was gone, and the room was empty. She felt so crushingly lonely, lonelier than she'd ever felt, yet at the same time overjoyed.

———

Her body was slow to recover, probably due to the lack of nutrition, and every time she sat up, her head spun with the injury. Finally, a tired-looking doctor who was also a prisoner with no name that she knew of released her, warning her not to get on the wrong side of his comrades again. She walked stiffly back to her hut and was just glad to be outside.

The time in the hospital had been excruciatingly dull and so depressing. She had spent many days alone. As she shuffled across the compound, it was evening and everyone was just back from the factory. On arriving at their hut, all the girls crowded around her to help her. Gaia came forward to examine her injuries and told her she had some plants she had picked surreptitiously and she would make her something to soothe her pain.

On seeing her, Nadia burst into tears and, grabbing hold of her, held her so close she appeared to forget that Tasha needed to breathe. Trying to pull away to get a breath, Tasha mumbled into the layers of sour-smelling clothes that her sister wore. "He's alive, Nadia. He's alive."

Nadia pulled away and looked at her sister quizzically.

"I saw Luca," she confirmed, her chest heaving with the emotion of that statement. "He's alive."

Nadia's gaze softened into compassion and concern. She didn't appear to believe her.

Tasha was persistent. "In the hospital he came to me."

"You had quite a blow to the head, Tash. I'm not sure what you saw—"

But Tasha cut her off. "He was real, as real as you are. At first I thought he was a ghost too, but he kissed me and then I knew. He's here and wants me to meet him at the end of the fence in the evenings."

Nadia looked concerned. "That would be too dangerous, Tasha. You can't possibly—"

Her sister cut her off again. "I love him, Nadia. If I don't see him, I will die in here. I will probably die in here anyway." Her voice started to crack with the emotion.

"How could you possibly get out at night after we're locked in?"

"I know a way," came Gaia's sing-song voice, as she continued to sew her latest creation. She stole scraps of fabric and needles and thread from the factory and was always busy in the evenings making something.

Tasha looked at Nadia with pleading eyes. And Nadia, as always with her sister, gave in and let Gaia explain.

"Take the job of emptying the toilet buckets from Carlene in the next hut. She hates it anyway and you can say she's sick. The Germans don't care as long as someone does their dirty work." Gaia elaborated as she broke a piece of thread between her jagged teeth, "She's the last one out at night and is given special permission to be out late to clean up after the officers. While they're eating and our huts are already locked for the night, there are few soldiers guarding. If you hurry, you could have ten minutes between emptying the refuse and coming back."

She agreed, and after making the arrangements the next night with Carlene, who was more than happy to hand over her job, she headed out after dark, rushing to empty the toilet buckets and then making her way to the area of the fence where the male and female camps intersected. As the cold of the night chilled her to the bone in her thin clothes, she stood shivering and waiting, standing there as long as she felt she could without it becoming obvious. But Luca never came. And the discouragement was crushing as she made her way back to her hut and a guard let her in. The next night she did the same, and the night after that, and when he didn't arrive on the fourth night, she began to fear that something was wrong or, worse still, the whole thing had been an illusion.

So when she approached the fence on the fifth night, her spirits and expectations were very low. She walked up and down as she had each evening, rubbing her arms to try to keep warm. Tonight, it was particularly cold, but with its chill came a thousand stars on a clear night. As she shivered, she stared up at the sky, placing yet another prayer between them. She was so engrossed with staying warm and mesmerized by the beauty of the night she didn't hear a person approach.

"Beautiful, isn't it?" Luca said as he placed both his hands on the wire netting and stared up at the sky. "Difficult to believe such beauty and such horror can belong in the same world."

She caught her breath and approached him slowly, feeling coy for some reason. Afraid that if she moved too fast she would frighten the vision of him away.

She placed her hands atop his and pushed her palm into his, feeling the warmth of his own even with the wire between them. They were roughened and blackened with endless days of hard work, but these were the hands that had caressed and loved her, cradled her and touched her.

She placed her head on the fence and he touched his forehead to hers.

"Oh, Luca, I've missed you so much. I was beginning to think you weren't real."

"They had us working out of the camp for a while. We had to sleep rough along the road. It was hard, but all I could think of since I saw you was that there has to be a God. Because how else can you believe that we would both survive what we have been through and end up in the same camp? I love you, Natasha," Luca said, using her full name with emphasis as their fingertips grazed one another. "And I can't bear that I can't hold you."

Tasha held back a sob, whispering, "I'm just glad you're here."

"How are your wounds now?" he inquired gently, his face pulling away to search hers.

"I'm healing," she sighed, "but everything still hurts."

"You have to stay alive," he insisted. "I couldn't bear it if anything happened to you."

"You too," she responded. "What do you do in the camp?" she asked him.

"They make me hit rocks until my arms, legs, and knees hurt. Sometimes I transport dead bodies. It's horrible. Who would've thought a world like this could exist?"

Tasha shook her head with regret.

"How is Nadia?"

"She's doing the best she can. We all are..." Her words drifted away as she tried to think of how to tell him. "I have a secret."

His eyes searched her face, and a half smile drifted across his lips, as if he was reminiscing about times gone by when secrets were something they shared on a frequent basis.

"You're digging a tunnel," he joked as his eyes scanned her face and centered on her lips.

"I wish I had the energy," she joked back, then paused slightly to deliver the news. "Nadia is pregnant with Ivan's child."

Luca looked at her incredulously as if he was trying to reconcile the beauty of new life with the hell they lived in. "How is that possible," he whispered, the corners of his eyes brimming with tears.

"The usual way, I think. You have been in here too long." She smirked.

He shook his head and pressed his forehead to the fence. "It's just unbelievable, the hope of new life in all this death."

She pushed her fingers through the wire and wiped away a stray tear.

"It's like a message from God telling us to hold on, Luca. If a child can survive through all of this, then so can we."

He slowly nodded, kissing the tips of her fingers. "You have to take care of each other."

Tasha nodded. "We will. You too."

Just then, a searchlight wheeled around the compound. They quickly pulled away from each other and crouched down to a squat.

"Can you meet here again tomorrow?"

"I think so," he hissed back. "I'll try. But please don't take any unnecessary risks."

Her mouth curled with a smile. "Don't tell me what to do."

He laughed quietly and pressed his face against the wire. She placed her cheek next to his. His face felt frigid with the cold.

She closed her eyes, thinking it felt like just a short time before that the two of them had been together as children. And then friends and finally lovers. How could this harshness be a part of their journey?

The spotlight swept the compound again, this time danger-ously close to them. Both of them instantly pulled apart and started to move away.

"Tomorrow," he hissed towards her, his words disap-pearing into clouds of icy breath.

"Tomorrow," she whispered back. She winced with the pain in her head as she tried to hurry herself towards her hut.

That night, as she lay huddled close to her sister, the usual cold didn't penetrate her, and she went to sleep smiling, reliving in her head every wonderful thought she could remember about Luca. She pushed away the fearful thought about the chances of them surviving this and chose ones of flying, making love, and laughing with the man she loved.

52

Tasha

Tasha and Luca continued to meet every evening. He had a special dispensation to clean off some tools, and she continued to do Charlene's job for her. They would only get about five to ten minutes, but it was enough just to be able to connect with one another each night. In between, he would leave her little gifts tied to the bottom of the wire fence, a ribbon that once blew into the camp, a flower he'd found in the dry dirt of the compound. Little things that couldn't draw attention if a soldier happened to notice it.

When Luca approached the fence one evening, she could see there was a look of concern on his face. It was a frigid night, and they sat huddled together, back to back, against the fence, which they found the most warming and also the way they could connect their bodies the most.

"What is it, Luca?" she said.

He shook his head. "Nothing. Just something I've heard. How are you? How was your day?"

"About the same."

He pushed a finger through the wire, and she locked her little finger with his.

"Sometimes I wake up in the morning and can't believe I'm here. It's like a nightmare that never goes away. Sleep sometimes is the only way that I can escape."

She heard him sigh in response.

"I know what you mean," he said. "It's the small things I miss. The freedom to walk down the street, hand in hand with you, flying together, being with our friends, and just having fun. That seems such a long time ago now, doesn't it?"

She sighed. "I feel like I've been through so much since the war started. Life was so simple. Flying, making love to you, listening to my babka while she sang her songs."

"I miss my family too," he said earnestly. "I took them for granted when I lived there. My mother was always there cooking, my father always willing to listen. But I was so caught up in my own life I didn't realize how important all that was. Promise me, Tasha, when we get out of here—which I know we will, because I can't think of an alternative—we will not take each other for granted, ever."

"I promise you, Luca, I will never take you for granted. Do you regret joining up?"

He turned and looked at her then. "I regret the way I did it. I should have talked to you. Maybe you would've talked me out of it. But I don't regret what I've done. I don't regret flying for my country. I don't regret fighting for the Allies against the Nazis, and for freedom. But I regret what I took for granted."

She nodded.

"What about you?"

"I wish I would've thought more about all of this. I've always been so compelled to do things, but I'm realizing as I get older, though that gave me a thrill, a sense of adventure, sometimes I make mistakes that way—big ones. But, no, like you, I don't regret joining the squadron to fight. I regret other decisions. I shouldn't have taken us over enemy lines. I should never have dragged Nadia into this. She's here because of me, and I feel incredibly guilty especially because she is pregnant." Luca nodded, the joy and fear intermingled in his expression as she continued, "And I spend all day being fearful that someone will find out about her. And if anything happens to Nadia, I'm not sure I could go on."

They turned then, the cold air cooling both their cheeks. He placed his hand on the fence as she placed hers on top of his, and she felt the warmth of his palm against hers.

"We're all going to get out of this. You and I are going to get old and fat together. And Nadia's going to have her baby and live just down the street from us."

Tasha smiled. "It's hard to imagine. That we'll somehow get out of this." She scanned the camp, tired-looking brown buildings, the ripening moon hanging heavy over the whole place. The barbed wire ran around the entire compound—the hard, brown dirt of the parade ground.

"Everything's so brutal and harsh. But I have to believe," said Luca, as he looked around too. "Because I think if you give up, I've seen people die that way here. When the men give up their hope, it's like they have nothing left to live for, and then they die. You and I both have something to live for. Let's remember we made each other a promise about that."

She nodded. "Luca, why were you so concerned when you arrived?"

He let out a deep, slow sigh. "There is talk, only talk, mind—that they may be moving some of us on from this camp. They need a group of us to go elsewhere in Germany, maybe even Berlin, to work in the factories there."

She caught her breath, the pain ripping through her body. The only thing that kept her going each day was knowing that she would see Luca.

He must have seen the pain on her face. "There's only talk,

Tasha. We don't know. I just thought you should be prepared if we're separated again for some reason. I'll always look for you, though. I'll find you again. I promise you. And we always have our sunrises. Never give up hope."

She nodded her head as tears stung her eyes.

He kissed her fingertips through the wire, and they nodded. Their time was up. But as she walked back to her barracks that night, an ominous feeling took over her, and she feared that, once again, she'd be parted from him.

———

She was on her way to work two days later when she saw it, activity in the male camp next door. The men were all lined up, moving towards the gate. Something about the way they moved alerted her that this was something more than them just going to work. They weren't looking down and slowly shuffling along as they usually did; they were being forced to march fast in a straight line, and the soldiers were shouting at them. Suddenly she knew, and her heart caught in her throat. They were moving them as Luca had feared. She quickly scanned the group. Nadia noticed what she was doing and turned to her.

"What is it? What's wrong?"

"Luca said they might move them. Look, look, Nadia."

Nadia looked across. "It certainly looks more active than I've seen it before. They may not take all of them. You can't be sure they'll take Luca."

Tasha gasped with shock. "Oh my God, there he is, in the line, I just saw him." And then he was gone. Did she imagine it? Did she really see him? Her heart breaking, she broke from their group who were all getting ready to go to the factory and ran to the fence, looking frantically from one face to another.

One of the guards saw her and shouted, "Get back into line, now!"

But she couldn't move. Still clinging to the wire, she screamed after him.

"Luca!" she screamed over and over again. "Luca!"

But none of them could hear her. Instead, they marched off at such a clip she was afraid they would never get there alive, wherever they were going.

She looked desperately from one of the ragged creatures to the next, looking for the one that was hers.

"Luca, I love you, Luca!" she screamed out again.

Then she saw someone twitch, lift a shoulder, afraid to do anything more than that; otherwise, they may be beaten before they'd even started the walk. But she knew it was him.

She screamed out in terror. He was leaving her again.

The guard reached her and pulled her roughly from the bars. "Get back into line."

Nadia quickly came beside her, grabbing her sister from his grasp and pulling her back towards their group before he could hit her, as Tasha sobbed. The other women held her up as she walked to work. She had this terrible sinking feeling that she would never see Luca alive again. He had already cheated death once. She wasn't sure he would be lucky enough to cheat death again.

At the factory, Nadia must have told Hans what had happened, because later in the day he came to speak to her. "I've made some inquiries amongst the guards to try and find out more details about the camp evacuation. And I'm afraid it's not good news. They're marching them all across Germany, closer to Berlin. To a big ammunitions factory there to help build more bombs. The march is hard enough, especially with the malnutrition, and they expect to lose people along the way. I'm so sorry. That's all I could find out."

A guard appeared at the end of the row, and Hans squeezed her arm gently before quickly moving away.

Once the guard was gone, Nadia moved to her sister's side and held her as she gently sobbed in her arms. "He'll be okay,

Tasha. He's strong and young, and he has survived this far. Have hope."

Tasha nodded her head but still couldn't shake the creeping fear that preoccupied her.

53

Tasha

Typhus continued to rip through the camp, causing girls to fall down in the lines for roll call. Also, it wasn't uncommon to see one or two girls being carried away from the machines. The infirmary was full, so the Germans turned one of the barracks into a place to keep the women. The nursing staff didn't want to go in, as they didn't want to catch the disease, and they would send in the other prisoners to take care of them.

One day, their bunk-mate Hannah came in again. She was panicking. "Alice is dead. She's dead. None of us will survive. That's four people in my section today. I'll be next." She started to become hysterical, screaming.

Gaia jumped down from her bunk and grabbed her by the shoulders. "Stop," she said with such determination it shocked her into being quiet. "Survival is a moment-by-moment choice. Sometimes you fight. Sometimes you make yourself so small you are barely seen. But always, absolutely always, you believe in a different tomorrow. So, stop creating problems today. You have to be strong and fight."

"But are you not afraid of dying, Gaia?"

"No," she said decisively. "No, I'm not afraid of dying. I'm afraid of continuing to live. If I die today, tomorrow I will be free." She sighed then. "But still today I have to fight, and so do you. We all have to be strong for one another. Every one of you, look at me," she said, commanding the room. "If one of us lets go, then we will all go too. You have to decide that despair is not an option, and then hope is all you will see."

"I just want it to stop," sobbed Hannah. "I just want this to go away. Just one day when I'm not scared and hungry."

Gaia pulled her close as the young woman sobbed into her shoulder.

"You must free yourself of the hope that the waves will stop," she said, stroking her brittle hair. "The waves will not stop," she whispered gently. "These are the tides of war. Instead, you have to learn to jump those waves, avoid them, trick them, bargain with them, turn your back on them if you must. Still, you cannot stop the waves, but you can survive them. Do you hear me, Hannah? Even if you get this horrible disease, you may survive it. You must not lose hope."

She put out her hand, and the group stepped forward and took each other's hands and squeezed them.

"We are all the family we have, and we have to be strong for one another. Do you hear me?"

They all nodded. This was all they had now, their strength and hope.

All at once there was a swooshing sound and Nadia's water broke and spilled out onto the floor from beneath her skirt. The women all froze, knowing what it must be.

"No," cried Nadia. "It's too early. My baby isn't due for another month."

Tasha grabbed her sister and pulled her close. "It's going to be okay. I'm here."

The women surrounded Nadia and began to help her, making a bed for her, bringing anything dry and clean they could find. Gaia brought some herbs that she said would help with the pain, and they prepared for a night that they hoped would usher new life into the world.

Nadia labored hard through the night as all the women tended her. She tried to cope with the pain, as Gaia, who had birthed many babies, knew exactly what to do.

"It is more challenging without water or clean fabric," she said, "but we'll do the best we can."

But as the night wore on, even though Nadia's labor was so intense, it didn't seem to be going anywhere.

They were all exhausted by the time morning came, but still, there was no sign of her baby.

"She's still not ready to give birth," Gaia said. "It could be hours from now."

Tasha looked to her sister as she mopped her brow. Nadia looked exhausted already. They now had a new problem. It was morning and they would all have to go to work. Nadia would have to come with them because the Germans wouldn't let her stay behind. If they said she was sick, she would have to go to the infirmary, where they would find out she was pregnant.

"Nadia," Tasha said, stroking her hair, "you'll have to go to the factory. Hans will help take care of you when we get there."

Nadia nodded, and the women helped her up as she groaned in pain. Then, shuffling out for roll call, Tasha held her sister close as she winced with the pain. They called out their names. As they started to move into formation, the guard looked over at Nadia.

"What is wrong with her?"

"She's just not feeling well," said Tasha. "Her stomach is upset."

"She should go to the infirmary," the soldier said.

"She's fine. She wants to work. I'll take care of her."

He looked put out. "I don't want her to be any trouble or to fall down."

"She won't," Tasha said. "I'll take care of her."

They moved out of the compound, and Tasha supported Nadia. As soon as they got to the factory and the guards were out of view, Hans came quickly to attend to her.

"Bring her into the office. She will be safe in there."

Gaia and Tasha helped, as Nadia had to keep stopping, gasping for breath from her strong contractions. While the women got Nadia as comfortable as they could on a small sofa in the office, Hans pushed her machines out of sight so it wouldn't be obvious that anyone was missing. Tasha sat with her sister. Hans was so gentle and kind. He brought her water, some medicine they had in first aid to help with the pain, some clean strips of fabric, which he gave to Gaia, and everything she might need after the birth. Then he sat stroking Nadia's hair, talking of his love for her.

It was a frightening day, keeping their secret away from the guards as they took turns attending to her. But by the end of the day, Nadia had still not given birth. Hans was frantic as she got up to leave.

"You can't take her with you."

"But they will know during roll call," said Tasha. "It will be worse if she's not there. But thank you, Hans."

He gave them his food ration, and, turning to her, there were tears in his eyes.

"I love you, Nadia," he said as he kissed her hot cheeks and held her. "Tomorrow, you will have a young one, I'm sure. You will have new life and we will celebrate and I will find a way to get your baby to safety."

Tasha didn't like to say that would bring problems of its own. How on earth were they going to hide a baby in the camp? But they did manage to get Nadia back home and into the bunkhouse.

As they went into their second evening of labor, Nadia grew tired and weary, and Tasha could see the concern on Gaia's face.

"She's not doing as well as I would like," she said. "I'm concerned she won't have the strength for what is ahead."

Tasha looked at her sister, who was feverish and tired. "You've got to do this, Nadia. You've got to hold on."

Nadia's eyes sprang open. She nodded vaguely as they continued through the night. Eventually, a tiny pink baby was born into a dark and dismal world just after midnight.

It was such a surprise to see this tiny one, so clean and new and fresh. It brought tears to everyone's eyes as Gaia held it up into the moonlight so they could look at it. "A beautiful baby girl," she announced.

Tasha shook her sister, trying to wake her. "You had a baby girl, Nadia. You have a daughter."

Nadia nodded, and then passed out again into a fitful slumber.

"She's lost more blood than she should have," Gaia said, using the supplies that Hans had given her to clean up Nadia and to cut the cord. "She will need to rest. She'll not be able to work tomorrow."

Tasha wavered between holding her sister's burning body close to hers and holding her new niece, who lay small and fragile in her arms. The other women took turns, too, holding and cradling the baby. The new life, such beauty in a place of such cruelty. Some women cried with the memory of their own children that had been lost to this war. Other women found it hard to hold on to the dream of ever having children of their own after what they had all been through.

Tasha just wanted her sister back. She held her fevered body close to her and whispered into her ear, "Please, Nadia, stay with me. Don't die. I can't do this without you. You just have to hang on for a little bit longer. Nadia, just a little longer."

Nadia would sometimes flutter her eyelashes as though she wanted to respond. But most of the time, she was somewhere else in a fever dream, a place that no one could reach her. The only other time Tasha would see her stir was when the baby would cry, and one of them would place the baby to the breast to be fed. Apart from that time, Nadia was lost to her. She didn't know what she needed to do to bring her back. It was so hard; she wanted her so badly it hurt her inside, but there was nothing she could do.

54

Tasha

It was the sound of the airplanes that woke Tasha a few hours later. She had been in a deep sleep, exhausted from the birth, dreaming about being in her own plane, about being back with her squadron in the midst of a mission. When she was suddenly woken by the familiar sound, her eyes stared at the bunk above her as she concentrated and listened intently. They weren't Russian, and they weren't German. The sound, she was sure, belonged to British planes. The hum of the engine was so distinct. Why were they flying so low?

Making sure her sister and niece were sleeping soundly, she gathered one of the thin blankets around her shoulders and raced to the door. Pressing her ear against the wood, she closed her eyes to listen. Another one flew directly overhead, and, opening her eyes and squinting through a knothole in the wood, she got her first glimpse of one of the British bombers, or was it a fighter? No, it was definitely a bomber. She could see it outlined against the drifting moonlight and there was more than one. She started counting them and got to six before she heard the first bombs being dropped far off. The sound was so familiar to her. They were attacking some sort of brickwork; she could tell by the sound of the masonry exploding. As she huddled against the wooden door, she felt great fear, almost like a premonition, that something was going to happen.

All at once Gaia sat up in her bunk, her eyes wild but intense. "It's time," she rasped. "It's time."

"What do you mean, Gaia?"

Gaia just shook her head slowly. "We should prepare," she whispered.

It started off as something small. At first, Tasha thought it was rain. The obvious sound of water gathering and pooling somewhere, which was strange because there was no sound of the raindrops on the roof, and she could see through the hole in the door that the night was clear and dry. But from somewhere there was the unmistakable sound of something wet and gurgling, building and coming towards her. She had never been to the beach, but this was the sound she imagined she would hear as the tide turned and waves came in. Staring through the cracks in the wooden door, she noticed water and dirt were collecting in pools all around the hut. What was it?

Then something more ominous, louder, farther away. Like the sound of a train thundering towards them. The women were waking up now and looking around in disbelief. Raised soldiers' voices sounded in alarm. One of the women who spoke good German translated. "They said there is water coming down the hills towards us, that they need to run. They're leaving. They're leaving us in here. Someone is telling them not to worry about us, that we will die anyway, and why not as drowned rats."

There was a collective gasp around the bunkhouse as the women started to rush out of their beds, grabbing clothes, blankets, or any belongings. The thundering sound of water was building in pitch, and now when Tasha looked outside, it was like there was a river running through the camp.

Hannah began to panic and started pounding on the door.

"Let us out, let us out, you bastards." But there was nothing but the sound of other the women screaming, raised voices from all over the camp.

Draped in a blanket she had patchworked together from discarded fabric, Gaia took control. "We have to do this ourselves. Grab hold of the bunk. We will try and use it to break down the door."

All the women except Nadia, who was still too weak, heaved up one of the bunks, and dragging it to the door, they thrust its bulk at the wood repeatedly until it began to crack. Even from the small amount of wood they managed to splinter, water began to gush in at an alarming rate.

"The dams must have broken," said another woman who was very familiar with the area. "Farther up the valley, there are dams."

"The bombers," said Tasha, "they must have hit the dams."

"Oh my God, we'll all be drowned," Hannah panicked.

As the roar grew in intensity, the women worked more frantically, trying to pull out the strips of splintered wood with their frozen fingers. As the second wave of water entered the camp, icy water poured in through the holes they had made, soaking their clothes and bare feet. Tasha helped her sister out of bed and bound the baby to Nadia's chest as tightly as she could, hoping if they had to swim that Nadia would be strong enough.

With a final ear-splitting crack, the door was splintered enough that they could pull pieces of it away and create a big enough gap to get through. Tasha clung to her sister as she helped her outside. All around them the women from her bunkhouse cried out and shivered with the cold and fear as they waded through the surging water. Already the whole camp was waist-high, but what was scarier was Tasha could see now clearly a third wall of water, looking twice as large as the previous ones, rolling and crashing towards them. In its wake it dragged the remnants of buildings, vehicles, and all manner of debris. That appeared more dangerous than the water itself as it thundered towards them.

"We need to get as high as we can," Tasha screamed to her sister to be heard above the deafening roar.

Grabbing her sister by her clothing, she heaved her up as high as she could onto a cement post where, ironically, the hated Nazi flag was raised, now sagging limp and wet. Using the sodden, thin blanket she still had draped around her shoulders, she knotted it hard around their waists, tying the two of them to the post. As the wall of water reached the camp, it flattened the high wire fence as if it were made of paper and gushed into the parade ground in a fast-moving surge as women who had made it out of the huts raced for higher ground. All around them, the terrified screams of the women still trapped in their bunkhouses were frantic and high-pitched.

Wrapping her arms around Nadia, she held on to her so tightly, her fingers became numb as she pressed her sister against the cold cement post. As the new wave of freezing water reached them, the shock of it took their breath away and woke the baby, who began to scream. Gasping with the cold, Tasha tried to bear the pain of the surging water that pummeled their bodies over and over again as it rolled in waves over them and through the camp. The feeling of cold was like a thousand knives stabbing at her body. Nadia screamed out as a stray piece of driftwood hit her in the head. Grappling for her sleeve, the only thing she could reach, Tasha pulled her sister towards her and yelled into her ear as she noticed Nadia seemed to be losing consciousness. "Hold on, Nadia, you've got to hold on!" she screamed.

It felt as if this surge of water lasted for hours, though in retrospect it was probably only minutes, but in that time, the force of the water created such mass destruction all around them it was surreal, smashing, engulfing, and swallowing the whole camp with its power. Tasha watched it rip apart bunkhouses as if they were made of matchsticks, and she saw women with faces of desperation caught up like ragdolls in the water, their eyes wild with fear as they gasped for breath before being caught in wild eddies, their hands frantically grasping for anything to take hold of before the water finally dragged them below the surface. Many went down and never came back up.

Anything that was loose was swirling around, caught in the whirlpools. Tasha continued to cling to her sister and Nadia gripped tight to her tiny daughter. All at once, one last surge arrived to do its worst, and the flimsy blanket she had used to bind them tore with the strain. They both were flung into the icy water, the two of them driven swiftly down through the camp.

Tasha swam furiously, calling out desperately for Nadia, over and over again. All at once, she heard another voice just above the sound of the raging water. It was also calling Nadia's name. She glanced towards where she'd heard the sound come from, and there was Hans, swimming furiously towards Nadia's body that Tasha suddenly saw bobbing in the water, just about to go under. Hans grabbed hold of her by her shawl and, lifting her up, turned her over onto her back as he swam towards Tasha, who had grabbed hold of a piece of wood from the bunkhouse and was using it to float.

"Take her," he screamed. "Take her quickly."

Tasha grabbed at her sister and dragged her towards the floating wood that looked as if it had been part of one of the beds; as she heaved Nadia upon it, another giant wave ripped through the camp and dragged Hans from her side.

Nadia suddenly sucked in air and screamed out, the pain and fear acute in her tone. "Hans! Hans!"

But he was gone, the surging water catching hold of him. And the last they saw of him was his head bobbing up and down as he got swept from the camp.

Tasha clung on to Nadia with one hand and the bunk with

the other, maneuvering Nadia on top as best she could. Her arms burned with the weight of holding her sister and keeping herself afloat as she frantically tried to keep her head above the water as they were driven down through the stream.

She saw Gaia out of the corner of her eye, the older woman flailing in the water too. It wasn't just the feel of the freezing water in the middle of the night; it was the sheer volume of it. It was gushing and pulling and dragging them through the camp without them having any control of their direction as women all around her tried so desperately to save their own lives. It was terrifying, and Tasha prayed that she would live. Just when she thought she would not be able to hold on any longer, the water started to recede and return to waist height as it continued its trip through the valley.

Pulling Nadia to her feet, they both hunched over, gasping for breath as the baby mewled desperately, strapped to her mother's chest. Tasha coughed and spluttered, her stomach filled with water, her lungs feeling as if they would burst with the pressure, the water stinging her eyes and throat. As they began to catch their breath and Nadia slowly nursed her baby to comfort it, the eeriness of the aftermath was strange, quiet and ominous, as they got the first look of the devastation left behind. The camp was unrecognizable. Women's dead bodies were splayed everywhere, pale and limp, some caught in debris, wrapped around remnants of the bunkhouse, others floating facedown in the shallow water.

As Nadia sat on the bunk bed that had saved them, Tasha waded back through the knee-high water to see if she could find their friend. "Gaia," she called out. "Gaia, where are you?"

She eventually found the woman. She was still alive, catching her breath, clinging to a post left behind by one of the bunkhouses that had only been partly destroyed.

"I'm all right, child, I'm all right," she whispered between rasping breaths.

"Gaia, look, the gates of the camp have been smashed open with the weight of the water. All the soldiers have already left. We can get away, Gaia. We can get away."

Gaia shook her head. "You go and take Nadia. You have to look after that little one. If they come back and find her, they will take the baby away, but I have my work here to do." She swept her hand around the camp. Women lay in shock, huddled in groups, overcome with grief and exhaustion.

"We should stay and help."

"No," said Gaia firmly. "You have to get away, for that child's sake. I will take care of them."

"Will I ever see you again, Gaia?" Tasha asked as she looked deeply into the woman's intense eyes.

"You will always be able to see me again, in your dreams, if not before." Hugging her tightly, Gaia pulled something from her neck and thrust it into Tasha's hands. "Now go!" she demanded.

Tasha looked down at the sodden scarf that had been around her friend's neck and saw the word "Hope" sewn exquisitely into the gray army uniform fabric.

"So you never forget there is always hope. Take care."

Supporting her sister, Tasha waded through the gaping hole where the gates had been.

Nadia's eyes rolled as she tried to stay conscious. "Hans," she murmured through her chattering teeth.

It was just as they left the camp that they found him, Hans's limp body lying across a rock, his face so pale, his body so still. Nadia limped towards him and threw herself down on top of him, screaming over and over, willing him to live, but he was gone.

As Nadia sobbed, Tasha took control.

"We have to keep going, Nadia. His death will have been in vain if you let them catch you now. We have to keep going."

"I can't leave him," she spluttered.

"We have to. You have to think of your child. Now,

come on."

Tasha practically had to rip her sister from his body. She cried out like a wounded animal, waking the baby, who howled again. But Nadia had no strength to fight Tasha, who dragged her towards the road, away from the many bodies, away towards her freedom. Nadia sobbed as her sister half-carried her.

They stumbled to the outskirts of the town. The devastation was unbelievable everywhere they went. It was hard to believe that just water could cause such destruction. But the farther they walked, the lower the level dropped. Soon the water was at a point where they could just wade ankle-deep. As they walked through a nearby village, a woman with a child in her own arms saw Nadia with her baby and brought her a dry blanket and napkins, which Tasha quickly wrapped around the baby, who fussed with being disturbed. She seemed oblivious to the danger she had just lived through.

The woman also pressed milk into her hand. "From our cow. It should keep you going."

Tasha was grateful and started to thank her profusely as she gave some to her sister, but they couldn't stop. It wouldn't be long before the camp would be discovered and the Germans would be sure to try to round them up. Hopefully, because of the many deaths behind them, they would have to deal with those first and would be preoccupied for at least a little while. Tasha did not stop moving, practically carrying her sister and even the baby too. They walked all through the day and the following night, stopping to sleep for a few hours here and there. Without shoes, their feet were cut and dirty, but she was determined to get Nadia to safety.

On the second morning, they stumbled into a village that had not been affected by the rising water. A lot of people from all around the valley had been coming to be taken care of there. When they saw them, an older woman reached out to Tasha and insisted she take them into their home.

Exhausted, Tasha agreed, for Nadia's sake at least. They were now many miles from the camp, though she did not dare tell them who she was and where she had come from. The older woman helped them with the baby and gave them all dry clothes, and grateful but exhausted, they all fell into one of the woman's warm beds and slept like the dead.

When Tasha woke again, she had slept through the rest of the day, then the night, and now the sun was high in the sky again. Nadia was still sleeping soundly by her side. Maybe she was getting her strength back. It was then that Tasha realized that they were free. It had been such a desperate time for her to get away, she hadn't had a moment to think of that until right then. But she and Nadia and the baby were now free.

When she felt well enough, she prepared herself for the trip. They still had to get across Germany and Poland. This would be really challenging without papers. It would take all of her skills.

The older woman would not let them leave straightaway, not until Nadia had regained her strength. She fed them some food and took care of them both. And over the next few days, as Nadia grew a little stronger and her tiny baby continued to thrive, Tasha had hope for the first time in a long time. Placing the tiny sewn piece of fabric close to her chest, she re-read Gaia's word over and over a hundred times a day, almost as if the word 'hope' was a prayer. But even with this shelter she had found, Tasha knew their enemy was all around them. With her heavily accented German, she would easily be recognized as Russian if anyone questioned her, so she knew it wouldn't take long for an informer or even soldiers to find them. So even though Nadia was still really weak, three days later, she made the decision to keep moving towards the Russian front and said goodbye to the woman who had cared for them after the flood.

55

Tasha

As they stumbled through the darkness the next night, Tasha helped her sister. She was still so weak from giving birth, and Tasha was concerned about how pale she was. But, on the other hand, her little one was quiet and still, smaller than she should have been because of conditions in the camp, but so content in her mother's arms. Nadia had her strapped to her chest, a blanket holding the baby in place.

"I will need to rest soon," said Nadia breathlessly as they moved through a dense forest.

"Just a bit further," Tasha replied. "The further we can go on in the dark, the better."

She suddenly caught sight of something ahead, moonlight glinting off tarmac. She imagined it was a road, but as she got closer, Tasha could see what it was.

"Nadia, look."

Nadia had been looking at the ground, breathing heavily, not really taking in anything around her.

"Look, it's an airfield."

"With planes?"

"Yes. If I can get in, I could steal one."

Nadia shook her head as they both got closer to the low fence. "Don't be so ridiculous, Tasha. You would be caught and killed before you even got inside."

"You don't know that for sure. Look, there are hardly any guards. It's nighttime."

"How would you fly one?"

"How is a German plane going to be any different? Maybe we can find something small, like we're used to being in."

She sat Nadia and the baby down under a tree while she surveyed the area and walked around the whole perimeter to figure out the best way to approach it. She watched for a while and could definitely see only three guards. The area was well lit. She would have to be really careful. She went back and told Nadia her plan.

"I'll get in, and once I have an aircraft, you need to be ready to leave, then I'll take us back home."

Nadia was breathing very heavily but nodded her head slowly. She was feeding the baby.

As Tasha got up to leave, Nadia grabbed her hand. "Tasha, I want you to know that I love you. I can't believe what we've been through together, but I couldn't have done any of this without you. When we were young, I thought your reckless-ness would be dangerous. But now I see that there's a place for it, particularly in wartime. You are made for this."

Tasha leaned down and hugged her sister tightly. "We'll get away, and you can tell me how wonderful I am later." She laughed. "But right now, I need to get you and my niece back over Russian lines."

Stealthily, Tasha moved towards the field, trying to avoid the light as much as she could. She'd already located a recon-naissance plane that she thought would be easy for her to fly.

Back at her own camp, the Russian ground crew kept the planes ready to go, just in case there was an assault or they needed to move quickly. She hoped the Germans did the same.

She saw the two guards go to the end of the field, so there was only one who she couldn't see. She finally located him, under a tree at the other end of the field, smoking a cigarette. Carefully she raced towards the tiny plane, her heart pounding in her throat.

She was just about to hitch herself up into the cockpit when she felt a hand on her shoulder.

"What do you think you're doing?" said the man in German.

Tasha turned in shock. There was a fourth guard, one she hadn't noticed before. She looked at him, remembering all her hand-to-hand combat training, but he had a gun drawn in front of her. There was a chance he could shoot her before she'd have time to wrestle it out of his hand.

"Oh my goodness," she said, crying, trying to speak in her best German, as she had made a real effort to learn it since she had been in the camp. "My sister is sick in the woods, and I need help. Do you have a doctor here? Someone that can help her?"

The German looked surprised but was entirely taken off guard. "What are you doing in the woods close to this camp?"

"We're just trying to get food. We're going to the next village, and she became sick. Can you help me?"

The guard lowered his weapon and turned his head to look towards the other guards, and while it was turned, Tasha struck, pulling the gun from his hand. She pushed him down and clipped him on the back of the head with it as he fell to the ground, unconscious.

"Female wiles win again," she said to herself with a smile, thinking back to her training.

She wasn't sure how long it would be before they'd look for him, so she had to move fast. First, she needed to figure out if she could fly it. She jumped into the cockpit. Though everything was in German, the instrumentation was familiar. It was luxurious compared to the plane she'd been flying, everything so neat and put together. Navigation maps tucked carefully on the side, radars and radar equipment, headsets, not that she would need any. Suddenly she was grateful of the hardships the night flyers had been forced to endure. She wouldn't need to rely on anything but her instincts, a compass and a map. She was however relieved to see the fuel tank was full and everything was ready to go. All she needed was to get her sister into the plane and to get them safely up into the air.

She rushed back to the spot in the woods and explained to Nadia what was going on as she picked her up and helped her towards the plane. After nursing, the baby was now tucked back in her arms, sleeping soundly. They moved as fast as they could with Nadia's condition to the aircraft, and Tasha helped her up as they stepped over the body of the German soldier.

"You remembered your hand-to-hand combat?"

"I did," said Tasha with a smile. "My version of it anyway. We'll need to get going as soon as we can."

"I can navigate for you," said Nadia breathlessly as she moved into the navigation seat. Her eyes were closing, and Tasha knew she was frail.

Tasha started up the engine, knowing that the guards would come running as soon as they heard it. She jumped out of the plane, spun the propeller, and it roared into life. Rushing back, she jumped into the cockpit, and thrusting the throttle forward, she began to move towards the edge of the field. She could hear the guards shouting from behind her, but she continued to advance. Then she heard gunfire. She kept her head down. She roared the plane into action and took off as quickly as she could.

"Oh my God, we made it," she shouted back as she soared into the sky. She knew she would have to go east towards home. She glanced down at the compass in front of her feeling jubilant. "We made it," she said again to her sister, "can you believe it?"

She turned around. Nadia was slumped forward, her head drooped on her chest.

"Nadia, can you hear me? Is everything okay?"

Nadia didn't answer, and suddenly Tasha felt scared.

She turned around to look at her sister, and then she noticed it. Nadia's body was bleeding. One of the bullets must have hit her.

"Nadia!" she screamed. "Speak to me!"

Nadia's eyes flicked open as she stared in front of her.

"Oh, thank God. Hold on, this won't be long. I'll have you home before you know it."

Nadia spoke haltingly, in obvious pain. "If anyone can get me home, it's you. Promise, if for some reason I don't make it, you will take care of my daughter."

"No! I won't promise you that because you're not going to die. Promise me you won't die. I'm going to fly you home as fast as I can. You've got to hold on, Nadia."

As Tasha flew east towards Russia, she did a quick calculation using the map. Knowing from other newer prisoners roughly how far the Russians had advanced, she estimated she would just about have enough fuel to get there.

Her eyes misted with tears as she prayed her sister would hold on. She kept the map and the flashlight on her lap as she guided her way there, looking at landmarks as she went.

She flew low under the radar, knowing that she would have to land before she hit Russian lines. She didn't want to be shot out of the sky by her own troops, flying in a German plane. Finally, as she hit the Russian searchlights and heard the artillery, she felt safe at last and came down close to the lines. When she saw the uniform of her own countrymen, she began sobbing.

The Russian troops came rushing towards her, guns drawn, and were shocked to find two women and a baby instead of German fighter pilots. She raised her hands, calling out in her native language, explaining who she was and where they had come from. Then suddenly a voice came from the crowd.

"Stand down, this is Natasha Petroffskaya, a decorated member of the 588 Squadron and a damn good pilot."

Tasha looked out in the crowd to see who it was, and coming towards her was a familiar face. His mustache was now thick and bushy and his body had filled out, and there was a scar under his left eye which marred his once-boyish looks.

"Sergei?"

"At your service. I see we are now even."

"Oh, thank God! Nadia has been injured. She's lost a lot of blood. I got her here as fast as I could."

Carefully, he helped her take her sister out of the plane and they laid her on the ground.

"Nadia, speak to me," she cried, looking into Nadia's pale, still face, rubbing and tapping at her hands that were so cold.

Nadia's eyes twitched a little. She held her sister's hand, and weakly and slowly she guided Tasha's hand till it rested on the baby still swaddled on Nadia's body.

Then she let out a deep sigh and closed her eyes.

Tasha sat there horrified, unable to believe what she was seeing in front of her.

"Nadia, listen to me, you have to wake up. Do you hear me? Wake up. Don't leave me. Not now. You can't leave me now. We're home. I got you here safely. Open your eyes, Nadia, you've got to open your eyes!" she screamed at her sister. "Please, Nadia! Please don't leave me!" she screamed again, which woke the baby, who then started to bawl.

Tears streamed down Tasha's face as she tried desperately to revive her sister. She tried over and over again as Sergei helped too. She wept openly as the ambulance crew arrived and took the tiny baby, unstrapping her from Nadia's chest, and handing her to Tasha, who strapped her to herself. Holding her tiny niece close to her, she kissed her little head.

She couldn't believe it. Sergei looked at Tasha and shook his head. Her sister was dead.

It felt unreal as they put them all in an ambulance to be taken to the hospital. She would not let go of Nadia's hand. All the way she spoke to her.

"I'm so sorry, Nadia, that I let you down. I was reckless. I should have thought it through. I should have thought like you. There had to have been another way. You would have thought of it. How will I go on without you? Please, please forgive me. Oh my God, what I am I going to tell your baby girl? That I am the one who has left her motherless?"

She took her sister's cold hand and held it to her wet cheek and looked at Nadia's beautiful face. She looked so peaceful, and Tasha felt so incredibly alone.

They officially pronounced Nadia dead at the hospital, and as Tasha stroked the back of the tiny bundle now in her arms, she realized they hadn't even had a chance to name her yet. She decided right there and then that the baby would also be called Nadia. Nadia. Hope. Her sister would live on through her daughter.

It was as she sat slumped in the waiting room that Sergei found her and knelt beside her.

"Tasha, Tasha, can you hear me?" Tasha turned and stared at him. She was so numb, normally feeling so emotional about things. It felt strange to her to feel nothing as Sergei continued speaking. "I'm so sorry about your sister. She was an amazing pilot and she will be greatly missed."

"It's all my fault, Sergei. I'm just too irresponsible. She was always telling me it would be the death of me, but it ended up being the death of her, and that guilt is just too great to bear."

She covered her face with her hands and sobbed as he slipped his arm around her.

"Tasha," he whispered, "you can't hold on to the guilt. It will destroy you."

"What do you know of guilt?" she spluttered back, angry that he was trying to make her feel better when she wanted to wallow in her pain.

"Because, Tasha, I have had to live through it myself, and it is hard to bear, trust me."

She stared at him and saw the pain in his eyes as he continued.

"I owe you an apology. Not just for what I said to you during training, and not just for the way I made your life hell during that time, but also because of Luca."

She continued to stare at him, trying to understand what he was saying.

"What about Luca?"

"The night that he went missing, I was flying with him."

"You were navigating for Luca when he went down?"

Sergei nodded.

"What happened?" she asked. Luca had not gone into any detail when she had spoken with him at the camp.

"We were flying over the enemy lines, dropping bombs in the daytime. We had just circled back to return to base when a German fighter hit upon us. As you know, Luca is a tremendous pilot, and he managed to dodge and weave his way out of trouble before taking out the other plane. What we didn't realize was that a stray bullet had hit the gas tank. We were leaking fuel everywhere. I suddenly started to smell it and let Luca know about it. The only hope would be for us to land. He began to look for a safe place. We were still over enemy lines, but it was the only way. He brought the plane down, but on the landing, it ignited the fuel, and the two of us had to leap from the cockpit in order to be saved. I was knocked out and Luca pulled me to safety. As we watched the plane go up like an inferno, he pulled me free, even though he himself had broken his leg.

"As I came around, he started to bind it, when we heard German forces. He told me to go, he told me to leave him while he held them off as long as he could, and I'm ashamed to say I did. I didn't have the kind of courage that you have, Tasha. That tenacity that made sure I got in the plane during the time you rescued me, that made you get your sister into the plane tonight, that takes a special kind of courage, and I've regretted what I did every day. I should have helped him, the way you helped me; even if it had slowed us both down, it would have got him back over the lines, back to safety. It taught me a great lesson, and I have been full of guilt ever since then. You see, we have no clear answers, Tasha. If you hadn't got her in that plane, she still may have died some other way. Recklessness on your part didn't kill her. This war did. You made the best possible decision in a very difficult situation, and it was the right one. I never saw Luca again. I can only pray he had a swift and painless end."

Tears shone in Tasha's eyes as she felt a little hope. "He is alive, though, Sergei! I've seen him, and I believe that I will see him again. I can't imagine a world without him in it. And don't feel bad. I've known Luca all my life. He would have insisted you leave. He's stubborn that way."

The relief on his face was indisputable. She bent down and kissed him on the cheek and Sergei blushed slightly.

"Thank you for your words," she said, tapping his cheek.

He began to chuckle. "Never in a million years did I think you would ever do that. What I didn't tell you in training, because I was too proud, is that I actually always had a crush on you."

She started to laugh. "What, the pretty girl with the ugly hair?" she parroted back to him, reminding him of his words to her so long ago.

"Well, let's just say that the hair doesn't make the person or the pilot. I would be proud to fly alongside you any day. I still can't believe you didn't take the chance to leave me when you saw who it was on that mission."

"I would never have got a good commendation for a dead pilot. I was only doing it for the medal."

He laughed.

The baby started to stir in her arms. It would need feeding soon, and the nurses had given her a good supply of milk. Tears stung her eyes. It was her job. Tasha had to take care of her from now on.

———

After her sister was buried, Sergei offered to drive her to her old camp, which was close by on the front, as always. Then she would need to figure out what to do next. She looked across at Sergei as he drove. They had both grown up a lot in the last few years. But the seriousness of war could do that to a person. Even so, it did feel good to finally be taken seriously by some of the male airmen, and she thought about Major Raskova's words right back when they had arrived at the training school, how she'd assured them that they would eventually win over some of the prejudices that were so prevalent in their ranks. Maybe, she thought, just maybe chinks of light were finally starting to creep through that wall of bias.

She felt exhausted as they traveled. Tasha needed to get home to Babka and take Nadia's baby with her. But first, she would go to her other home, to the women who were family, and break the news of the loss of one of their finest pilots.

56

JUNE 1943

Tasha

Her squadron, as always, were on the front lines, working hard, and they had made quite a name for themselves throughout Russia. In honor of their service they had earned the title of Taman Guards and were now known officially as the 46th Taman Guards Night Bomber Aviation Regiment.

Sergei had told her about it on the way and how the Russian papers were full of the stories of how Hitler was being slowly defeated, the harsh winter of 1942–43 helping with their cause, even at the cost of so many Russian lives. It was as if Stalin was happy to sacrifice as many men and women as it took, just so long as they won.

The number of dead and wounded was unfathomable to Tasha. This war had changed everything for her motherland. But finally, they had Hitler on the run, and they had retaken most of Russia's borders.

As she walked onto the airfield, she saw the sight that made her heart warm with joy: the tents all set up in their neat rows, and beyond those, the airplanes glinting in the waning spring sun. Around in a circle the girls sat with a couple of easels, and their embroidery. Tears stung her eyes as she embraced the sight of a place that was home to her in her heart.

As she thought of the companionship she'd known in this group, she felt overwhelmed, and the strongest feeling she had was love.

Her best friend saw her first. She was out of her tent cleaning off her boots. It was 3 p.m., and many of the girls were either already awake or about to get up. Eva's eyes grew as large as saucers when she saw Tasha. She didn't come to greet her at first, just watched her walk into the camp as if she didn't believe it was her. As if she was looking at a ghost, and maybe she was. Tasha had lost so much weight that she was thin now, her face gaunt, and her hair had grown long and wild while she'd been in the camp, way beyond her shoulders. But not long and full as it had been when she had been younger. The starvation at the camp had also taken its toll on that, as her hair was stringy and its copper color had faded to a dingy brown. Still, she was not complaining. At least she still had hers. So many women she knew there had lost it with the shock, horrendous treatment, and malnutrition.

Finally, Eva whispered her name. "Tasha, is that really you?"

Tears streamed down Tasha's face to see her best friend. She had feared the worst when Eva had been injured in their plane, and the joy at seeing her alive was overwhelming.

"Oh my God, Tasha!" Eva screamed as she raced towards her, throwing her arms around her friend.

"Eva, I'm so glad to see you too. I feared you were dead!"

"I thought the same of you."

The friends hugged each other tightly as baby Nadia cooed up at her from beneath her clothing.

"Who is this?" asked Eva, astonished, as she noticed a tiny pink face peeking up through Tasha's wraps.

"This is my niece. My sister's baby. She's also called Nadia." Tasha's eyes grew large with tears.

"And your sister? She is with you?"

Tasha slowly shook her head. "She is all I have left of my sister. But my sweet niece will continue her mother's legacy."

Eva's eyes filled with tears too.

Hearing the commotion, many of the other girls came out of their tents and, noticing Tasha, started to crowd around her. It took everyone a minute to really realize who they both were. They all had a thousand questions. Where had she been? What had happened? How was Nadia? Slowly, she started to answer them one by one, told them about the camp, told them about the hard labor she'd been under, the starvation. Then haltingly about her sister's death and baby Nadia's life.

"I'm here to speak to the commander," she finally told them after a short time of them catching up.

They all wanted to play with baby Nadia. Each of them took turns holding her and cooing with her, tears brimming in their own eyes. So many of them appeared to realize that with the great loss of men there may not be an opportunity for them to get married or have their own families on the other side of this war. They had been soldiers for so long that they had forgotten they were also women who could be mothers. It was beautiful to see the joy that baby Nadia brought to the whole group. The same pleasure that Tasha had felt, being with her sweet niece.

"I'll be back in a moment," she told Eva. Then, she made her way to the command tent.

Walking inside, she saluted her commanding officer, who looked as shocked as the other women had been.

"Natasha Petroffskaya?" she whispered. "I can't believe it. We gave you up for dead months ago. I should have known that somehow you would've cheated death."

"I'm here to face whatever you wish to do with me. I know I did a terrible thing and never thought I would learn, but I've been through a hard time, although that doesn't stop me from wanting to face what I need to face here. I let you down. I let the squadron down. And most of all, I let my sister down."

"Nadia is not with you?"

Slowly, Tasha shook her head. "Nadia died escaping the Nazi slave labor camp where we were imprisoned. She was very weak after she gave birth to her baby and she was wounded."

The commander's eyes grew wide. "Your sister was pregnant?"

"She got pregnant when she saw her husband on leave, and she hid it from all of us. Even me. I didn't even know when we got captured. She didn't tell me for months. It's astonishing that the baby survived, but now she is thriving."

"I'm sorry for the loss of your sister. She was a superb leader, pilot, and a truly wonderful person. I know your heartache will be great." Tasha fought back the tears that were brimming in her eyes. "It seems, Airwoman Petroffskaya, that you did indeed disobey your group and disobey my orders. You flew a plane into enemy territory, when you should have come back here. You lost a plane and two of my best flying officers were captured. But I can see you have paid a high price for all of that. I'm not going to reprimand you at this time because, to tell you the truth, I could do with you back here. Would you be willing to come back and fight again?"

That was when the tears started to fall. She tried to control them. This was what she wanted more than anything. "I would," she said. "I need to come back."

She did. She needed to come back to fight for both of them, for Nadia and for Luca, if he still lived. She needed to keep the hope of that alive.

"Nadia's baby is with you?"

"She is. She's with the girls." Then she added with a smile, "They're enjoying her."

"I would like to see her too, if I may. If she has half the

spirit of your sister, she will grow up to be an amazing woman."

Tasha nodded.

"What will you do with her now, though?"

"I'll take her back to my grandmother and see if she will raise her until the war is over. She did an excellent job with both me and my sister."

The commander smiled and nodded. "Then I want you to report to us as soon as you can, when you feel well enough."

"I'll be back soon."

She left the tent and saw Eva cuddling little Nadia, rocking her in her arms and cooing and singing her a little song. Tasha then told the girls she would be returning, to their absolute, unbridled joy. "We can't wait to get you back. You've been sorely missed," Eva said in delight.

Tasha nodded. This would be the first and the easier of her journeys home.

———

Taking the train, and then the bus, she made her way back to her home village. It felt so strange to her. The world had seemed so large when she'd left, but now it seemed so small, sadder somehow. Everyone around her that she saw on the train or on the bus looked shabbier, thinner, more tired. She had forgotten that the war had affected everybody.

Getting off the bus in her village, she looked around her, the familiarity warming her heart but also making her sad. She passed the flying club, where the two battered planes they used to fly had been requisitioned for the war; the bar where she and Luca had spent so many of their days, and the store where she would shop for Babka. They were all the same. And yet Tasha was entirely changed.

She made her way back to the little house that she'd grown up in. Babka was out in the garden, apparently fighting with some vegetables. It looked like it was turnips that she was pulling up. Tasha stopped to watch her for a second as her heart overflowed with love. This remarkable woman had managed to make it through two wars and the revolution. And yet, she never seemed to age to Tasha. She, too, was of course thinner like everybody else, but her expression was as resilient as ever.

Babka sat back on her heels and wiped her forehead. Then she saw Tasha and slowly rose to her feet, the shock evident on her face. She whispered her name, and Tasha nodded. Then she ran to her and allowed her to take her in her flower-scented embrace as she sobbed on her shoulder. Home at last.

When she introduced her to baby Nadia, Babka's eyes lit up with the joy of new life. However, when she told her of her mother's death, Babka's eyes shadowed. She shook her head and shut her eyes. Burying her face into her large, callused hands, she wept as Tasha held her. Then when baby Nadia started to cry too, she wiped her face and took young Nadia into her arms and held her tightly.

"She looks so like your sister when she was a baby. It's hard to believe that she's not the same person. I don't know what we'll do without our sweet Nadia to keep our family on an even keel. But thank you, God, for giving me Tasha back, and giving us both this beautiful child, who will help turn our miserable days into joy."

She held the baby to her chest then, and they went inside and made tea. Tasha told her everything that had happened, about being in the prison camp and the fact she had worked in a German factory. But she didn't tell her how hard it had been. She knew all this would be devastating enough for Babka as it was. So, she told her about what she'd done and how she had found Luca.

"Has there been any news of him here?" she asked hopefully.

Babka shook her head. "All the young men are gone. It's

just old men and women here. We've heard nothing of those at the front. I'd heard nothing of you until today. Will you stay, Tasha?"

Tasha shook her head. "I can't. I have to go back and fight. But I will come back for you and the baby after the war."

Babka understood. "And I will take care of this little one, then," she said, cuddling the baby, "until you come back."

Tasha nodded. And watching the older woman, she felt once again all the love in this home.

57

APRIL 1945

Tasha

Tasha stood to attention with the rest of her unit on the yellowing grass, beaten and muddied by the many boots that had trodden it down. They had been in their present location for over six weeks now, taking part in the East Prussian Offensive after spending late 1944 freeing Poland from Hitler's forces. They were all constantly pushing forward, hemming the Nazis in, and they'd celebrated the day that they no longer had any hold on Russia. As the commander continued to give them instructions, Tasha looked down the line of girls, so few with her now whom she'd trained with all those years before. Some had been moved on to other units, some gone to take care of their families, others killed in action. Instead, there were new faces now, many of them spurred by the fame the Night Witches had achieved throughout Russia, women who wanted to serve alongside their sister comrades and destroy the Nazi evil.

There were still a handful of familiar faces, but the atmosphere had changed. The feeling of sisterhood was still here, but the naivety, the sense of excitement she remembered on the first train journey, the feeling of awe at being women and being able to serve that they'd all felt at the beginning was gone now. Snatched from them by a long war that had jaded them, changed them to the severe and intense group of women they'd become.

The commander was talking about their achievements as she stood to attention.

"Since you were first deployed three years ago, this unit has successfully destroyed seventeen river crossings, nine railways, two railway stations, twenty-six warehouses, twelve fuel depots, one hundred and seventy-six armored cars, eighty-six firing points and eleven searchlights. In addition to bombings, the unit performed one hundred and fifty-five supply drops of food and ammunition to Soviet forces. You have successfully completed over twenty-three thousand sorties with only twenty-six precious sisters lost."

Tasha's minded drifted to what all that had meant to her: the nights of no sleep, the nightmares, dropping bombs night after night and the loss of friends and family.

All at once, there was clapping around her, and Tasha was pulled from her reverie. Her commander was once again giving out medals. It seemed that every week one of them was being commended for their work in the field.

She finished off the presentation by making an announcement. "I have some important news that I have kept till the end, as I know you'll be excited to hear this. Through our chain of command, I have heard that our leader has decided to grant us a great honor because of the work that you have done. Over twenty-three thousand sorties with so much destruction fighting against the enemy. So, he wants to give you all a place in history as the Allies and Mother Russia close in on Hitler. His front is now shrinking so much that we believe that just one bombardment on Berlin will take him down completely and for good. So, Comrade Stalin has decided that this unit has been chosen to be one of the units that will take down this final city, to reward you for your work throughout the war."

There was a buzz of excitement all down the rows. For years, it felt like they had been under the radar, working against all the prejudice, the lack of equipment, and the shame of being relegated to bombing at night and now, at last, they were being given this important mission alongside the other Allies.

"The Americans will continue to bomb in the day," their leader continued, "and you will join the forces at night to take down Berlin and win our final victory. I know I can count on you all. And I want you all to be aware of the significance of this privileged assignment we have been given by our great leader and the woman who started this all, Marina Raskova. And in her name, I want you to fly with honor and complete the mission set before us."

There was a sadness as Major Raskova's name was mentioned. She had died in battle in January 1943 leading the 587th Bomber Aviation Regiment, at just thirty years old—a great loss to their country and their morale.

The commander continued. "It will be the biggest mission we have taken on so far, and we will need all of your skills to complete it. But I know that you can do this. You are dismissed now. Go and prepare, and I will give you your missions for this evening so you can start this work that we have been given to complete."

The girls beamed at one another with pride, and the camp was abuzz as they continued to talk about what this meant as they made their way back to their tents to prepare for that evening of sorties. Tasha was also making her way back to her tent when her commander called out to her.

"Airwoman Petroffskaya, may I speak to you in my tent, please?"

Tasha turned and, following the commander inside, saluted and stood to attention at the other side of her desk.

The woman looked at her, a compassionate smile on her lips. "How long have you been with us? From the beginning, no?"

Tasha nodded. "Yes, Commander."

"You have been a great asset to Russia, even though you haven't always followed the rules. I can't tell you how disappointed I was when you defied orders and took a plane over enemy lines and the loss of life that followed."

Tasha swallowed down the pain, as she did when anyone talked about Nadia. Nothing ever took the guilt from her. Her stomach twisted uncomfortably as she tried to find words to respond. When she did, her voice was tight with emotion.

"I'm very sorry to have let you down, Commander. I vow that will never happen again."

The commander nodded her understanding and walked behind her desk, staring at the picture of Joseph Stalin that hung there for a moment before continuing. Then, slowly, she swiveled on her heels. "I believe that is true. They wanted to reprimand you and make an example of you, but when you made it back and with a German plane, I felt that you had been through enough suffering to pay for your disobedience. So, I have had to justify keeping you on. Your skills and bravery I have always admired, even if your judgment sometimes has not been correct."

Tasha nodded, and the commander paused again, as though she was trying to find the right words.

Her tone became gentle. "You have spoken before about your young man..."

Tasha looked across at her with surprise. This conversation was going in a very different direction. "Yes, Commander. He was taken as a prisoner of war."

"Not unlike yourself."

Tasha nodded again. "His name is Luca. We were from

the same village. He was taken to the same camp as I was but then he was moved to near Berlin. That's what he told me at the time. I don't know for sure."

Tasha pushed down the tears. This she already knew, and tried not to dwell on. Instead she focused on sorties night after night and tried to not think about the consequences of what was happening in the war in other places.

"If you are part of this bombing crew, you'll be going into Berlin to bomb. And there is a chance that he may still be there."

Tasha nodded. "This I am aware of," she said in a tiny, tight voice.

"Can I count on you, if I send you in? I can't send you in if I believe for one moment you'll pull a stunt like you did before. Our leader is depending on us. And the last thing I can have you do is bring shame to our country. It would be a huge embarrassment for us and a black mark against our squadron that I can't allow to happen."

Tasha rolled back her shoulders. "You can count on me. I've learned my lesson. Haven't I proved it a thousand times since? When Nadia..." She wanted to say the word "died," but it didn't seem to be able to come out of her mouth for some reason. So, she began again. "When we lost Nadia, something changed in me. She would never have taken the chances that I did. And if I'd been more like her, she would still be alive now."

The commander understood. "There is room for both in this war. You have always been courageous and very cunning. There is no doubt your sister had her skills, which is why she led the unit. And sometimes you need somebody who will take a risk, but it has to be a calculated risk. That's what I want to do with you right now, take a risk on you, because I believe in you. And I think your sister did too. I'm not saying what you did was right, but you may never have got out of Germany if you hadn't done it. And I think she knew that, even if outwardly she reprimanded you for your recklessness. So, I'm asking you this one question: can you go and bomb Berlin, knowing that you may be killing the man that you love if he is in one of their armament factories? When he was the reason you left us in the first place. Do you think you can do this?"

Tasha looked down at her feet as she thought through all of what the commander was saying to her. Then, meeting her gaze, she looked resolute. "I can. I have to trust in fate. If Luca and I are meant to be together, somehow, we will find a way. He may not even be alive. It has been two years since I've heard from him and the camps were not easy. The Russians were horribly mistreated. As were all the people there. Although, now that the death camps in Poland have been liberated, we know that we were in fact lucky."

The commander nodded. "I'm sorry for that."

"You can trust me. I promise you."

"I'm glad you said this because, Airwoman Petroffskaya, I think it's time for you to head up your own mission."

Tasha looked at her with surprise. "I don't have the skills for that. I'm not of that kind of mind."

"I think you are. I think you're ready. I'm going to ask you to lead the group that will bomb Berlin. I trust in you as you trust in me. And I believe you can do it."

Tears sprang to her eyes then, and she realized since Nadia's death, since her mistake of getting them shot down and then taken to a camp, she had not trusted in herself, not in all this time. She had done the work that needed to be done, and inside of her, she had hoped that maybe she would die in action, punished, a remedy for the guilt that she felt. But as she stared at the eyes of her commander, she suddenly felt a renewed hope and slowly nodded her head.

"Thank you for this privilege. I promise you I will not let you down."

The woman came over and placed her hand on her shoulder. "I know you won't. Now go and get ready. You have a group to take up."

Nadia put on her flying cap and saluted. She moved towards the tent flaps and looked back. "Commander."

"Yes?"

"Thank you."

The older woman nodded. "Thank *you* for your sacrifice and your hard work. Now go and make us proud."

As soon as Tasha looked down at the target for that evening, she understood why her commander had needed to confirm her loyalty. Acidic bile forced its way from her stomach, collecting in the back of her throat as she tried to swallow down her fear. Then, forcing away the thought screaming in her head, she strode to her crew, waiting to hear from her now she was their squadron leader.

As she walked, she spoke under her breath. "Nadia," she whispered out to the air, "Nadia, I need you more than ever. This will be the hardest thing I've ever done, and I can't do it without my sister." She felt the burning in her heart that she always did when she thought about Nadia. She put her hand to her neck, the talisman her sister had given her when she completed her training. As she clutched her necklace, she felt a warmth spreading through her body, as if Nadia was smiling down on her. And with that, she had her answer. She just knew her sister would be with her, guiding her all the way.

Reaching her crew, she swallowed down her fear as she began to speak to them.

"Tonight, we have been given the great privilege of working with all the Allies to bring Hitler to his knees. I don't have to remind any of you of the cost of this war to Russia so far. We always knew the Nazis were evil, but since our Allied brothers liberated their diabolical concentration camps, we have seen the depths of human horror and we know we are fighting for what is right."

Tasha waited, looking around the group of women. Their eyes were cast downwards, arms slipping around shoulders to comfort one another. They remembered siblings, friends, fathers, husbands, and the overwhelming death toll that Russia had suffered over the four long years of war.

She carried on. "Tonight, we have been ordered to bomb a target just outside Berlin. It is an ammunition factory that may have created many of the very weapons that have robbed us of so many of our loved ones."

She paused to gather herself. She did not want to dwell on that one selfish thought that attempted to pound its way out of her head and rob her of her composure. Her crew was counting on her to be strong and to lead.

Swallowing down the lump in her throat, she continued. "I want you to do your very best to stay on task and bring an end to the last traces of what Hitler has in his arsenal. I am proud to fly with every one of you. This is a perilous assignment. There's undoubtedly live ammunition in this factory. And though we want to destroy it, we do not want to destroy ourselves in the process. So be there for your sisters, but don't take any unnecessary risks. Do you understand me? In other words, don't be like me."

There was a subdued snigger around the circle. Tasha's exploits were well known, even though she had done every-thing by the book in the last two years.

"May you all be safe and support one another, and let's finish the job we all set out to do."

As she finished, they all stood a little straighter with the encouragement and then, hugging one another, wished each other good fortune as they did every night.

Tasha strode out to her plane. Eva was close behind her and raced to catch up with her.

"Tasha? Tasha, stop for a second."

Tasha knew what she was going to say. And she didn't know if she was ready for this conversation.

Finally, Eva reached out and grabbed her arm and stopped her in her tracks. "Tasha, an ammunition factory?"

Tasha turned as tears stung the corners of her eyes. Then, drawing in a deep breath slowly, she nodded her head. She didn't have to say any more. Eva knew everything about Tasha's life. They had been flying together for years now, back together again as soon as Tasha had got back from the labor camp. They still made an incredible team, the best of friends with a relationship deeper than sisters. Without saying anything, Eva knew that an ammunition factory just outside Berlin was the last place that Luca had been forced to work.

Eva didn't say any more. She just took her friend in her arms and held her as she whispered into her ear. "Can you do this? Are you up for this?"

Tasha pulled away and wiped the tears from her eyes. "I have to be, Eva. This is my job. Hitler must be crushed. And I will always love Luca. And anyway, you know as well as I do that the chances of him even being alive right now are very slim. I've heard nothing for the last two years."

Eva nodded her head compassionately. "But even so, this is hard for you."

"Of course it's hard for me. But you know what I've learned, Eva? I always thought that I could get away with everything. I thought that I would always be lucky. I felt that if I just did things my way, somehow, they would work out for me. And for a long time, they did. Till the day I flew us across enemy lines without properly calculating the risk to my sister's life. As I looked at her dying body, I knew that I had gambled all that time. And I'd just been lucky up till that point. I'm not saying that she wouldn't have died some other way, but having her death on my conscience is the hardest thing that I've ever lived with. It was because I did it my way.

"Now, I have to trust in something bigger than myself—a

plan. Even a God, maybe. Something that's keeping all of this moving, recognizing that I am a tiny cog in this huge machinery of war. And that means I can't change a damn thing. But I can take care of my sisters tonight. And I can do the right thing for a world at war. And for the thousands of brave fighters like Luca ahead of us to be born, who will be free to live and love. And that's all I can do right now. This will be the hardest thing I've ever done. But you see, I have no choice. I will roll the dice, and God will decide how they fall."

Eva nodded. Tears were now in her own eyes. "You are the bravest of people. I'm proud to serve alongside you. And have been for all of these years. You will be an exceptional squadron leader."

Tasha smiled halfheartedly. Somehow the promotion didn't mean the same to her as when she had desired it so passionately at the aviation school.

Buttoning up her leather flying cap, she bounded towards her plane for the hardest sortie of her life. As they prepared for that evening's campaign, the sound of the artillery guns was constant. Russia had been bombarding Berlin for days now. The rockets fired every few seconds, one after another, day and night. The sound was deafening and, at night, it lit up the skies like thousands of fireworks. The experience was traumatizing. And yet it was also the sound of victory. She could do nothing but concentrate on them all being free. She started her engine and made her way down the field, pulling into the sky for what felt like the thousandth time, checking her altitude, her instrumentation, and checking in with Eva as she always did.

It didn't take them long to find their target. Berlin was reduced to rubble. The devastation was unfathomable to believe unless you witnessed it. In every area of the city, fires were raging out of control, filling the night sky with the smell of creosote, burning wood, and cordite. A blanket of thick black smoke surrounded them as they flew towards the target, and she relied on Eva's incredible navigation skills to get them there as she kept a close eye on her squadron. From behind her, Eva confirmed their position.

Tasha looked down at the unassuming building on the outskirts of Berlin. A building that could have housed the love of her life for the last two years. A building that she now had to destroy. The pressure in her chest was overwhelming as she tried to suck in a breath and not think about the consequences of what she was about to do.

She heard Eva behind her. "Eight hundred feet. Seven hundred feet. Six hundred feet. Steady on course and altitude." Tasha focused on her altimeter. As Eva prepared for the release, Tasha kept the plane straight. She heard the thud of Eva's hand on the release lever, and her heart leaped to her throat as Eva cried out, "Bombs are away!"

Then the panic came, ripping through her body, squeezing the smoky air from her chest, her stomach clenching into a stiff ball with the pain. She whispered to her sister, "Please, Nadia, please." As she did, she stared at the little piece of tattered cloth Gaia had given her that she always kept on her dashboard. The word *"Hope"* sewn into it so bold and encouraging. Thinking of the Romany woman's words from so long ago: "If despair is not an option, then hope is all you see."

All around her, the rest of her crew completed their drops. And it was as the third set of bombs hit their target that a deafening explosion lit up the ground, rattling their plane and beginning a rolling cavalcade of smoke and fire, rivaling anything being wrought in the center of Berlin right then.

The plane steeply climbed high into the sky to escape the heat of the burning building below her. She signaled to all the girls to move quickly away from the scene as she coughed and tried to clear smoke and dust that had found its way under her goggles and into her eyes.

It was only as she swiped at her eyes that she realized tears were streaming down her face as her last vestige of hope, the hope that somehow she may find him alive, seemed to disappear into the sky with the soot and ash that threatened to clog their engines.

All the way back to reload, she sobbed quietly, unable to take her thoughts from what she had just done. She had to trust now. Had to trust in the power of their love. And hope that, somewhere in heaven, Nadia would be taking care of Luca, either up there or down here.

As she finished the last sortie, there rose the most glorious sunrise, breathtaking, a rainbow of reds and gold. Eva caught her breath.

"Look at that, it's gorgeous," her navigator cooed.

Tears stung as Tasha closed her eyes and thought back to the young man she had met in the woods so many long years before.

"Hello, my darling," she whispered to herself. "I will never forget you; no one will ever have my heart but you."

Once she had landed her plane, her commander came to find her. The older woman's admiration was evident in her eyes.

"You did well, Squadron Leader Petroffskaya. Nadia would be proud of you."

Tasha drew in a deep breath with the mention of her sister's name, then nodded and prepared to go up again and continue her fight. She would fight until this enemy was utterly destroyed. That's all she could focus on now. That was all she could do.

58

Tasha

After Berlin fell, the exuberance at their airfield was unbelievable. They drank vodka, they sang, they danced, they cried, and they held one another. Finally, after four years of fighting their enemy, it had been announced that Hitler was dead and the war for them was finally over.

Once the Allies had declared victory in Europe, Tasha and her unit were used to fly supplies into Germany and to help out where they could. The first time she had flown over Berlin in the daytime, she had wept. Though having no connection with the city itself, the devastation was unbelievable. There was nothing in the city that was recognizable. Mounds and mounds of concrete and dust, burned-out vehicles, and people aimlessly wandering the streets. She was sure now that Luca was dead. If he had been even close to Berlin, working in an ammunition factory, she couldn't imagine he would still be alive.

A week later she was taking in bandages and supplies to a hospital on her humanitarian mission, when she heard somebody talk of Russians who were there in the hospital, rescued from a camp. With her heart almost beating out of her chest, she asked the nurse if she could go and speak to them, telling her she was Russian as well. The nurse gladly agreed, thankful for the supplies that she had brought. However, nothing could have prepared her for what she saw when the nurse pointed out her countrymen. Skeletons of beings, bodies battered with work-hardened hands. Their heads looked almost too big for their bodies. They looked frail and aged, though she surmised many of them weren't much older than herself. She made her way tensely down the row of beds, looking from one to the other, looking for one familiar face. A man called out to her in Russian, asking for a drink of water.

Pouring some from a jug, she brought it to his lips, and he thanked her. Then he asked her, looking at her flying suit, "You are Russian?"

"I am, comrade. Where did they bring you from?"

He told her the name of the work camp that he'd been kept at.

Then, swallowing down her fear to prepare for the answer, she asked him, "Do you know somebody called Luca Baranov?"

His eyes pierced her as he searched her face, the sadness deep and looming in his eyes as he slowly shook his head. "That name is not familiar to me. So many were killed, even before the bombing. Only a few of us survived from that camp."

The pain twisted in her stomach, as it was obvious she would never see him again. She nodded her head.

"You were close to him?" he asked, his voice low and gritty.

"I'm in love with him."

The man's face shadowed. "I'm so sorry. This war has taken many good men." He thrust his hand towards her and grabbed her own. His was like a claw, just sinew and bone and an odd shade of gray as it latched on to her. "There will be better times now. You will have better times."

She nodded, tears catching in her throat. Not for her. Life could never be better without the man she loved. She scanned all of the beds, checking twice with the nurses, who confirmed these were the only Russians in the hospital. But with great sorrow, she had to accept he was not there.

As Tasha began to leave, another comrade called out to her.

"There are others, I heard the nurses talking," he said. "Not at this hospital, at the one across town. There may be a chance."

For a second, she felt a sense of hope. If these men had survived, Luca could have.

Leaving the ward, she asked the sister for directions. More than anything, she wanted to dash over there, search the whole of Berlin. That was what the old Tasha would have done, been impulsive and reckless. But instead, she reminded herself she would need to get permission. So, she flew back to her camp with a sinking heart, knowing she was never going to do anything without counting the cost again. She would never do something without consulting her commander first. That was what Nadia would've done. That was what Tasha would do from now on.

When she spoke to her on returning, there was a look of concern in her commander's eyes. It was apparent she didn't hold out any hope, but she granted Tasha permission to go to the other hospital to see if Luca was there. After flying in another load of supplies, she approached the desk with a trembling voice.

"Excuse me," she said in her best German. Then she asked about Russians.

The sister shook her head. "I don't think we have any here."

But then one of the other nurses stopped her. "There were a few, Sister, on the other end of the ward. I heard them talking in Russian."

The sister nodded. "Ah, yes, they just arrived. Yes, you're right. I'm afraid there are not many, though."

"Was there anybody there called Luca Baranov?" Tasha asked, barely above a whisper.

The sister shook her head. "They only just arrived. Some have barely been conscious in that time, so I'm not sure of their names. But you can go down and look for yourself if you like. This nurse will take you."

The nurse led her down the ward, and as she passed bed after bed of the injured, her stomach churned. As she looked at the exhaustion and hopelessness on every face, all at once she was afraid to find him. What if he looked like one of these people? How had the war marked him? She didn't care for herself. She'd love him no matter what state he was in, but how would it be for Luca? Would he be a broken person even if she did find him?

One patient was sitting up awake, an older man with gray hair. She spoke to him in Russian. "Excuse me. Is there anybody here that you know called Luca Baranov?"

At the sound of her voice, the man in the furthest bed with his back towards her slowly turned over. At first, she didn't recognize him. He had aged so much, his face was heavily lined, his hair already turning gray, and he was so thin, even thinner than in the camp that she'd seen him in before. If it hadn't been for his eyes, which were still the same bright shade of blue, she would not have known him. Their eyes locked as he peered at her, looking as if he was in a state of shock, as though he didn't believe what he was seeing either. Tasha was rooted to the spot as she hitched her breath, willing her legs forward but unable to move. She had honestly expected him to be dead, and after years of the work camps, how could he still be alive? It had to be an illusion.

"Tasha?" he called out to her, breaking the tension.

His voice was dry and raspy, and she saw an angry red scar running down his face.

Slowly, she moved towards him, passing the beds until the truth sank in, and then she started to run, racing towards him. Reaching his side, she drew in a breath and whispered, "Is it you? Is it really you?"

Tears brimmed in the eyes she never thought she would see again as slowly he nodded his head.

"Oh my God, Luca, Luca," she gasped, trying to catch her breath. "Oh my God, oh my God." She drew close to him, scared to touch him. Not knowing where he was hurt.

But before she could decide, he grabbed her hands and pulled her down towards him, gripping her against his chest. She closed her eyes, listening to his heartbeat, trying to take in this information. She was with Luca. She was with the love of her life. He had survived so much. He had survived a plane crash, two camps, the attacks on Berlin, and this was his heart beating. Unable to believe it, she forced herself up to look at him.

"You're hurt."

"I have been, but I'm much better now. Most of the wounds I have are not on the outside of my body, and there have been times I have never wanted to go on living. But I refused to give up because I made you a promise."

"A promise?" She searched his face, trying to make sense of what he was saying.

He scanned her own as though he wanted to drink in all of her before speaking again. "I promised you I would not die. And I never break a promise. Especially to the woman I love. Sometimes that promise was the only thing that kept me alive."

Gently, he pulled her forward, his dry, cracked lips kissing her own, his hands caressing her face. And even in the discomfort of a hospital bed, the strangeness of the circumstances, her heart skipped a beat, her stomach tightened with the excitement of being close to him. Her Luca was alive. Gently she pulled away and ran her hands down his face, carefully circling the angry, new scar. Only then did she realize the other men on the ward were cheering.

"Oh, Luca," she sobbed. "I've missed you so much."

He nodded his head. "My thoughts of you were what saved me. I would get up early every morning just to watch the sunrise no matter how tired or ill I was, just so I could be with you. Through all the grueling work, through night after night of bombings, even through the beatings... I knew there would always be a sunrise." He trailed off for a second, his past thoughts haunting him, then he swallowed it all down as he adopted a more cheerful tone. "And look at you." He gestured at the medals on her uniform. "They commended you? They will never want you at the circus now."

She beamed as she realized with relief that within this broken body was the man that she knew and loved, the man that she'd known her whole life. Then, nestling her head back into his shoulder, she closed her eyes as he stroked her hair.

Eventually pulling away, he stared deep into her eyes with all the love she had ever known from him brimming there.

She took both of his hands and gently kissed his knuckles, her voice quivering as she spoke.

"I have loved you all of my life, even before I really knew it. We have been through a long, hard war together and seen and done things no human being should ever have to experience, but I have held this one hope for years, the hope that I would get a chance to say this to you." Her voice dropped to whisper. "Luca Baranov, will you marry me? Marry me and make me the happiest woman alive."

Tears streamed down his face as he pulled her so close, his breath tickled her cheek as he whispered into her ear, "Nothing, and I mean nothing, could give me more joy than to become your husband."

She nodded, her tears mingling with his and she placed her forehead against his and felt the warmth and contentment of the love that passed between them. Then threading her fingers through his, for the first time she actually believed this was finally over.

———

It took a few weeks before Luca was able to leave the hospital, but Tasha went to meet him when he did. He had grown stronger over the weeks and started to regain some weight and look more himself. Cuts and bruises and his healing injuries were unimportant compared to the beaming face that he had when he saw her ready to pick him up.

"I've been given permission to fly you back to our camp," she said.

He put his arms around her and pulled her in tightly.

"I still can't believe you're here," he said. "I've imagined you for so long." He nestled her head into his chest and kissed her hair gently. "And my body still seems to remember you," he joked as he became aroused.

She pushed him away, laughing, and took him back out to her plane. He had a limp from some of the injuries he had sustained, but he looked really good to her.

When they reached it, he climbed into the navigator seat.

"Sure you don't want me to pilot?" he asked.

"No, you'll have to just be at my mercy." She laughed. "I promised to be gentle with you." She started her propeller, then jumping into her cockpit, she set off.

When he got to the camp, all the girls were glad to see him, fussing around him and treating him to a meal. It was hours before they were alone, and they went out for a walk close by the camp. She had to tell him something significant, and she looked over at him to see if he was strong enough for the news. She rolled back her shoulders. Best just to get it over with.

"Do you remember before the war, we were going to fly off together?"

"I should have taken you up on it," said Luca with regret.

"We may have to do that. We can't return home."

He looked at her with surprise.

"There's news leaking out that prisoners of war are now being killed when they return to Russia, because Stalin is ashamed of them for being caught. So, we can't risk that happening to us."

"The man is a brute," Luca spat out. "No better than Hitler, in many ways. I have heard that they are talking about over twenty million Russian deaths because of this war. Twenty million, Tasha! The man just sacrificed our troops without a care. Someone told me he would send out foot soldiers with one gun between two men. When the first was shot the second was expected to pick up the gun from his fallen comrade and keep fighting."

Tasha nodded her understanding of his resentment; she had heard many of the rumors herself.

"Unofficially I have permission for you to stay overnight at my base, and then I'm going to resign and we can escape together. I have heard the Americans will take care of us. We can have a new life in a new country. My best friend Eva has promised to find Babka and help get her and baby Nadia out of Russia, so they can join us over there."

She heard him draw in a long, ragged breath beside her, and she knew he was thinking of his own family.

Slipping his arms around her waist, he pulled her close, and she could hear his voice full of emotion. Tears rolled down his face.

"I'll miss seeing the world that shaped my childhood. But we will find a way to make sure my family can visit and Tasha, as long as you are by my side, that is all the home I need."

She looked at him and kissed him. "Me, too. We will find a way to bring them to us and as long as we're together, that's all that really counts." She pulled him closer then, holding him as tight as she could, never wanting to let him go.

EPILOGUE

Tasha woke up with a start. She had been dreaming again, dreaming of a war that never really left her. She couldn't count how many times she had woken in her bed, her hands in the air grasping an imaginary throttle, her eyes in sleep trying to focus on a target. Even though it had only been four years of her life, those years were the ones embedded in her bones, even after all this time.

From somewhere else in the house, someone called out to her again, and she realized that was what must have woken her.

Getting up from her bed, she pulled open her curtains and looked out the window across her view of the cornfields of Kansas, her home for many years now.

Her granddaughter Evie appeared in the doorway.

"Were you taking a nap? Nadia is here to take you to the plane."

"I was just resting my eyes for five minutes," Tasha responded as she smiled at her granddaughter. Evie had all the fire she remembered from her own youth but tempered with the tender heart of her grandfather. Evie loved deeply, just like Luca.

Tasha's niece, Nadia, was already waiting for her in the front room and she drew her auntie in for a hug. Tasha still caught her breath whenever she saw her. She looked so like her sister. Though this Nadia was a completely different character with a lot of the intense passion of her father, Ivan, Tasha still caught glimpses of her sister's spirit in her.

Luca shuffled in from the porch where he'd been sitting, and there was that smile. The one he kept only for her. In the many years they had been through together since the war, their love had only deepened. Their bond had grown stronger, especially since Babka had died just two years after they had arrived in America. Her grandmother had loved Kansas. Babka had settled into her new country for the last two years of her life with the great joy of a child. Leaving Tasha to take over the cooking, she had spent endless days sitting out on their sprawling front porch, soaking up all the sun a mid-west summer could offer her.

Luca placed his arm around his niece. "So you're taking my wife up in a plane, are you? Be careful she doesn't grab the controls from you. You know how she likes to have her own way."

Nadia smiled as she kissed Luca on the cheek. "I'll take great care of her. Don't worry," she said, patting the side of her uncle's chin.

As Tasha prepared to leave, she noticed Luca pick up his book and move back to the porch.

"You're not coming with us?"

He shook his head. "I've seen enough warplanes to last my lifetime. You take care of yourself, though, none of your circus tricks."

Then, leaning forward, he brushed her lips with a kiss. Tasha couldn't believe that he still made her heart quicken even after all these years. As he drew away, she tried to read her husband, searched his face with the scar that had faded to a thin, white line, looking up into his blue eyes that never changed. There Tasha saw a glimpse of the past horrors he had never wanted to share with her. Even though the bad dreams still came in the middle of the night, when she would hold him tightly until he stopped shaking and sobbing. Tasha understood and wasn't going to press him.

Before she left the house, she slipped back into her bedroom and took out the precious necklace her sister had given her so long ago. She also glanced at the framed piece of tattered, gray uniform fabric that hung over her dressing table with the word "Hope" exquisitely sewn into its threads. How often had she thought of her old friend's words over the years when her world had seemed bleak? She whispered the words she knew by heart to herself as she fastened the necklace. "If despair is not an option, then hope is all you see." She would need both Nadia and Gaia's strength today for this foray into her past.

On the way to the airfield, Nadia talked all about the "fly day" they were going to, and Tasha began to feel nervous. How would it feel? How would it feel to see one of the planes she had flown in?

Arriving at the aerodrome, she was shocked to see just how many people had come out to see some old planes. She had expected maybe thirty people, old war flyers like herself, perhaps some from the American military, the odd grandson or two but nothing like this. Instead, the aerodrome was heaving with people. Families, veterans, and many people dressed up in vintage WW2 clothes; in the background, a brass band was playing a lively war number.

As they entered the field, Tasha sucked in breath as in front of her on a huge banner flapping in the wind was her face. It was a photo of her, Tasha's arm around her navigator Eva, taken right before one of the missions. The words "WW2 hero Natasha Baranov" were emblazoned across it.

She looked over at Nadia with great bewilderment.

"I knew if I told you about all this fuss, you wouldn't come;

they want to honor you, Aunt Tasha; the war was won with the help of the Night Witches and people want to recognize that."

It had been a few weeks before that, with great enthusiasm, Nadia had informed her aunt that this local organization had managed to find and restore a Soviet Polikarpov Po-2 vintage plane. And eventually, she had managed to talk Tasha into coming along to this open day as the airfield was so close. But Tasha had never expected anything like this. Bands and flags, people in crisp new WW2-era uniforms celebrating and glorifying a war that had never been this glamorous.

All at once, Tasha's head started to swim. She wasn't sure she could do this: Luca had been right; she should have stayed at home and read beside him on the porch.

Nadia must have sensed her fear. "It's going to be all right, Aunt Tasha, I promise you. You won't have to do anything you don't want to."

As soon as they arrived on the field, Tasha was surprised to feel like a celebrity. A dashing young man in an American GI uniform escorted her from the car. Nadia had asked her to wear her medals, and she had helped her attach them to the jacket that she now wore.

"Mrs. Baranov, we can't tell you how honored we are to have you here today," he said with deep sincerity, his face so alive with the admiration obvious in his eyes. She had never been recognized before like this; it was surreal. The man escorted her to the stage, where she sat and listened to Nadia give a short speech. Tasha's eyes filled with tears as Nadia spoke with conviction about her mother's sacrifice and how Tasha's squadron had hardly been acknowledged for their bravery and astonishing success. She heard Ivan in her niece's passion.

Tasha was too overcome to speak; she just stood and waved when Nadia introduced her; in response, the crowd jumped to their feet and cheered.

As the band struck up another patriotic tune, the same young man in the GI uniform came to escort her out to the planes.

The Po-2 stood apart from the others, so much smaller and simpler than Tasha had remembered. How could this little plane have survived a whole war and made it all the way over here to America?

As she approached it, she wasn't ready for the wave of emotion that flooded her. It was beautiful and heart-wrenching all in the exact same moment. The first thing that struck her was how clean it was. None of their planes had ever looked like this. They had always been dirty, working hard night after night. She started to look it over, and as she placed her hand on the fuselage, it felt so familiar to her as tears streamed down her face. As she allowed the intense emotion to wash over her, her other hand stroked the necklace at her throat.

"Oh, Nadia," she said under her breath. Her niece turned, thinking she was talking to her.

"Are you okay, Auntie Tasha?"

"I was thinking of your mother," she said, smiling wistfully. "Nadia should be here too." Her niece nodded, her own loss etched on her face as they continued to look around the plane.

"She is a beauty, isn't she," the GI enthused as he gave her a rundown of all the plane's stats and restoration information. "We can't be sure which one of you flew this, but—"

Tasha cut him off.

"This was Irina's plane," she said confidently, as he looked at her, bemused. "They were like our children; we knew them all. She was an incredible pilot, and this was hers."

He looked at her in awe as she chuckled. "When you live with these planes day in and day out, and they keep you safe night after night, you learn a few things about them. They have their own characters. It's not magic, even though I am a witch," she added, raising her eyebrows conspiratorially.

Nadia approached her auntie; in her hand she held a very new-looking leather cap and goggles, which she handed to her.

"Are you ready?"

Tasha stared down at the cap and paused; she wasn't sure if she was.

"It would do us a great honor," encouraged the handsome GI, "if you let us see you flying once more. This was an amazing time in history, and we would like to see you seated back in one of your planes." Feeling this young man's sincerity and the fact he reminded her of Luca at that age, she found herself nodding. How could she resist such a handsome face?

Tasha rolled back her shoulders and, hitching her breath, stepped up onto the wing, which seemed further up than she remembered, and, climbing in, she took the navigator seat.

The feeling inside the cockpit was surreal; every memory came flooding back. And for a second, it was as though she'd never left.

Her niece climbed into the pilot seat as all around the crowd clapped and cheered. A member of the ground crew started the engine, and the familiarity of that sound caused Tasha to catch her breath for a minute, and she wanted to climb right back out, but grabbing Nadia's necklace for courage, she willed herself to stay.

Buckling herself in, Nadia taxied the plane out to the airfield as the jarring cheers and tinny hum of the patriotic music through the speakers disconcerted her. She felt on display, playing a part in a world that had never looked anything like this. As Nadia started to pick up speed, Tasha fought her desire to take hold of the throttle though she couldn't help but monitor all the instrumentation. She held her breath at the familiar pitch of the engine lifting as Nadia throttled up with her mother's elegance, and they ascended into the sky. In the air, Tasha felt more at home and was enjoying the cornfields below her until she was pulled back to that memory of the worst night of her life. As she continued to feel paralyzed and gripped by the pain of the past, all she felt was sadness. The brutality of the war and the loss of Nadia and all her friends, so many of whom were now dead, even her precious Eva.

Then all at once she heard a high-pitched squawk just above the hum of the engine and, opening her eyes, she caught sight of a magnificent bald eagle. It soared high above them, its white head glowing in the sunlight, its sable-colored wings splayed outwards, rippling in the wind as it glided in gentle circles on the warm thermals. And suddenly she was lost in its splendor, as she remembered the beauty of the world in the sky. Then, pushing past the sad remembrance, incredible memories flooded back to her. Breathtaking sunrises and sunsets, cloud formations and the incredible view of the world below her from the air. It wasn't sad, and it wasn't horrendous or heartbreaking. It was a gift she had been given.

Even wearing this recreated leather flying cap and goggles, the freedom of flying felt like breathing to her. And as she watched the eagle in awe, a memory came back to her with a jolt. Something she had forgotten, something she had said to Luca years before about needing to free the bird that was trapped inside her. Flying in her squadron, being with those amazing, brave women and defeating their enemy had, without her realizing at the time, opened the door to the caged bird inside her; as hard as the war had been, she had fulfilled her destiny. The destiny that this flight was now celebrating, and the realization of that brought her so much peace.

"Want to take the control for a minute, Auntie Tasha?" her niece shouted into the communication tube, bringing her back from her reverie. Tasha picked up the shining tube that smelled of oil and fresh paint.

"Yes, I do; want me to show you how to loop the loop?"

"*No!*" Nadia screamed in sheer delight, apparently hearing the edge of humor in her aunt's tone as, with a shaking hand, Tasha took control of the plane.

At that moment, as she took hold of the familiar joystick, with the air rushing past her and the familiar hum of the engine pulling her forward, she was no longer an older woman living her life in a retirement community in Kansas. Instead, she was twenty-year-old Airwoman Petroffskaya, a proud member of the 588th Night Bomber Regiment, flying with the Allies, defending the world against Hitler's evil regime.

Except now, she was flying in celebration of that precious freedom, and that thought gave her great satisfaction.

"This is for you, Nadia," she shouted out into the sky. "This is for all of you, wonderful Witches of the Night."

A LETTER FROM SUZANNE

I want to say a huge thank you for choosing to read *We Fly Beneath the Stars*. If you enjoyed it, and want to keep up to date with all my latest releases, just sign up at the following link. Your email address will never be shared and you can unsubscribe at any time.

www.bookouture.com/suzanne-kelman

This is, no doubt, the hardest book I've ever written. Not only because of the intense scenes of battle, the death of female pilots, and the depiction of the harshness of work camps, but because I was going through one of the most challenging times in my own life, dealing with a lot of losses on a personal level. I have to be honest: there were times when I wanted to give up; it seemed too hard to be up in the air fighting for my life in the mind of a female pilot when everything inside me wanted to curl up and die. But the bravery of these women's voices from the past kept me going. Their story needed to be told, not only because there is so little written about them, but because I think we all need to be reminded daily of the indomitability of the female spirit.

I was about halfway through this manuscript when Russia invaded Ukraine. And my heart broke again for another tyrant who felt he had the right to attack and destroy a free nation. As I watched the war unfolding in the east, I had serious concerns as I continued the writing process: would writing about Russian fighter pilots seem insensitive during such a horrific time? But after much soul searching, I realized something significant. This time, more than ever, was the time to write about women's bravery and how any nation's tyrants should never be allowed to succeed. Instead, they should be challenged and defeated. In 1940 the name of that tyrant was Hitler; today, it is different. Just because these women were Russian didn't take away anything from their incredible bravery and the fact they fought for our freedom alongside their western brothers. As you read this, I hope you will feel the power of these remarkable women and their story, and something of their courage will whisper its strength to you to keep going as it did for me.

I hope you loved *We Fly Beneath the Stars*, and if you did, I would be very grateful if you could write a review. It'd be great to hear what you think, and it makes such a difference helping new readers to discover one of my books for the first time.

I love hearing from my readers—you can get in touch on my Facebook page, through Twitter, Goodreads, or my website.

Thanks,

Suzanne

www.suzannekelmanauthor.com

facebook.com/suzkelman

twitter.com/suzkelman

ACKNOWLEDGMENTS

First, as always, I want to thank my incredible publisher, Bookouture. It is so wonderful to be supported by such a talented and hard-working team. A big thank you to my phenomenal editor, Isobel Akenhead. Thank you for being so enthusiastic when I first pitched this idea and showing me so much compassion and kindness as I had to extend deadlines to deal with family bereavements. I am so grateful not only for what you do on paper but for how you support and encourage me and my work. I feel exceptionally fortunate to have you as my editor.

Also, I thank the rest of the incredible Bookouture team: Jenny Geras, Peta Nightingale, Alexandra Holmes, Alex Crow, and the others who shepherd my books to completion. To the dream team Kim Nash, Noelle Holten, and Sarah Hardy, who work tirelessly to promote my books, organize blog tours, and root out every possible opportunity at launch to get the word out. You guys are stellar.

A huge thank you, as always, to my wonderful husband, Matthew Wilson. Thank you for being there over this challenging year. I am so grateful to have you by my side every single day.

To my wonderful son, Christopher, you are such a gift to me. I am so proud to be your mum. Your kind heart, infinite wit, and wisdom are a daily gift to me. I love you with all my heart.

As well as my own little family, I am so blessed to be loved by an American family of the heart, honorary sisters, and a brother, which form the circle of love in my world. To my sweetest friend Melinda Mack, thank you for your kindness, compassion, and friendship, especially through this last year. I'm so grateful you are in my life. Also, big-hearted thanks to my brother of the heart, Eric Mulholland; I'm so glad we are friends. To my sweet "bezzie mate" Shauna Buchet, I love you. Also, to my number one writing buddy, K.J. Waters, thank you for being my number one cheerleader. I have so appreciated your fantastic support and friendship over the years.

Lastly, thank you to you, my readers. Thank you for choosing my books when there is so much choice out there to read. I so appreciate every one of you.